RAISING FIRE

"Leave me be. Let *them* be. Please."

"No." Mauntgraul gripped his shoulder. His hand had become a claw, the black talons dragging Ben upright, drawing him close. "You and I are alone, are we not? The last of our kind. I can feel it. Your love for humans has murdered us all. You will not turn away from me now."

Ben tried to shrug him off, but the White Dog gripped him fast. In response, Ben was changing, crimson scales slipping over his skin. But Mauntgraul was not dissuaded, his wings and tail folding out, fifteen tons of scarred white flesh reducing the ramparts behind him to rubble. Black claws spread across the turret roof, gouging the stone like chisels. Together, they rose, Mauntgraul and Ben, carried skyward by their thrashing wings. Ben kicked and wriggled, forcing all that he had left against the vice around his shoulder and neck.

"The kindest thing would be to kill you," Mauntgraul said. "Instead, I will make you watch."

By James Bennett

Chasing Embers
Raising Fire

RAISING
FIRE

James Bennett

www.orbitbooks.net

ORBIT

First published in Great Britain in 2017 by Orbit

1 3 5 7 9 10 8 6 4 2

Copyright © 2017 by James Bennett

Excerpt from *Wake of Vultures* by Lila Bowen
Copyright © 2015 by D. S. Dawson

The moral right of the author has been asserted.

A CIP catalogue record for this book
is available from the British Library.

ISBN 978-0-356-50665-4

Typeset in Plantin by Palimpsest Book Production Limited,
Falkirk, Stirlingshire
Printed and bound in Great Britain by Clays Ltd, St Ives plc

Papers used by Orbit are from well-managed
forests and other responsible sources.

Orbit
An imprint of
Little, Brown Book Group
Carmelite House
50 Victoria Embankment
London EC4Y 0DZ

An Hachette UK Company
www.hachette.co.uk

www.orbitbooks.net

For Dad
In memory

The Dreamer awakes
The shadow goes by
The tale I have told you,
That tale is a lie.
But listen to me,
Bright maiden, proud youth
The tale is a lie;
What it tells is the truth.

Traditional folktale

PART ONE

Choir Invisible

Here in the civilised world
Stranger events by far occur
Than in the Country of Cropped Hair;
Before our very eyes
Weirder tales unfold
Than in the Nation of Flying Heads.

Strange Tales from a Chinese Studio,
Pu Songling

ONE

The North Sea

This is my fairy-tale ending.

It wasn't much. As Red Ben Garston flew into the storm, the wind and the rain battering his snout, he couldn't suppress a surge of resentment. It shouldn't have been this way. According to the Lore, he should've been safe. He certainly shouldn't be here, flying in the face of a February gale, his ears ringing with a hateful song, a silvery plucking of strings that he had long ago forgotten, the music calling, calling him on. As the melody, the *signal*, grew stronger – finally clear beyond doubt – he had thrust himself away from his tumbler of Jack in the Stavanger docks and, cursing, left Norway's rain-swept coast with a leap and a leathery snap of wings. He'd dumped his clothes behind a shipping container on the cargo pier. A thick woollen jumper, jeans and boots reduced to a cloud of rags. Seven tons of red-scaled flesh speared up and over the sea, a shadow fleeting under the clouds.

An hour later, here he was, the rain ricocheting off his horns and flanks like bullets reminding him of the injustice. Winter storms loved this sea, had made it their battleground

3

for many a year, a place to show off the worst of their calamities, but this, the weather, was something else. *Unprecedented*, the newsreaders said, *since records began*. Ben could've told them that a hundred-odd years wasn't that long, considering. Everywhere, seagulls laughed, making sport of the churned-up fish. Thunder rumbled in the leaden bellies of the clouds. Oh, the tough red shell of his body could withstand whatever the storm threw at him, no worries about that. In recent months, he had endured lightning and worse. The muscles between his shoulder blades throbbed with draconic strength, the wind shrieking down his long plated neck to the arrowhead tip of his tail. His claws, each the size of a rhino's tusk, hung under his belly, a sheaf of knives raking the squall. But inside his cavernous heart, bitterness beat like a drum.

And with it, the usual cynicism.

Same old story, sweetheart. This isn't 1215.

Back then, in a time that no Remnant would seriously call *the good old days*, King John had pressed his seal to the Pact, binding Remnant and human alike. It was the oath under which they all lived, the secret compromise of centuries, the stipulations as familiar to Ben as his own changeable flesh. As long as the Remnants, the magical creatures and fabulous beasts who still endured in the world, agreed to withdraw from society, refraining from meddling in the future progress of civilisation, then the King and his subjects would do them no harm. This ongoing arrangement was known as the Lore, an arrangement that, in word and in deed, had far surpassed the reign of one puny king, not to mention the medieval age.

4

In the end, everyone had been tired of the stalemate, the endless war between the Remnants, the denizens of the Old Lands, and humanity with its push for advancement. And so the Pact came to pass. Only the chosen leaders of each Remnant tribe, be they dragon, troll, griffin, vampire, wizard or witch, had been allowed to remain wakeful and active in the world, albeit in secret, hidden in human form. The other creatures, the unchosen, had been lured and lulled into an enchanted slumber known as the Long Sleep. Naturally, the Remnant leaders had been reluctant to face a future that rendered them no more than myths, shadows of their former selves. Still, being forgotten was better than annihilation, better than extinction. Common sense – or whatever the Remnants liked to call it – had prevailed. That and the assurances of King John, who had placated them all with the temporary nature of the Pact, reminding them of the ancient prophecy, spoken ages ago by the Queen of the Fay upon her people's departure from earth.

One shining day, when Remnants and humans learn to live in peace, and magic blossoms anew in the world, then shall the Fay return and commence a new golden age.

That hope smouldered in the hearts of all Remnants. When the long-vanished Fay returned as the legends promised, then the Pact would be fulfilled, the Lore annulled, the Sleep undone and—

And everyone would get their bloody happy ending, Ben thought, his fangs bared against more than the weather. *Once upon a time, I actually believed that.*

Once upon a time being eight hundred years ago. Now, the sea spread out below him, a surging wilderness, frothing canyons of grey. Heavy clouds enclosed the horizon and he shot onwards, squinting through the downpour, a thunderous mist swirling in his wake. Racing low over the waves, he kept his membranous wings taut and steady. Half blinded as he was by the spume and that shrill music rattling in his skull, his navigation skills also weren't helped by the fact that he had no idea where he was going.

The source. You have to find the source of the song. It's been days now . . .

The water below should have soothed him, eased the cramp in his juggernaut gut. The wind, a shrieking harpy, stole away any chance of primal comfort. Rain hissed off his bladed spine and through the gills under his wings. The storm screamed like a living thing. Sometimes, Ben knew that it was.

But for all this, only the song, the incessant strings, comprised the weight of his unease. It was the kiss of moonlight on an Arctic plain. The flutter of butterflies rising from a poppy field. At the same time, it was a razor blade slipped under a fingernail. Or like opening a door onto an unexpected hundred-foot drop.

He knew this music. This *lullaby*. And with an ache, an urge that he imagined all Remnants would share in his position, he wanted the damn thing silenced.

The sea went on forever, a foaming wasteland offering no clues. If he continued at this pace, he'd be flying over Yorkshire by dusk, and despite the length of his wanderings, he wasn't yet ready to return to England, to face the emptiness of home.

Or the consequences of last year. Let's be honest here.

This in mind, he greeted the sight of the oil rig below with a feeling akin to relief, a kind of eager dread. His ears prickled, his balls shrank, the intensifying melody informing him that he had located the source of his headache. His summoning.

There were several of these rigs dotted about the North Sea. With oil prices plummeting around the globe, many of the rigs had been decommissioned and stood, their rusting steel legs fixed to the seabed, like the skeletons of krakens rising from the waves. For all their technical ingenuity, the rigs had become titanic hotels for seagulls and terns, the drills silent and the pipes dry. The men in the Stavanger bars, many of them part of the laid-off workforce, had muttered and grumbled enough about it. The economic downturn. More than thirty oil fields shut. A market teetering on the brink of collapse. After the EKOR refinery explosion last year, Ben barely plucking Rose from the flames, he couldn't tell the men that he was sorry.

It didn't surprise him to find one of these wrecks out here, the derrick cables rattling in the wind, the cranes shuddering, the flare stack dead and the vast circle of the helipad rain-washed and empty. And the irony of the location wasn't lost on him either. In the endless jungle of pipes, the latticed framework of stairs and walkways, Ben saw an echo of that dangerous showdown last summer, but he couldn't make out any signs of life. The music, however, was scaling towards crescendo, the sound twisting his guts into knots. And this kind of music, of course, would require someone to play it.

It's a harp. The *harp. Or a piece of it . . .*

As soon as he thought it, the strings fell still, their silvery intrusion lost to the air. Echoes rebounded through the machinery and gridwork, skittering into silence, swallowed by the wind. Ben experienced a second of blessed relief and then his instincts were shrilling in alarm again. His nose, this time. Catching a familiar scent.

Human.

"Come out, come out, wherever you are. You stink more than the fucking briny."

He growled this as he made a pass, sweeping around the towering crown block in a broad half-circle, veering back towards the open space of the helipad. Whoever waited for him below – his flyby suggesting that there was more than one person present, possibly several – he knew it was unlikely that they'd understand him, decipher the *wyrm tongue* spitting from his mouth. All they would hear would be a roar through the storm, the primal bellow of a beast whose age had long since passed but who remained fearsome nevertheless, ready to kill if the bastards left him no choice. The harp would assure his summoner of his arrival; he merely announced his presence to remind them of this.

He had already made up his mind who he was dealing with, anyway; there were only three possible options, three representatives who would have access to the magic that summoned him. The Guild of the Broken Lance. The Whispering Chapter. Or the envoy extraordinary, Blaise Von Hart. Only the three official branches of the Curia Occultus, the ancient council that had drafted the Pact in the first place, possessed a fragment of the instrument that had put all the other Remnants to sleep. King John had chosen the roles of his conclave well. Military, ministerial and magical. The Guild had the administration, of course, overseeing the Lore for centuries. The Whispering Chapter had taken care of all matters moral and spiritual, appointed to pacify the nation's fears about the magical creatures in its midst, which many saw as an abomination, as demons and devils, an affront on Creation. And then there was Von Hart, the last Fay representative of magic. Von Hart had retreated into shadow with the rest of the Remnants, there to live at the beck and call of the ancient council should the need ever arise. An ambassador. An envoy between the human world and that of the Remnants.

Scanning the oil rig, Ben wondered which of these organisations would pick such a godforsaken place to face him. The Guild? In disarray, if one believed the rumours. The Chapter? Dormant, underground for years. And as for Von Hart . . . Well, he was far from human, but Ben wouldn't put it past him.

He was puzzling over the *why* of his summoning as he landed on the helipad, his wings flapping, dwarfing the surface. Claws splayed, he alighted on the concrete as gently as possible, the raised structure groaning slightly under his weight. Overhead, a crane loomed, its hook swinging in the gale. The space around him remained empty apart from the lashing rain. Whoever had called him here didn't seem keen to make themselves known.

"Hello? Anybody home?"

The wind snatched his words away, carrying them off and away over the water. Peering up at the blocky buildings around him, he sensed no activity at all. The smell of humans lingered, however, stronger now, closer than before.

Terrific.

He had come here because of the music, because the nature of the harp had left him no choice *but* to attend. Whatever sense of duty he might or might not feel, the artefact had drawn him here against his will, the ancient magic a yoke around his neck, irresistible to all Remnant kind – for now, focused only on him. As the silence thickened around him, his haunches bulged, preparing to take flight again. Just like in London last year, he suspected he had blundered into a—

Snap.

He heard the dart zip past his ear moments before the thing bit into his neck, piercing the softer flesh of his throat. Snarling, he reared back, his wings gusting billows across the helipad and rattling the walkways above. Hearing a cry, he swung his head in that direction, catching sight of the huddle of figures above, a blur of slick waterproofs, tiny faces washed out by the weather. All of the figures struggled to stay on their feet as the walkway shuddered and groaned, punched out of true by Ben's shifting bulk. He caught the glint of metal, the raised guns, infrared beams sweeping through the haze. There were four or five people up there, he reckoned, each one crouching behind the railing and aiming down at the dragon in their midst.

An ambush. It's a fucking ambush.

His attackers quickly recovered their footing, displaced air popping in his ears, another couple of darts thudding into his chest and flank. One bounced off his scales, clattering to the tarmac between his forelegs. Narrowing his eyes on the foot-long spike, he saw the fat silver barrel fixed to the end of it. Considering his bulk, the darts were little more than bee stings, but Ben bellowed all the same, lurching back on the helipad, his claws raking the shuddering surface. The feather on the end of the dart related the news and none of it was good.

Tranquillisers. Great.

Bladed neck winding towards the walkway, his fangs parted in a jet of flame. Dragon fire splashed against metal, two of his assailants jumping clear, landing in a tangle of limbs on the adjoining mezzanine, one retreating inside the station overlooking the helipad. In a fiery bluster, he saw the two remaining bastards on the walkway go up like Roman candles, their waterproofs shrivelling along with their skin, their screams cut short by the incredible heat. The resulting aroma, sweet and sour, only served to anger him further, a violation of his bestial appetite, long ago suppressed. He focused on the damaged structure, looking for weaknesses, preparing to claw the walkway to pieces. Even the railings were melting in the blast, liquid metal dripping from above, charred holes spreading in the latticcwork.

Ben sucked in, gathering his breath for another volley. The sacs in his lungs throbbed, the belching gas bitter in his throat. Whether he was facing agents of the Guild or the Chapter no longer concerned him. Tranquilliser darts or no, he wasn't about to let the arseholes put him in chains. He had to get away from here, and fast. Tail lashing out, toppling barrels stacked on the edge of the helipad, he rounded on the gunmen on the steps, his claws unsheathed, ready to skewer them, turn them into human kebabs.

Through the drifting smoke, he saw another figure emerge

from the stairway up to the helipad. At first, the rain shrouding the space between them made it hard to tell whether the newcomer was a man or a woman. His prickling instincts soon informed him that she was the latter, despite her height and stocky frame – seven feet tall, he judged, and half as broad – her jaw and shoulders set. She was dressed in faded military fatigues, but it was the cross shaved across her closely cropped skull that betrayed her as a True Name, a servant of the Whispering Chapter. The cross, a symbol of old slayer saints, related the woman's rank in the order.

Assassin.

Ben's eyes grew narrower as she came striding towards him, bold as you like. Her fatigues didn't quite match the pedestrian look of the other agents, who traditionally favoured threadbare attire, if Ben remembered rightly, the stuff of thrift stores, clothes that the Salvation Army wouldn't put in a jumble sale. How long had it been since he'd encountered a True Name? Two, three hundred years? These days, the Whispering Chapter was all but defunct. Or so he'd thought.

No. Scratch that. Hoped.

Something large, silver and round gleamed on the woman's back, a shield of some kind, catching the early light. He watched her draw a sickle from her belt as she approached. *A sickle? Might as well come at me with a toothpick.* Ben snorted, flame fluttering inside his nostrils, but he was quick to realise that the helipad rippled with more than just the ensuing heat haze. He plucked at the dart in his throat, but he was already having trouble, his claws scrabbling on concrete, clumsy and slow. Whatever the agents had packed

12

in the thing, the dope was doing its work, the toxins pumping into his veins. He shook his head, the drifting smoke clouding his vision, the oil rig around him blurring, swimming in and out.

Got to . . . get the hell out of here . . .

As he swayed back and forth, his tail thumped down on the platform. A wing unfolded, a tangled sail flapping along the ground, and he lost balance, staggering to the left. His shoulder crashed into the base of the crane, the girders screaming.

Grinning, confident of his intoxicated state, the assassin, the True Name, came striding towards him, her boots splashing through the puddles.

Mustering the last of his strength, Ben reared up, a serpent ready to strike. The assassin drew to a halt a few feet before him and the look on her face, an undaunted web of scars, gave Ben pause. His breath caught in his throat, choking back a barrage of flame. Planting her boots firmly apart, the woman raised her sickle and brought it down, slashing at something on the helipad before her.

Snick.

Ben heard a rope whip across the platform, trailing a jumble of hissing metal pegs. In the rain and confusion, he hadn't noticed the taut lines stretched across the concrete, the tightly woven steel mesh that he was standing on. In a matter of seconds, the snare leapt upward all around him, the connecting wires released from their fastenings and whistling up to the arm of the crane over his head. Ben found all seven tons of his red-scaled bulk wrenched up off the helipad in a snarl of claws, tail and wings. He roared, but only spirals of smoke emerged from his throat, his inner gases doused by the tranqs, his muscles too numb to respond. Above him, the sky wheeled, a blurred carousel of grey. Distantly he heard cheering and, he thought, an approaching judder, the *chop chop* of rotors through the air.

Idiot.

That was his last thought before everything went black.

TWO

In the darkness, Ben drifted, remembering. After Africa, after witches and mummies and the destruction of the East Katameya Oil Refinery, he'd had his fill of dust and death. That was why he'd drifted, into the ice. With the funds in his bottomless bank account and official-looking papers mailed to him by Delvin Blain (his dwarf accountant in Knightsbridge moaning down the phone about Ben's recent financial arrangements), he had flown to Finland. First class. Direct. Donning a *vinterjakker* lined with goose feathers, he had headed inland, letting the snow cool his inner heat, his inner pain. He'd spent the winter trudging across the tundra, heading up to the Gulf of Bothnia, helping to mend roofs, load trucks and haul fishing nets in nowhere places like Pooskeri, Kristenstad and Vaasa. He drank whiskey and thought about Rose, his lost love.

Stay away, she'd told him. *From me. From us.*

Wherever she was, she'd taken herself and the baby in her belly far away, and Ben knew better than to pull too hard on that particular string. He wanted to see her. Didn't want another knockback. He wanted to hold her. Had learnt that affairs with humans were futile. Destructive, even. Over the weeks, his hair and his beard had grown long, a crimson mane curling between his shoulder blades. He had become a wild man, a stranger from the hills, his troubled gaze piercing the blizzards. The stares of the locals bothered him no more than the short days, the long nights, the endless dusk of the Arctic Circle. He found himself numb, too numb for fear. The weak light couldn't hurt him. Kamenwati, the undead priest who had almost dragged the world into hell a few months ago, had shown him darkness, darkness everlasting, deeper than death. Ben trudged on, steeled against the north and the sinking sun . . .

Then, two weeks ago, he had realised he wasn't alone. At first, he'd caught sight of his shadows in bars, the men and women in drab clothes, watching him over their drinks, waiting. Later, the odd fisherman or trucker told him that people were asking after him. Where was he heading? Had they noticed anything strange about him? Ben understood that he was a hunted man – or rather, a creature in the guise of a man. Tracked by agents. The Guild or the Chapter. He wasn't sure.

Around this time, the music had started up, the tinkling of the harp. He hadn't wanted to trust his instincts, preferring to believe that the faint strain he heard in the air was simply his imagination, a memory, a ghost. Something he could easily dismiss and get back to his drinking. But the music had only grown louder, invading his dreams and then his waking life, drawing him across Norway, tugging him like a magnet. Sometimes the song, the summons, was just out of hearing range, then it became clear again, stark, leading him onward, an unshakeable leash. Each time, his tracks would change course in the snow, dragging his feet to the coast.

And this morning, on the Stavanger docks, the song had grown louder than ever, dragging him out to sea . . .

He had fled into the ice and darkness, seeking solace in the northern wilds. But now it seemed that he had found only light. Or perhaps the light had found him. Silver shards, glimmering in his mind like hooks, hauling him back to consciousness.

"Good afternoon, Signor Garston. I trust you had pleasant dreams."

Ben moaned. Then he grunted and spat. His profanity earned him a swift kick in the ribs from the shaven-headed assassin who, through the pervasive and needling glare, Ben squinted up to see standing to one side of him. He grimaced, his complaint for the other figure standing over him, the source of the silvery light. And the music. The music was back, drilling into his ears, sweeter, sicklier than before.

"People are always . . . waking me up."

He found himself sprawled on his back on the helipad, the rain still hammering down, the slap of a chilly hand. Taking a second to mentally probe for any broken bones, he found himself whole and in human form, his skin-tight suit, a meshed costume of tiny black scales, stretched over his leaden muscles. Rain slicked the symbol on his chest, the red *wyrm tongue* sigil encircled by yellow. Sola Ignis. The lone fire.

With his extraordinary healing abilities working to sweat out the toxins in his blood, he tried to sit up, the weight of the loosened net around him keeping him down. His crimson hair straggled in his face, his beard dripping. A flash of will, the urge to sprout horns and wings, met a flash of silver in his mind, a harsh white wall resisting his efforts. Binding him. The reason for his hindered transformation shone like a baleful star above him – the harp, a fragment of the harp, cradled in his summoner's arms. The radiance thrown by the thing hid her expression, but he could make out a bony broom handle of a woman, standing in a plain grey dress a few feet away. She'd scraped her hair back in a strict ponytail, the ashen strands rendering her nondescript, a rainy smear in the fluttering light. Behind her spectacles her eyes gleamed, hawkish with the scorn of the old.

"You should thank us. Saints alive, we have prayed for you. And there is only one reason why you're still breathing."

"Let me guess. You fancied yourself a dragon-skin jacket."

"Look at you," the woman said, her fingers caressing the strings – the ghostly suggestion of strings anyway, the harp unmade, one of three pieces, a fragment of a greater power. "Nothing more than a myth. Once formidable, now merely a story to frighten children. The great Benjurigan. The great beast. Fallen at our feet."

"You flatter yourself. It isn't like I came here willingly." With a sneer, he nodded at the two-foot-long spar of wrought silver resting in her arms. He had never seen the legendary *Cwyth*, the mnemonic harp, up close before; he'd only seen the instrument depicted in woodcuts, tapestries and paintings, or read about it in books. Anyone else might have taken the moulded and embossed spar, broken as it was, for a piece of a statue. Its flat triangular length suggested some beast or other, perhaps a griffin or a lion. An experienced eye like Ben's knew the object for what it was – the soundboard of a harp, shaped to resemble a prancing horse's back. Or a creature much like a horse . . . "King John granted the Chapter a piece of the harp for safe keeping," he said. "You're not supposed to use the damn thing."

His derision wasn't just down to bravado. Although the harp exerted a certain power over him – as it would over all Remnant kind – an individual fragment, once strummed, could only lure him and lull him into human form. He was one of the chosen, the Sola Ignis, guardian of the west. Eight hundred years ago, the envoy extraordinary, Blaise Von Hart, had sung his name into the Fay enchantment, rendering him immune to the spell that had sent all his kind, most Remnantkind, into an enchanted slumber. There was no way that the woman with the harp could send him into the Sleep. All the same, she could hurt him. All the same, he was afraid.

"Who will we answer to?" the woman said. "Look at this storm." She cricked her neck, indicating the barrage around them, a slight shiver in the gesture. Excitement? Dread? "Global warming. The shifting Gulf Stream. Giant waves battering the coast. The end comes, Benjurigan. The end of all ends. It's only a matter of time before we all get swept away. Still, one can pray, yes?"

"If that's your poison." *Yeah. Excitement all right.* The woman sounded European – Italian, of course – her voice snappy and cultured, a prima donna berating the forces of nature. Or inviting them in. A slight slur softened her words and he wondered whether maybe she'd had too much to drink. Christ knew he hadn't. "Does the Guild know about this?" Again he nodded at the harp. The slack steel mesh around him. "How about the Cardinal? What does your boss think about you breaking the Lore?"

The Guild and the Chapter were different, of course. The former remained tolerant of Remnants, respectful of the knightly code bestowed upon them by King John, and each successive chairman had sworn to uphold the Pact. The Whispering Chapter had been less . . . enthusiastic, to put it mildly. It was sheer luck that the administration of the Pact hadn't fallen into *those* zealous hands. If it had, Ben doubted he'd have made it as far as 1218, let alone Norway. But the Chapter still lived under the Lore, as they all did. His capture, this wielding of the harp, was supposedly illegal. Except . . .

"The rules have changed," the woman told him. "The Guild is in disarray. Compromised. As I'm sure you're aware."

"I might've heard something."

"As for our Cardinal. Well, he was old. Ineffective. Let's just say it was time for him to step down."

"Sure. I bet the Chapter offers a great retirement package."

"Our new Cardinal favours the old ways. The old values," she said, strumming, strumming the strings. Bright pins stabbed his eyes, his head. "We've been tracing your movements since Cairo, the Sister and I." The old woman tipped her head at the shaven-headed brute standing next to her, the assassin with the scythe. "Our agents have told us much. Several illegal manifestations. Damage untold. Rumours of *relations* with humans." Her inflection on the word told Ben exactly what she thought about it. "You've been busy, old dragon."

"You don't know the half of it."

But he wondered how much she did know. For ages, he'd taken so much care to stay in the shadows. Out of sight. Out of mind. Last year had put an end to all that and he'd been on the run ever since. He wished he could say that running was a new thing. In his eight hundred and sixty-one years, there'd been more bastards than he could recall who had seen him as the Holy Grail of all turkey shoots, and that didn't just mean the vengeful Fitzwarren family. Now it seemed that the Chapter wanted a turn.

This was bad. Very bad.

"Ben Garston, you are under arrest." The woman drew herself up, spitting the formality with obvious relish. "In your absence, we held a council. It was imperative that we got to the bottom of the breach in the Lore last year. The Chapter deemed it the Guild's responsibility, a lapse in security that saw a goddess rise from the grave and dragons battling in public. Not to mention the collateral damage. Have I forgotten anything?"

Rose. You forgot Rose.

He counted this as a small mercy. "I think that just about covers it."

"*Buono.* Then you can see why we had reason to challenge the Guild's authority. With no elected Chairman of the Guild, our new Cardinal declared a state of emergency. All agents are now subject to the one remaining functional branch of the Curia Occultus. The Lore rests in our hands."

"Wonderful. Why doesn't this sound good for my health?"

"You, my friend?" Her spectacles were lamps, boring into his skull. "Our verdict *in absentia* was execution."

Holy fuck.

Ben went slack, the steel mesh clanking around him. His breath came out in a groan, his limbs straining against the light.

The woman intoned, "*It is the King's command that hence-forth no Remnant in the land shall assume True Shape nor apply abilities wyrd without the permission of the Curia Occultus. His Grace, the barons, the cardinals and the white mage have all sworn that this shall be observed in good faith, lest a Remnant face the penalty of trial and the fitting punishment of—*"

Ben spat, his lungs full of damp air. "Sounds like the same old bullshit to me."

He chewed his lip, glaring up at the woman with the harp. The quoted passage mentioned a trial. *Did I blink and miss it?*

The woman gave him no time to protest. Stepping back, she nodded at the Sister. At first Ben thought the assassin was reaching for her scythe, preparing to pass sentence there and then, leaving his head to rot out here in the middle of the sea. Instead, she dipped into her pocket and brought out a thin circular object. Silver flashed under the clouds, joining the glow thrown by the harp.

Ben glared at the shimmering horror. *Lunewrought. The ore of Avalon.* When the harp originally shattered way back in the Old Lands, its unmaking had left the three fragments along with several splinters. All *lunewrought* was one metal, the alien substance of the Fay, an alloy of mineral and magic. As shards of the harp, the metal retained the power to trap and bind him in human form, in a weakened state, vulnerable to harm. Around the time of the great council in London that had resulted in the Pact, the Curia Occultus had smelted the splinters into a handful of shackles for the sole purpose of restraining Remnants, should the need ever arise.

It appeared that the woman above him had a journey in mind. Judging by the throbbing in the air, the *whoomph whoomph* of approaching choppers, his head wasn't going to rot out here after all. Another small mercy. Kind of.

"Keep that thing away from me," he growled at the approaching assassin, the manacle in her hand. "Unless you want to dry off real quick."

The old woman, the broom handle, laughed. It wasn't a pleasant sound.

"Signor Garston. There really is no need for aggression. As I said, there is only one reason why you're still alive. Tell me what I want to know and I promise that your death will be swift."

"Since we're trading advice, why don't you shove that trinket where the sun don't shine?"

"A shame. I was hoping for your cooperation." The old woman sighed, disappointed. "Von Hart keeps his own fragment of the harp. The envoy plays a part in all this. And you *will* tell us where to find him, I assure you."

"Von Hart? What's he got to do with—"

He cut himself short. In his confusion, he hadn't noticed the assassin kneeling at his side. The manacle snapped shut around his wrist, the chill of the metal, a burning sensation akin to frostbite, tingling on his skin.

At once, the old woman's fingers stilled, the fragment in her arms falling blessedly silent. Its restricting magic was no longer needed, replaced by the *lunewrought* cuff. As the light faded, Ben looked up at her, growling under the sting of his restraint. He noticed that the left side of her face was askew, her eyelid, cheek and lower lip like melted candle wax. The result, he guessed, of a former stroke and the reason for her noticeable slur. Her dead nerves sat at odds with her sharp, aquiline nose, her fine bone structure. And her eyes, those opals, never leaving his face.

"We'll just have to persuade you," she said. "I'm afraid it's going to hurt."

The assassin reached forward and yanked at the net around him, dragging the mesh away from his body. She grabbed his shoulders, intending to haul him to his feet, carry his sorry arse off to the chopper awaiting him. Christ knew she had the muscles for it. Even with the shield on her back, she could probably sling him over her shoulder, a sack of wet cement, and deliver him to whatever unholy torture chamber the Chapter had in mind.

He couldn't let that happen. Gathering his strength, he kicked out, aiming for the Sister's stomach. With a gasp, she stumbled back, clutching her gut – but not before Ben had grabbed the hilt of the sickle hanging on her belt and ripped it free. The old woman shouted something, her warning lost in the storm, and the assassin, snarling, came lurching towards him for another try. A clumsy slash of the blade and she pulled back, cautious, measuring him with hard eyes.

I'm still a meathead like you. I won't make this easy . . .

Ben used the gap between them to stagger upright, the sickle slashing out as he swayed drunkenly on the platform. The steel mesh, fine as it was, slipped against the wet concrete, threatening to tangle his feet. Taking small steps, he shuffled backwards, retreating to the edge of the platform, the Sister coming after him, slowly, her arms held wide.

The old woman was laughing again.

"Oh Ben. Stop this nonsense. Where are you going to go?"

Tottering on the brink of the helipad, he glanced over his shoulder. At once the source of her amusement became clear. A hundred feet below, the sea swirled, a raging mass of white and grey. If he jumped, he could probably survive the fall. But stuck in human form? It was a long way to swim back to shore. His kind might have a primal connection with water, but he didn't like it *that* much. He wasn't betting on his chances; there was no way in hell he'd make it.

The Sister was edging closer, one hand fumbling behind her back. He realised she was reaching for a weapon, maybe a knife, maybe a tranquilliser gun. In his foggy state, he didn't want to take his chances with her either, and that left only one option.

Between a rock and a hard place. As usual.

The old woman stopped laughing when he dropped to his knees. The assassin halted, surprised. He took a second to flash them both a grin and then raised the sickle over his shoulder. Closing one eye – the other needed for aim – he brought the blade down as hard as he could, slicing down on his wrist.

"*Stop him!*"

Ben howled. The oil rig wheeled around him, fire shooting up his arm and into his brain. In a second of exquisite, drawn-out pain, he saw the sky above him grow dark and the bristling black shapes cutting through the clouds, two or three choppers approaching the helipad. When he heard the faint clank of metal, the *lunewrought* manacle rolling away from his severed hand, his howl became a roar, shaming the thunder.

A blink, a push, and his red-scaled bulk was eclipsing the helipad. His tail uncoiled, a bladed chain swinging over the edge of the platform, the ballast of its tip pulling him into the air. He fell, tumbling towards the waves, grimacing as his pinions snapped out, letting the wind catch him. Wings spread, he rose over the helipad, a shiver of satisfaction in his breast as he watched the Sister and the old woman blasted back across the concrete surface, sheltering their heads from the stirred-up squall. The soundboard of the harp slipped from the old woman's hands, the metal fragment skittering away in the wind and spinning over the edge of the helipad, clanking through the latticework down to the lower decks. That would buy him some time.

Too weak to muster fire, he hauled himself upward, flapping awkwardly clear of the rig. Blood showered down from his foreleg, the wound left by his missing claw splattering the helipad, drenching the old woman and the Sister in a brighter kind of rain.

Fury whirled in his mind, stoked by pain. The wound would heal, he knew, and fast, his fabulous flesh mending and forming a fresh, albeit scarred, appendage. Growling, he swallowed his rage, understanding that the injury, the drugs in his veins and the fragment of the harp made this no time for battle. Against all the odds, he had lived to fight another day. He took advantage of the fact while he still could.

"Amen, fuckers."

He thrust himself up into the clouds, a great red arrow loosed into the storm.

Down on the rig, the Sister climbed to her feet. Turning her face to the sky, the wind howling around her cross-shaved skull, she watched the abomination vanish into the rain. The downpour sluiced down her neck, soaking her military fatigues a darker shade of grey. Shoulders slumped, she bore the weather without so much as a shrug; she had endured flails, from both herself and others, with far more righteous bite.

She turned as she heard footsteps, finding her mistress, the old woman who went by the name of Evangelista, approaching through the squall.

"Console yourself, Sister," Evangelista said, her blood-streaked features attempting a smile. "He won't get far. We must take the utmost care with the harp, but *lunewrought* answers to *lunewrought*, remember? Ben Garston has been touched by the stuff, one of the shackles in our keeping. It should make tracking him so much easier. But you had better get going."

Evangelista lifted the shackle in question and handed it to the assassin. Just like the broken soundboard, the metal glowed like moonlight in the gloom, throbbing with an alien power.

To show her allegiance, the Sister tugged her scars into a grimace and raised her sickle, recovered from the bloody ground, the curved blade sharp and deadly in the haze.

"Remember you are a Sword of God," the old woman told her. "You bear the Arimathean Shield, one of our holiest treasures."

The Sister bowed her head in benediction. All in the Chapter knew the tale, how long ago, St Joseph himself had gifted the shield to Sir Percival, the legendary knight of the Round Table. With it, the knight was said to have defeated a terrible dragon – a typically cherished story of the Chapter and one that couldn't fail to excite the assassin who heard it.

"May your pursuit be just as glorious," Evangelista said. Her smile was gone, replaced by a coldness in her eyes, the deep chill of devotion. "You have your orders. Find that misbegotten spawn of serpents. Bring him to our temple in the mountains. Bring him to the Invisible Church."

The Sister, all seven foot of her, offered a grin of her own.

"There we will pluck the truth from his tongue, extract the envoy's whereabouts. Ben Garston will answer for his crimes. And your Cardinal will take his head."

THREE

It's the harp. The Chapter want the harp.

Nursing his bloody stump, his nerve endings screaming louder than the wind, Ben burst through the cloud layer, chased by the worst of his fears. The clouds were inside his mind as well, his prodigious system fighting to throw off the tranqs, but even through his lingering stupor, the reason for the ambush seemed clear. Why would the Whispering Chapter postpone killing him when its agents had the chance? The old woman, whoever she was, was looking for Von Hart. There could only be one reason for that, surely.

Like the Chapter, the envoy extraordinary guarded a fragment of the harp. Indeed, dredging up his memories, it was the envoy who had brought the *Cwyth* to the great council on Thorney Island in the first place, wasn't it? As the last of the Fay, present at the Battle of Camlann, which had seen the fall of King Arthur, the Fay quit the earth and the Old Lands surrender to history, Von Hart must have kept the shattered instrument for centuries. In 1215, he had stood before King John to re-forge the damn thing, serving the royal edict of the Pact to bring about the Sleep. Yes, it had been a simple matter. Such power, if Ben credited the tales, conjured by the effortless act of fitting the broken pieces back together. *Lunewrought* melding to *lunewrought*. At the foot of the throne in Westminster Palace, the harp had blazed and sung in Von Hart's hands as he mustered his people's alien science, singing the names of the chosen Remnant leaders into the music. And of course, the lullaby had worked like a charm. The spell was more powerful than the King, the Curia Occultus and all the Remnants put together could have imagined. Kings had died and other kings had taken their place, but the Lore remained, the Sleep advancing. In the space of a hundred years, the lullaby had circled the globe . . .

Ben soared higher. The touch of the manacle added to the healing sting of his wounds, the *lunewrought* leaving a frosty residue to remind him of the power of the artefact to which it had once belonged. Nor did he feel safe up here, even at this altitude. He didn't think for one second that the Sister and the other agents wouldn't pursue him. He had seen the approaching choppers himself, all of them loaded with weapons, machine guns and rockets to shoot him from the sky. That was the least of his worries. It was only a matter of time before the Chapter recovered its fragment of the harp from the oil rig's lower decks and used its magic to summon him again, drawing him into the line of fire. Next time, he might not be so lucky. He had to get out of range of the song as fast as possible. The greater the range, the greater his chances of resisting its lure.

And then there was the matter of Von Hart himself.

You know where I am if you need me.

That was what the envoy had said last year, his exact words. Last year, the pale fairy had prevented Ben from becoming dragon steak on two separate occasions, once in London and once in Cairo. Five thousand feet up, with ice crystals forming on his snout, his inner gases keeping him warm, the memory of the Lurkers, the Walkers Between the Worlds, still prompted an unbidden shiver. He had never been a fan of magic. Less so of Von Hart's help. Hell, the envoy was probably watching him now, his strange violet eyes peering into whatever shiny ball he used for scrying. *Prying.*

Alongside his unease, caution snickered. He wanted answers. Who better to provide them than the envoy? But things weren't that simple. He couldn't be sure how the cards lay, whether the envoy was in hiding or not. On the one hand, he wanted to warn him, even though he doubted that the fairy was blind to the threat.

We all live under the Lore, Ben. He'd said that too, standing on the desert dunes in Cairo as they'd watched the refinery burn. *This changes everything.*

He had already tried to warn Ben. About a council. A possible trial. As a creature who loved a gamble, would the envoy risk the Chapter catching him napping? Unlikely. Ben settled on the feeling that it probably wasn't wise to lead his pursuers straight to Berlin. Von Hart, presiding over his secret neon realm of Club Zauber, would hardly thank him for it.

Like it or not, Ben was in over his head. This wasn't a matter of a resurrected goddess and an undead priest, an old rivalry threatening to plunge the world into darkness. This stabbed at the very heart of the Pact: the Long Sleep. The enchantment upon which the Lore rested. If the

31

Whispering Chapter was after the harp, then the new Cardinal might already have his grubby hands on the Guild's fragment, confiscating the artefact from the collapsed brotherhood of knights. And if the Chapter succeeded in reforging the blasted instrument, then—

A burst of silver in Ben's skull disintegrated the ominous thought. *The song? The lullaby? Already?* The smarting at his wrist, cold and brief, told him otherwise. It was the residue of the *lunewrought*, he thought, his fangs grinding, the ancient Fay magic responding to something below. It must be below. At this altitude, there was nothing around him but acres of sky, a clear blue prairie emerging from the tattered fringes of the storm. The odd seagull. He couldn't see a plane or hear the choppers, but he knew they'd come after him the minute the gale subsided, exhausting its wrath over the sea.

The faint blue glow drew his eyes towards the earth, the distant skerries of Denmark or the Netherlands appearing from the stratospheric sheen. He traced the luminous curve of an arc sweeping out to sea – an arc that he knew with a dragon's eye had nothing to do with the horizon. Huge it was, perhaps a mile or so across, much like a rainbow sweeping into the distance, albeit one that had been pushed over flat and comprised one colour, that depthless cerulean gleam. Twinkling. Fizzling with energy. *Magical.* As he flew lower and drew closer to the shore, it struck Ben, with a familiar cramping in his guts, that the arc was *inside* the land. Buried somehow. Rather than being superimposed, it ran like a stratum in stone, a visible quartz made up of light.

There were symbols down there too, he noticed, vast

sigils and glyphs bound by the edges of the curve, each one the size of a village or a small town. What the symbols meant, he couldn't tell, the gigantic alien alphabet marching off into the land, over forests and hills and rivers and roads, into the rounded haze, the limit where the earth met the sky. In the other direction, out to the ocean, the arc continued, perhaps reaching the tip of Scotland or Iceland further to the north-west.

What the hell am I seeing? Some kind of terrestrial brand or tattoo that one could only discern from thousands of feet up, and even then, Ben guessed, probably only when recently touched by *lunewrought*. Or spiked by tranquilliser darts. Something told him that the latter wasn't the case, but before he had a chance to investigate further, he noticed that the arc – what looked to him like the segment of a much wider circle, marching off to God knows where – was fading. Growing indistinct. It was decaying before his eyes, dark ragged holes growing in the landscape, the odd symbol winking out as though unseen flames were gradually eating through the fabric of the earth.

He blinked in the wind, and when he looked again, all he saw was the sea below, the coastline of Europe coming up fast. Whether magical vision or drug fugue, he couldn't be sure, but as though glimpsed unawares and evading his sight, the arc through the earth was gone.

Strange days indeed.

Ben flew onward, deciding on a course of action. There was no point wasting time on the unknown when the known was all around him and pressing – the mystery of the mnemonic harp and the Chapter's quest to recover it, if his detective skills were up to scratch. Danger threatened again, gushing into the smoking chasm left by the breach in the Lore. This time, he would do his best to stay ahead of the game. He needed information and, much as it galled him to admit it, help. He had to find Von Hart or at least make contact in some way, get a message to him. If the Whispering Chapter found the envoy before he did, well . . . his gut told him that it wouldn't end well.

Despite all this, suspicion mingled with his intent, stoked by the reappearance of the *Cwyth*. All the shit that had happened last year. He recalled his unplanned visit to Club Zauber last summer. Hadn't Von Hart quoted a verse from that old poem shortly after his arrival?

Foggily, Ben dredged up the words.

> The King's harp shattered in three
> re-forged then unmade a silver key
> a severed song the watcher's keep
> locking the door of endless sleep

Yeah. He had. At the time, Ben had dismissed the verse as a subtle taunt, Von Hart reminding him that most Remnants hadn't *chosen* to go into the Sleep. That in many cases, the harp, the key, fitted the padlock to what amounted to an enchanted prison. Now he wondered. Secrets and lies, unseen plans and events, lay like scattered cards on the table of his past actions, some in the suit hiding a darker underside.

Damn you, fairy. What were you trying to tell me?

Above all else, the envoy loved riddles. *Cryptic* was his

middle name. There was a point to all this, a game even. Ben had suspected as much in Egypt, and here it was again, that unshakeable feeling that the fairy was testing him, preparing him for something – something he might not like.

The history of the harp goes way back, back into legend and myth. And you were there at the start, weren't you? Bringing the harp to the Curia Occultus. Travelling to distant lands to ensure the progress of the Sleep. Who the hell knows what you got up to? Who the hell knows what you started . . .?

Ben cut off that particular line of thought. Distrust wouldn't help him here. He had a day, two days at best. And he owed the fairy a favour; it was a matter of honour that he couldn't ignore. The Chapter had managed to track him down, after all. It might take longer to track the envoy, but like the Guild, he imagined that its reach was long.

Into the south then, across Holland and down into France. It was hardly as out of range of the harp as he would've liked, but for now, he had limited choices. The envoy extraordinary was out of reach. But there were other keepers of secrets. And certain ways to extract them.

Even if he was too late, there were some, he knew, who had an ear for the dead.

Jing ~ mirror

Xanadu, 1275

At first, the Great Kublai Khan had resisted the idea of the *Tiaoyue*, the English Pact and the coming of the Sleep. He had sat, straight-backed and clutching the elephant-shaped arms of his throne, as his sorcerers, mandarins, emissaries, warriors, concubines, mystics and monks descended on the chamber in a restless flock, the vast white pillars resounding with the news from the west.

Jia Jing, a small green-and-gold shape crouched on a cushion at the Khan's feet, had struggled to pick out anything meaningful from the babble. Mention of some *lullaby* or other kept resurfacing from the milling audience below the dais, the shaven heads shaking this way and that, the raised hands and the snapping fans waving as though to swat points of the debate out of the air, dismissing the rumours as hearsay. No, as *tonghua*, as fairy tale.

And, as it happened, *tonghua* wasn't that far from the truth. Scowling at his subjects, the Great Khan had risen to his feet, a hand raised for silence. Jia, observing custom, rose along with him, awkwardly shuffling her hooves on the dais, her foal-like form flowing into the shape of a little

36

girl, her long dark braid coiled atop her head in the customary fashion. To all intents and purposes, she looked as human as any nine-year-old girl, but she kept forgetting about her hooves, and once she had made the transformation – a matter of shimmering seconds – it always felt too late to change them into silk-bound feet, a concession to embarrassment that would not go unnoticed. She was painfully aware of the stares darting from the Khan to where she stood beside him, her cloven hooves, both a glimmering gold, prompting whispers and pointed fingers from the throng. Why should she feel so uncomfortable, so out of place? Was she not one of the wonders of Xanadu? The Mongol invasion had not seen the Middle Kingdom shake off its faith in myths, clinging to gods both old and new with the same timeless reverence, a soul-deep devotion that Jia could not imagine the people renouncing. Magic endured in the soil here, in this, the most sacred, the most central of realms. Who among the noble houses and palace servants was unaware of the fact that the Khan enjoyed the counsel of ancient beasts, remnants of an older, wiser world? Long had the children of the *Xian* attended the Dragon Throne.

Oh yes, people speak of you, the Khan had assured her, *even in the lands beyond the Yellow River* . . .

That day at court, Jia had detected envy in many of the gazes and – oddly – she had noticed derision too, the reason for the latter soon becoming clear.

The Khan's new guest, the dusty Italian merchant with his sage-cum-guide standing at his shoulder, stepped forward and cleared his throat, thankfully stealing the attention of the court. After begging the Khan for patience, the merchant spoke at some length (pausing now and then for the sage to translate) about the infamous song that, over the course of sixty years, had wound its slow but inevitable way from England.

"It was a simple thing, Oh Wise One," the merchant said. "Such power, conjured by a re-forged harp. An ancient enchantment, the work of Fay magic, the lullaby was more powerful than the English King, the Pope and all the court put together could have imagined. A lullaby to cross oceans, to touch all lands." The merchant's voice trembled as he spoke, a feverish undercurrent of wonder. "You would have wept to see it, lord. The silver tide washed out from the hall on Thorney Island, striking the bells of Westminster Abbey, the old shrine resonating with fairy music. The echoes shivered across London, the notes sounding in every steeple from St Clement Danes to St Paul's and beyond. The music rippled over the city walls, across the fields and into the land, igniting every church along the way like . . . like dead trees in a forest fire! Windsor, Winchester, Rochester. On and on. By nightfall, even the bells in Scotia were said to have rung."

The lullaby, the merchant went on, had drifted on the winds across the sea, across the Holy Roman Empire and Byzantium, into far, dusty Pi-p'a-lo and the Caliphates of Persia. It was in the air. In the sky. In the fabric of things, he said, an enchantment flowing out in all directions, echoing off still water and between hollow trees, eventually spilling into the east. As the song progressed, the magic amplified, weaving outward to encompass the world. And wherever a Remnant heard the song – be they dragon, giant, troll, goblin, wizard or witch – the music would entrance and calm these creatures, the ground under them bubbling and seething, swallowing hundreds down into the Sleep, down into deep, though temporary, graves. *Such* mo shu*! Such power!* The lullaby, as the merchant called it, was not without its ambassadors, its diplomats and traders. Envoys like himself, the merchant said, who rode a day or so ahead of the musical tide to speak with the rulers of foreign lands, to press upon them the turning of the age. The envoys travelled at great personal risk to herald the advancement of all that was human, to stress the importance of magical suppression, the enthralment of the ever-warring Remnants.

It is my honour and my duty, the merchant said – through the mouth of the sage, of course – *to present this great golden compromise of choosing one representative from each Remnant tribe to remain safely awake among humans. As long as said Remnant swears to uphold the Lore and refrain from interfering in human affairs, then my sage will gladly sing their name and the lullaby, the enchantment, will not touch them.*

The rest of the Remnants, however, must fade and dwindle into the Sleep, safely removed from the ages, a historic truce to end all discord. At least, he continued, the Remnants must sleep until such a time came when the *Xian* returned, the climate for peace dawning again, commencing a new golden age where the darkness had passed and Remnants and humans could live in peace. All the legends claimed that the *Xian* had promised to return, did they not? Everybody knew that.

Many rulers, like the Khan, had resisted the idea, the merchant confessed, scoffing at the Pact as folly, a truce bound to break – but each king, queen, baron, contessa, sultan, tsarina, pasha, rani and shah soon found themselves inspired by the dream of growth and wealth and power. Of *progress*.

The sage, white-haired and dark-eyed, had looked up then, and addressed the Khan in his own voice, making it clear that he was no mere translator, no mere servant.

Look at the troubles in your lands, he said. *Look at the battle between Remnants and humans. Tell me, where do you see its ending?*

Gradually, her heart sinking to depths that only the young can feel, Jia had watched, helpless, as Kublai's scowls melted into frowns and then into hesitant smiles. The Khan was listening, and, to her horror, nodding in agreement.

She had looked at the merchant, this Marco Polo, his tongue working overtime as he seduced the Khan, laying silk upon silk, and she could see his hunger as plain as day. For trade. For glory. For rank and power. Frowning, she'd turned her attention to the other envoy, the wandering sage, who for all his thinness and long white hair was not yet old, an impression that had puzzled her at first. Alarm scattered all her perceptions as she realised that he was staring directly up at the dais.

As she met his strange violet eyes, he bowed slightly in greeting.

That was all weeks ago. The lullaby had wound its way into the Middle Kingdom with the Great Khan's blessing

– an unusual move from one so staunchly resistant to foreign influence – and Jia Jing, the chosen Imperial ward, could do nothing but watch as the creeping spell ensorcelled her kith and kin, putting the last ragged remnants of her herd under the Long Sleep. From a high watchtower, the white-haired sage had sung her name into the dusk, or so she was told, unable to hear him in the achingly sweet yet terrible music resounding from every temple, every hall, the lullaby taken up by every zither, lute, drum and gong in Xanadu.

In the wild-flower meadow beyond the palace wall, she had wept and kissed her parents goodbye, stern Ziyou and gentle Ye, who were as gods to her. No more would the three of them run wild with the wind across the northern plains, Ziyou whinnying laughter as he goaded Jia to leap gullies and streams, Ye chiding her husband and warning of stones and broken legs, laughing all the same. No more to sit on her mother's lap in human form, her father cradling them both and a yellowing storybook from the palace library, reading the old tales of the realm, his voice rising to mimic the fright of the Monkey King as he raced from Ox-Head and Horse-Face at the gates to the underworld.

No more. Jia had listened to her parents' parting advice, to serve the Khan well, and to heed their reassurance that all would be well.

We will return one day, daughter, they had told her. *When the world is ready for magic again. When the Xian return from the Dark Frontier. We too will come home.*

Jia had one hope and one hope only, and that was to believe them. There was no room to focus on the alternative if she expected to go on with a sound mind, to live. And so the music had come weaving through the trees, an invisible serpent hushing over the grass, bringing loss and loneliness and change and sleep. Then, slowly, one by one, the gathered herd had slumped to the ground and the ground had bubbled and churned, opening in deep, dark funnels of molten earth. Down, down, her parents went, the wild flowers closing over their heads. In moments, the lullaby faded and her mother and father were gone.

This morning, Jia sat and pouted on the palace steps, remembering. *Pining.* She missed them. Already she missed them with the aching bewilderment of an only child left to wonder why neither of them had contested the Khan's will, why they had agreed to leave her behind. At nine years of age, her green silk dress tattered at the hem and her long black braid woven with happenstance leaves, Jia didn't quite understand why the Khan had chosen her alone to remain. She was the youngest of the herd, true – barely a foal – and thus most useful to the Wise One and all the shining dynasties to come, but what dark fate lay ahead of her? What purpose? Why had her parents refused to tell her? Were they afraid she might refuse?

At the high altar in the temple, she had bent to sign the merchant's Pact, nothing more than a tatty bit of scroll, and intoned the sacred words, repeating the chief monk's oath. "To serve the Emperor of Zhongguo, the Middle Kingdom, for all the time to come." All of the priests and all of the people had witnessed this, a declaration of Remnant alliance and loyalty.

You serve the Dragon Throne now, the monk had hissed at

her, a hunched, wizened elder with no teeth. *And you have sworn to uphold the Lore. Make no mistake, your survival depends on it!*

Much as she disliked this warning, the honour was indeed a grand one, and publicly she displayed a quiet gratitude, bowing where necessary, kneeling when required, a distant yet agreeable smile balanced on her lips.

Privately, it was no use. Sitting on the steps, Jia wiped an eye. Ziyou and Ye might have left these lands like all of her kind, but the memory of them still galloped across the plains of her dreams. Like it or not, she was the last of the *sin-you* – what the Italian merchant called a "unicorn', though she disliked the foreign term, disliked hearing her unique and extraordinary kind reduced to nothing more than a European counterpart when she had never been anything other than herself. And every day, she felt the same ache, the same longing, the same need to remind herself.

They are not dead. They are sleeping.

To take her mind off her loss, she turned her thoughts to her guardian, her protector (she refused to entertain the word *keeper*, although she knew, as all her kind knew, that *keeper* was the uncomfortable truth). This recent change in the Khan's outlook, his shift from stubborn pride in the realm's existing state of affairs to a growing concern over its position, lay firmly at the newcomer's feet, Jia thought. These days, the Khan spent so much time with the dusty Italian merchant, Jia felt just as abandoned by him as she did by her parents. Kublai and this Marco Polo, who'd spent years trekking down the Silk Road and now walked the stone paths of the great garden, chatting through the linguistic efforts of the little scribe bobbing between them. Listen to them! The Khan and his guest. Laughing in the shade of the willow trees!

Jia scrunched up her face as she heard them, the Khan's chuckles rumbling up the dazzling marble steps where she sat in the shadow of the watchtower. Like a spindle for the sun, the edifice loomed above her, the Great Khan's summer palace, Jewel of the North, the rooms of which were all gilt and painted with figures of men and beasts and birds, and with a variety of trees and flowers, all executed with such exquisite art. The beauty of the place had dwindled somewhat in the weeks since the Khan had capitulated to his guest and agreed that the dragons whispering high through the air and the wailing ghosts and the fearsome hopping *jiangshi* would prove a sword in the cog of any future world empire. Not to mention the skin walkers, the fire-eating goats and the rampaging *raksha* demons. All must give up. All must give way.

And as for me? I do not belong here . . .

All Jia had to do was lift up her dress a couple of inches and look at her glossy golden hooves on the sun-drenched steps to know this.

She was thinking this when the shadow fell across her. She started, looking around and up at the silhouette on the terrace behind her. It was the other one. The sage who had arrived with Polo, guiding him across the Taklamakan Desert by all accounts, this tall wanderer with the long hair and fine-boned face, both so white that they shone silver in the sun. Why hadn't she heard him approach?

"Good day to you, Daughter of Empires."

He moved into the shade of a pillar where she could see him, take in his long robe, the red silk patterned with stars, the formal garb tied loosely at the waist. She recognised the foreign garb as a kimono, an imported luxury – or a stolen bounty – from Japan, and she was already scowling. He probably fancied himself as some kind of sorcerer or prophet-of-the-sands, muttering this and that cosmic nonsense into the ears of fools.

Jia, who was in no mood for chatter, screwed up her nose even further. She had not forgiven him for singing her name from the watchtower weeks ago, whatever the bidding of the Khan.

"I am the daughter of Ziyou and Ye, both fallen into the Sleep. And there is but one empire to my knowledge, the greatest upon the earth. I linger here at the wishes of Kublai Khan. Who are you to creep up on one under his protection?"

To her frustration, the man in the robes chuckled, his scrawny shoulders shaking. Calming himself, he leant down towards her, his strange shadowed eyes like fragments of twilight.

"An honoured guest, Miss Jing," he told her, the sound of her name, unoffered, startling her. His accent was as strange as his eyes, a soft, guttural twang from Deguo, the Kingdom of the Franks, that for all its outlandishness courted her attention. His familiar tone, however, nettled her. He smelled of rice wine and dusty scrolls, a combination that she wished she could find unpleasant, seeking a reason to mock him. "I have come to Xanadu – or Shangdu or Cambalu or whatever you like to call it – to foster peace with the

45

Middle Kingdom, to ensure Master Polo's safety and advance the progress of the Long Sleep. Perhaps I hoped to make a friend or two of the Remnants in these parts, offer my comfort and my counsel, help them adjust to life under the Lore. Alas, all I see is a rude little girl."

"Then you don't see enough," Jia said, glaring up into his porcelain face, his sharp nose perched above her, casting a shadow of amusement. "For I see more than an interfering sage, dressed in the guise of a man. I see one who would never care about peace, friendship or another's safety without a heavy price. I see one who doesn't belong here any more than I do. A creature just as lost and abandoned as—" She caught herself, her breath hitching in her throat. "Oh!"

Jia had thought this was reasonably clever, up to the point of her shock. As a *sin-you*, a living, breathing symbol of justice, she had the extraordinary talent of perceiving truth from lie, a talent inherent to all her kind and one that, naturally, made her invaluable to the Great Khan's court. It was like breathing; as Jia regarded the sort-of-man before her, there was no doubt in her mind about his real nature. And once hitting on the truth, it was hard to keep a grimace of shame from edging through her expression, which only grew deeper when the man straightened up to laugh. Echoes skittered up and away into the palace like doves released from a cage.

"You wound me." He pressed a hand to his chest, his eyelids fluttering. "Why, it's almost as if you're the first person to ever point that out. Such insight! Such wisdom! Where would the Khan be without you?"

"I didn't—"

He cut her off. "It's a shame you do not like me, child.

46

The truth is I'm not unused to such greetings. Humans fear what they don't understand. Which leaves me wondering – what's your excuse?"

"I . . . I am not afraid of you."

"*Wunderbar.* Your courage will serve you well in the days ahead. Our business here is done, you see, the Pact signed and sealed in the east, but the Khan has asked me to stay on longer. I'm afraid you'll have no choice but to endure me."

Jia's heart sank to new, uncharted depths.

"Here? In Xanadu?" Why was she trembling so? Could he tell? "Why?"

"Oh, something about an education," he said. "The taming of ill-mannered wards. That kind of thing."

Just like that, Jia was scowling again.

"And you were happy to accept, of course," she shot back, looking to prick him in return. "For a price."

His mirth resolved into a thin-lipped smile.

"I had heard that your kind see much, truth from lie, the real from illusion, and it fascinated me so. How could one stand before such a creature, his heart rendered as naked as a babe?" He told her this and then, all seriousness, his nose came swooping down towards her again, almost meeting the end of her own. In one swift, graceful motion – the flick of a fish in a pond – he pressed a finger firmly to the middle of her forehead, where the curved point of her secret nature lay hidden beneath her skin. "Well, I'll tell you. I am a fairy, one of a race that you call the *Xian*. We are known for our glamour and tricks. And don't you ever forget it, you naughty green filly."

47

Jia was on her feet – her hooves – at once. All outrage and wonder, she knocked the sage's finger away and would have delivered a rather sharp kick to his root-thin shins if the Great Kublai Khan and the dusty Italian merchant hadn't broken through the trees at just that moment, walking onto the broad stone terrace that spread out from the foot of the palace steps.

". . . built this place when my awful grandfather burnt Zhongdu to the ground," the Khan was saying, his long golden robes glittering in the sun. "Here I have entertained many marvels – from fox spirits to firewalkers – and pleasured many wives."

This boast might have impressed the famous Marco Polo, but for all the little scribe's deciphering chatter, the dark-haired young man in the ragged tunic couldn't quite seem to grasp the sense of it. *Pleasured?* he enquired. *Wives?* Then he gave up, making a strange little sound in his throat, his cheeks turning red. Kublai, who had emerged from the trees with much the same grace as a water buffalo, stifled a chuckle. The hand rising towards his mouth twisted into an elegant summons as he noticed the pale sage and the little girl standing on the steps.

The sage and the girl bowed, their argument forgotten. Or perhaps postponed.

"Ah, Master Von Hart. Welcome, lord, once more to our lands. After all, are you not written into our legends, having fought the white wyrm in the mountains east of here three-score years ago? Are you not older and paler than the walls of Xanadu herself?"

"All this and more, Great Khan."

48

"Come, Jia, show some courtesy. Bring our envoy extraordinary down here beside the pool. My servants will serve us some tea." The Great Khan clapped his hands. He clapped them right next to the little scribe's ear, so no one could be in any doubt who he meant by "servants", and the little scribe hurried off, rustling down a path between the trees. "I am passing the hour with your courageous friend Master Polo, who really does tell the most remarkable tales. Ghosts in the desert, wasn't it? And visits to cities years out of his way." The Khan winked at the young merchant. "Jia Jing, of all my subjects, will happily tell us the truth of them."

Polo spluttered at the joke, but he took his place easily enough on the low stone wall around the pool. Now it was Jia's turn to redden, embarrassed by the thought of the Khan putting her on show. She stared into the pool, the afternoon sun glimmering in the water like the coins strewn on the bottom. Cherry blossoms bobbed on the ripples made by the white and orange koi, both liquid in the scattering light. So much was scattered these days. So much lost.

The little scribe reappeared from the bushes bearing a rattling tray with a teapot and several cups set out upon it. He was setting this down before the Great Khan as Jia in her tattered green dress and Von Hart in his long red robe joined them on the terrace.

"Jia, my petal, why do you look so glum?" the Khan asked when the two of them drew near. "Speak up now, my girl. You mope around my halls like a ghost and barely pay attention to matters of state, which is where your lessons will lead you in time. Tell me that your downcast eyes are due to the heat or the brewing war with the Shogunate Regents of Nippon. Anything but the *Tiaoyue!*"

The Great Khan rolled his eyes at Master Polo, who tittered in that way of his, even before the scribe had a chance to translate. Polo, of course, would know the *Tiaoyue* as *Il Patto*. Or possibly just as the English Pact, a name people currently whispered, or so Jia had heard, in every tavern across Europe. The mandarins claimed that the mysterious contract was already fast becoming a rumour, destined to become the secret of the age just as its founders had intended . . .

Thinking of the lessons ahead of her, days spent with the sage at her side, she mustered a boldness she didn't feel.

"I miss my herd," she said. Her voice was smaller than the blossoms floating on the pool. "I miss—"

"We have all made sacrifices," the Great Khan said and took a sip of tea. His words were consoling, but his face was not, as he looked down upon this all-but-orphan in his care, this pale, pretty waif, who was adrift and utterly miserable in paradise. "Your parents have made the greatest sacrifice of all. You must honour them, Jia. While they sleep, we will build a heaven on earth. I see no reason to cry, little one."

Nevertheless, tears burned in Jia's eyes. She knew that they must shine like pearls, betraying her sorrow to everyone present. Mocking the strength that she had promised to show the Great Khan, her parting oath to Ziyou and Ye. As Kublai poured more tea, his grip threatening to break the handle, and Polo found something interesting to look at in the sky, the white-haired sage who in truth was a fairy said,

"My Khan, if I may?"

The Khan grunted. Von Hart bowed, taking this as royal assent. When he spoke, he turned to face Jia.

"As Master Kung teaches, the heart of the wise should resemble a mirror, which reflects every object without being sullied." When Jia met his eyes, the envoy hastened his words. "But you are young and yet to grow wise, Jia Jing. In this, I will give you three gifts. My time, a tale and a choice. Do you accept?"

"If the Khan deems your gifts fitting," she said, pointedly aloof. But when the Khan simply grunted again and sipped his tea, Jia bristled, unable to contain a rush of hostility. "I am sure he paid handsomely for all of them!"

"Jia Jing!" The Great Kublai spluttered over his cup, wheezing as he sat forward.

Von Hart held up a palm.

"Be at peace, oh Wise and Merciful Ruler of the Northern Plains and All Zhongguo from the Great Wall to the Southern Seas." As the Khan flushed with pleasure at this somewhat excessive address, the envoy followed up his flattery with a smooth piece of business acumen. "But perhaps the child is right. And to be frank, my tale would be better served by an example. If it please you, we should conclude our dealings here, out in the open, for all to see."

And now the Khan flushed a deeper shade, shifting his bulk and coughing behind his hand, revealing that he was all too aware of the little trap of decorum into which he had fallen.

"Think no more of it," he said and clapped his hands.

Out of the trees at the edge of the terrace, a team of six servants emerged wrestling a large, unwieldy and angular object. As they came closer, Jia realised that the object was a mirror, framed in some kind of dark wood, perhaps mahogany, perhaps teak. Unlike the mirrors dotted around the palace, the frame, an octagonal border at least a foot thick, bore no carvings of any kind, no dragons, no phoenix, no symbols for health and prosperity, no warnings against vanity. The lack of decoration surprised her – the artisans in Xanadu would have painted the flowers if the Khan had let them – but any calls for modesty, in this case, would have been unnecessary. The mirror was so dirty, the glass was black, betraying the artefact's untold age.

Grunting, the servants clunked the mirror down, clods of filth and dust falling to the flagstones. The huge frame rested on its stand in the middle of the terrace, the top of the thing looming two or three feet over Von Hart's head – and a great deal more over Jia's. Apart from its size and the dirt that covered it, she found nothing more remarkable about the antique, and threw the envoy a puzzled, and vaguely triumphant, look.

"This was your price?"

Von Hart wasn't listening to her. It was clear that the white-haired sage did not share her indifference, gazing at the mirror in evident awe, a hand trembling out, the tips of his fingers stroking the frame as one might stroke a beloved cat.

"So it's true," he said, in barely a whisper. "The Eight

Hand Mirror has endured. I hardly dared believe otherwise, but . . ."

"There is nothing beyond the power of the Dragon Throne, Master Von Hart." The Khan, puffed up by the fairy's flattery and presently enjoying some of his own, leant back on the poolside wall. "I realise that your tutelage does not come cheap and I imagine you thought your price impossible. As I said, I do not promise what I cannot deliver. Some weeks ago, one of my raiding parties discovered the relic in an island shrine off the coast of Japan. What the Shogunate will not give, we will take, yes?"

The Khan laughed. Von Hart merely smiled, without taking his eyes off the mirror.

"It's an old mirror," Jia said, too mystified to mock.

"Or perhaps a door," the envoy murmured, mostly to himself. "A door without a key. The Eight Hand Mirror is one of our oldest trinkets, child, left behind by my people when they departed this world, abandoning us to our fate. I have travelled many leagues to find it."

Jia sniffed. "Forgive me, but it does not look like much to me. It looks like you lack skill in bargaining, to be fair. And it certainly doesn't look like a tale, which is what you offered me."

Von Hart shook his head, his hand falling from the frame. As he turned to face her, a sly expression stole across his features, once again drawing her into the orbit of his confidence.

"Very well. Then here is my tale," he said, and with no more ceremony, began. "In the days of the Yellow Emperor, lord of the old gods of Zhongguo, the world of mirrors and the world of men were as one. Two worlds, with two peoples, both quite different from the other. The old gods had fashioned the humans from the earth, but the mirror children, it is said, were shaped by the *Xian*, which most call the Fay in my part of the world."

Jia narrowed her eyes. Was the envoy making fun of her? Everyone knew that the worlds of Remnants and humans were different, a division based on fear, yes, but also on origin. The old gods had made the humans and when the old gods fell, becoming the *Xian*, these debased powers had created the Remnants – it wasn't hard to see the allegory in Von Hart's tale. Or that he wasn't just telling it for entertainment. The arrival of the Eight Hand Mirror, a convenient prop for his story, struck Jia, at that moment, as a touch too rehearsed. Was this tale simply for her benefit? A way to make her accept her new circumstances? He hadn't lied *outright*; of this, she was naturally sure. All the same, insincerity wafted on the breeze, making her ears twitch. She listened to the rest of Von Hart's tale in bunch-shouldered, knowing unease.

"Both kingdoms, the human and the specular, lived in harmony. The mirror, you see, is simply a metaphor. Figurative." Jia snorted to show that she wasn't stupid – at least the envoy admitted it – but he went on regardless. "A symbol to show that an object and its reflection are two wildly different things. Sadly, in time, a war broke out. There were many reasons why, not least the departure of the *Xian* into the Dark Frontier, to distant shores across the gulfs of infinity, but at its roots, the tale tells us that the humans and the mirror children could no longer share the world in peace. Thus, they say that the armies of men gathered and trapped the *Xian*'s wayward creations in a mirror kingdom, thereby binding them in a cage of reflections and forcing them to repeat all the actions of men. They stripped these creatures of their magic powers and reduced them to slavish dreams, ghosts of their former selves, forever locked behind glass."

There was a silence. The metaphor was clearer now, or so Jia thought. *Locked behind glass.* Surely this meant the *Tiaoyue*? The English Pact and the Sleep?

Ghosts of their former selves . . .

Imprisoned.

"It is said that when one looks through the glass and sees the bitterest truth," Von Hart continued, "on that day, the mirror will break."

At first, Jia didn't realise that the tale had ended. She expected the envoy to go on, thinking that there would be more. Instead, to cover for the fact that she had grown curious, rapt even, she let out a sigh, wilfully jaded.

"You mean me, don't you? You mean *us*. The Remnants."

Von Hart put a finger to his lips, but he was smiling, as cheerful as a canary.

"Shhh. We cannot speak of such things as freely as we once did."

It was the first time that she had felt any warmth towards him. Her own smile, playing at the corners of her mouth, evaporated as his tone turned serious, harsh even.

"And now to your choice," he said. "Will you turn away or look into the mirror? I must warn you, I offer you this but once and once only. And once you have chosen, the consequences are entirely yours. There can be no going back."

"Master Von Hart," she told him, quite plainly, "I looked into your mirror and all I saw was dirt."

"You can look again, if you wish," he replied. "Or you can walk away, believing whatever you want to believe. Believing that you have seen an old mirror, a fairy's fancy. Nothing more."

Her lips took on a wry slant.

Is this a game? Is he testing me?

She glanced at the Khan, but he was simply watching, apparently as mystified as she was. Who could guess at the intention of fairies? So, happy to play along, she said, "And what, may I ask, lies in your mirror?"

"Why," he said, "your heart's desire, of course."

Jia sighed, her shoulders falling, defeated by his absurdity.

"Very well then," she said, echoing his sombre words. "Astound me."

Von Hart walked over to the mirror. With a shrug that informed her that there were no tricks here, no special incantations or complicated ritual, he waved one alabaster hand before the glass. *Just look.* And so Jia looked again. This time, on closer inspection, she found that she was no longer looking at a dirt-encrusted surface, an archaic silver disc buried under filth, but that the glass itself was black, as smooth, as lustrous as obsidian – or as deep as a well. As she drew closer to the mirror, she realised that the Great Kublai and Master Polo had noticed the change too, both of them shooting to their feet, the tea tray rattling, their mouths hanging open. The little scribe forgot all about his duties as a servant and leapt into the nearest bush.

Von Hart withdrew to the edge of the frame as Jia advanced. Standing before the glass, she waved a hand. Then she glanced behind her at the Khan and the merchant, at the garden beyond them. Then she frowned at Von Hart.

"None of us are in the mirror. It only reflects the trees around us. How?"

"It is not that kind of mirror," Von Hart said. "Look."

Jia looked. At first she thought that the coiling mist was a combination of her recent tears and the afternoon sunlight, an illusion captured in the glass, but then the mist gradually parted and she found herself looking into a deep, dark space. Even though the flagstones warmed her hooves as she stood in the shadow of the Khan's palace, she was gazing into a yawning cavern, black and measureless, and a vast flat space before her that she took for a sunless sea, without waves, without so much as a ripple on its surface.

Pulled by a string of awe, her petulance forgotten, Jia moved in a trance towards the mirror. Von Hart stood beside the frame, watching her, his strange eyes glittering.

"The Eight Hand Mirror answers the desire of the one who stands before it," the envoy said. "And you can see them, can't you?"

"Yes," she told him. And she could. Ziyou and Ye lay upon the dark shore, their faint green shapes recumbent and curled around each other, their haunches relaxed, their manes covering their eyes. Their bellies rose and fell with their slumbering breaths.

Catching sight of the unfolding vision, Master Polo took

a step back, almost tumbling into the pool. He jabbed out a finger at the fairy.

"And that's where the Remnants belong," he said, visibly shuddering inside his tunic despite the heat of the day. "You said so yourself, Von Hart. Our worlds can never be one."

But it was the girl who replied.

"That, Master Polo, is a lie."

FOUR

Paris. The City of Light. Ben came wheeling down from the night, his wings spread to embrace her. Montmartre twinkled and shone, a mound of jewels above the weave of streets. The Eiffel Tower was a lighthouse in the dark, a spotlight beaming from its crown of steel ingenuity. Ben swept across its path, coasting over La Chapelle, rattling the trains on the elevated Métro line. A minute later, his passage stole the hats from late-night shoppers in the Square André-Tollet. He banked, following the river of the boulevard. By the time anyone looked up, questioning the sudden gust, he was already gone, out of sight.

Paris might be the City of Light, but she harboured pools of darkness too, the broad parks like lakes of tar at this late hour. It was darkness he sought now – reluctantly, urgently – the labyrinthine arteries of Père Lachaise cemetery, a city within the city. A city of the dead.

Last year, the threat had arisen from darkness and death, from whispering ghosts and buried tombs. A cemetery struck him as a good place to dig for information. Besides, the one who resided here – the one who lingered – was always open to a bargain. At least, he had been two hundred years ago, at the end of the French Revolution. Ben was banking on the fact that the Remnant's appetites lingered too, along with his curiosity. His – and the February cold filled him at the thought – *spies*.

Fifteen feet off the ground, Ben extended his will, a cerebral push from bestial to human – and he was a man in a dark-scaled suit dropping from the sky. *Thud*. Despite his caution, masonry buckled, some vault or other cracking under his weight, his reduced tonnage trailing him like an echo, a ripple of inertial mass. He kicked grit from his toes, throwing off the chiding of the graves.

Sorry about that, bones. You see, I'm the third-generation spawn of a long-extinct mythical lizard and something bright and slimy that squirmed inside a glass alembic. This human form is just a disguise, a clever way to move from A to B. You could say I'm a glorified guard dog . . .

Ben snorted to himself in the gloom. He was long past the point of kidding himself.

All around, the silhouettes of mausoleums and tombs marched off down the tree-lined lanes of the Avenue Circulaire. The cemetery was closed, of course, but he would have to watch out for patrols. He didn't want any trouble. Père Lachaise, the largest boneyard in the city, was a daily draw for thousands of tourists, come to pay their respects and marvel at the graves of novelist and poet, dancer and scientist, composer and painter, surgeon, activist and rock star. There were no lamps to light his way, only the moon and his serpentine vision, which kicked in now, his retinas shining like coins. Dust and the scent of decay drifted to his nostrils, mingling with flowers dying and dead. Reverence hung in the atmosphere. Carved faces watched him as he padded into the murk, winged angels and bearded busts, all silent, mossy and grey.

But not everything here was asleep. Not everything here was at rest.

He reached the Monument aux Morts and stood before the famous tableau, the angular edifice shaped, ironically enough, to resemble an Egyptian mastaba. Weeping figures flanked the centrepiece – a large rhomboid doorway leading into dark. A man and a woman, both naked and pale under the moon, stood on either side of the egress, their limestone backs turned to him, the woman's hand draped on the man's shoulder, perhaps reassuring him as they prepared to enter the place where, in the end, all must enter.

Including Ben. He crouched, flexing his legs, and leapt up onto the ledge between the statues. Few knew that the monument wasn't just for show. The shadowed doorway led down into the catacombs that snaked under Paris, a labyrinth of dust and bones. Even the Remnant who dwelt here couldn't claim to have reached the end of every stairway, every tunnel, and he was nine hundred years old . . .

A few steps and Ben reached the iron gate barring his way. Most would have been lost in the gloom, but Ben could see well enough, the soft radiance thrown by his gaze picking out the heavy padlock and chain. Padlocks and chains meant little to him. Unlike the small symbol etched on the gate.

✝

It was one of the old ones, all right. Not as old as *wyrm tongue*, perhaps, but archaic and forgotten all the same. The symbol belonged to one of the Five Families of the *vampyri* and marked this place as a *Maison du DemiVivant*, a House of the Half Living. The Families were gone now, of course, fast asleep in a box somewhere, dreaming their long dark dreams through night and through day.

A thump, a kick, and the gate was scrap metal at his feet. To hell with manners. Du Sang would either answer him or not. Fuck the ancient customs. This wasn't 1793.

Grit crunched underfoot. Ben trudged down steps and into a chamber, alcoves on either side of him, filled with the splintered remains of coffins and pale jags of bone. The musty smell was stronger here, lichen and rot. Things squirmed and skittered in the dark, disturbed by his presence. *Worms and rats. The least of my worries.* On the far side of the chamber he made out a brick archway, a curtain of cobwebs fluttering across it. He tore through the veil (his severed hand was all but renewed now, the skin a little red from the wound) and stale air whispered around him, wafting from the depths beyond. Was it his imagination or did he hear a word in the draught? A dry, soft breath, chill on his flesh.

Benjurigan . . .

Yes. He was expected. Of course he was. The creature that made this pit his home had eyes everywhere. Ben couldn't hope to catch him unawares.

He pressed on, his shoulders brushing the corridor walls, which sloped gently downwards. Embrasures in the vaults above let in shafts of moonlight, but he could already see that he was in a gallery of some kind. He passed paintings as he went, rendered in the Romantic style, the images slowing his steps. It struck him that the series of paintings looked so modern because someone hadn't wanted to forget the old tale. Lord knows no human would find this story in a book, for either children or grown-ups. All the same, he had to tear shrouds of cobwebs away from the frames to confirm what he was looking at.

The first painting depicted a battle. A snowy valley, stained by the light of a dying sun. By smoke. By blood. In the fray, Ben made out men and women in shining armour, lances set against all manner of beasts – goblins, dwarves, witches, trolls. Giants loomed over the clash, dull flecks of red representing the mess left by their clubs as the weapons swung through the rabble, flinging handfuls of knights into the air. Overhead, dragons raked the skies with flame, some of them mounted, some of them strapped with empty saddles. It was an idealistic image, Ben supposed; he had heard that some Remnants fought against King Arthur too, choosing the side of the Usurper, Mordred. Either way, when a pavilion at the edge of the battlefield drew his eye, it was clear that he was looking at a portrayal of the Battle of Camlann, back in the sixth century. A pennant flapped gaily from the top of the tent. From its place on the wooded hill, all who fought below would see the crimson symbol of the Pendragon.

Where all this shit started . . .

In the next image, Ben found himself peering at the inside of the pavilion. A sad tableau spread out before him, the paint as timeworn and dreary as the scene. A grey-bearded man in armour sat with his head in his hands at a round wooden table. He had liked round tables, this man, and Ben didn't need the obvious symbolism to place the figure as Arthur, the legendary King of the Britons. At his belt hung a sword with a jewelled pommel, another giveaway. Caliburn, the Sword of Albion. Next to the King, a dwarf wearing a cap with bells was bringing Arthur a foaming jug, no doubt one of a few judging by his pose. But it was the woman on the other side of the tent who caught the whole of Ben's attention. Earth-skinned and snow-haired, her braids coiled high upon her head, her eyes the typical violet shade. He recognised her from a hundred legends, a hundred tales known only to Remnants and the few humans privy to the secret history of Britain, a land once known as Logres, the Old Lands. He recognised her with an ache in his breast and a lump in his throat, an unbidden longing. Those same legends referred to her as the Lady of the Lake. Nimue. Our Lady of the Barrow. Queen of the Fay.

In her arms, the Lady bore a harp. The harp resembled a unicorn, the silver and ivory column crowned by an equine head and a tapering conch-like horn. It was the *Cwyth*, forged from *lunewrought*, the ore of Avalon. The story went that during the final battle between the King and Mordred, Nimue had offered Arthur the magical relic. Eager to turn the tide of the war, to preserve the shining Example of Camelot, the Queen had told the King that by strumming the ancient instrument, he could put Mordred and his army into an enchanted sleep until the cavalry arrived in the form of Sir Lancelot, the White Knight.

It hadn't gone down well.

Ben moved on, his breaths slow, his feet shuffling through dust. In the third painting, the King was on his feet, his sword in hand. The blade was slicing down on the *Cwyth*, the harp flying apart in three fragments, silvery splinters showering the scene. The dwarf was falling back in horror, tankards of mead splattering around him. The Lady, however, stood with her spine straight and her arms folded, her proud stature betrayed by the sorrow in her eyes. Ben remembered that in the tale, Arthur had refused her gift. Mistrustful of the Fay and believing that the Queen was offering him a coward's way out, he had shattered the harp. And, in his pride, he had damned them all.

The fourth and final painting, more faded than the others, as though touched by many hands, depicted the outcome. The scene was outside the pavilion again, its pennant limp now, the sun setting on the Pendragon banner. Between the trees, figures moved, or perhaps ghosts, a scattered crowd of slender men and women drifting up the hill. Ben could see through many of the figures, their transparent dresses and cloaks like gossamer thrown over the snow-laden branches and the pristine ground. But he knew that he wasn't looking at men and women, not really, nor any earthly creatures. The figures, the Fay, each with backs turned, moved up the rise towards what appeared to be a blazing black sun, a broad dark circle on the summit. Some were vanishing into that darkness, winking out like stars.

The Fay. Leaving . . .

Disgusted by human weakness, the Lady Nimue had led the Fay from the earth, abandoning both Remnants and humans to the dark days ahead, to days of blood and war and centuries of bitterness . . .

Ben wiped dust from his face, grunting at the unexpected moisture on his fingers. Shaking himself from his awe, he made to turn away when a figure in one corner of the painting grabbed his attention, drawing him back to the frame. He swallowed, then frowned. The man – who was, of course, no man at all – stood watching the Fay depart. The thin figure also had his back turned, his white-gold hair tumbling between his slumped shoulders and spilling onto his robe, the red silk patterned with stars. At his feet, in a silvery pile, rested the fragments of the harp.

Oh man . . .

With a sigh, Ben turned away, shaking his head. Yeah, it was the myth of the Lady, all right. A fairy tale for fairy tales. Some Remnants saw the ancient sorceress in a nigh-on messianic light. Others saw her as the worst kind of traitor, a villain who had left them to die. Ben couldn't call that one. The Fay had fucked off into the nether six hundred years before he had hatched, leaving them all to their fate – all Remnants knew the tale. After all, it was their provenance, the reason why they were Remnants. And most Remnants hoped that one day, when pigs flew and trees sang and the moon married the sun, the Fay would return as the Queen had promised . . .

One shining day, when Remnants and humans learn to live in peace, and magic blossoms anew in the world, then shall the Fay return and commence a new golden age.

Ben shared his feelings with a snort.

Dragons and unicorns. And fairy ladies singing lullabies. Right.

Shrugging off the ache in his chest, he found his way to a narrow stairway that wound around the walls, spiralling into the heart of a well. For all he knew, the pit might stretch to the bowels of the earth. Here and there, in the nooks and crannies, skulls grinned, their eyeless sockets somehow watchful. Claws slipped from his feet to grip the steps, one hand tracing the crumbling brickwork. He drew his hand back as something fat and hairy skittered over it, his cry resounding down into darkness, then back up at him, a distorted echo. Frowning, he balled a fist to squash the offending bug – and then realised that the wall was covered in spiders, crawling out of socket and jaw of the surounding skulls, a black surging mass clicking and rustling beside him as he made his way down.

By the time he came across du Sang, Ben was peeling webs off his cheeks and out of his hair. The spiders followed and watched, a million shiny eyes upon him. He was thinking of drawing a breath, incinerating the lot of them, when du Sang spoke.

"*Bonsoir*, Monsieur Garston. To what do I owe this uninvited pleasure?"

FIVE

Le Vicomte Lambert du Sang reclined in the middle of the pit. It took Ben a second for his eyes to adjust, to see that du Sang lay on a tangled net of cobwebs sagging from the surrounding walls. The web bowed slightly under his weight, the lightless depths showing through the gaps.

Ben halted, looking down at his quarry from a cautious distance.

"Let's not pretend," he said, nodding at the walls, the spiders halted along with him, an army of shiny eyes. "You always were a nosy bugger."

"Oh, don't mind my little spies. It is in their nature to gossip." Du Sang stretched and yawned, a sound like leather drawn over gravel. "From New York to Cairo, how they like to chatter. And how I like to listen."

"Then you know damn well why I'm here. You're looking . . ." *Well?* No, he couldn't say that. He changed tack. "It's been a while. How is life – death, whatever – treating you?"

Du Sang made a sound in his throat. It might have been a chuckle.

"I thought your kind had fabulous vision. How does it look like it's treating me?"

The creature below looked like a boy to Ben, young,

sinewy and pale, but a boy who had gone to his grave several
years ago and perhaps after a horrible accident. Du Sang
was so grey that he blended with the web around him. Bones
lay under his wrinkled flesh and not all of them matched
up, an elbow, a shoulder jutting in the wrong direction. The
rags he wore couldn't hide the mess. Worst of all was his
face, which was simply a skull, upholstered in fly-blown
skin. A tuft on his brow, curling and brown, only highlighted
his wasted condition. His eyes, however, remained bright.
Raked-up rubies on a bed of ash.

Ben shrugged. Du Sang didn't seem to expect a compliment.

"Speaking of things owed," he said, "I seem to recall a
certain necklace. One of a set, commissioned by Louis the
Fifteenth for his mistress, Madame du Barry. The Queen
wasn't happy about it. There was that whole scandalous affair.
I'm sure you remember. You were there. Oh, what fun we
had! All those orgies in Versailles! Then the Queen lost her
head and I lost track of the diamonds. And . . . well, wasn't
that around the last time I saw you? *Quelle coincidence, non?*"

Ben glowered. It was a chapter in history he'd like to
forget, the days he'd spent on the banks of the Seine,
attending *la tavern* and *la bordel*, relishing the rich scent of
buxom duchesses and the earthier one of servant girls. He
had spent a decade drunk, as far as he could recall, with
the once charming Lambert at his side, a friendship born
from longevity and boredom. Their friendship had taken
them tottering on high-heeled shoes to the palace of the
Ancien Régime and all the decadence that waited inside –
some of it his.

He was reminded of a gift he'd presented to Rose a couple of years back and which she had politely declined. He would prefer to forget about that too.

"The past is the past. We all make mistakes. I'm interested in the present."

Le Vicomte du Sang – a title that was surely self-appointed or stolen – gave that same husky laugh. "We've all lost our sense of humour since the signing of the Pact. The Lore leaves no room for *rigolade*. Very well. To business. But there is a price . . ."

"I know what you want, du Sang." *It sure as hell isn't diamonds.* "What you always want. And by the looks of you, what you haven't been getting much of lately."

Du Sang drew his lips into a pout, waving a hand for Ben to continue.

"This morning, the Whispering Chapter tried to trap me on an oil rig. The agents were using a fragment of the harp." The touch of the silver relic smarted still, a memory of his bondage. "And they were looking for Blaise Von Hart."

"So I suppose you are too. Well, let's face it, where would you be without him?"

Ben was about to protest, but du Sang was on the move, crawling towards him over the web. Ben swore that he could hear the boy's bones, the creak of his crooked limbs.

What the fuck happened to you?

"Now, let's see . . ." Du Sang reached out a trembling hand and plucked at one of the strands, bending his ear to the vibration, catching a sound beyond Ben's hearing. He looked up and shook his head. "Nothing from your old foe, House Fitzwarren," he said. The strand thrummed across

70

the well, shivering up to the wall by Ben's shoulder. "The family is still sweeping up the ashes. Doubtless the patriarchs will train another in due course. Fulk Fitzwarren the . . ." Du Sang cocked his head, counting. "*Mon Dieu!* You have to admit, they never give up."

"Tell me about it." The vengeful attentions of House Fitzwarren had been the bane of Ben's life, son upon son determined to claim his head and win back the deeds to Whittington Castle, a crumbling ruin in Shropshire. Last year the latest Fulk had tried and failed. Badly. "But I'm asking after Von—"

Du Sang was already tweaking at the web. Again he lowered himself to listen. Something in the way he sat back and pursed his lips told Ben that he was enjoying himself.

"Hmm. The Coven Royal won't be cooking up any more trouble. Those kinds of spells have a way of coming back on a person. Well, that and a ten-ton dragon landing on your head. The witches are gone from this world."

The creature below him looked oddly regretful. Ben was getting annoyed.

"If I wanted to go through my enemies, I'd grab a telephone book."

Du Sang tutted. Again he bent his ear to the web. Then he leant in even closer, frowning. After what seemed like a goodly long while, he sat back scratching his head. He looked up at Ben with puzzled eyes.

"Silence," he said.

"Silence? What do you mean by—"

"All I hear are whispers. Whispers from the past. I hear nothing in the present."

Ben let this sink in, a cold fist closing around his heart. "You're saying that the envoy is dead?"

"*Non.* I'm saying he isn't in the world at all. I'm sure I would've marked his ending. He simply isn't . . . there."

"That's impossible." But Ben knew that it wasn't. Hadn't he gazed into the darkness last year, the endless gulf of the nether? Goosebumps prickled on his skin. "He must be travelling. Travelling along the Silver Leys." But to where? And why? "I can't blame him for hiding."

Du Sang ignored him, his face to the web once more, straining for something that Ben couldn't hear.

"An old mistake," the boy muttered. "A thorn in the lullaby. A stain in the fabric of things, spreading, growing sour . . ."

"Give me the good news first." The envoy's absence stirred anger in Ben's breast, the paintings in the gallery and du Sang's mention of the lullaby like a finger in an old wound. "That fucking song. The Pact. All of it." He struggled to find the words, uncomfortable with the idea. "There were, what? A few thousand of us left? We were hardly a threat."

Du Sang stopped babbling and looked up.

"Oh come now. London Bridge, 1212. Don't you remember?"

Ben scowled. He didn't much like to recall those days. The withering crops, the spreading plague, the ships wrecked upon the shore – all these disasters, the astrologers had said, signified that the land was crying out at the devils in their midst. The strange moon, the "bloodstained light", had already foretold King Richard's defeat in the Crusades, proof of the Remnant curse. And as the sages pored over their charts, they said there was worse to come.

They were right. In 1206, appalled by King John's laxity in dealing with the Remnants – which Rome deemed infernal, a blight on Creation – Pope Innocent III placed England under an interdict. No church bells rang, their steeples falling silent from Dover to Berwick. Canon law forbade all communal rites until King John recognised a new Archbishop, one hell-bent on ridding the land of fabulous beings and beasts. Dispatched from the Eternal City, a conclave of priests arrived on English shores to observe and report on the ongoing struggle, the long war between Remnants and humans. And to press the Pope's will upon the King. A King who found himself with no choice but to entertain them, these grey clerics, this Whispering Chapter that lingered in every corner of his palace, their ears bent to the throne. Still John hesitated. He was neither the wisest nor the bravest of kings and he feared that an all-out attack on Remnants would have grave consequences, graver than the scorn of Rome.

But Ben knew that du Sang was right. There had been several . . . troubles, he recalled. A witch making off with an entire village shoved into her bag, the tiny residents screaming in the windows. Goblins raiding a wagon in Sherwood, stealing chests filled with gold, a fat share of the King's taxes. Giants trampling over planted fields, gobbling up cows and sitting on farmsteads . . . King John had reluctantly borne all these things as long as his backside stayed warm on the English throne. And besides, he'd argued, the Remnants were hardly climbing the palace walls. The troubles were out there in the country, in the mountains and fens, and who was going to mourn a few peasants? Now and again he made a show of suppression, sending this or that knight into the Marches, sword in hand. On the whole, he played a more cowardly game. Let the Remnants nibble at the edges of his realm. Let sleeping dragons lie and all that . . .

Then, in 1212, Rakegoyle had come to London.

"Yeah." Ben looked down, murmuring at his feet. "I wish I could forget it."

"All those knights, charging about, currying favour. Hanging witches from trees. Poking lances into barrow and cave. All for a damsel's kiss and lands from the King. Well, they poked about in the wrong one, didn't they?" Du Sang looked happy to relate the event. "She was old, Rakegoyle. The last surviving spawn of Scawgramal, the legendary mount of Sir Mordred himself. You couldn't blame Rakegoyle for her air of nobility, nor her surprise when the knights came calling. I'm sure you haven't forgotten what she did to them. Only bones came rattling out of that cave. She ripped those men right out of their skins."

Ben wrinkled his nose, but not in sympathy. He was all too familiar with knights. When King John had sent Fulk to Mordiford all those years ago, the outcome had cost him dearly . . .

"They should've left her alone," he said. "She was in her last season anyway."

"Yes. Old, mad Rakegoyle took to the skies and flew off to London. Our Lady of the Canons lay in rubble by the time King John beseeched you for aid. He sent out riders into the Royal Forest, to the Hedgehog and Viper, that shithole of a tavern where you used to drink. Perhaps you

74

had downed a tankard too many, because you decided to answer the call. And when you reached the city, the winds had blown the flames south from the cathedral. The houses on London Bridge were ablaze."

Ben closed his eyes. It did him no good. The shards of that day were in his heart. Sure, he'd been bitter, but he had also been sick of the fighting. Sick of war and death. With Von Hart's guidance, he had chosen a different path, seeking to heal the rift between Remnants and humans. A tragedy like Mordiford would never happen again, not to anyone, not on his watch. Or so he'd thought at the time.

He pictured a pair of tremendous wings, white with age, their shadow falling over the tumbledown rooftops and crooked streets of medieval London, the pennants on the city wall snapping in the rush of wind. Inn signs had wheeled and doors slammed shut. Horses had reared, spilling carts of fruit as the shadow swept over the river, diving in low to envelop the sainted spires in a barrage of light and heat . . .

"There were three thousand trapped on the bridge that day, man, woman and child. Not one of them escaped." His voice was barely a whisper. "And Rakegoyle wouldn't listen to reason. She wanted to tear the city apart."

"So you stopped her and all the curses came true," du Sang said, relishing Ben's discomfort. "Do you see? Rakegoyle fell into the Thames, her wings smouldering, and her bones rot there still. But her death damned us all nonetheless."

Ben winced. An ache was growing in the middle of his chest, the indigestion of memory. The old dragon's death had proved a grim milestone in the history of Britain and the fate of the Remnants. Surveying the smoke coiling from Southwark, drifting from the ruined cathedral and the blackened bridge, King John had realised he couldn't fight a war on three fronts – with the barons, the Pope and the Remnants – and possibly hope to win. He had to do something, *anything*, to restore peace to the realm. In the end, he realised that his kingdom, his newly built townships a mill for wealth, would never be free of the threat in its midst.

Unless . . .

"You're saying this is my fault," Ben said. "You know we had no choice."

"Didn't we?" du Sang replied. "Do you fly over their rumpled beds and wonder, Ben? The too-angular slope of a hill. The muscular sweep of a valley. A river coiling like a tail . . . The secret bed of legends, exiled creatures of dreams, who now in turn dream, slumbering for centuries. Black Annis, the buggane, the fenodyree – where are they now? Grass has grown over their graves. Concrete grown over the grass. And yet here we are. The Remnants remain. And perhaps it was all for nothing."

"Fuck that noise. King John knew better than to make matters worse. The Great Fire of Southwark told him what to expect if he opted for a Remnant massacre. We were all sick of the fighting by then." Ben hadn't been present at that monumental meeting in Westminster Palace, but Von Hart had told him all about it. Thorney Island might've sunk with the weight of those summoned to hear the King's proposal, their lances and crosses flashing in the sun, their cries loud enough to ripple the Thames. *If we had given our peace to a dog*, the King told them, *it should not be violated.*

So then treat with Remnants. "We signed the Pact. We heed the Lore. It's been that way for eight hundred years."

"The King has been dead for the same length of time," du Sang reminded him. "It was a choice of evils at best."

Ben rubbed the back of his neck. He didn't like where this was going.

"Get to the point. It stinks down here."

Du Sang let that pass. The rot must smell like attar to him.

"I hate to be the bearer of bad news," he said. The gleam in his eyes somewhat put the lie to this. "So . . . is there anything else I can help you with? Freak weather reports? Miraculous storms? The unprecedented rainfall in Somalia?"

"You're a comedian, du Sang."

"The whereabouts of a Brooklyn waitress, recently spell-bound and scarred?"

"Shut the fuck up."

The way du Sang cringed told Ben that he had meant no offence. His offer was tactless, but genuine. *He must be hungry.* He felt colour rush into his cheeks. Wherever Rose was, she didn't want to be found. He had lied to her, left her to the CROWS and given her a burden that no woman should bear, especially alone. Sure, he wanted to know where she was. The information was gold dust, precious and tempting. He would've given his right arm to know (the limb in question would grow back anyway), but after all his selfishness, his excuses and evasions, was he honestly prepared to spy on her?

"No," he said, more to himself than the boy. "Not this way."

Du Sang clapped his hands. "Then there is only the matter of the price."

Ben shuffled to the edge of the step, the black well tugging at him, longing to draw him into its depths. Head wheeling with questions, the whereabouts of the missing envoy, he was only half aware of his hand extending into a claw, the tip of one talon hanging over his outstretched forearm, ready to pierce the scales of his suit and open up a vein . . .

"Here. This should keep you going for a few years."

And it would. Dragon blood was like Popeye's spinach to the creature below him. Ben had seen it before, long ago. In a matter of seconds, the furrows of age on du Sang's face would blush, tighten and fill out, his lips engorging to a sensual pout, his skin renewed, a downy pink. The scrap of hair on the boy's skull, a last sorry lock, would flourish into glossy brown curls, spilling over his pointed ears and down his elegant neck. Ben would watch as his joints reset, clicking and jerking into place, flexing with limber muscle. His clothes, of course, would stay the same – there was nothing deathless about rags – but as he tasted the drops from Ben's veins, a vision would soon be wearing them, to all intents and purposes a nineteen-year-old boy, only much older and much less naïve.

All the same, du Sang didn't crawl forward, crab-like, and extend his tongue. His eyes, chips of malachite, burned still, but with a mournful heat, as he looked up at Ben.

"*Non*, Benjurigan. I'm afraid that won't do."

Ben's claw closed up like a Venus flytrap. "What? We agreed—"

"Did we?" Du Sang turned his face to the spiders on the

wall. "We have a million witnesses. Would you like to hear their take on it?"

Ben glanced at the bristling arachnid army. He could imagine their voiceless verdict, the hiss of their legs rubbing together, their mandibles snapping, but other concerns eclipsed his revulsion. Were the webs around him thicker than before? He made out the faint strands, delicate and newly spun, adding to the ones that ran piano-like from the web to the surrounding walls. A spider dangled past his face, slipping down a silent wire as he stood and watched. He slapped it away, disliking the soft tearing sound as his arm came unstuck from the wall.

What the hell?

"OK, so you don't want the sauce. What do you want?"

"Nothing," du Sang said. Before Ben could respond, the Vicomte sighed and went on. "Ever since I signed the Pact, years ago in these very catacombs, I have held my appetite in check. Oh, a nibble here at some chevalier's neck might go unnoticed and unpunished. The Five Families sleep deep in coffin and crypt, no longer rising with the moon. As long as I don't kill anyone or turn another, I endure in that narrow tract between Loreful respect and taking liberties. It is tiresome. I grow bored."

Du Sang's face was a scratched mirror, reflecting the past. Perhaps he longed for the Age of Light, when he had been the freshly risen victim of some ghoulish duke or other. It must have been a feast to him, a banquet of visionaries under the stars, drunk on wonder and wine.

Ben, who could guess where this was going, said, "We do what we must to survive. No one said it would be easy."

"Strong words, but your voice trembles. You lost your way too, isn't that so? In whiskey and in women's arms. What is it folks say these days about denial and a certain river?"

"Don't turn this around. We all agreed to do our duty."

Du Sang smiled, a sorry sight. "*Oui*. But duty does not sweeten the taste of a youth strutting along the Canal Saint-Martin, his skin doused in cologne, his veins awash with cocaine. Even when you visit the *supermarché* just so you can siphon the meat trays in secret, the hormones stick in your throat, making you retch, making you want nothing at all. What good is duty then?"

"It's the Lore." Ben realised how weak this sounded, particularly now that the same Lore had placed him on death row. All he could offer du Sang was a drink. "I don't see the problem. If it's blood you want—"

"No. You don't see. Fabulous vision clearly doesn't mean fabulous insight." Du Sang shook his head, his dry tendons creaking. "Your compromise is false. A war of attrition, just as the Curia Occultus intended: . . . *but one of each Remnant may endure, awake and unfettered under the Lore, governed, protected and guided by the Guild of the Broken Lance, hereby appointed wardship of this bond for all the time to come.* It was blindness. Blindness." The boy merely looked sad now, beyond frustration. "I heard how you did for Jordsønn, you know. A hole near a bridge, a flash of fire, and the troll was ash."

"What did he expect? He was out of control, eating humans."

"Is that what I must do? Run riot from Picardy to the

Pyrenees, flouting the Lore by infecting people with undeath?"

"Don't be absurd. Jordsønn was different. The Guild charged me with the task, and in the end it came down to—"

"Duty," du Sang said. "And the Three? Was that duty too?"

"I didn't kill the Three." *But Lord, I would've loved to.* "Atiya—"

Du Sang waved his fingers, dismissing Ben's protest. "One of each. Awake and unfettered under the Lore," he said. "Tell me, Ben, which troll and which witch has been woken from the Sleep to replace those deceased?"

The question was simple, but the truth of it shot through Ben's breast like an arrow. Would the world see the likes of those Remnants again? *Hopefully not.* Still, it made him wonder. He couldn't recall any provision in the Pact for awakening a new representative or perhaps sending one into the Sleep. The harp, the lullaby – well, he'd thought it was ancient history now, pretty much done and dusted. A relic on the heap with all the others. Of course, all that had changed this morning. And nor could he ask the Guild or Von Hart about it. He sure as hell wasn't about to ask the Whispering Chapter . . .

Reflex jogged a hand towards his neck, but his elbow jarred, held by dense clinging strands.

"Tell me, which scion of the Families will the Chapter rouse to replace me?"

Spiders were swarming around him, a thick cloak sweeping over the skulls and binding him to the wall. He felt hundreds of the bugs on his skin, hairy, silent and quick, cobwebs lacing through his hair and over his cheeks, muffling his cry.

"What are you doing, du Sang? This is fucked."

"I told you. I am bored." The Vicomte crept across his bed in the middle of the well and hooked his fingers into the brickwork, climbing the staircase towards him. Another spider, larger, paler, but no less deadly. "Do you know what it's like? Can you imagine? You walk into Notre-Dame and your shoes smoke a little. You swig holy water and catch a touch of flu. You wait for the dawn and the sun gives you blisters, soon healing in the dark. You are too old. Too seasoned. Too *hard*. And you discover that the myths surrounding you are mostly a pack of lies."

"C'est la vie."

Du Sang ignored him, creeping closer. "So, what can one do? A leap in front of a train at rush hour and you dust yourself off and walk away. A fall from the Eiffel Tower and five minutes later you're bawling on a bench in the Champ de Mars. A jump off the Pont Neuf and the chains around your ankles carry you down, into the weeds and the filth, simply to float there for days, watching the keels of tour boats go by. You rot, but you endure. Eventually the chains slip off your bones and you float to the surface, cursing. Can you imagine?"

Ben *could* imagine, up to a point. Sword, gun, rock fall – hell, even a tank shelling – he had survived all of these things. Nevertheless, he wasn't immortal. Take his head and he would die. "You don't . . ." He struggled in his bonds. "You can't want this."

"I miss the old days, my friend." Du Sang was on him now, his skeletal hands gripping his shoulders, his breath rank in his face. "The way you could suck out a baby's eyeball and let the juices gush down your throat. Or seduce some young artist or other, bite the heat in their *pantalon*, revel in the shooter of blood." The boy's eyes blazed with remembered gluttony. "I am a foul thing. A frayed thing. And I am tired. *Dragon fire* is the answer."

The spiders scuttled over Ben's hands, his feet, his face. A hundred spinnerets worked overtime as they hurried back and forth, cocooning him in silk – but it was still only silk. Nor was he troubled by du Sang's teeth, lengthening, poised over his neck. His skin was a carapace, iron tough. This attack was so futile that Ben could've laughed, but for old times' sake he held his scorn in check along with his flames. Despite the Vicomte's confession to several grisly crimes, he only felt a weary sympathy. Lambert du Sang was far from the first Remnant to go cuckoo.

He was about to say so when the tremors struck.

A rumbling surged out of the dark, rattling up the well. The walls shook, bricks and skulls punched out of true, bouncing off Ben's shoulders and shattering on the steps. The spiders needed no further warning, disappearing into the widening cracks, an ebbing tide of legs and eyes. Dank air bellowed from below, thick with the stench of rot and the sewers, making Ben gag. The shifting earth roared up the pit like the groan of some subterranean beast. In the uproar, he picked out a strain of music, distant and achingly sweet, a silver thorn plucking at his heart.

It can't be . . .

Du Sang's shriek drowned out the melody. A cascade of rock, muck and bone crashed down around him, wrenching the boy from his perch on Ben's chest and hurling him into the well. The Vicomte clung to the ragged remains of his bed, his eyes bright saucers of blood.

"What . . ." Ben shouted through the dust. "What's happening?"

Du Sang's head turned this way and that, tracing the thrumming of the strands, the web vibrating in time with the convulsing walls. When he glared up at Ben, his words were garbled, threaded with fear.

"A shattering of glass," he said. "The turn of a key. A black door opening."

Ben had no time to question him further. The web broke under the boy's weight and Lambert du Sang was gone, the bricks around him crumbling inwards, carrying him down into the dark, his howl echoing to silence.

It was time to leave. Ben's wings made short work of his cocoon. Pinions scrabbling at the walls, claws sparking off stone, he thrust himself up and out, the staircase collapsing under him as he headed for the light.

Half an hour later on the Boulevard de Belleville, Ben walked in off the street and took a table in the Wu Palace, one of the many restaurants in the Chinese quarter. Paper lanterns hung outside the joint and the carved screens offered a refuge from curious eyes, folks who might enquire after a six-foot, broad-shouldered man with unkempt red hair and beard and only bare feet in the middle of winter. Dust cloaked his dark-scaled suit, obscuring the *wyrm tongue*

symbol on his chest. Back in the cemetery, he had burst
from the monument in a mess of shattered earth and graves,
hurling cherubs and headstones aside.

Shaken by du Sang's news – or rather the lack of it – and
the boy's feeble suicide attempt, Ben didn't care what the
public made of him tonight. He was oddly heartsore,
surprised that the thought of Von Hart's absence should
leave him feeling so empty and lonely. Was he even coming
back? Let them stare if they wanted to stare; there wasn't
much point to anything if the last of the Fay was gone.

He needn't have worried. Apart from a TV in one corner
and a tank full of koi, the restaurant was empty. The waitress, a city-looking girl with blossoms protruding – a little
wildly, he thought – from her bobbed black hair, took his
order with a smile and left him to half watch the news.

The usual carousel of doom and gloom slid across the
screen. Melting icecaps. War in the Middle East. A baboon
of a president . . . It was enough to give anyone a headache.
He was rubbing his temples when his food arrived and he
attacked it with abandon, swallowing the dumplings whole
and shovelling down the rice. In human guise, a full stomach
would satisfy the hunger of the beast within. He had a
feeling he was going to need his energy, even if he wasn't
sure about his next move. His encounter with du Sang had
shaken him more than he'd like to admit. Things, it seemed,
were falling apart, whether brought on by the breach in the
Lore or the grind of modern times he couldn't say. Either
way, the Remnants were a mess. *Endangered species*, wasn't
that what the witch had told him last year? He had seen
too much since to deny it.

He ate, gathering his strength. Was running the only option left?

He guzzled down a bottle of beer, washing the taste of the graves from his throat. Belching, he picked up the fortune cookie that the girl had left beside his bowl. The cheap confection of sugar and flour crumbled to pieces in his fingers, as if it wanted to open itself. He rolled out the narrow strip of paper, preparing to snort at the twopenny prophecy.

Instead, he read the words and sat bolt upright.

When the time comes, let me fall. VH

The elegant handwriting would have given Von Hart away regardless of his signature. Ben was too relieved at this proof that the envoy still lived to question the message straight away. Exhaling, he pushed himself away from the table and, eyebrows raised, watched the strip of paper go up in flames, curling up in embers and a wisp of smoke.

Magic. Some kind of spell. And for once I don't mind.

He was halfway to his feet, looking around for a sign of the *hexenmeister* himself, when he heard a moan. Turning, he saw the dark-haired girl standing by the entrance to the kitchen, her hands covering her mouth, framing her dinner-plate eyes, the blossoms in her hair shaking in denial.

Ben followed her gaze to the TV in the corner. That was when he saw the earthquake in Beijing.

SIX

Zhoukoudian, China

Thirty miles west of Beijing, dawn crept into the Zhoukoudian hills. The mist was lifting, swirling over Dragon Bone Hill, where a cave yawned, as though sucking up the darkness. The figure standing before its shadowed mouth knew that the cave was one of several in the area, part of a system winding back into the hills, old and deep. Dragon Bone Hill had been a world-famous site ever since archaeologists had dug up human remains here a hundred years ago. The fertile lands beside the river had been home to China's most distant ancestors – the figure knew this too – squat men and women in furs, mastering the primal magic of fire . . .

Old, old lands.

Zhongguo.

These days, the legacy of *Homo erectus* was the museum at the foot of the hill where, for a small fee, one could enter and enjoy all the plaques and the lifelike statues. At this hour, the museum was closed. The museum square, later to welcome the meagre footfall of low-season tourists, skirled with leaves, some dancing around a large bronze bust of Neanderthal man that gazed solemnly in the still.

Look how you've grown, the figure before the cave thought. *Look what you have done.*

For all its importance, Zhoukoudian was a grave, the stone having offered up an ancient bounty, hints and clues of human evolution. But a more recent tomb rested here too, one built by chance and necessity. For eight hundred years, the makeshift tomb – or perhaps a cell – had lain dark, silent and undisturbed.

Until today.

As the sun touched the cave mouth, only animals were present to hear the violation. A strain of music drifted on the air, a silvery plucking of strings, strummed by the figure's hand. The notes, rich and sweet, full of yearning, echoed down the hillside, reverberating between the trees. In the grass, snakes raised their heads, tongues flickering as if to scent the sound. Rodents froze, their whiskers twitching. Monkeys screeched and fled, a volley of icicles falling from the branches. This was a song they had no wish to hear. In an instant, the music was *everywhere*, shattering the still.

And then, as if it hadn't happened at all, the music stopped, a hand held over the strings. The hillside returned to silence, winter smoothing out her cloak. The figure standing before the cave knew better than to risk a repeat, to let the music rise to a crescendo. The instrument was broken – a memory in itself – and it would not do to summon the ghosts who haunted the Dark Frontier, drawn to the walls of Creation by the heady lure of magic.

Not here. Not now.

But the echoes were enough. The notes reverberated into the cave, blending with the shrinking shadows. Like burrowing worms, the short refrain bled through stone, resounding through the fissures and cracks, past bones and baubles yet undiscovered.

In minutes, the echoes seeped into a vault, a vast subterranean cavern, the obsidian bowels of the hill. The cavern – in truth a prison, bound and sealed by charms – stretched a hundred and fifty feet in length and fifty in diameter, ample space for the one who slept here, his dreams deep and dark.

Flames roared in his dreams. Distant screams echoed in his memory, a fugue of blood and war. The walls ran slick from his slumbering breaths, his heart pounding like thunder in the deep. Moisture dripped from stalactites that had lengthened an inch in each century of the dreamer's entombment, splashing on scale, horn and claw. Scars riddled his recumbent flanks, the griffonage of a thousand swords, arrowhead, axe and lance. In the damp and the dark, his scars remained a secret language, speaking of battles lost and won. The dreamer breathed in, the steam swirling. Breathed out in a rumbling snore. Condensation trickled from his skull, dripping from eyelids the size of a city clock.

The echoes rang from one end of the cavern to the other, a brief, glittering symphony.

And with the sound: memory.

In his dreams, Mauntgraul grunted, scenting the memory of the feast, a banquet of fire, panic and meat. He shifted his bulk and then stiffened, the glossy black barb on the end of his tail quivering. The echoes of the music faded, leaving a bitter taste.

Some had come to interrupt his feast. Some had stolen his freedom.

James Bennett

Pain followed on the heels of memory. A silvery light burned in his skull, building to blinding anguish.

He remembered the pale fairy and his harp, the rock face closing around him.

He remembered Red Ben.

In the deep and the dark of eight hundred years, the dreamer's eyes flew open, blazing like the blackest suns.

SEVEN

Considering their recent argument, Ben Garston told himself he'd rather call up the Whispering Chapter than chat with his dwarf accountant in London. That aside, he needed a plane ticket pronto and Delvin Blain, CEO of the Blain Trust, could provide him with one from any airport desk in the world, along with a passport and visa, both undetectable forgeries. Flying east in dragon form wasn't advisable, not when human agents were watching. *Hunting.* The Sister was no doubt hot on his tail. The fear, a quiet swarm in the pit of his stomach, made the receiver tremble in his hand as he placed the call from a phone booth in the Couronnes Métro station.

"You," grumbled the dwarf down the line, in a grumpier tone than usual. "Do you know what time it is?"

"Yeah. Late. For all of us if I don't catch a flight to China like yesterday."

"China? Nudd's bells! Why do you—"

"Something is up, Blain. Something bad. It's to do with the mnemonic harp. I have to find Von Hart . . ." And he did, didn't he? It was his duty, no matter what. Plus there was the fear, bubbling away in the background, a suspicion so ominous he couldn't quite look at it directly. Not yet. "There's been an earthquake in Beijing."

"Don't tell me you've taken an interest in seismology . . ."

Ben swallowed, hard. "The news says the epicentre was at Zhoukoudian. Do you remember what we put in those hills, Blain?"

Silence for a good long minute. Ben let the memory sink in. Then he heard rustling, coughing, a brief murmuring to one side of the receiver in London, the striking of a match. Ben could picture the scene easily enough. Having sat up, dismissed his latest secretary for the sake of discretion and sparked up a cigar, the CEO was all ears.

"I'd say you were starting at shadows, Mr Garston. But all that business last year . . . it isn't over, is it?"

"Take a lucky guess."

A sigh. "And I thought all I had to worry about was smuggling gold."

"Blain, can we put the jousting on hold right now? If there's been another breach, then—"

"You'll get your plane ticket. Have I ever let you down? All the same, it sounds relevant, after a fashion. I was going to call you first thing in the morning."

"Problem?"

"More of an . . . irregularity. My dealings with certain bodies on the black market turned up a matter of interest. I hope you're sitting down."

"When do I get time to sit down? Just spit it out."

"Suit yourself. I was talking to Bolgoth Clave last night. You know the goblin racketeer down Whitechapel? Looking into new fencing avenues for you. Hell, what's a few more laws?" Another cough. "Sorry. In passing, I mentioned the Lambton armour falling into the possession of House Fitzwarren – we were chatting about all the shit last year – and Clave . . . well, he told me that the suit had been up for auction in Newcastle the year before last. The latest heir of the Lambton estate wanted nothing to do with the damn thing."

I don't blame them.

"So?" But the lump was back in Ben's throat. "House Fitzwarren had to have acquired it from somewhere."

"That's just it. The Fitzwarrens didn't. They weren't even at the auction. The suit sold to the highest bidder for almost twice the asking price. Quite a fierce battle, if one can credit a goblin."

"Cut to the chase. I have a plane to catch."

"Ben. The name of the buyer was Herr Von Hart."

More silence. Ben remembered the suit with its bristling array of spikes, jagging from the greaves, gauntlets and hinges. The helmet, beaked and vulturine. He wasn't likely to forget it. What the fuck had the envoy wanted with the Lambton armour? Last year, House Fitzwarren had sent the suit as a gift to Paladin's Court and the latest Fulk had been wearing it at the time. And inside Fulk – the worst kind of Trojan horse – a lost soul hungry for power, hungry to conquer death . . .

Never trust the Fay, Ben . . .

"Out of curiosity, I tracked the sale of the item," Blain went on. "Not much of a paper chase, to be honest. It seems that our envoy extraordinary gave the suit to the Fitzwarrens as a gift of some kind."

Ben's hand fell from the side of the booth, balling into

a fist at his side. And the swarm in his belly exploded into frenzy.

"He did *what*?"

Fear isn't a good travelling companion.

Ben started awake, gripping the arms of his seat. Dreams were fleeing his skull, a retreating billow of flame, an echo of a scream . . . Slowly, he relaxed. As much as he could, anyway. The fear had sat next to him on the flight out of Charles de Gaulle, the jet veering south above the City of Light while he stared numbly out of the aeroplane window. The dawn crept through the streets below, a map of the cold creeping through his veins. Fear swirled in his plastic cup as the plane roared into the morning sky, the sweet Jack warming his bones, but failing to soothe him. Fear muffled the in-flight movie and the landing gear dropping and the sands of the Middle East stretching off to the horizon. In the lounge, waiting for his connecting flight, the fear paced around between the rows of seats, footsteps measuring out his disquiet.

He was travelling incognito, of course. Crowds churned around him, a sea of suitcases, people heading from who knows where to any place. Departure boards trickled in digital amber. Tannoy systems pinged. Anodyne music wafted from speakers. Ben had no way of knowing if he was followed, if anyone watched. A man in a grey suit passing him on the escalator. A woman pretending to look at postcards in a gift shop, peering at him over her sunglasses. A teenager kicking the back of his seat. How could he know the reach of the Whispering Chapter, the extent of the order's network? The Sister had rocked up on an oil rig. What was to stop her

94

rocking up in an airport, manacle in hand? OK, so the Chapter had used a fragment of the harp to lure him, but if she happened to appear, it could still spell the end of him. In a leather jacket, T-shirt and jeans – the clothes snatched from the first open store in the *Quartier Asiatique* – Ben looked like an everyday traveller, clothes rumpled from the plane's tiny seats, eyes puffy with jet lag. His straggling beard was far from stylish and his hair was starting to creep towards the middle of his back, so red that some might mistake it for dye.

What did it matter? Considering the Chapter's sentence of execution, there was nothing he could do to worsen his predicament, no crime he could commit, no fate worse than death. Was there? Either way, he had slipped through the net. He was on the run, a fugitive from the Lore. The last thing he wanted was to draw attention to himself.

Besides, to risk the miles ahead in true form was to court exhaustion as well as exposure.

This isn't 1215. They've had telescopes since the seventeenth century and radar operators won't think you're a sign from God.

Ben shuddered. Memory of his first long journey to China, all those centuries ago, added to his unease. The end of that journey was a stone cast into the pool of history, and how strange that he should feel the ripples now, after all this time. How *unsettling*. He tapped his fingers on the arms of his seat, reminding himself that keeping his head low was now a secondary concern. Hiding was far from a new thing. Neither were earthquakes in China, but when the news had cut to the site of the tremors, Ben was out the door of the restaurant and in the back of a cab before his dim sum could climb up his throat.

Fear joined him again on his next flight into the Asian night. A man across the aisle attempted conversation, but Ben only managed a weak smile and the man returned to his magazine with a "Don't like flying, huh?" He dozed for a while and all his dreams rang with screams, a city burning beneath the shadow of vast white wings . . .

It had all been so long ago. The memory faded. When he'd last travelled this way, eight hundred years ago, he'd had the envoy to guide him, Von Hart's robes fluttering in the wind as he'd sat in the saddle of Ben's withers, muttering this or that spell to protect him from the cold. *The good old days.* Now the past came swimming into focus, a sequence of reluctant tasks flashing across his mind.

In that distant summer of 1215, Von Hart had come to him in the Royal Forest, finding him in the Hedgehog and Viper. The envoy had told him about the great council taking place on Thorney Island, the knights and the priests who had gathered to form the Curia Occultus. The Hidden Court, as the envoy dubbed it, was discussing the future of Remnants, their continued existence in these lands. Or the end of it. Ben, growling over his tankard, had asked the stick-thin man in the starry red robes what the fuck he wanted. Hadn't Ben done enough for King John by taking down Rakegoyle? Von Hart had smiled his smile.

Oh, it isn't what I want. Ben vaguely recalled his reply, plucking his words from the mists of time. *And the threat is far from over. News comes from the east of a screaming horde, an empire in flames. The King would ask another boon of you, mein freund. A sign of good faith . . .*

And so they had flown east, he and Von Hart, to challenge

Mauntgraul, the White Dog. High up in the hills of the Hebei Plain – a place that the map called Zhoukoudian – the envoy and the soon-to-be Sola Ignis had confronted the renegade dragon, a terrifying breed with a barbed sting on the end of his tail and a battle cry to level trees. That battle hadn't gone as planned. Mauntgraul, gorged on blood, enraged, had wounded the both of them.

Tail lashing, his deadly sting aimed at Ben's heart, the White Dog had been moments from triumph. In a desperate attempt to salvage their mission, Von Hart had strummed his fragment of the harp, making a dangerous compromise. Unable to slay Mauntgraul, the envoy had imprisoned the beast in the hill instead, managing to send him into the Sleep. A matter, Ben had argued at the time, that was likely to come back and bite them on the arse, if the Fay (it had still been *when* back then) returned to the earth. Then the times had progressed. Ben had forgotten. All of them had forgotten. And in the forgetting, a false comfort, a false sense of security, an illusion as deep as an enchanted slumber . . .

He awoke to the sound of the captain making an announcement in a language he recognised as Mandarin. The news had finally caught up with him. Due to the earthquake, Beijing International was diverting all flights to Xian, a city a thousand klicks to the south. The jet landed and Ben found himself in a queue for the ticket desk, passports waving, complaints snapping in his ears like firecrackers.

When his turn came, a beleaguered stewardess in a skewed little hat yelled into his face.

"No flights! No flights!"

Ben regarded the woman with red-ringed eyes.

"Wanna bet?"

He made the change behind some trucks in the terminal car park. Dawn was coming around on this side of the globe and he shrugged off his human guise like a cloak, his wings climbing into the fading dark, heading north-east.

Into the fear.

Dragon Bone Hill – what was left of it, anyway – rose from the pine forest swathing the lower slopes. Fog shrouded the valley. And smoke, coiling from the maw in the rock face where the upper cave had sundered, collapsing into a fissure that split the hill from summit to foot. The ruptured peak jagged at the sky like a broken tooth. The exposed chasm was a smouldering doorway framing Ben as he stood atop the strewn boulders, the rubble that had hurtled down the hillside. Something large and strong had burst from the hill, a pale horror breaking from a shell.

With keen eyes, Ben gazed into the sepulchral depths, making out the obsidian gleam of the cavern, and he needed all his strength to stay on his feet. His flight from Xian had taken three hours, with only dread to drive him on. With the rock warm under his feet, he couldn't even muster a snort. His journey to China had taken a day and a night and he'd lost his way twice since leaving Xian, painfully aware of the time slipping through his fingers and his jet-lagged state.

I'm not up to this shit.

He couldn't tear his eyes away from the hillside, the open wound of disaster. That was what it was, *disaster*, and he couldn't kid himself otherwise. He could barely hear the noise from the valley floor, the grumbling of military trucks and fire engines around the museum, the occasional bark of a soldier at the sneaking approach of journalists. The building lay in ruins, every pane of glass shattered, the roof collapsed, the road leading into the hills a cracked river of tarmac. The large bronze bust in the square had rolled off its plinth and lay in several pieces on the churned-up flagstones, a random Dali-esque sculpture. The authorities were turning their efforts to searching for people buried in the rubble, staff and tourists alike, although the quake had struck just after dawn and the digging was more likely a salvage operation for the relics housed inside the building. In the fog and the smoke, no one noticed the sixty-foot-long red-scaled beast that swung down out of the sky, rippling and dwindling as he descended, a man in a glossy black suit landing on the rocks.

As what he was seeing sank in, Ben covered his mouth. *No. Jesus, no.* He wanted to tell himself that the breach was impossible, the Lore inviolate, but of course it was much too late for that. But whatever, *whoever*, had awoken the sleeper in the cavern, they could only have done so with a fragment of the harp. Why did he find that fact the most terrifying of all?

History. Because you know what's coming.

"You re-forged the harp, didn't you?" Ben murmured, speaking to the hill and the absent envoy. "You told the Curia Occultus that you had the means to enforce peace. And once the Remnants went into the Sleep . . ."

The harp had been dismantled, yes. A fragment given to each of the branches of the Curia Occultus for protection, the Guild of the Broken Lance, the Whispering Chapter (a typically cowardly act by King John) and the envoy extraordinary himself, the latter swearing to guard and restrict all magic and remain hidden from society until the Fay returned or . . .

"Yeah. Until hell froze over."

Re-forged, the mnemonic harp held the power to lull every Remnant into the Long Sleep – or awaken them from it – the magic as complex as any fairy spell. Dismantled, a single fragment of the harp held the power to rouse or sedate one Remnant. One Remnant every time a hand strummed the instrument, striking up the lullaby in a certain way – not to lure, not to summon, but a specific sequence of strings to resonate with the ancient enchantment. Of course, no one but a madman would think that wise. This was surely what had happened at Zhoukoudian, someone in possession of a piece of the harp, rousing the beast that Von Hart had foolishly put to sleep . . .

Could the Chapter have got here from Norway so fast? In two days? Well, it's just about possible. And why does the Chapter want the harp anyway? To put the last of the Remnants into the Sleep? It would explain why the Cardinal was after Von Hart . . .

But this, this was an awakening. Nausea churned in Ben's guts. Looking up at the broken hill, his memory eclipsed all other thought, curdling with a deeper emotion that he didn't want to name but recognised as guilt.

"To hell with it," he said into the maw. "We did what we had to do."

He tried to focus on the mystery before him. The Guild,

the Chapter, the envoy extraordinary . . . three possible suspects and one of them supposedly an ally. Or someone else, someone who had come to possess a fragment of the harp, via theft or otherwise . . . Suspicions aside, he had to find Von Hart. That was painfully clear. This wasn't just bad news for humans; it was dangerous for Remnants as well. The harp held the power to lull them all. And the monster that had broken free from Zhoukoudian wouldn't spare those he felt had betrayed him, least of all Ben.

Ben surveyed the valley around him, the trees snapped like cocktail sticks, the fallen branches, the strewn stones. Did the hillside ring with echoes, silvery and bright? The kind of echoes that gripped your heart, squeezing out every last drop? The kind that crawled into your skull, chiming until your eyeballs popped? Ben thought so.

And as for the envoy . . .

It seems that our envoy extraordinary gave the suit to the Fitzwarrens as a gift of some kind . . .

Despite the apparent chicanery, the knowledge of Von Hart's hand in matters, assisting, manipulating Remnant sedition (and almost costing Ben his life), he found it hard to see the fairy opening the vault in Dragon Bone Hill, causing the destruction before him.

And setting the nightmare free . . .

Nonetheless, the fact remained that Blaise Von Hart was one of three bodies on earth with the means at his disposal. With the *power*. The envoy had a habit of making odd comments, but at this moment, only one stuck out in Ben's mind. In Club Zauber last year, when Ben was caught up in the evils of the CROWS, Von Hart had said, "Perhaps this change in regime is inevitable. Perhaps it is our turn again . . ." Looking at the shattered hillside, Ben found it hard to allay his suspicions, however reluctant they were.

Never trust the Fay, Ben.

"The thing is," and he realised that it was true even as he said it, "I've never trusted you."

There was only the sky to answer him. Even the birds had fled. And there was more in the air than echoes. Ben breathed in, catching a scent he hadn't known in centuries, a combination of cinders and sweat, of scaly, protean flesh. *Eau de wyrm.* It was the scent of the fiery past and the terror of the future.

First things first.

Swallowing fear, he spread his wings, preparing to trace the source.

Sixty miles north, skirting the western edge of Beijing, Ben reached the Juyong Pass. Snow clung to the peaks and layered the valley, the monuments and the buildings down there draped with ice, resembling elaborate cakes. The Great Wall of China snaked up from the pass, an ancient brickwork marvel climbing into the peaks. The battlements zigzagged across the wooded crests, climbing up to the watchtower on the summit, a squat, square turret. How many hands had carried blocks up these slopes, prisoners in the sun and rain, lending their bones to the barrier? Hundreds, thousands . . . and in the end, this whim of emperors, this colossal scheme that verged on both genius and madness, hadn't exactly worked. The Middle Kingdom had fallen to Mongol invaders, to the horse lord Genghis Khan.

Ben snapped out his wings, slowing his descent towards the watchtower. The creature he sought stood on the parapet, man-shaped, naked and gazing to the south. This creature, Ben knew, had been the first to breach the wall during that long-ago battle, his wings a blade crashing through stone, the might of his draconic form. He also knew that he wouldn't give a shit about dead slaves, especially if they were human.

Ben landed as gently as possible, shrivelling to man size out of courtesy. If he could avoid a fight, he would do so, though he realised this was wishful thinking. His quarry would sense he was here, of course, had probably smelled him coming from miles away. But the man at the battlements didn't turn around. His bare back and buttocks, dark, muscled and riddled with scars, remained another wall to the one who pursued him.

"I was wondering at the stench in the air," Mauntgraul said. "Smoke? I thought. Or shit? Now I have my answer."

"Hello, Maunt." Ben managed to keep his voice steady. "Got out the wrong side of bed, I see."

"Yes. Such a deep sleep." Mauntgraul sighed at the tree-tops below him, perhaps not grasping the saying. "The sights I have seen since my rousing suggest that I dreamt for longer than hours. Days? Months? God's bones, Benjurigan, pray don't say it was years!"

"You know damn well it was." *And no one says God's bones any more,* he thought but didn't say, biting down on the taunt. "A lot has changed."

"In truth? Forgive me. I left Albion in the ashes of the Anarchy, flying east to these lands. Much was changing in my homeland as it was and I had no stomach to embrace it. Soon, I found a new sport. A great leader and a tribe that worshipped me like a god. Unbound, unchecked, I agreed to help them take an empire. And yet some would deny me my freedom." He continued, brightening. "Why, this meeting reminds me of another one not far from here – what? Three, four centuries ago?"

"Eight." Ben was not fooled by the White Dog's conversational tone, nor did he miss the slight slump of Mauntgraul's shoulders at his admission. "And the last time we met, there wasn't shit in the air, but screams. We came here to silence them. To silence you."

"You bent the knee to King John," Mauntgraul said. "You and that ridiculous fairy came riding across the skies to Zhongdu and threw salt all over my game."

"Game?" Ben said. "You turned the plains out there into a blood marsh, ravaging crops, poisoning rivers, reducing villages to ash. For over a year, Genghis Khan laid siege to the city, his hordes surrounding the walls. He let the million-odd people trapped inside them slowly starve to death."

"Granted, Genghis was less merciful than I. I asked him several times to let me put Zhongdu to the flame." Mauntgraul shook his head. "Later, the Jin themselves begged me, crying out from the towers where their dragon bows sat unused. And then, one morning, the city offered me a sacrifice, appealing to my heart. Oh, you should have seen them, Benjurigan. The white ladies of Zhongdu. Thousands upon thousands of women lined the battlements. Together they leapt, falling like petals into the moat. And still the Khan waited."

Ben had no words for this, his hands trembling at his sides.

"Only when the emperor opened the gates, the city falling to the tribes, did Genghis invite me to show my compassion."

"You razed the fucking city to the ground!"

The words flew off Ben's tongue before he could stop them. How could he forget the charred, skeletal bones of the city when he and Von Hart had arrived, sweeping east across the Yellow River? Weary and fraught, they had seen the wasteland for the first time. The rotting cattle. The mounds of corpses. The circling vultures and the wolves. The Hebei Plains might have been the Fields of Hell, the war machines left abandoned in the muck when the Khan had moved on, already bored with his conquest and hungry for the next.

But Mauntgraul, having smelled their approach, had turned back to greet them . . .

"A new beginning." Mauntgraul spread his arms, encompassing the snowy vista. "Many great things rise from the ashes, wouldn't you say? Am I not one of them?"

"You don't know this world, Maunt. You haven't seen—"

"Then show me, brother wyrm. Let's fly together, you and I. You can show me the worth of enslavement. And I will show you destruction."

Mauntgraul turned, revealing the grim set of his jaw. Despite his tone, Ben could see that he wasn't joking. The White Dog had lost none of his physique, none of his presence. He was a tightly bound knot of dark wood, his limbs a model of strength. Veins braided his arms, his neck, the generous member between his legs, all speaking of vitality.

His draconic blood pumped through his frame, the way he held himself, his vigour coiling inside. His midnight eyes made a proud bust of his head, his human form passed down from the hands of the Fay, seeded through dragon's egg and dragon's egg. Only at his temples did his great age show, streaks of silver through his close-cropped hair.

Ben remembered this mask, this guise of the Wandering Moor. He remembered the terrors hiding behind it. He held out a hand, palm flat and facing upward, and in *wyrm tongue* he made his appeal.

"The old war is over. It doesn't have to be this way."

"Have we known any other?" As Mauntgraul's shadow fell across him, a chill crawled into Ben's bones. "This is our destiny. Why we first hatched. Even when Scawgramal and Pennydrake fought tooth and claw under Dinas Emrys, this was our fate. And when Myrddin released them from the pit, the two dragons symbolised our struggle, the Red and the White. Our enmity runs through our bloodlines, reborn with every snout that breaks a shell. It is blood on snow, Benjurigan. Old as dust. And it will last until the end of time."

"No," Ben said. "You're in love with your own legend. You *choose* to rend and destroy."

"I am all that you are not," Mauntgraul told him. "Vengeful where you forgive. Strong where you are weak. Free while you are a slave."

"I am my own man!"

"Man? *Man?*" The White Dog laughed, throwing back his head. Collecting himself, he drew even closer, his lips curled back in a snarl. "Who gave you birth? You have forgotten her, haven't you? Jynnyflamme, the spawn of Pennydrake. Your mother, who wheeled in the skies above Grasmere like a teardrop from the sun. Who abandoned her egg in the habit of our kind, hoping that you would grow strong and find her. Instead, you suckled on a human teat. Isn't that so, *milk drinker*?"

"That isn't what happened. She—"

"Even in your youth you turned your back on us. One by one you watched us fall. And that was not the worst of it." Mauntgraul's nose was level with Ben's now, so close that his next word crisped the hairs on Ben's cheeks. "*Traitor*."

Ben roared. With all his strength, he raised his fists and brought them down on Mauntgraul's chest, pummelling his flesh. Through his rage, he was aware that it would do him no good. The dragon knew just what buttons to push. And he was a fool to respond.

Mauntgraul staggered back a pace, a sneer crawling over his face.

"What will you do?" he said. "Where is your family now? Where is your greedy king and all his rapacious knights? Where is your envoy with his little harp, to make the earth sing and close around me, the darkness dragging me deep? *Where?*"

Ben stumbled back to the battlements, the questions like mallets thudding on his skull. The horror of his situation was sinking in, icy fangs biting deep. The White Dog's resentment, his anger, his *blame* was a wall of heat he struggled to withstand.

"Leave me be. Let *them* be. Please."

"No." Mauntgraul gripped his shoulder. His hand had

become a claw, the black talons dragging Ben upright, drawing him close. "You and I are alone, are we not? The last of our kind. I can feel it. Your love for humans has murdered us all. You will not turn away from me now."

Ben tried to shrug him off, but the White Dog gripped him fast. In response, Ben was changing, crimson scales slipping over his skin. But Mauntgraul was not dissuaded, his wings and tail folding out, twelve tons of scarred white flesh reducing the ramparts behind him to rubble. Black claws spread across the turret roof, gouging the stone like chisels. Together they rose, Mauntgraul and Ben, carried skyward by their thrashing wings. Ben kicked and wriggled, forcing all that he had left against the vice around his shoulder and neck.

"The kindest thing would be to kill you," Mauntgraul said. "Instead, I will make you watch."

With that, he slammed Ben into stone, the watchtower flying apart.

EIGHT

Minutes passed in stunned orbits of pain. Then, growling, Ben shrugged off the rubble, the broken blocks booming into the treetops below. Nursing his shattered ribs, he scanned the skies, locating Mauntgraul between two peaks, a pale shape sweeping south. The sight drew bile into his throat.

Adrenalin kicked him onto his feet. He winced and cursed, haranguing his healing abilities to greater speed. Bloody, bruised, he had somehow survived, but the dragon's parting words left no room for relief. Dread eclipsed all other concerns. He couldn't see Beijing from here, but he could picture it – the city rising from the northern plain, her skyscrapers hazy in the smog. Unsuspecting. Undefended.

Deadly and true, Mauntgraul levelled his wings, gliding towards the buildings on the horizon.

And the people. The millions of people.

Fuck.

Ben sped in pursuit. Death, his old friend, was grinning again, and this time his skull bore fangs. Motorway bridges, smokestacks and cars went blurring past under his wings. Too soon, the pan-flat fields gave way to high-rises and cranes, smoky slums crouching in their shadow, the northern fringes of Beijing.

Down a canyon of tower blocks Mauntgraul swept, his scaly length reflected in a thousand windows. Cries rose from the round-the-clock traffic, the curses of drivers and cyclists. After the mountains, their alarm felt like a punch in Ben's guts. The people below had seen the dragon. Seen him. They looked up at the sky open-mouthed as the beasts came hurtling towards them, a wall of fangs rushing out of myth. Out of *nightmare*.

All he could do was shoot through the smog, the pollution thicker here, stinging his eyes and coating his throat. If he could catch up, bring the White Dog crashing to the ground, then maybe dust would cover the scene. Let disbelief do all the rest . . .

Dread pushed Ben into the city proper. He'd been getting away with this for far too long, and seeing Mauntgraul up ahead, he could sense his luck running out.

The White Dog slowed to circle the Bell Tower, the ancient stone building rising from the low rooftops of Dongcheng. Seeing the tourists on the broad balcony edging the building, Ben grasped the reason for the dragon's distraction. A scent, after eight hundred years, that would surely prove irresistible. Today, the huge belfry was silent, the giant bell still, but Mauntgraul swept down, lashing out his tail, come to strike the hour of destruction.

Tiles, brick and wood flew. A sculpture took flight from the eaves, sending plaster and stone spinning down to the square below. The people on the balcony broke into a panicked chorus as the structure gave way, sagging under a barrage of debris. Lurching from dislodged beams, the balcony peeled off the face of the edifice, spilling people into the air. By the time Ben reached the tower, Mauntgraul was thrusting further into the city. All that remained was a mess of rubble and broken bones. People wailing, calling for help, their anguish drowned out by the tolling of the bell.

This isn't happening.

Death had come to Beijing. Fresh screams rose from the *hutongs*, the riddle of alleyways around the site. A sleek red missile, Ben flung himself in that direction, following the thrashing trees and telephone lines, chasing terror and chaos.

Mauntgraul shot over the urban grid, over the streets and the flat-roofed houses huddling under his claws like prey. He veered to avoid a hotel, smashing through the neon sign on the roof, the Chinese letters reduced to shrapnel. He spun down on the other side of the building, a barrel roll sweeping him into the city centre.

An uproar announced his arrival on Wangfujing plaza. The shoppers milling along the mall forgot all about shopping as the shadow of wings fell over them. At once, the crowds scattered into a babbling mass, stampeding for the nearest subway station or Jianguomen Street beyond, the traffic there screeching to a halt. Fenders met fenders with a crunch. Metal thudded into flesh.

Ben drew a breath, preparing to spew fire, but his lungs shrank as he realised that he would only roast the fleeing people alive. The White Dog would resist his heat anyway, his hide as tough, as durable as armour. He was left to watch, helpless, as the older dragon dropped into another dive. Wingtips skimming storefronts, snapping awnings and sparking off the huge neon advertising screens, he arrowed down the street, his claws extending, daggers made of night. Ben winced as he scooped up people from the crowd, one or two flying free from his grip – a policeman, a tramp, a wailing girl – falling to smack on the concrete below. The rest of his catch Mauntgraul shoved into his maw, a clutch of flailing limbs between his fangs.

With a roar, Ben gave chase, the blood mist of the carnage peppering his snout.

Gunshot snapped from the streets below, guards outside the high red walls of the Forbidden City putting rifle to shoulder and firing at the threat blasting overhead. The moment he saw them, Ben knew that the guards would make no distinction between the White Dog and himself. Metal zipped off his scales, hot pinpricks that did nothing to slow him.

Ahead, an open space spread out before him. Tiananmen Square, the largest square in the world, at least offered a safer battleground. With a snap of his wings, he pushed himself after the dragon, flying beyond firing range. A moment of grace that he knew wouldn't last. He was already too late.

The crowds were scattering, a sea of umbrellas and dropped cameras, whipped into frenzy by the monsters above. Screams struck off polished stone, but Ben barely heard them. Fangs bared, he drove his weight down, down into Mauntgraul's back, his talons raking flesh. Together the dragons tumbled through the air, smashing into the flagstones below.

Dust flew outwards, blasting the fleeing crowd. Ben rolled with Mauntgraul in the chaos, jaws, legs and tails locked, claws scraping at scales. Fighting for breath, he tried to muster fire, but the White Dog's grip closed around his throat, lifting him off the ground like a doll and hurling him across the square.

He found himself caught, a prisoner of gravity. Air screaming in his ears, the square became a blur interrupted by the screaming crowds, the Forbidden City wheeling past. In a heap of crumpled wings, he smashed into the Great Hall of the People. A cloud billowed from the grand government building as he touched down, pillars crashing in around him, shattering on scale and horn.

After a minute or two filled with stars, he dragged himself up, rubble clattering off his spine. Bones straightening, he shook off his wings, looking around for Mauntgraul. *Where is the bastard?* Weak cries drew his gaze, reluctantly, to the littered ground between his claws. Dust-and-blood-covered shapes groaned in the debris, but he couldn't think about that now, couldn't let their anguish slow him. In the distance he heard the wail of sirens, and he prayed that the police were bringing meat wagons as well as rockets and guns.

He leapt skyward, his wounds complaining about his renewed pursuit. Weaving above the panorama of the square, his nostrils flared, straining to catch the scent of his quarry. His eardrums gave him the bad news. Screams rose from somewhere to the south, and wheeling in that direction, he saw a pale shape snaking between the distant high-rises. Drawing in his wings, heart thudding, he followed.

The high-rises marched into the suburbs, row upon row of them. Beijing provided a dragon with ample space to hide; the tall buildings were packed close in a concrete and steel maze. But Mauntgraul, he guessed, was only hiding for the fun of it. *He isn't afraid of me.* The intermittent screams told Ben that the beast flew onward, wanton and without shame. He caught glimpses of him between the tower blocks. A wingtip brushing a window. A grille of fangs reflected in glass. On the tip of his tail, his sting went swishing back and forth, loaded with deadly green venom.

Ben held his breath as he approached, coasting and silent. He stretched out a claw to grab Mauntgraul's tail, keep its danger away from him. One strike of the spiked black barb on the end of it would make this the shortest battle of his life.

Sensing his approach, Mauntgraul snapped his snout around, fangs bared. Too late, Ben realised that the dragon was only waiting for an audience, allowing him to catch up. He watched, gasping, as Mauntgraul dwindled in mid-air, his human form slipping through his closing grip. Feet first, he dropped like a stone towards the earth – towards the intercity railway line and the sleek shape of the bullet train speeding along it.

Before Ben had a chance to react, Mauntgraul was thudding into a carriage roof, the train's velocity absorbing the shock. Claws sprouting from his feet, he crouched against the smooth surface, catlike, secure. In a second, he was gone, a dark shape flashing under a motorway bridge and out of sight.

Ben dived after him, his wings folding. Judging the distance, his bulk shrank in time with his descent, falling through the buffeting air. His snout and horns flowed around his skull, his flesh melting into a glowering face, his crimson hair streaming out behind him. Scales compressed, sliding over one another until his symbiotic suit wove around his body, black, glossy, emblazoned with *wyrm tongue*. He landed, gracelessly, on the last carriage of the train, denting the streamlined caboose. Throwing out a hand, his fingers formed a makeshift grappling hook, his legs flailing. Metal squealed as he gouged long lines in the roof, fixing himself to the train. Flat on his belly, he looked up with a curse, glaring at the White Dog.

Mauntgraul was five or six carriages ahead. Ben could see the track curving ahead through an area of low buildings, the outskirts of the city. Claw over claw, the dragon was crawling towards the snub-nosed driver's cab. If any passengers inside had heard them land, no one sounded an alarm, and the scenery continued to rocket past, the train speeding south at several hundred klicks per hour, a white missile with wheels. High-rises, factories and cranes were giving way to the flat plantations of the plain, the city skyline receding, the smog relenting in scraps of cloud. The morning sun shone through the haze, giving Ben a clearer view of his quarry – clearer than he'd like. The White Dog was perfectly still, his muscles holding the lustre of teak, bunched against the wind. When he glanced over his shoulder, Ben could feel his gaze across the distance, patient and fierce. He was waiting, all right. He wanted Ben to see him. Wanted Ben to watch.

Satisfied with his attention, Mauntgraul gave a grin – *and now for my next trick* – and, keeping low to avoid the masts and wires zipping overhead, continued to crawl towards the engine. A dragon-sized claw in the gears would spell certain disaster for all.

Limbs aching, the air raging in his ears, Ben hauled himself after him.

The train shot over a river, past platforms, whistling alongside the highway parallel. Billboards and road signs smeared across Ben's vision with the giddiness of some frantic cartoon. Another train roared past, the buffeting wind threatening to throw him from the carriage and into the surrounding fields.

Looking up, he saw the White Dog changing. A sheen of scales rippled up over his buttocks and back, his black horns protruding from his skull. Half dragon, half man, Mauntgraul climbed to his feet, facing Ben with a grin. The move was ill judged. A railway mast smacked into his spine, the strut squealing with the impact. Jags of metal showered around him, thumping along the roof. Ben yelled as the debris tore at his arms, spraying blood down the carriages behind him. Grimacing, he pulled himself onto his hands and knees, spurred by the sight of the White Dog standing on top of the driver's cab. Mauntgraul was unfolding his wings, the green-veined pale pennons springing from his tensed shoulder blades. Bunching his fists, he raised his arms over his head, his elongating horns lending him the look of a biblical demon.

The train accelerated across the plain. The White Dog meant to step on the brakes.

Ben pulled himself into a crouch, preparing to leap the space between them, rugby-tackle the dragon from the train. As he did so, something caught the corner of his eye, an object to his right, moving faster than the traffic on the highway. Faster than the smear of the buildings and fields.

Fighting against the rushing air, his eyebrows rose despite himself, his lips a puzzled sneer.

Something was racing beside the train. The object was moving too fast to trace, a motion blur rippling in its wake, a green-gold streak through the day. As it drew parallel, Ben made out a muzzle, a windswept mane and galloping hooves.

What the hell? Unless he'd lost the plot completely, even a racehorse at full tilt couldn't keep up with a speeding train. And to his surprise, the beast was steadily overtaking, leaving that dazzling blur, the emerald sheen of its hide.

Before he could question the newcomer's presence, the galloping beast leapt for the train. A beast leapt, but a woman landed, alighting on the carriage ahead, halfway between Ben and his goal. The impact shuddered under him, heavy feet on steel.

No. Not feet. *Hooves.*

In a second, the woman had steadied herself with a sword of some kind, stabbing the blade into the roof. Her equine form was gone – a shape thrown off – but her skin-tight suit matched the colour of its hide, a dark green silk, the cuffs a burnished gold. She held her arms close to her body, her slender muscles coiled like springs, a stance that Ben recognised from a thousand kung fu movies. Another sword appeared in her hand, a mirror to the first. The single-edged blades were broad and short, all curving crossguards and knuckle-bows. Fancy, but sharp enough to slice through scales? He doubted it.

Crouching, her eyes were only for the White Dog.

"Get out of the way!" The wind snatched his words away. "He's—"

117

Did she know? Did she care? Mauntgraul's appearance, horned and clawed, betrayed the fact that he wasn't a man. Just as her hooves – shit, her *presence* – had betrayed her. When she shot a look at him, her long dark braid flying around her face, he saw determination, not fear. A silent warning, too. *Stay back.* She was Chinese, perhaps in her early thirties, but her eyes were anything but human. She was a Remnant, that much was clear. Her breed, however, was unknown to him, originating from Asian climes. From unfamiliar myths.

Whatever she was, listening to him wasn't one of them. Before Mauntgraul could bring his fists down on the driver's cab, she was on the move again, her hooves thrusting her forward, closing the gap between them. Arms held out, swords level, she leapt over a passing mast as if it was a skipping rope and went sailing downward, a hoof connecting with the back of Maunt's skull.

The White Dog staggered forward, fighting for balance. He lost his footing, the smooth surface defying his claws, and went tumbling down the nose of the train. The woman landed in the space where he had stood moments before, sheathing her swords on her back.

Ben was sending mental applause when Mauntgraul reappeared on the carriage roof, an arm whipping out, lashing at her legs. He cried out, but she was already flipping out of reach, climbing the pummelling air like a ladder. When she landed again, her hooves slipped on the polished surface and she flattened herself against the roof, preventing herself from tumbling from the train. The move, however, cost her the advantage. Pressed to steel, she couldn't avoid Mauntgraul's tail, swollen to draconic proportions and whipping out like a flail.

Ben winced as its length crashed into her, swatting her like a fly. It must've hurt, but the woman didn't vent a scream. In silence, she relinquished her grip on the sword hilt. She bounced once, twice along the carriage roof and went flashing past Ben, a green-gold tangle of limbs. He reached out, making a grab for her, groaning as his fingers closed on air and he watched her roll down another carriage and slip off the train, vanishing from view.

Nice try.

He had no time to ponder her intervention. Mauntgraul, in full dragon form now, was rising atop the driver's cab. His wings fanned out, keeping most of his weight off the carriage, his hind legs scraping steel. Beyond him, Ben made out an approaching interchange, the roads looping in a raised concrete knot around some satellite town of Beijing.

The bullet train sped on, shooting onto a viaduct alongside the interchange, fifty-odd feet above a river. Ben didn't need to see the glint in Mauntgraul's eyes to realise that he had chosen this site for his killing blow.

Somewhere, distantly, he heard the screech of brakes, smoke from the traumatised engine billowing around him. He could only imagine the driver's terror when the scaled demon had rolled across the windshield, a clutch of claws and fangs. But the driver had slammed on the brakes way too late. The train would take about a minute to slow, a minute that Ben no longer had.

Up ahead, Mauntgraul was twisting his claws, digging deeper into metal. Thus secured, he stretched out his neck, a scarred snake bristling with knives. There came a wash of flame, acid green, the heat inside him escaping his lungs.

Then the White Dog screamed.

Dissonance pulsed along the train. Inertia struck, gravity trying to peel Ben from the carriage. Moments before the sound wave followed, the surface of the carriage rippled like water. An overhead mast buckled inward, disintegrating into shards. Wires snickered overhead, sizzling and then evaporating, reduced to sparks and dust. All the carriage windows blew inwards, the sound like corkscrews jammed into his ears. The roof under him was melting away, liquefied metal streaming between his claws. Skull ringing, Ben found himself flying backwards, the White Dog's shriek blasting him from the train.

Deafened, he watched Mauntgraul paddle his wings, thrusting skyward. He could feel the judder in the air as the dragon shifted the cab from the viaduct. Its derailment shuddered down the length of the train, the carriage wheels skewing, dancing from the tracks. The next moment, the connected carriages jackknifed, torpedoing one over the other, wrenched upward by gravity and speed. The foremost cars slewed across the bridge, crashing headlong into the huge cantilevers supporting the structure. The rear carriages hit the obstruction with a thump, an impact that Ben felt in his guts and balls, his teeth biting through his tongue.

Whoomph.

Pluming smoke, one carriage burst through the latticed fence of the viaduct, sailing across the gulf and smashing into the interchange, crumpling like a used cigarette. Tyres squealed, the traffic up there skidding to a halt. The remaining carriages took an unscheduled detour and shot over the edge of the bridge, plunging into the waiting gorge, the river exploding in fountains of dirt.

Ben observed the crashing train in slow, shuddering seconds. The sky spun, spewing steel and flame. Then his back hit something hard and cold, sparing him the scene.

When he came round, people were screaming.

"Your English king feared my vengeance." And closer to him, he heard Mauntgraul, a winged shadow blocking out the sun. "That's why you and the envoy chased me to Zhongdu, all those centuries ago."

Ben shook his head. The old serpentine language, *wyrm tongue*, hissed inside his skull, wrenching him back to awareness. He took in his surroundings, a foggy patchwork. The wide river. Carriages protruding from the water. The bank on which he lay, human-shaped and covered in mud. The broken bridge above him. The bodies strewn across the slope. Scraps of metal. Bloody limbs. Some, he noticed, moving weakly. Survivors from the crash. He took in the interchange next to the bridge. The concrete pillars loomed over him, impassive mourners by a grave.

And the White Dog. The crowds peering over the edge of the expressway were screaming at the dragon as well as the carnage. Camera phones flashed in the sun. Sirens wailed, distant but approaching fast. Drifting smoke obscured the sea of faces, masking the tears, the pointing fingers. Everything stank of fire and death.

Ben groaned, tasting blood.

"Rakegoyle," he said. "She burned London Bridge to the ground."

Feebly, Ben tried to sit up, howling as pain shot through him, igniting every nerve. He collapsed in the mud again, whimpering. Whatever had happened to his spine, his extraordinary flesh had yet to heal it. Mauntgraul might as well have nailed him to the ground.

"Did the old bitch have any choice?" the dragon spat, his fangs coming closer, a black portcullis. His breath was the stench of an abattoir on a hot day. His tail arched over his shoulder, the barbed tip swishing back and forth.

"But you brought her down, didn't you?" It wasn't a question; it was a statement of fact. "You killed her. Your own kind."

Ben found that he had no words. Mauntgraul stamped down by his shoulder, his claw throwing up muck, the ground shuddering.

"*Didn't you?*"

"To save us . . . all . . ."

But the White Dog was roaring now, lost in his rage. His voice shrill, a door off its hinges, banging in a high wind. Bordering on hysteria.

Ben wanted to reach out, explain the sacrifices he'd made. *It doesn't have to be this way . . .*

He never got the chance. Mauntgraul's tail came spearing down, lightning quick, the barb on the end of it striking Ben's chest.

"You killed my mother."

PART TWO

Death Music

Nature is not human hearted.
Lao Tzu

Miào ~ temple

Mount Song, 1356

In the stance of the crane, one knee raised and tensed, Jia stood in the temple courtyard as her master and friend Blaise Von Hart lowered another stone onto the stack that trembled atop her head.

"To be *youxia* is to be an example," he told her, and she could swear his pale face was holding back a smirk. "In the old days, the *youxia* wandered the land, upholding justice, setting right to wrong. You would call them knights-errant in my part of the world. In Zhongguo, they were warrior monks, more likely to break your head than bless it. The *youxia* – knowing darkness, knowing chaos. Choosing light."

She hissed something through her teeth that may or may not have been *yes, teacher.*

"The way of the *youxia*. It is to walk the golden mean. To be the balance in the world."

"*Shi . . . laoshi . . .*"

He is enjoying this.

Sweat trickled down Jia's brow, stinging her eyes. Sweat as bitter as the pain in her heart. Upon her arrival at the temple three weeks ago, she had committed the unpardonable sin of not being male; her presence breaking the traditions of centuries, all the known customs. And the monks appeared to take daily pleasure in reminding her of this. In turn, she projected her displeasure at all the men here, apart from her thin, white-haired and typically objective master. Besides, knowing his true nature, could she honestly think of Von Hart as a man? He was *Xian*. Fay. Different. Other. Perhaps even more than a man.

She had never wanted to come here, had only done so on the orders of Toghon Temur. The Khan, the sixteenth ruler of the Yuan Dynasty, was nothing whatsoever like the Great Kublai. Like all the petty, weak – and thankfully brief – khans who had succeeded the Wise One, Toghon stood like an ant in his shadow. Small and constantly drunk, his head barely rose from the bosoms of his concubines to attend to matters of state. No wonder the empire was crumbling.

Still, her duty, her oath stood firm: "to serve the Emperor of Zhongguo for all the time to come".

Von Hart grasped her reluctance only too well, not that it made any difference. He spoke of *honour* simply to prod her, she thought. The faces of the monks remained impassive whenever they looked up from inking their scrolls or lighting the incense at the sight of her whimpering on the ground, once again beaten by her training, but their frowns spoke volumes. Naturally, with her inherent talent of perception, she sensed their silent disapproval at her presence here, a woman in the temple, of all things! She could understand their resentment, even if it galled her. Her brothers had left everything behind – even their shoes – to take up their place in the temple. She had not chosen to come. The monks might have no choice but to tolerate her, her mythical nature and her pathetic attempts at *wushu*, but she would not give them the satisfaction of letting them see her bested. No, never that. And so her ordeal continued.

"Breathe."

As ever, Jia took Von Hart's instruction. Standing in the courtyard, the mist coiling around her straining body, she could smell the dense vegetation, the vines clutching the tombs in the forest of pagodas and strangling the pillars of the mountain gate. The roots of the mangrove trees crawled across the flagstones and riddled the shallow set of steps leading up to the temple proper, the heavenly palace hall. Up there, the thick wooden doors stood locked and bolted, the shrine beyond claimed by Von Hart upon his arrival, the sacred space serving a purpose other than prayer. In his curt Frankish tone he had forbidden the monks from entering the place, and his eyes, so darkly violet, so very unlike human eyes, had been all they needed to obey him. They grumbled, of course, but the order had hurt Jia the most. The shrine represented her wayward emotions, her longing, but also her comfort. Access had been denied her too and yet the temptation remained.

Behind the doors rested the Eight Hand Mirror. She knew that her fellow monks didn't resent simply the barring of the shrine, but also the housing of the relic in this, their holiest site. Here on Mount Song, one of the kingdom's Five Holy Peaks. Umbrage lingered in every hooded glance that slipped towards the thin, pale creature who had landed in their midst, bringing a woman and black glass with him. In the courtyard during Jia's lessons. As the brothers sat in the hall, inking scrolls or eating bowls of steamed rice. If the envoy noticed this (and she believed he did), he paid the monks' displeasure no mind. And the monks, Jia sensed, were too fearful of the mirror's provenance to mutter about its presence too loudly.

The Eight Hand Mirror is one of our oldest trinkets, child, left behind by my people when they departed this world, abandoning us to our fate.

Yes, the monks were probably right to fear it. Several had shrunk from the mirror as others – with gritted teeth and ashen complexions – had unloaded the artefact from Von Hart's cart and hefted it into the shrine, where it now stood on the altar, shrouded in shadow but never forgotten. Nobody had wanted to touch the thing, that much was obvious, an aversion that stood in complete contrast to Jia's feelings on the matter; she would rather have died than leave the mirror behind.

At first, she had heeded her master, resisting the urge to disobey him. There had been no such rules in the city of Dadu, where she could come and go in the envoy's chambers of her own free will, standing before the large plain octagonal frame whenever the need took her, which was often and deep. Why had Von Hart hindered her now, removing her one small joy? Comfort had become a habit and loneliness was its own devil, whispering in her ear at night.

One moonlit night, she had found herself padding across the courtyard and, employing the vines that wove all around the temple, climbing hand over hand to the roof. It had been an easy thing to drop down through the hole that served as a chimney and make her way across the floor to the altar, a ghost whispering through pale beams. That night, the Eight Hand Mirror had stood dusty and dark, the glass, as usual, reflecting no one, only the darkened chamber behind her, the urns of incense and the sculpted gods. For this, Jia was thankful. She had not wanted to see herself, to all intents and purposes a sixteen-year-old girl, breaking the faith of her master.

Oh master. The thought pricked a tear from her eye, the memory of all she had lost. *How has it come to this . . .?* A hand stretched out, fingers trembling; she had touched the glass, as cold as ice under her palm. The mirror was a window, of sorts. *Or perhaps a door.* Wasn't that what the envoy had said, all those years ago? *A door without a key.* All Jia had was her frosted skin and her heart's desire, her closeness to the glass. As ever, she shivered, her guts cramping in the presence of magic, but knowing that her discomfort was a small price to pay for the vision awaiting her, the mirror rippling, the blank darkness swirling and shifting, a curtain parting on hope. For hours she'd sat there, cross-legged and gazing into the glass. Into the cavern deep under the northern plains where her parents, Ziyou and Ye, slumbered on undisturbed, bound by the Loreful enchantment. Oh, how she missed them! How she wished that she could feel Ziyou nickering in her ear as they grazed beneath Xanadu's walls, or her mother, Ye, swatting her flanks with her emerald tail at something her father had said, their foal braying with laughter between their legs . . .

Only when the first rays of sunlight crept under the locked

temple door did Jia rise, her heart leaden with guilt. She spared the black glass one last longing look before she returned to her room.

That was the first time, but there had been others since. She had come to look forward to clear and moonlit nights almost as much as looking into the Eight Hand Mirror.

The mirror was her only peace in these dismal days. Toghon Khan, finally accepting that he couldn't make use of Jia for his own ends, had banished her from court. Well, he said that he had sent her to the temple on Mount Song to toughen her up, prepare her for the coming war. But they both knew what this was. Punishment. *Exile*. Toghon loved wine and whores and money. He had no great love of Remnants.

It had taken all of Jia's resolve not to run away, flee Dadu and take to the hills, a fugitive roaming the land. Still, her honour bound her. Honour and memory. On his deathbed, the Great Kublai had gripped her hand, thanking her for her years of service. Reminding her to guard the Dragon Throne for all the time to come. How could she refuse her oath? Stand in denial of the Lore? In the end, she had swallowed her pride and, head hung low, joined Von Hart on his way to the temple, the wheels of his cart creaking under the weight of his mirror. Today, Xanadu felt very far away. So did the Great Kublai. The Wise One was seventy years in his grave, having spluttered his last in gluttony and gout.

Now, as she stood in the courtyard with the stones on her head, there was only Von Hart, who, knowing her grief, had only intensified her lessons, bending her to the point where she might break.

"The Khan laments," the envoy said, as though catching the scent of her sorrow along with her sweat. "The empire crumbles. The Red Turban rebels roam the land, setting fire to the fields and sacking temples. And you have spurned your duty at court. You who remain of all of your kind, appointed by the Great Kublai himself, raised to serve as your father served the Iron-Faced Judge Bao Gong and his father served before that and back and back down thousands of years." Von Hart caught his breath, fighting to overcome his dismay. "There is . . . chaos, child, spreading in the land. Spreading everywhere, I think. A chaos I feared, yet hoped to forestall, the signing of the Pact keeping us safe. A worm gnaws at the heart of things . . ." He appeared to have forgotten her, muttering to himself. "*Ja*. I must check on the circles, strengthen the walls . . ."

"Circles, master?"

"Hope can blind us, Jia. Perhaps all I saw was what I wanted to see. We can all be guilty of that."

He cocked an eyebrow at her, a look that was as enigmatic as it was knowing, and one that she did not like very much. For some reason, she thought of Ziyou and Ye asleep in the mirror and felt her cheeks redden with more than the pressure of the stones.

"Master?"

Did he know about her moonlit visits? Why did he always evade her perception, smoke under glass, his truth out of reach?

He flashed her a smile and patted her arm, threatening to dislodge the stacked pile on her head.

"Oh, don't worry about me. I will be fine, as ever."

"But I wasn't—"

"It's everyone else I worry about, Jia. The mortals. You Remnants. I'm a terribly powerful creature. The last of the *Xian* on earth. Remember that I used to teach Merlin, the greatest wizard in the west."

"*Shi . . . laoshi.* You said."

There was no point in arguing. He was old, she knew, older than the first days of Camelot, but not yet old in the last. When she had been a little girl in the gardens of Xanadu, Von Hart had told her all those colourful stories of kings, knights and dragons in faraway Albion. She had sat rapt by his knee as he described the fall of Arthur Pendragon, the end of the Old Lands and the departure of his people from the earth. In fact, all through her childhood, he had filled her head with knowledge like water in an ever-brimming cup. Had there ever been a teacher as wise, as strict, as kind as Von Hart? The gods, the stars, the law, the land and the mathematics of all these things went wheeling around the inside of her skull like diamonds in a void, the light of his wisdom pushing back ignorance. Making her strong. And one day, his teaching had led her to an appointed position in court, one that only she could hold, that she was *born* to hold, according to the Wise One and all the khans who came after – the sacred position of judge.

You can see the truth from lie, child, Von Hart had said, in feeble consolation. *Can you not see your worth to the Empire?*

Jia could see all right. For year upon year she had stood beside the throne, hearing the pleas of the accused. Indeed, she'd stood on the dais in full *sin-you* form, all green mane and golden hooves, the better to inspire dread in the ones below the dais. Oh the tears! The hand-wringing. The excuses.

The bribes. The threats. Once the charges had been read, the pleas made, she would turn to Kublai – or Kulug or Jayaatu, as time went on – and signal, with a raised head, the innocence of the man or woman bound before the throne. Her single horn, a golden antler-like blade curving up from the middle of her brow, would sparkle in the sunlight, presiding over an ocean of sighs. More often than not, over an ocean of sobs. With a lowered head, her horn tipped to the courtroom floor, she would signal the guilt of the thief, the traitor, the murderer . . . Then she would turn away, her purpose served, as the court set about extracting a confession and doling out swift justice. In fifty years of service, no Khan had commanded her to play the role of executioner.

But that was not enough for Toghon.

Stubborn, belligerent beast! She remembered Toghon's words, hot in the face of her refusal. *The gods have cursed us. Flood, famine and drought blight our lands. Rebels run amok as our enemies rise in the south. Still you refuse to make of this man* (he'd pointed to the prisoner, stripped to the waist and bound in the middle of the throne room floor) *a bloody example, a warning to all.*

And she remembered her answer. Biting back anger, she had shaken off the gasps that met the appearance of her womanly form, standing in her sheer silk dress on the dais.

The gods have not cursed us, Toghon.

So now she stood with stones atop her head, her limbs aching, holding her position. Her tunic was wet, a sponge for sweat. Her hair was long, lank and unwashed. The dust of the temple was in her mouth. And her wise old master, his features as smooth and pale as the flagstones at her feet, hissed philosophies of pain and truth in her ear, watching her discomfort, sharing her fall from grace.

A worm gnaws at the heart of things.

"Master . . ." She spoke into the envoy's silence, disliking his ominous words.

"Think no more of it," he told her. "Your training is all but done. Time will teach you other lessons, I think. The value of sacrifice. The price of the truth. You will be ready, I promise you. When the time comes."

Ready for what? she wanted to ask, but before she could question him further, he was clapping his hands and leaning forward. "Now, one more stone, I think." And for a fleeting moment Jia could have forgiven all the indignities and kissed him. "One more stone and then to your supper. But you must fetch this one yourself."

Jia's heart thudded in her breast as if the stones were already falling, falling through her, falling into a future of failure. Rejection from court. Eternal exile. Shame upon the herd. She blinked away sweat, met Von Hart's strange-coloured eyes, the suppressed laughter glinting there. Unlike the mirror, his gaze didn't spare her. Here, she found herself reflected, a sinewy waif who had seriously thought to endure this torture and emerge *youxia* – a warrior, a monk – on the other side.

Through the drumming in her ears she heard herself say, "Yes . . . teacher . . ."

Another breath, a deeper one. Let the mountain and the forest fill her lungs. Let the silence of the temple soothe her. Let time slow and pool, as placid as the Eight Hand

Mirror atop the altar, as she gently, gently tensed the tendons in her neck. The stones rattled ever so slightly as she sank in inches of agony, the drip of a water clock, towards the flagstones and the pebbles arrayed there. One-footed – and the urge to let that foot swell and harden, become a *hoof*, was like sweet fruit dangling before her nose. But she knew that such a transition would earn her another day of hardship from Von Hart and so she fought to resist. The spindle of stone weaving on her skull, Jia lowered herself, jaw clenched, into a crouch.

Von Hart took a step back as she stretched out a hand, splayed fingers trembling, for the nearest stone . . . She corrected herself and swallowed all emotion, a shroud thrown over her eyes, over her mind, as her palm closed around the coolness of a pebble.

Then the chaos that the envoy had mentioned erupted all around them.

The first thing Jia heard was a cry, somewhere off in the forest. *One of the monks*, she thought. *Hunting.* The cry scaled into the setting sun like the chirring of a nightjar, amplified by the distance, echoing into a silence that was somehow worse. The heavy silence of threat.

Von Hart tensed. "*Verdammt!* They come—"

In a cascade of stones, Jia bolted to her feet, the crane taking flight from her mind, fluttering and squawking away. Pebbles clattered down all around her, a hard rain on her shoulders and feet. Behind her, the smashing of bowls and tumbling of tables, harsh in the still. Monks came pouring down the temple steps, a flood of grimy tunics and shaven heads, a bristling forest of staves. As her brothers swept around her, Jia followed their charge to the mountain gates, her eyes wide as an opposing tide roared between the vine-choked pillars, equally dirty and wielding knives. Ten men, she counted, each one wearing a red turban, each one with fire in his eyes. That the rebellion should reach here, as far north as the slopes of Mount Song, drove a cold blade of fear through her mind. She stepped past Von Hart as if he wasn't there and stood, breathing hard, as the monks and the rebels clashed.

In an agony of indecision, Jia hopped from one foot to the other, watching the battle commence. Along with denying her access to the Eight Hand Mirror, Von Hart had also forbidden her from assuming natural shape anywhere in the temple, for the sake of the monks, who, he'd said, struggled enough with her presence as it was, without added strange-ness. This was another habit that she found hard to break. Hesitant, fearful, she stood like a novice at the edge of a ball, the dancers weaving and swirling across the floor. The dance before her was less elegant than that, a whirl of staves and flashing blades, scattering blood and screams, but she could see the technique nevertheless, the practised art of *wushu*. The monks held the animal forms in torso, neck and limb, the leopard leaping, the snake striking, the dragon wheeling, all fluidly changing from attack to defence, the space between the gates a clamour of flesh meeting flesh and a cloud of dust.

Dare she vault into the fray, green-maned, golden-hooved, taking her chances with her own fledgling skill? What would Master Von Hart say? Despite herself, her muscles rippled under her skin, her fists clenching and unclenching. In her mind, she pushed down her bestial shape and summoned up the form of *Single Tiger Emerges from Cave*, preparing to attack . . .

The Red Turbans, she noticed, fought without grace, their fists flying, knives slashing, flinging feathered darts wherever there was room. Most of the rebels, or so she had heard, were little more than farmers, untrained and untried. Rustic young men aggrieved by the taxes levied by the Khan and provoked by tales of his lechery. The recent chain of floods, the Yellow River drowning crop upon crop, had stirred the peasants like a ladle in a pot, the bitter broth of rebellion reaching boiling point. These rebels were Chin, Jia knew, not Mongol. The men came here under the banner of a Buddhist sect, with red turbans on their heads, and she sensed that they would have no qualms about spilling blood, even here on holy ground, in their fight to break the chains of their horse lord oppressors.

Thrown from thought of attack, Jia clutched her throat, the understanding drumming through her. In a flash of insight, she knew what she was seeing. If the bandits were here, then Nanjing had fallen. How else could these men have marched the six days west, armed and unchallenged? With no Mongol troops to stop them, the war band had forged its way to Mount Song, hungry to set a flag on the summit, as red as the sun setting on the Khan, unfurling in the wind for all to see! *And to hide their desecration in glory* . . . Jia could taste the rebels' ambition like wine on her tongue, earthy and sweet. The coiling mist couldn't hide the truth. The Yuan Dynasty would fall.

Bloodshed. Ruin. Change.

Faced with the Shaolin monks, the Red Turbans would usually have stood no chance in battle, the brothers routing the rabble back down the mountain easily enough, back into the restless south. There was something else here, some strange presence. Jia could feel it. A secret in the mist. The Red Turbans came with a weapon in their ranks, old, raging, eager to kill . . . Her forehead creased with the impression. The rebels might have broken the walls of the empire, but they had not done so alone . . .

Jueyuan!

The thought shuddered through her, wrenching her back to the here and now, even as the weapon in question burst from the forest and gripped the pillars of the mountain gate, forcing the barrier apart. A huge simian hand wrenched one of the granite posts from the earth and, paying no mind to either rebel or monk, hurled it into the fray, the courtyard shaking with the impact. Men screamed, crushed by stone. Blood tinged the rolling dust.

The *jueyuan* shouldered through what was left of the gates, grunting and hooting. In the haze, Jia took in his massive body, thirty hands tall and almost as wide. The creature resembled a gorilla, with the same small glittering eyes and the same heavy knuckles thumping the ground, levering his bulk into the courtyard. The only features that set him apart, betraying him as a Remnant, were his glossy blue pelt, his elongated snout and skull, and his baboon-like fangs. The rare and quite mythical ape was said to haunt the upper reaches of the mountain forests, a slow, shy creature that most would have thought harmless if not for his habit of carrying off the odd villager, sometimes as a mate, sometimes as a meal. Such attacks were unheard of these days, of course. As with most Remnants, the lullaby winding out of the west had lulled the *jueyuan* into the Sleep. The beast before her was the last of his kind – the last one *awake*, anyway – left to retreat into the mist-wreathed forests of bamboo, sinking into loneliness and legend.

Along with the rest of us . . . The knowledge reminded Jia that not all Remnants shared the same abilities, the same intelligence. The *jueyuan* was simply an ape, or something resembling an ape, yet another inexplicable creation of the long-departed *Xian*, a creature that, for all his rarity, human beings would only see as a monster, a horror, a threat. One they might cage and cajole, beating him into submission . . .

"Where did they find you?" Jia muttered under her breath, pushing down an unbidden surge of sympathy. "Where?"

As if in answer, the *jueyuan* bellowed, thumping his chest. The beast, having broken through the gates, was bringing his fury to the battle. Everywhere she looked, she saw rebels swept aside by a hairy blue arm the size and weight of a tree trunk, the men tumbling across the flagstones in a snarl of turbans, curses and dropped knives. The great ape snatched a monk up off the ground, his struggling body dangling upside down, his legs trapped between thick leathery fingers. Roaring, the beast swung the monk downward. Jia squeezed her eyes shut at the wet crack of bone, the sight of brains painting the flagstones . . .

When she opened her eyes, the monks were fleeing, heading off in a confused mass towards the forest of pagodas in search of a decent hiding place, escaping the monster in the courtyard. Dazed, bloody, the remaining rebels climbed to their feet and gave chase, knives out and flashing.

That left Jia, Von Hart and the *jueyuan*. The beast bunched his haunches, preparing to leap after the battle, crash through the rows of tombs. Then he paused, grunting, something catching his attention. Jia cried out as his massive head came swinging towards her. He growled, baring his fangs – but his menace couldn't hide the confusion in his eyes. She watched, holding her breath, as the beast scratched his armpit and reared up on his hind legs, his nostrils flaring. *Smelling* her.

Had the *jueyuan* caught her magical essence? Von Hart's alien nature? Yes, she thought so. Sweat and dust aside, the ape's eyes grew wider, the gleam of longing sliding under the surface, savage and raw. He blew out his cheeks, a gust that sent leaves rattling across the courtyard. There was more here than the scent of *humans* alone, and the beast was obviously trying to fathom it, this new and unexpected threat. To fathom *her*. He tipped his head, questioning.

Tentatively, Jia raised a hand in greeting, her palm held out and open. Stealing a breath, she took a small step forward.

Von Hart gripped her shoulder, a silent warning, but she shrugged him off, addressing the creature in the courtyard.

"That's right, old one. I am like you."

The *jueyuan* grumbled in his chest. Then he whined and hooted. If he decided to attack, no barrier stood between them; he could bound across the space with ease and rip her limb from limb. Jia's heart punched against her ribcage as she watched the *jueyuan*'s eyes, bright, wary, hounded. Scars criss-crossed his snout and there were several patches in his dull blue pelt, making her wonder what kind of indignities he'd suffered, captured and caged by the rebels. What were his wounds if not a mirror to her own?

Another step. She stretched out her hand. Maybe if she could reach him, soothe him, she could—

The *jueyuan* threw back his head in a howl. He pounded his chest with his mallet-like fists, the canopy shaking overhead, twigs and leaves showering the courtyard, dust drizzling from the temple eaves. Echoes rebounded through the forest, bouncing between the mangrove trees, hissing through the bamboo. The battle, playing out between the tombs, faded into a background roar.

Von Hart gripped Jia's shoulder again, this time less gently. He had seen enough.

"So much for diplomacy. Come on. We can shelter in the temple."

Jia spared the ape a last frustrated glance and then the envoy was dragging her over the flagstones. The ground under her rumbled and shook as the beast brought his fists down, chips of stone flying as he levered his bulk after them. Von Hart, all decorum, held out his robe from his waist, his bare legs whirling like snow towards the temple steps. With a savage grunting in her ears, hot breath on the back of her neck, Jia leapt up the shallow incline. She sailed over the twisted roots and the cracked slabs to find the double doors locked and bolted. The chain rattled against old wood as she hurled her weight against it, then threw a desperate look at the envoy, who was racing up the steps behind her.

A roar shook the temple eaves, grit and leaves showering down. A yawn of fangs took up the space at the bottom of the steps, the foul blast of the ape's breath speeding Von Hart up to the doors. He fumbled in his pocket, retrieving a large rusty key. Before he could protest, Jia snatched it from him, spinning on her heel to shove the key into the lock, turning it with a screech of metal. The moment the door swung wide, she grabbed the envoy and pulled him into the gloom beyond, whirling to shove her back against wood, the entrance slamming shut.

Boom!

The next thing she knew, she was tumbling through the air, hurled by the force of the *jueyuan* ramming the temple. Blocks of marble rumbled from the eaves, statues of dragons and monkeys shattering on the terrace, the pillars crumpling, a section of the roof sagging inward. Splinters flew, the lock and chain reduced to scrap metal, daylight spearing through the entrance. Dust billowed everywhere.

Shielding her head, coughing, Jia looked up from the broken benches and the overturned braziers among which she found herself sprawled. A shadow fell over her, the great blue ape ducking under the archway to crawl into the temple. He sniffed, then sneezed, a halo of dust leaping off his pelt. Through the murk, Jia made out Von Hart lying on his back a few feet away, his eyes wide and dark, his robe splayed around him like a pool of blood. As carefully as she could, Jia caught his gaze and pressed a finger to her lips.

Don't move.

The ape, grunting, rolled on his knuckles right past them. Reaching the middle of the floor, he drew to a halt, surveying the altar. For the longest time, there was silence. In the distance, the noise of the battle went on, fading down the mountainside. Then the *jueyuan* gave another hoot, his excitement echoing across the floor, stirring the dust into fresh clouds. The afternoon breeze hushed through the forest, a sigh to match the one coming from the *jueyuan*, an exhalation of longing that prompted a gasp from Jia as she realised that the ape had laid eyes on the Eight Hand Mirror.

A mixture of jealousy and fear kicked her back onto her feet. She chanced a step forward, then froze when the *jueyuan* didn't turn around, having lost interest in her and the battle outside. Following his gaze to the Eight Hand Mirror – *her* mirror (she thought of it as such) – her stomach clenched and her throat grew tight. She hadn't thought about the magic in the glass answering to anyone other than her, but the black surface was rippling and clearing, opening up on a deep dark space.

The Eight Hand Mirror answers the desire of the one who stands before it.

She remembered Von Hart's words well. For all its origins, the Eight Hand Mirror was merely a tool, ancient, magical and yet belonging to no one, not truly. Perhaps not even Von Hart. Held by the octagonal frame, a deep cave swirled into view, a different cave to the one where her parents, Ziyou and Ye, slumbered upon the underground shore. This one was smaller, with dead foliage piled up to the walls, the dry branches forming some kind of nest. In the nest, Jia made out several huddled shapes, the hint of limbs, long and strong, the rise and fall of simian chests. The mounds of sleek blue fur . . .

The *jueyuan* howled again. Then, warbling in his throat, fists and feet pounding the floorboards, the great ape forgot all about the rebels and the monks and Jia and the envoy and headed for the Eight Hand Mirror. For his troop. His tribe.

"No!"

Jia's cry was futile, falling on deaf ears. The beast bounded up the steps to the altar, his arms flung wide in embrace.

Jia winced. There was a sound like the striking of a gong, the reverb shaking rubble from the beams overhead. Teeth rattling, she saw the beast smack into the mirror, the glass meeting his hairy bulk without so much as a shudder.

Dazed from the impact, swaying, the *jueyuan* recovered his footing and tried a more cautious approach. Snout extending, nostrils flaring, he sniffed the artefact, the large wooden frame, plain and unadorned. Then he lumbered around it, scratching his head as he surveyed the back of the relic, clearly unable to fathom the paradoxical dimensions, the yawning cavern in the glass and the shallowness of the frame. In silence, he came around to the front again, drawing himself up to his full height, his sloping brow level with the top of the frame. Without warning, he reached out and grabbed the mirror, giving it a rough shake.

Jia made to dart forward, but Von Hart's hand was gripping her arm, advising restraint. Her head swung around, startled, fierce. She hadn't heard her master approach. The envoy met her desperate gaze with a small shake of his head, and biting her lip, she could only watch as the ape set the mirror down with a grunt and a thump. When the dust cleared, she let out her breath, seeing that the glass was unbroken.

It is said that when one looks through the glass and sees the bitterest truth . . . Wasn't that what the fairy had said, all those years ago in Xanadu? . . .*on that day, the mirror will break.*

Jia had no idea what that meant, but relief blossomed in her breast all the same. Of course the big blue monkey couldn't break the glass! No more than he could step into the frame, shake the other apes awake, dispel the binding enchantment. Hadn't Von Hart taught her the truth of the matter? The troop of *jueyuan* was no more present in the temple than her parents had been, Ziyou and Ye slumbering on under the northern plains. The Eight Hand Mirror was merely a window, a magical lens from a distant age, and it was no great mystery that the ape should share her desire, her private longing. Abandonment, loneliness, loss – these were the ghosts of all Remnants, weren't they? Haunting them down the long years . . .

The Eight Hand Mirror stood firm on the altar, as solid, as strange as ever.

But her relief withered and died as she realised that the ape wasn't going to leave the matter there.

Slowly the *jueyuan* lifted his arms and brought them down, pounding his fists against the glass. Dust trickled from the beams, and under Jia's feet, the floorboards shook in time with the beast's hammering, sorrow and pain punching into her bones. Wide-eyed, a hand climbing to her mouth, she watched as the ape pummelled the cold black glass. The echoes, metallic, dull, reverberated through the chamber, plucking at her nerve endings, setting her teeth on edge. Minutes passed as she stood there, frozen by an anguished uncertainty, her hands slipping around her face to cover her ears. It was only as the beast's pounding gradually slowed, his bulk slumping, his breaths ragged, that she saw the blood streaking the mirror.

Clutching her head, she spun to Von Hart.

"Make it stop! Make it stop!"

And the envoy, perhaps waiting, perhaps not, obliged her.

An inexplicable blast of wind came up, his robes fluttering around him, livid tatters of red. Eyes bright, lips dancing with some charm or other, the fairy spread his arms, a fiery radiance, liquid and hot, balling around his outstretched fingers. With a cry of released *chi*, he brought his hands together, flinging the collected burst of energy at the *jueyuan*.

At the mirror. Gods . . . !

Prismatic light bleached the temple, devouring every shadow. Jia shielded her eyes as the colourful glare flooded outwards from the altar steps, a rippling, shimmering wake prickling on the inside of her skull. The blast shook hangings off the walls and widened the cracks in the floor. Mount Song itself rumbled for a moment, before falling still. When she opened her eyes, she witnessed the spindly form of Master Von Hart, a foggy aura, a rainbow seen through mist, fading all around him. She thought she heard a howl – the *jueyuan*? – but she couldn't be sure in the rumbling chamber. As she counted her heartbeats, the echoes receded, falling away, leaving only silence.

Hardly daring to peep through her fingers, Jia looked up at the Eight Hand Mirror. It was only then, in that breathless moment, that she grasped the strength of the magic, the artefact unscarred, a smooth black octagon absorbing her alarm.

The glass unbroken.

The ape was gone. Jia didn't ask where, thankful that she didn't have to look at his charred dead body strewn across the altar. Perhaps he was ash, a pile of dust lost in all the rest. It was impossible to tell in the gloom. She choked back unease and, drawn by the mystery, made her way across the chamber and up the altar steps. Shivering, she stood before the frame, her flesh growing cold at her approach, numbed by the glass. Frowning, she stared harder into the darkness. Through frosty plumes of breath, she thought she could make out the shapes in there, equine, recumbent, green-maned and golden-hooved . . .

Overcome, she sank to her knees in the dust.

Von Hart, however, had no words of comfort.

"This shouldn't have happened," he said. "Matters must be worse than I thought, when Remnants join with humans in war. The Pact was supposed to prevent such a—"

"Why?" Jia spoke over her shoulder, her head hung, hiding her tears. "Why did . . .?" She couldn't find the words. "There must have been another way."

"Another way . . . yes." Was he even listening to her? "What is this foulness I smell? A sour pall like milk on the turn. The circles . . ."

Jia started, sensing change. Shuffling around on her knees, her hair straggling in her face, she turned from the mirror to find Von Hart standing at the foot of the altar steps. His long red robe shimmered in the gloom, catching the daylight slanting through the broken doors.

"Master?"

"I must leave you," he said. "I must return to the west. Back to where all this began."

"Leave? How can you—"

"Your training is over, child. I have shown you all I can."

"Then I'll come with you! Guard you on the road!"

He might have laughed at this, but instead, in a gentle tone, he reminded her of her duty. "Jia, you took an oath to watch over the east, just as another watches over the west, safeguarding the Remnant world. A lone sword. A lone fire, *ja*? Will you forsake your honour, abandon the realm?"

To serve the Emperor of Zhongguo for all the time to come . . .

She climbed to her feet, her face like stone. He knew she could not.

"You will take the Eight Hand Mirror," she said. It was a statement of fact, cold and flat. A measure of the loss he would leave her with, here in this nowhere place. "Won't you?"

Tears welled up in her eyes, hot and unwanted.

For once, Von Hart looked like he didn't know what to say.

"Come now." His words were a whisper in the still. "It is time to put away childish things." His brow troubled, he offered her a feeble smile and tapped his chest with his bony fingers, a little left of centre. "Remember that you can always see them in here."

In that moment, the two of them were no longer master and student, but simply old friends. She wanted to fly down the steps and into his arms, bury her face in the smell of worn silk, the comfort of ginger and cinnamon. At the same time, she wanted to grab him by the shoulders and shake him, demand that he never leave her side, never take her mirror away . . .

But she did neither of these things, knowing that he was right. Comfort had become a habit. A crutch.

Time will teach you other lessons. The value of sacrifice. The price of the truth.

Was this what he'd meant? Had he been preparing her for this parting earlier? He remained inscrutable, a mystery from another world, but Jia reckoned so. And the point of the lesson was clear. If she was to walk the path of the *youxia*, then she must learn to stand alone. That was what he was telling her. The tear that trickled down her cheek was only for him; how much she would miss his counsel. His . . . love.

"Dry your eyes, Jia," he told her. "I will return soon enough."

But Jia could tell this was a lie. He did not mean to come back for a very long time.

NINE

Dragon dreams are deep and dark. And so is the nether.

Are my eyes open? Ben wasn't sure. It was like staring into a fathomless well, a vertiginous darkness in all directions, rendering him a mote, an atom. Insignificant. Adrift.

Am I dreaming? The thought flashed through his mind, a spark in the lightless womb. *Am I dead?* When he exhaled, a plume of breath frosted his beard, putting the lie to his fear. Pins and needles warmed his chest; his body was attempting to heal. He was alive. Asleep, but alive.

This was the nether, all right. He recognised the emptiness, recalling its chill. Dreaming, dazed, he somehow drifted in the gulf between worlds. Wasn't that how Von Hart had described it? Even the *unreal* was real, he'd said. The paradox of existence. A dark dimension shifting with the tides of the unformed, the shadow of all that lived.

Wake up.

Who speaks? Ben turned his head, searching the darkness. *No. Nothing. Quite literally, nothing.* He had a sense of depth, a void all around him. At once, his heart shrank at the memory of the Lurkers, those pale watchdogs of Creation, spectres haunting the absence. The Lurkers mindlessly wandered the gulf – spawned, appointed by

God knows what – stirred to purpose whenever an earthly incantation drew on the nether, channelling magic. The nether comprised a kind of fuel, a raw, empyreal substance (again, the envoy's words), dormant in its natural state, but energised by an arcane word, a complex arrangement of symbols, an occult gesture on the earthly plane. When siphoned in small amounts, many a conjuror had gotten away with it. Summoning an imp. Shifting the weather. Making a princess fall for a frog . . . But greater spells required greater energy. Too much energy and the Lurkers would go swarming towards the source, drawn like sharks to blood, tentacles and claws extending, drooling for a bite of the *real*.

Wake . . . up.

Ben drifted, his veins burning, his thoughts swirling under thick green glass. *Venom. Mauntgraul's venom.* Afloat in the darkness, he heard a scream come scaling through the void, scattering his self-examination. Thin, faint – but an electric bolt, nevertheless, jolting him to alertness. And under him, a light was growing, pallid and wan.

There were shreds down there, glowing, translucent. He made out tendrils, the distant shapes of pincers and bulbous eyes, and a ball of ice spread out from the middle of his chest.

Lurkers. A misbegotten swarm.

The phantoms swam in a straggling school, drifting like snowflakes out of the dark and melting into a blazing white sun. Or what looked like a sun. Even from afar, Ben could tell that the thing was huge.

He made out its colossal head, its domed and many-horned

skull, the array flickering like moonbeams. Great tentacles, each one viscous and ghostly, dangled from its bulk, writhing as though underwater. Ben counted six to eight of them, the vapour trail left in their wake confusing his count. A grille of bones met where the ghost-beast's mouth should've been, reminiscent of a visor or a faceguard, the edges curving outward in sharp silver tusks. Behind the grille, a forked tongue pulsed and slithered, so bright that Ben had to squint to look at it. The feverish wail was echoing from the creature's throat.

Ben had seen Lurkers before. But he had never seen a Lurker like this one. Far below him, a narrow silvery line shot through the emptiness, stretching from a tiny circle of light (no: an octagon, he reckoned, cut in the darkness) towards the spectral giant, which writhed above the shining road, a grotesque guardian. It was a bridge of some kind, stretching from nowhere to – to whatever the hell he could call the thing below him.

The bridge. Is it one of the Silver Leys? he wondered. *What the hell am I seeing here?*

A dream.

A death.

His head was spinning, his senses overwhelmed. Arms wheeling, he tried to retreat, as if this non-place had tides that would carry him back to shore. Instead, stuck in the glue of dreams, he found himself drifting towards the giant phantom, slowly, relentlessly, as if the thing could wait forever, for longer than infinity, measureless and cold.

The great ghost-beast, this king of Lurkers, reached out for him, a tentacle uncoiling.

A voice chimed in his head, sharp and clear.
"*Ben.*"
And his eyes snapped open.

A butterfly. He was looking at a butterfly, perched on the end of his nose. Black wings fluttered in time with his return to consciousness and, flapping a hand, he swatted the insect away. Groaning, he let the world filter in. Birdsong. The breeze through the branches above. He breathed in, sucking in the fragrance of trees and flowers, a heady scent that failed to cleanse his memory. By now, the Chinese news channels would be buzzing with reports of the destruction, the chaos in Tiananmen Square, the high-speed railway crash. *Dragons* . . . China wasn't the most open of countries, so how long the news would take to hit the international channels, he couldn't say. *Chemical spill. Mass hallucination. Terrorism.* He had a feeling that such mundane impressions weren't going to help him this time.

Where was Mauntgraul? The White Dog had struck his killing blow. Wherever the dragon was now, whatever havoc he hoped to wreak, he was done with the Sola Ignis, that much was clear. It was likely that he thought Ben dead.

Ben closed his eyes, shutting out the screams. The fear. The blood. All those deaths. Under his horror, the old enmity smouldered.

I had a lucky escape. But I am not done with you . . .

Blinking, he sat up, patting his chest. He found his *wyrm tongue* sigil whole and unbroken, the symbiotic nature of his suit healing along with his flesh. The wound felt tender under his touch, but the pain was abating, the green fire quelled. *Healed*. But how? He knew that his own abilities couldn't have withstood the White Dog's venom, not for very long. He should've been facing a slow and painful death. In his mouth, he tasted ginger and honey, masking a hint of something earthier and fouler. Medicinal.

Where am I anyway?

He rose woodenly, and the ground swayed like the deck of a ship, tilting under his feet. Blotches fluttered across his vision, larger, darker butterflies. *Get a grip, arsehole.* He stretched – and immediately doubled over, retching a thick green soup. *Lovely.* For a few dizzy seconds, the vomit burnt his stomach and throat with the same dull fire as his wound. Then, gritting his teeth, he straightened, taking in his surroundings.

Trees all around. He was up in the hills somewhere, out in the wilds. His nostrils confirmed the fact, the noticeable lack of pollution. Limping, nursing his chest, he made his way through the thicket. A deer bounded out of his way, stirred by his heavy tread. The woodland sang with life, bees and dragonflies zipping around him, and by the time he reached the clearing, his head was swimming in the sunlight.

He stood at the edge of a broad dappled glade. In the middle of the space, a small pool glimmered beneath a rushing waterfall, fish twinkling in the depths. And on the rocks at the edge of the pool sat the woman from the train.

Her skin-tight suit caught the light, an emerald sheen reflected on her smooth round face, her gaze fixed on the water. Down her back, which was half turned to him, her long dark braid followed the curve of her spine. Her womanly guise was appealing enough, but entirely betrayed by her golden hooves, glossy upon the wet stone. She was staring at them in a way that Ben recognised, an inward contemplation that went back years, centuries, ages, and found little comfort in the past.

In the way that she shook off her apparent sadness, he could tell that the woman knew he was there, just as he knew that he wasn't looking at her true form, the horned equine figure that had raced alongside the tracks.

"You healed me," he said by way of introduction. "You saved me from the White Dog."

The woman said nothing, neither to confirm nor deny her assistance.

Ben tried again. "Things happened so fast, I didn't catch your name." He swallowed. Was he slurring? He tried to sound casual, in control. "I'm Ben Garston. Red Ben to my friends. The Sola—"

"I know who you are." Her voice was curt, devoid of emotion. A cold statement of fact. "In the Remnant world, you are the Guardian of the West. As I am of the East. Like you, I am a student of Blaise Von Hart, the envoy extraordinary. Or at least, I was."

He gets around.

"Great. Then you know I'm not your enemy." A pause. Then, "Don't you?"

She didn't seem interested in making friends. Instead, she turned to face him with her own question.

"You saw him, didn't you? The Ghost Emperor."

"The what?"

"The Lurkers in the nether. Amassing. You were mumbling in your sleep."

Amassing?

Ben stumbled to the edge of the pool. A few feet away from her (what might or might not be a safe distance), he placed his hands on the sun-warmed rock, bending to look into the water. His bearded and bedraggled face stared back at him, gaunt with the ravishments of fever, cuts and bruises on his cheekbones and brow. With a shiver, he shook off the dregs of his dream. Or perhaps his vision. The radiant ghost, the behemoth in the void, tentacles writhing. Its maw a maelstrom of light . . .

"I had an interesting . . . nightmare," he said.

"The Lurkers are merging in the nether," she replied. "Something is drawing them to the earth. Something has caught their attention. Something big."

"Magic," he told her.

"*Muo shu*, yes. Powerful spells. Or rather their decay. The magic of the Fay is growing old. The circles of protection are souring."

"The circles—"

Ben cut himself off. Through the receding fog of the venom, he recalled another vision, one he'd experienced over the North Sea, sparked by the touch of *lunewrought*. The great blue arc had glimmered with symbols, marching from the ocean off into the haze of the European hinterland. Some of the symbols had been fading, winking out.

Before he could confirm this notion, the woman continued.

"The binding enchantments have grown weak. Great spells branded into the earth to ward off the ghosts in the outer dark, permitting the Fay their magical age. But the Old Lands are done. The Fay departed. The spells corroding.

And the stench of their corruption draws the Lurkers to its source. The phantoms are amassing, becoming one. Preparing."

Like flies to a shit heap, Ben thought but didn't say.

A notion struck him. When he'd been lured to the oil rig, finding himself bound by the magic of the harp, there had been no sign of the Lurkers. No strange churning in the air, no bristling shadows moving behind the pipework, pressing against the skein of reality. In the face of the energised Fay artefact, surely the beasts would have made their ghostly presence known. Wouldn't they?

It occurred to him then that the Chapter's cautious use of the harp might be down to the fact that the agents feared attracting the Lurkers. He didn't know the range of the song to judge this by (quite far, considering Norway), but his speculation fit well enough. Would the Chapter know about events in the nether? Doubtful. A colder thought followed on the heels of this one. Without the appearance of the grey ghosts, he wondered how long such caution would last.

Still, what the woman was saying kind of made sense. If the phantoms had their attention elsewhere . . .

He shivered. "Your Ghost Emperor."

She nodded, flashing him a look. "Pray we are not too late."

Too late for what? Ben was freewheeling, a little dazed. His wounds might have healed, but recent events had left their mark. And he wasn't enjoying the conversation.

"We? Besides, I'm not one for gods," he said. "I've had . . . a bad experience."

This earned him a sharp tilt of her head. Her eyes, a clear jade, darkening.

Seeing he'd offended her, he tried a different approach.

"Anyway, I'm grateful. Thanks for . . ." He gestured at his chest. "You know. This."

"Sacred herbs and eagle's blood will serve as a makeshift antidote," she said. "The poison of despair runs deeper. That is your own affair."

"What would I do without you?"

"You are a clown," she said, but she wasn't smiling. "I brought you up to Yesanpo for one reason and one reason only. Information. Dead men tell no tales, isn't that what you English say?"

In some cases, the dead never shut up, Ben thought, but kept to the point.

"What makes you think I know any tales? But if you're suggesting I owe you something, it'd be nice to know who's keeping score."

She weighed him up with those needling eyes. Eyes to look right through him.

"I am Jia Jing, the appointed judge of the court of Kublai Khan, Guardian of the East, Keeper of the Lore. And you are Ben Garston – or Benjurigan in your native *wyrm tongue* – a dragon who claims to uphold the Lore, but who spends most of his time drinking, bedding women and making trouble. Satisfied?"

"Charmed," he said. "I can tell you're a fan. Would you like me to sign something?"

"I think we both know your signature doesn't count for very much."

Ouch.

"The Lore is broken," he said in a growl. "But I didn't break it, honey."

Christ, he felt tired. Old. Then again, his arse had just been dragged through a near-miss arrest, a vampiric attack, a brawl with a dragon, a high-speed train crash and a venom-induced coma. Maybe he should cut himself some slack.

She got to her feet, facing him. "That isn't true."

The woman, Jia, said this with a conviction that took him aback. Her composed exterior couldn't hide the tautness of her lips, the whiteness of her knuckles on her folded arms. He wondered at that, why she should be so angry when they'd only just met, but it didn't take a genius to realise the common denominator here. Pale, inscrutable and missing without a trace.

"Sounds like someone has been telling his own tales." He rolled his shoulders, disliking the way she was looking at him. "Where is he, anyway? Von Hart? I've been looking for him."

"If I knew that, I wouldn't need you."

The envoy could be anywhere, Ben knew. In the world or out of it. With a shudder, he recalled du Sang's words from the vaults under Paris.

I'm saying he isn't in the world at all . . . He simply isn't . . . there.

He coughed, covering his unease.

"Seems I'm a popular guy," he said. "So come on. Spit it out. You want me to take on this Ghost Emperor for you? Kick his arse into spectral smithereens? You know, Miss Jing, this isn't my first rodeo."

The equestrian reference pricked her, he saw. She looked away into the trees, her jaw grinding.

I'm getting under her skin. Good.

"You are far from a hero, *Mr* Garston. I am on a mission to warn the watchers. I am looking for the Curia Occultus. I think you can help me find them."

He barked a laugh. "Are you serious? I'm the last person you want, lady. Von Hart has gone AWOL. The Guild is in a shambles. And the last time I ran into the Chapter, they were talking about chopping off my head. It wasn't pretty."

Jia looked up to meet his sneer. She didn't seem interested in his excuses. Instead, she gazed into the pool again, her voice soft, holding back ice.

"I remember when I first heard the Ghost Emperor. It was a whisper behind the sky. The space between thunder-claps. Cannon fire across a misty river. A new god approaching the earth, pressing his eye against a hole in the world, looking in, hungry. And then reaching out . . ."

Ben could have waited for Jia's description.

"Listen—"

"Do you know what it's like out there in the nether? How endless? How cold?"

He did.

Now she looked at him again. "Are you really prepared to let what's waiting out there come here?"

He didn't like the way she said this, her eyes moons of unspoken judgement.

"You can think what you like," he said. "Hell, you can use me as a bad example in the future, a Remnant gone to seed. All I know is that the Chapter was using a fragment of the harp. Do you realise the power of that thing?" He guessed she did. All Remnants would know the story. Fresh in his mind from du Sang's tomb, he conjured up the painting of Nimue, the Queen of the Fay, presenting the harp to King Arthur during the Battle of Camlann. His sword, Caliburn, shattering the harp. "The instrument pre-dates both of us by centuries." He was guessing at her age, but she didn't correct him. "Folks used to call it the *Cwyth*. The mnemonic harp is just the trendy modern name. If the Chapter catches up with us – with me – I won't have the strength to fight them. And neither will you. What makes you think they'll even listen to you? The Cardinal isn't exactly a fan of Remnants. Especially now."

"So we find the Guild. We use them as a go-between. To send a warning."

"Sure. I can point you in the right direction. You'll find an empty mansion in London."

"This is your duty. You swore to uphold the Lore!"

He was bluffing, of course. Under his apparent reluctance, he wanted to get to the bottom of the matter just as much as she did. And he wanted to find the envoy, now more than ever. He was in way over his head. Either way, he wasn't about to wear his heart on his sleeve, make his next move common knowledge. He had been played one too many times.

He looked up and saw that she was changing, growing taller, thinner, as she approached. An emerald sheen rippled over her face. Her head bulged and widened slightly, her flesh puckering. The next moment, a long golden horn was sprouting from her brow, bloodlessly parting her skin. It tapered up like a scimitar, notched and as sharp as a blade. On golden hooves she came to a halt, keeping a small space between them. She had retained most of her human form, her shapely legs and torso lengthened into a statuesque column covered in a cropped green hide. Her singular horn – more of an antler, really – sparkled in the sunlight.

Having partly revealed herself, she looked down at him with penetrating eyes.

"You do not trust me," she said.

Again that cold statement of fact, devoid of emotion. But it was true, all the same. There was something a little too neat about this set-up, her rescuing him only to press him for information.

"Lady, I don't trust myself."

She was a Remnant, that much was clear. He had seen her true form next to the train in Beijing. Some kind of equine beast, green-haired, gold-hooved and a little larger than a horse. She belonged to a breed beyond his knowledge, an old Chinese tribe lost to mythology. Regardless, she must be the only one of her kind, awake and walking the earth, if the Pact was anything to go by.

Maybe he had learnt his lesson after all. She was up to something, he reckoned. For all her aloofness, he could tell she was afraid. *Desperate*. Hell, he could see it better than anyone. It was in the tremble of her shoulders. A sadness behind her eyes. Perhaps she needed something she couldn't name, an underlying reason for his presence here. Was she really asking him for help? Or was there something more?

"And I don't work well with others," he said. "Didn't Von

Hart tell you that? Kidnapped girlfriend? Exploding refinery? No? I'm kind of bad for business."

"Let me put this another way," she replied. "Von Hart has gone missing with his fragment of the harp. The Lore states that as guardians, we must inform the Guild of any clear and present threat. I don't know where to find them. You do. If you refuse to help me, that places all of them in danger. And consequently, all of us."

"Christ, you mean from Von Hart, don't you?"

"I merely present the facts as I see them."

"Yeah? Well, *I* can't see them," he said. Or rather, he didn't want to.

Jia didn't look convinced. "Someone woke the dragon. Someone with a piece of the harp. Why would the Guild or the Chapter do such a thing? Their entire purpose depends on maintaining the Pact. Safeguarding the Sleep. Neither order wants us around."

Ben recalled the old woman and the Sister on the oil rig. *The rules have changed*, she'd told him. *Our new Cardinal favours the old ways. The old values.*

Even as they spoke, the Chapter was stepping into the Guild's shoes, the old tolerance crumbling, replaced by spiritual scorn. And now this Jia Jing wanted to make a house call on the Guild, warn the military branch of the Curia Occultus that this was no time for division between Remnants and humans. A call to arms before this Ghost Emperor of hers breached the walls of reality and brought about a cataclysm for all. Ben couldn't assure her that the disordered banner of knights would roll out the red carpet either.

And as for the envoy . . .

"Granted, Von Hart has the means . . . but still, it doesn't add up. If he'd decided to wake a Sleeper, why choose Mauntgraul? A *Cornutus Quiritor* – a Horned Screamer – isn't a breed known for its gratitude. The White Dog least of all. And back in the day, he was the one who put the damn beast into the Sleep. Why would he wake up a dragon that wanted to kill him?"

And me. But again, he left that part unspoken.

"I . . . remember something," she said. "An old legend about the envoy fighting a white wyrm in the mountains. The Great Khan mentioned it, I think. Years ago in Xanadu." She frowned, then shook herself back to composure. "But that means nothing. Times change and we change with them."

I was there. And ain't that the truth.

Ben squeezed the back of his neck. Delvin Blain's news about the Lambton armour wasn't doing anything for his suspicions. And he realised that doubts had been congealing in his mind long before he'd seen the crack in the Zhoukoudian hillside. What was it he'd said to Von Hart last year, the two of them standing on the desert dunes?

You knew all along, didn't you? Ghosts from limbo. The living and the dead trading places . . . And still you let me blunder into this. Why? To wake me up? To teach me a lesson?

And he remembered Von Hart's answer, his parting smile.

Never trust the Fay, Ben.

The envoy had bought the suit of armour at auction last year, and gifted it to House Fitzwarren, Ben's long-standing nemesis. And, well, he still bore the scars to relate all the rest . . .

Still, he wanted to argue.

"Von Hart is the envoy extraordinary, an ambassador between the Remnant and the human world. There's no way in hell he'd do such a thing. I'd trust him with my life."

"A lie," she said, simply. "And isn't there that saying? Never trust—"

"I know!"

In the great briar of fabulous beings, the Fay were like roses made of steel. The petals might look pretty enough, but if you didn't watch your fingers, you'd quickly find out that they were sharper than razor blades.

His head was tingling, caught by her unblinking gaze. The sensation wasn't a new one. He remembered Queen Atiya and her lightning, white fire scouring his skull, drinking in his secrets.

"How are you doing that? Get the fuck out of my head."

"I am Jia Jing, the last wakeful daughter of the *sin-you*. In this land, I am a living symbol of justice. I must warn you, Ben Garston. I see the truth. You can twist your words in any way you please, but deception will not serve you here."

Ben groaned. "This is turning out to be a horrible day."

"The days ahead will grow worse," she told him. "The envoy has vanished with his piece of the harp. The White Dog has woken, summoned perhaps by that very same piece. And the Lurkers gather, drawn to the failing magic. Drawn to the door of Creation."

Ben couldn't deny it. He had seen it for himself in the limbo between waking and sleep: the Lurkers shifting across the void, melting into a blazing white sun, the beast with light at its heart.

"If we do nothing," Jia said, "the Ghost Emperor will devour the world." She looked up to meet his level stare. Where they had failed to find accord in respect, they appeared to find it in fear. "We have both sworn to protect our lands. You *must* help me."

Ben found it hard to hold her gaze. Her sorrow was back, tears shining in her eyes. He felt weak in the face of it, the venom drawn out of him, his struggle back to health leaving him weary. *In need of a damn good drink.* Mauntgraul's sting would always be with him. He knew that. Another bad memory to throw on the pile with all the rest, like a newly formed scale prised from his side or the look in a woman's eyes as she had stood on the moonlit dunes . . . In the end, his suspicions decided for him. Besides, he couldn't stay in these hills forever, while the White Dog gorged on civilisation. Responsibility nipped at him, but doubt had blunted its teeth. Or maybe, though it was hard to admit, he was disappointed. The envoy extraordinary was one of two things: conspirator or coward. Hadn't there been a third thing? A friend?

No, I can't bank on that.

Annoyed, he asked her, "How do I know you're not working for the Chapter?" It couldn't hurt to rattle her, to see what might fall out. "Trying to get me out in the open."

"You dare to—"

"Oh yeah, I forgot. You're a unicorn. Truth, honour, justice." He snorted, letting her know what he thought of these high-and-mighty ideals. "All that jazz."

"I am no more a unicorn than you are a *long*," she said. "The dragons of my country numbered many. Elemental creatures of peace, ruling over nature and the weather, serving the gods. You are simply a western beast, an overfed lizard, a creature of destruction and fire. And you fly in the face of death."

"Well, in case you hadn't noticed, I'm the last one standing." The conversation was over as far as he was concerned. "Look, I can't help you. You're on your own. Go to Paladin's Court if you must. Any old Remnant will show you the way. But I've got my own fish to fry."

So saying, Ben extended his will, scales covering his flesh. He spread his wings, Jia staggering back in the churned-up dust, her protest lost in the noise. With a leap, he took to the skies, spiralling up from the woodlands.

Groggily, he snaked skywards, a red shadow pushing up to where the air grew thin, his tail swallowed by cloud. Dog tired, he clawed his way to a safe altitude. Then, wings spread to catch the easterly wind, he turned his snout for home.

TEN

Mauntgraul speared on through the night, his wings spread and tail weaving, over Hampstead Heath. His snout was an arrow trained on the building ahead, a throng of gables and turrets thrusting through the trees.

Paladin's Court.

The sight stoked the coals in Mauntgraul's heart, green fire hissing in his veins. The mansion was unfamiliar to him, of course. In his time, the only buildings on Hamestede had been a farm, a chapel and a couple of windmills. And an old hall where this one now stood, serving much the same purpose, surrounded by a peaceful rural community. Well, peaceful apart from the occasional passing dragon who would pluck clawfuls of sheep and cows from the fields, perhaps a yeoman or two for an after-supper treat (their sweat so piquant, a greasy delicacy). *The good old days*. Mauntgraul had thought them so, before the flames of the Anarchy had guttered out, forcing him to fly from English shores, abandoning his home to insufferable peace talks and the bastard Pact.

The White Dog folded his wings and spun towards the

earth. A rustle of wings, a snap of his tail, and a naked man dropped onto the lawns, his hungry gaze on the mansion's front door.

He walked right up and thumped on the oaken surface, ignoring the knocker, shaped to resemble a gauntlet, with a curling lip.

And I shall nail your head to my tree of shields, knight . . .

No one came to the door. He wasn't expecting them to, although the hour was far from late. Another thump, his fist swelling into a mallet of scales, and the door crashed inward with a boom.

He kicked his way through a pile of envelopes, tracking mud across the tiles as he strode into the hallway. An elegant staircase ascended through cobwebs to the upper reaches of the house. Colours dappled the steps, thrown by the moonlight falling through the large round stained-glass window above the entrance. Cracks riddled the window, the sign of recent restoration, but the image in the glass was clear, bringing him up short.

A growl rumbled from his throat.

Georgius the Palmyrene. The bladdered old lecher . . .

Music was coming from deeper in the house, loud enough to explain why his entrance had gone unnoticed. Flutes, horns and strings, he thought, though he did not recognise the melody. Someone started singing and a moment later another voice joined in, this one rougher and out of tune. Mauntgraul scowled in the shadows. Shoulders set, he took the corridor ahead of him, following the echoes like a bad smell.

Surprisingly, the dogs only noticed him as he set foot in

the library, the bookshelves soaring around him. The music had muffled his approach and the pall of woodsmoke and alcohol, a sour medley in his nostrils, must have obscured his smell. Not so now. Growling, the hounds shot onto their paws, catching his animal scent. Ears flat, whining, the two dogs edged in retreat, their trembling shadows merging with those weaving across the threadbare rug. Beyond the hounds, a man leant against the side of the fireplace, staring into the flames. He wore a rumpled blue suit and the dragon placed his age in his middle seasons, tufts of grey showing at the temples of his tousled hair. Mauntgraul had just finished throttling the second dog, letting the carcass fall to the floor beside its twitching companion, when the man noticed him, the shuddering floorboards catching his attention. His singalong snagged in his throat, the glass in his hand slopping on the hearth, the liquid hissing, carrying the faint whiff of brandy.

"Ah. One need not call the devil, isn't that what they say? He will come knocking regardless."

The man slurred over the music. He didn't appear to mind the intrusion or the dead dogs, sparing their corpses an inebriated pout. With a tut, he lurched from the fireplace and straight into a stack of books, half packed into a large wooden chest, one of several dotted around the room. He hiccuped and kicked his way through the scattered volumes. Most of the furniture stood around like ghosts, lumpy shapes covered in sheets, and the man bumped his way through this obstacle course to a strange, trumpet-eared device set on a table by the opposite wall. There came a scratch and a squeal and, with a triumphant grin, he spun back to Mauntgraul, brandishing a shiny black disc. A laughable shield, the White Dog thought, if that was the man's intention.

"Mozart. *The Magic Flute*," the man said by way of explanation, though these words meant nothing to his guest. "Music to soothe a savage beast, eh?"

Mauntgraul, who hadn't braced himself for hospitality, raised his eyebrows despite himself.

"You know who I am?"

"No, dear heart. Not particularly. Nevertheless, the blood is in the water, eh? Only a matter of time before one of you showed up." The man took a sip of his drink and steadied himself against the wall. "I suppose you might've been a bailiff, if not for the hour and the . . . you know . . ." He waved his glass at Mauntgraul's nakedness, which didn't appear to bother him either. "Lord knows our sponsors have all disappeared since that terrible business last year. Our agents have vanished like smoke and even the servants have washed their hands of us. The Broken Lance is, well, literally broken. I'm afraid I'm all that's left. And I never got my chance to take the chair."

"And who might you be?"

"Quentin Bardolfe, lord of the manor." He gave a laugh, the squeak of a mouse, but Mauntgraul failed to see what was so amusing. The man's eyes, red from lack of sleep, glimmered with moisture. "At least I have been since Daddy . . . died or what have you. The board never properly explained." He lowered his voice in a theatrical whisper. "I've been in hiding."

Lord? Mauntgraul snorted. *This fool is as drunk as one.*

171

"Still, despite the Chapter crawling all over the place, I knew they'd never find what they were looking for. I waited for them to lose interest, watching through the trees. And today I decided to take a look at my inheritance. Old bricks and cobwebs, more like. An anchor around my legs, carrying me down into bankruptcy. Mind you, at least the cellar yielded some quality plonk." To support this, Quentin Bardolfe raised his glass in a toast. "And, of course, there is the trinket we left behind."

"The Guild is no more?"

"Afraid so, old bean. Please forward any queries, complaints or debts outstanding to the Whispering Chapter. They're the ones running the show now."

"Those dirt-kneed, cross-kissing peasants."

"Now, now."

Under Mauntgraul's derision, a shiver of unease. He had come here prepared to face a host of knights, rip through a forest of lances and toast his ancient foe in their armour. But times had changed. His long flight from Beijing to London had shown him a world transformed, one that no longer huddled in rags around woodland fires, but blazed in the darkness, the roar of industry usurping the silence of the heavens.

Faced with this sot, this Quentin Bardolfe, he could see that things had changed indeed. Was this his only challenger? The best of all royal champions? Shrill bells rang in his head, imagined yet persistent. A part of him wanted to laugh, but he feared that if he started, he would never stop.

"Lament to your heart's content, knight. I only came here to kill you."

"A shame," Quentin said. He held up his glass to the firelight, swirling the brandy inside. "There are at least a dozen barrels left."

Mauntgraul clenched his fists. He hadn't expected this. Ever since leaving China, the thought of vengeance had driven him on, a seething, infernal engine. If Red Ben loved the Lore so much, then the White Dog would take the greatest pleasure in making good on his promise, letting the traitor watch his carefully ordered world go up in smoke. With green venom burning in his veins, Benjurigan would die understanding that he had failed, destruction and terror the last things he'd know . . . At the same time, Mauntgraul would exact a blood price for all serpentkind – all *true* serpentkind, that is, the ones with the balls to throw off the shackles of the long-departed Fay, heeding their instincts to rend and tear, and who had found themselves tricked and trapped, their fire quelled, snuffed out by the lullaby.

To the devil with the milk drinkers.

Standing here in Paladin's Court, Mauntgraul had found a wasted weakling instead.

But Quentin Bardolfe had a trick up his sleeve.

"I imagine that you came here for this," he said, setting down his glass. He bent towards the trumpet-eared device and, flicking a latch, lifted the lid. "It's lead-lined. Small, but sufficient. The Chapter's agents searched this mansion from cellar to attic, but no amount of *lunewrought* would've led them to Daddy's gramophone. You see, the Chapter may have unhorsed us, but they didn't take everything. And much as the new Cardinal insisted, there are no Loreful grounds that require us to relinquish the relics in our keeping.

Nevertheless," the word came out *never-the-lesh*, "in the spirit of sportsmanship, you are welcome to try your luck."

The knight lifted an object from inside the box. He held it out, a touch gingerly, as if the object might bite him. As he did so, silvery light washed over the walls. The shadows thrown by the fire retreated, chased by a fiercer flame. In a blink, Mauntgraul took in the offering, a metal bar roughly six hands long. A sword hilt? No. A series of raised furrows, elegantly carved, twisted around the narrowing S shape, the wider part of its surface dotted with what appeared to be pegs, tiny teeth of pearl. Lips peeled back, Mauntgraul made out a mane, soft and white, tumbling in a summer wind. He was looking at part of an instrument, the fragment comprising a neck, a harmonic curve.

A broken piece of a harp. *The* harp.

Despite its gleam, the fragment before him wasn't made of silver. At least no silver native to earth. Lunewrought. *It is* lunewrought. *The ore of Avalon.* The instrument, he knew, was incomplete. Dismantled, if one credited the tales, the harp's music muted, its magic impaired.

But not completely.

"Whatever is the matter?" Quentin asked. The shimmering scrap in his hand lent his grin a maniacal cast. "You'd think the news of our downfall would be music to your ears."

So saying, he passed a hand over the silver bar. The bar throbbed in answer, the light brightening. Mauntgraul winced. Every inch of him wanted to look away, but the instrument held him mesmerised, enraptured. The neck of the harp, the harmonic curve – for that was the fragment that Quentin held – gleamed in appreciation of his

174

touch, its aura resolving into faint lines, the spectre of silver strings.

"Stop this . . ." *Music to soothe a savage beast,* the knight had said, but as Quentin crooked a finger to pluck at the strings, the sound he produced was anything but pleasant. "Stop or—"

The notes filled the room, sickly and sweet. At once, Mauntgraul slapped his hands to his head. Shutting out the harp wouldn't do him any good. The bells were chiming inside him, tolling in his skull, an echoing peal that was part scorn and part sorrow. Anguish and joy warred in his heart, the light shining into deep, dark places. He knew this song. He had heard the lullaby twice before, once upon sleeping, once on awaking. Its beauty, its horror, was as familiar to him as his own fiery dreams. His head spun with unbidden reveries. Rakegoyle tossing him his first chunk of meat, the leg of some peasant or other. The combined hiss of silk dresses, cascading from a high stone wall . . .

The library was rippling around him, caught in the cruel osmosis of the music. The shelves and the furniture were melting, growing indistinct. The floorboards sagged, the old wood as soft as toffee. The earth, the deep, wet earth, was churning under his feet. The ground yawned, hollowing, preparing to embrace him in slumber once more.

Quentin Bardolfe strummed his fragment of the harp. When Mauntgraul caught his eyes, seeing the fright spiking through the brandy, he realised that there was another sound too, a shrill accompaniment to the mounting song. *Bells. The bells.* This music belonged only to him, swinging in the troubled belfry of his mind.

The bells were laughter, his own laughter, a carillon ringing in his ears.

The library was shrinking as Mauntgraul grew, the stacks of books and shrouded furniture beginning to look as though they might fit into a doll's house. Warbling, Quentin Bardolfe slipped down the wall, shaking his head in futile appeal. A claw closed around him, white as death, muffling the music of the harp. Rafters cracked and shifted under Mauntgraul's shoulders, unable to withstand his expanding bulk, the encroachment of his scaled thews. Paintings fell, plaster rained down and light fixtures sizzled as his horns speared the upper floor, impaling a four-poster bed and an escritoire, goose feathers and paper wafting through the haze.

Mauntgraul laughed. He laughed at the fate that had snatched vengeance from his fangs. And he laughed at the man in his grip, the knight's gasping, crumpling form. Mauntgraul squeezed. He squeezed until his claws dug into his palms, the pain making him drunk with excitement. A thick red drizzle trickled from his fist, shards of bone and intestines slopping on the shattered ground. Finally, only the scrap of silver, the *lunewrought* fragment, burned against his flesh. The magic, though silenced, echoed in his mind, merging with the bells. The White Dog threw back his head, smashing centuries of architecture into powder and grit. His tail lashed out, the fireplace, the furniture and walls vanishing in a sweep of rubble, the windows exploding, the night rushing in.

In a whirl of emerald flame, Mauntgraul spiralled upwards through the mansion, the staircase sucked into the maelstrom, and burst from the roof in a shower of stone and tiles. Smoke and wreckage trailing from his wings, he soared up into the darkness, the sleepless blaze of London shining on all horizons. The city clanged in his head along with the bells, a blaring, incessant fanfare, and he threw a claw over his snout, trying to shut out the light. The overwhelming stench of industry and change.

Of human triumph.

Laughing, shrieking, he spun towards the earth. He crashed headlong into Hampstead Heath, gouging a furrow across the hillside, benches, signposts and trees scattering all around him.

In the darkness, a naked man lay shivering in the mud, half in and half out of a broad chilly pond. The water bubbled and hissed with his heat, boiled frogs and fish bobbing to the surface. Clutching the fragment of the harp to his chest, he lay on the bank, nursing the relic as if it was a pet or a favourite toy.

When dawn broke, the man could at last hear himself again, laughing and sobbing. Laughing, sobbing.

The lullaby played on in his head.

ELEVEN

This is stupid. The Chapter could be anywhere.

The morning mist chilled Ben's skin as he stared, disbelievingly, between the gateposts of Paladin's Court. The gates loomed, monolithic and grey, the stone stags leaping on either side of the entrance, their antlers bent to lock over the driveway. Up there, between the trees, a mansion should have waited.

It had taken a lot for him to come here, but Jia's tale of the Ghost Emperor had spurred him to investigate. *Thanks for the tip-off.* Like it or not, she was right. He had sworn an oath, and with no other leads, all he could do was walk back into the heart of the fire. Alone. The last thing he'd wanted was company; he was called the Sola Ignis for a reason.

After alighting on the outskirts of Beijing and making another brief phone call to the Blain Trust, he'd managed to secure a flight back to London. And some everyday clothes, jacket, jeans, T-shirt and trainers to cover his conspicuous suit. Fourteen hours later and here he was, weary, uneasy and taking in the ruin of the Court.

According to the Chapter, the Guild was in disarray, the administration of the Lore fallen into the Cardinal's hands.

He hadn't expected to find anyone here anyway, only a start. Perhaps a couple of clues. Von Hart would have to wait. If Ben could find the whereabouts of one of the knights, he could warn them about the imminent peril, the Chapter's un-Loreful use of the harp and the gathering of the Lurkers. He certainly hadn't expected to find the mansion reduced to rubble, a heap of fire-blackened brick.

Was he looking at Mauntgraul's work? He thought so. The White Dog was hungry for revenge and the Guild of the Broken Lance would surely serve as the special on his menu. When Ben breathed in, he caught more than the scent of burnt timber, confirming his suspicions.

Dragon fire. He must have loved ripping this place apart, abandoned or no.

He'd taken a step through the gates when a rumbling behind him distracted him, dragging his eyes over his shoulder. At first, he didn't realise what he was looking at – a trail of dust in the distance, a thrashing of trees down the road from the Heath, dustbins falling over and car horns blaring in the wake of some impossibly speeding object. As the disturbance drew closer, approaching fast, he made out a familiar green-gold blur and his heart sank. Instinctively he shielded his head and dropped into a crouch as a great plume of dust billowed around him, grit peppering his shoulders and chest.

When the dust settled, he stood, coughing, and glared at his unwelcome visitor.

"You," he said. "You know, you should learn how to take no for an answer."

"I'm not following you," Jia said, her *sin-you* form melting into womanly shape, dust showering from her suit. She regarded him with her cool jade eyes. "And you're not the only person who can buy a plane ticket."

"Right. And stalking is just a romantic walk, but only one of you knows it. Next you'll tell me I'm out of milk."

"I told you. I'm on a mission to—"

He cut her off. "What's with the suit anyway? Another one of Von Hart's gifts?"

"I'm sorry?"

"The suit," he said. "When you shrug off your unicorn form, you're not exactly running around in the nuddy. A guy tends to notice."

"I'm not a—" Jia gave up, exasperated. Petals bloomed in her cheeks. "Some of us learnt how to control ourselves," she said. "A meditation. A focus. I shape my clothing out of my hide, using the power of my mind."

"Seriously?"

"I am *sin-you*," she said, as if that was answer enough.

"Like I could forget. But this suit trick . . . Miss Jing, you are full of surprises."

"And you are full of shit. We don't all need . . ." Jia frowned, searching for the word, "a nursemaid."

That stung. Sure, he'd been reluctant to accept his suit last year – Fay gifts tended to come with hidden price tags – but Von Hart had synthesised it from his scales, shrunken and charred, granted, but retaining his transformative ability. Like it or not, the suit was a part of him. Why not wear it?

His wounded look meant nothing to Jia. She resembled a porcelain statue; her spine so straight, her braid coiled over her shoulder. Attractive, in an athletic way. Her expression was aloof. All business.

"We're wasting time," she told him. "Time we don't have."

"I was on the case. And as I said, I don't do team-ups."

"Unfortunate," she said. She didn't look like she thought it was unfortunate. "I think the end of the world is slightly more important. Don't you?"

"Now I feel bad." He changed his face to convey the impression that he didn't feel too bad.

"Calm yourself. We are going to report to the Guild, as we agreed."

"We did?" He looked over his shoulder up the driveway, at the ruin waiting there. "Besides, I don't think knocking will do us any good, because—"

"Because you won't risk your head. I heard you."

He looked back at her and crossed his arms, a sneer sliding onto his face.

"You don't like me very much, do you?"

"I am *youxia*," she said. "Sworn to uphold the Lore. My feelings don't come into it."

"Could've fooled me."

But he was too tired to argue. Despite himself, the sight of the Court had taken its toll. If the ruined building represented anything, it was his own failure. *Your happy ending.* The thought made him choke, a thickness gripping his throat. As Jia's eyes bored into him, he found himself fighting to stay on his feet, stop himself from sinking to his knees.

Instead, he turned his back on her.

"I don't know why I'm doing this any more." He aimed

his words up the driveway, a murmured statement of fact. There was no point lying to her, after all.

"You are the Sola Ignis. Sworn to—"

"Uphold a Lore that wants me dead? Is that what you were gonna say?"

Jia said nothing. He continued in a growl.

"*The Pact is no truce at all, merely a cell where you wait for extinction.* Someone said that to me last year. She said I suffered the compromise because of hope, Remnants living in peace with humans. I didn't want to believe her at the time. Now I can no longer kid myself." He drew in a breath, exhaled steam. "The Remnants are dropping like flies. All of this – the mansion, the Guild, the Lore – all of this is changing. And not for the better. The Whispering Chapter wants to stamp us out. The Fay will never return. Don't you see? Everything I've done was for *nothing*."

He was shouting now, but he didn't care. Shouting held back the tears. His blood surged with frustration, quick and hot. He couldn't tell Jia the real reason for his pain, the knife sticking out of the wound. Perhaps he would have felt this way sooner if he hadn't met Rose. Was it his fault that he had seen his one-time lover as his reward? (Rose would've said *trinket*.) When all was said and done, weren't they all slaves to their nature? Her smile had embodied his love for humans, a reason to go on. In the end, her humanity had come between them (she would've said *lies*), forcing their worlds apart. Rose had left him. Turned her back on him. On the mask he wore.

No, he couldn't tell Jia that. He could only speak of his duty, the millstone around his neck. Dry, joyless duty, imposed by a dead king's council eight hundred years ago, demanding his loyalty up to and including curbing the crimes of other Remnants, venomous dragons, flesh-eating trolls . . . Curbing. *Killing.* His duty. Taking in the rubble where Paladin's Court had once stood, that duty no longer felt like enough.

His anger bounced between the trees, fading into silence. A bird trilled a weak remonstration.

"Change is the only constant," Jia said. From the softness of her voice, Ben could tell that she was picking her words carefully, reluctant to anger him further. "Do not presume to know destiny. No future is certain."

"Enough with the aphorisms!" He wheeled on her, an arm sweeping out. "You think I should just accept this? Accept death?"

She met his rage with the usual calm. "We have all made sacrifices," she said.

But her calm was also a mask, he saw. Even in the mist, he couldn't fail to notice the tear that streaked down her cheek, pricked by the blade of his words.

"You're not the only one who lost something," she said. "You are not the only one who has no choice."

"What—" he began, but a sharp *pop*, the sound of a log breaking in the thicket, arrested him.

He spun back to the gates to see shapes emerging from the trees on the edge of the driveway. A sharp intake of breath informed him that Jia had seen them too, seven or eight people rising out of the fog and walking down the track towards them. None of the newcomers hurried, he noticed, their approach cautious enough to tell him that they knew who he was, the danger he presented. That made these people agents and he was trying to decide which branch they served, Guild or Chapter, when frayed jumpers and threadbare jeans seeped through the mist, along with woolly hats and scarves. If he hadn't known better, he'd have taken them for the North Hampstead Rambling Club out for a morning stroll. As it was, the guns pointing in his direction, the muzzles raised to take a bead on his head, gave the game away.

Tranquilliser guns. It's the Chapter all right. Stepping up its game.

His jacket seams were popping, draconic brawn bursting from his jeans as the agents drew nearer. His trainers exploded in shreds, newly sprouted talons raking the muck. A carapace flowed over his skin, sleek and red in the murk, the nubs of wings bubbling at his shoulders. A ball of heat gathered in his chest, his swelling jaw, a lizardine snout, parting to reveal fangs. Smoke whispered from his nostrils, the intimation of fire.

Jia placed a hand on his arm. Snorting a patch of flame, he looked down at her, saw her quickly retract her fingers, stung by the heat of him. Nevertheless, she held her ground, spelling out her appeal with a shake of her head.

Don't.

Damn her. He mentally cursed her, because she was right. Much as he'd like to turn these dour God-botherers into human kebabs, he knew that the agents were only following orders, dispatched by the Cardinal to bring him down, drag him in chains to the Invisible Church. *And twist the old thumbscrews until they realise that I can't give them Von Hart*

184

. . . That wasn't going to happen on his watch, but turning the driveway into the Massacre of the Latins wouldn't exactly help his case. Reluctantly he dwindled back into human form, rags of clothing clinging to his dark-scaled suit. Jia gave a nod of approval, then turned her attention to the agents, measuring up the oncoming threat.

In a low voice, she reminded him that she had other concerns.

"We didn't come here to fight, Ben. Remember, we came to warn them."

"Those aren't agents of the Guild," he said. "They're True Names. Agents of the Chapter." A persistent thumping troubled the air, its source lost beyond the shuddering trees. Leaves and twigs swirled around his feet, tossed by the rising wind. He had to shout to make himself heard. "I shouldn't have come here."

"Those agents serve the Curia Occultus." Jia pointed at the approaching men and women, who were stooping now, holding their hats, the gale tugging at their raincoats and flowery skirts, both fashionable sometime around the mid-seventies. "The Chapter serves the Lore, as do we. I must warn them of the Ghost Emperor. My mission—"

A feathered dart pinged off the gatepost by Jia's head, brick dust showering down and forcing her towards Ben. He grabbed her arms, keeping her upright.

"Be my guest," he said, and then released her, shoving her in the direction of the drive. "I'm sure they'll stop shooting long enough to listen."

Jia looked at the agents. Then she glared at Ben. Again she surveyed the swaying trees leading up to the ruined mansion. She took a step, then spun and ducked as the earth at her feet exploded, bullets chasing her into the shelter of the gatepost. *Real* bullets, Ben noted. Not darts. The Chapter clearly had no qualms about wounding them, as long as the agents got what they wanted. Desperate times had just become frantic. A bullet shattered an antler of a leaping stag, chunks of stone thumping to the ground.

Pale-faced, Jia stared at Ben as he squatted beside her, his cynical growl greeting her alarm.

"Any more bright ideas?" he asked. "No? Good. Then *run*."

In a volley of gunfire and twirling leaves, Ben led the way back to the road, sprinting with his head down into the connecting street. He left it up to Jia to follow, but she joined him on the other side of Hampstead Lane, navigating the traffic red-faced and cursing, her butterfly sword in hand. It was only a matter of time before a passing driver called the police, but he couldn't worry about that right now.

With a twitch of his head, he directed Jia onto the Heath, the two of them racing down a beaten track, past an empty frost-jewelled playground, startled dog walkers lurching from their path.

Ben headed vaguely south, keeping to the cover of the trees. He judged his destination a twenty-minute sprint away, a quarter of that time if he changed into true form. In the meantime, staying small gave him the advantage and Jia obviously agreed, darting along beside him. The boughs rattled and thrashed overhead, leaves swirling around them in a yellow-brown funnel. Chancing a glance up through the canopy, he spied the unmistakable glint of metal, and the next moment the first of the helicopters *whoomph-whoomphed* over the treetops, its rotors making cotton candy of the mist.

Jia shouted something, but he couldn't hear her over the noise. The sight was warning enough. A second and then a third helicopter appeared above the Heath, their gun barrels tipping in his direction. Apaches, he noted, twin-turbo attack helicopters, designed and primed for heavy-duty combat. Ongoing conflicts in the Middle East and elsewhere kept an informative array of military hardware on the TV and in the papers, a running advertisement for human inventiveness, the old religion of Might Makes Right. It didn't surprise him that the Chapter should have access to such machines. If he took the Guild of the Broken Lance as an example, with MPs, judges and colonels on its books, then it was clear that the Curia Occultus had very long fingers, reaching into government war chests as well as the odd confession box. An organisation with roots that wound back to the Crusades wouldn't have survived as long otherwise.

Ben shouted at Jia, pointing at a path branching ahead of them, leading over a rise. Open ground, but if they could just make it to the next stretch of woodland . . . On his right, Kenwood House loomed out of the mist, the old stately home a compass point that told him he was heading in the right direction. The two of them emerged from the trees, the canopy whipped back like a tablecloth trick, prompting the vanguard Apache to discharge a missile. The rise ahead, a gentle knoll riddled with paths, broke apart like an upended jigsaw puzzle as the rocket thudded into its flank, showering Ben and Jia with clods of earth. There was no explosion. No fire. No heat. With a hiss, a yellowy fog billowed from the crater, wafting in their direction, a rolling, stinking cloud of chemicals.

The Chapter wants me alive, that much is clear. Over my dead body.

Enough halothane filled the air to take down a T. rex, let alone a humanoid. Ben had no choice but to change, his wings blasting the gas away. The *sin-you* followed suit, her bare feet bulging into hooves, her single horn sprouting from her forehead, a tapering golden antler. All the same, there was only one way to go, and that was up. For all her speed, she would never get clear of the gas in time. What could he do? Leave her to the cruelties of the Chapter? She claimed to have been one of Von Hart's students, and besides, she had saved his life, drawn out the White Dog's venom . . .

All his indecision happened in a second. Even as he realised the risk he was taking, he was closing a claw around Jia, lifting her from the ground. He could feel her struggles, her kicking against his plated flesh having little effect. The mist churned like a hurricane as he leapt for the unpolluted heights. For freedom.

Bullets snickered and pinged off his spine. He banked right, intending to soar around the craft, but its rotor blades came angling towards him, cutting off his escape route. Changing course, he found himself surrounded, the other two helicopters dropping through the cloud cover, their rotors forming a whirling wall, ready to turn him into a smoothie. Up close and personal, the Apaches held all the menace of wasps. Their thermal-imaging sensors, bulky protuberances on the nose of the craft, would show him up like an escaped prisoner under a spotlight; he couldn't hope to lose them in the fog. The Chapter wasn't messing around: the bristling array of rocket launchers and missiles invited him to a world of pain. The Apaches hovered above him, noses tipped to direct him to the ground. Through the windshield of the chopper ahead, Ben could see the gunner and the pilot, and neither of them was waving.

The sky is my backyard, buddy. You're just a tourist.

The Apache in front of him fired – an unseen signal passing between the three craft – but there came no stutter of bullets, catching Ben off guard. Before he could manoeuvre, twist away, a metal web was spreading through the air above him. Trap sprung, the Apache ascended and withdrew, whickering in retreat. Ben reeled, trying to throw off the net as it settled around him, the safari-grade mesh clunking on the ridges of his spine, wrapping around his tail and tangling in his wings, his pinions folding under its weight. He thrust upward, the wake of his struggle spinning the other two choppers in a blast of air, the pilots punching at the controls. It was no good. He could fight the True Names all day long, but he couldn't fight gravity. He roared and thrashed, the net making flight impossible. Surrendering, he tumbled towards the earth. Clutching Jia close to his chest, shielding her struggling form, seven tons of constricted dragon crashed headlong into Hampstead Heath.

Boom.

Minutes passed. Trees shuddered and creaked, relinquishing the last of their leaves. The tremors subsided, an unearthly silence settling over the Heath. Apart from the *thud thud* of rotors overhead, the chilly peace returned to the parkland. Birds twittered, fluttering from branch to branch. The ponds smoothed to stillness. The London skyline marched on undisturbed, the Gherkin and Shard deaf to the uproar.

The mist cleared. One of the choppers, the pilot leaning forward in the cockpit and scanning the ground, managed to veer out of the way a second before Ben came hurtling past, a red streak spearing into the sky. He clutched Jia in one claw, the net bleeding in melted runnels off his wings, a scatter of slag in the winter air.

The red streak shot south-east, flying from the park and fleeting over the surrounding rooftops, TV aerials quivering in its wake, then flashing over the traffic on Finchley Road. Driver and pedestrian alike looked up, alarmed by the turbulence, the blast overturning shop signs and rubbish bins, snatching hats from upturned heads. Snapping his wings in close to his body, Ben swept over a bridge and shot into the mouth of a railway tunnel on the West Hampstead interchange.

Settling dust obscured his vanishment.

TWELVE

The devil is in his hell and all is wrong with the world.

And this *was* hell, of that the tramp had little doubt. The day passed by in a stutter of startling scenes, each one rearing like a wooden grotesque in a mystery play, the devil come crawling out of clouds of flour in the village square to tempt a mummer saint. *Good old George.* But today, the devil was the champion, making the tramp dance through all the maddening sights. Later, at the bidding of some priest or other, the peasants would gather to throw the devil on the fire.

Dance, dance ye to the music of death.

The sun rose over Hampstead Heath. Had there been a fire somewhere? the tramp wondered. Smoke spiralled from the hill at his back, churning from the guts of a shattered building. *The Court,* he thought, wondering where he had plucked the name from. Could he hear bells? Or had that been earlier? Perhaps the bells were only ringing in his head. *Ding-a-ling-ling.* He clutched a narrow object in his hand, a short metal bar, bowlike and silver. Tuning keys dotted the scrollwork. He hated the thing, but he would never let it go. Mostly he was afraid that if he did, the bells would fall still and, in the silence, so would he. He trudged down the hill, wanting to get away from the noise, but having no success. Screams greeted his mud-streaked appearance as he slipped his way down the sodden bank and onto the path, his arms swinging out before him. Froth bubbled on his lips. His eyes rolled up in their sockets, bloodshot orbs scouring the fractured pieces of the past.

He saw the old man standing by the bench before the old man saw him. The little brown dog yipped on its leash as the tramp broke the old man's neck and shuffled into his plundered raincoat, the fabric ripping at the shoulder seams. Somewhere in his delirium, the tramp understood that his nakedness wouldn't serve him here. He was a creature of instinct, and instinct would guide him, even in his confusion. In a glimpse of terrible clarity, he could see himself as others saw him: a dark-skinned brute stumbling under the trees, leaves sticking out of his silver-streaked hair and his gaze searching, searching the tangled briar of his past . . . Then he was holding down the laughter again, holding down the sobs.

He stuffed the fragment of the harp under his coat, the bells muffled, but holding back the silence. Soothed, he flung the old man's body into the bushes and hurried on into the dawn. He had swallowed both the man's eyeballs, but hungry as he was, he was loath to touch the real meat. He didn't want to besmirch his new clothes. Didn't want people looking at him.

He needn't have worried. People swerved to avoid him. Even a madman could tell that his torn clothes had rendered him invisible. A man spat at him and told him to go get a job. Most of the people said nothing, looking up at the buildings or down at the pavement where his bare feet sloshed through the puddles. Mauntgraul (*Is that my name? Or the name of a ghost?*) barely noticed them.

Hands to his head, trying to shut out the ceaseless roar of the metal carriages shooting past, he staggered drunkenly down the road. Look, there a giant painting of a goddess! She stretched across the face of one of the countless towers, pouting down in rouge tyranny. Dummies stood in windows, blank-faced, watching. In other windows lay glittering stacks of trinkets, the purpose of each beyond his ken. Dials turned. Numbers flashed. Bells (*bells!*) went off. Down a corridor of stares, the tramp staggered along the road, bumping into the lords and ladies in their strange garb. Stumbling into the pageant, the mystery play. Into the fire.

In the pageants of old, there had always been a devil, wooden and crimson-painted. Horned. Fanged. Breathing fire. But he couldn't remember the right name for him (*A word. Another word beginning with D*) and the parade went waltzing by, shouting and laughing into black devices held up to mouth or ear, fingers tapping at the bright rectangular surfaces. To look into the past was safer. Easier. Nothing in the past could hurt him now. Not priests. Not knights. *Fuck them and their Lore.* He could smell the past all around him, a lingering trace retained in a shopfront or a stray cobble under his feet. In weathered stone that had seen fire and flood and thirsted for more. The bones of the city. London Town, gorged on the ages and grown fat. Oh, he would know this place in his sleep! This grave of serpents. This ancient smouldering feast!

Yes . . . The *dragon* city. The pageants had featured a dragon, a beast to symbolise the devil. *Dragons.* And he remembered a flight of the beasts, a sky that had swarmed with snout, wing and tail, the mottled flanks of gold, green, black and blue.

And red.

Why did his nails grow long at this last thought, his half-grown talons spearing his palms? Blood spattered the pavement, melting into the rain. No one stopped. No one looked. He had a feeling that no one would talk to him if his head burst into flame. Or if a tail with a barbed sting on the end of it came coiling out of his spine. *What a ridiculous thought.* In a shop window, a row of screens captured his every movement, mirroring his face. Why did he weep so? What was this voice in his head? Better to let the bells drown it out, a silver sea washing away the shore of his reveries. Mauntgraul, the White Dog, wailed and stumbled away, pushing his way through the crowds.

Oi, mate, watch where you're going!

Fucking twat!

Should I call the police?

He hurried along the street, stumbling further down the dragon's throat.

The pageant lurched on into night. Singing. Dancing. Somewhere, he had lost hours. He sat, shivering in his raincoat, on the steps of an elaborate fountain. The crowds surged all around him, but the people never came too close. Above him, a little stone god balanced on the fountain's topmost pinnacle, poised in the act of shooting an arrow. But the god's arrow was missing and his wings were stone, never to take flight.

Mauntgraul sympathised without knowing why. Like a

charmed snake, he sat mesmerised, watching the myriad shapes swoop and swirl across the grand building opposite, the reflections blinking in the puddles, impossible visions of light.

In his mind, the bells tinkled, ceaseless.

He didn't notice the boy until the boy spoke. One moment, he wasn't there. The next, a shadow separated itself from the crowds and the traffic and coughed politely behind his fist, announcing his otherwise composed presence.

"*Bonsoir, monsieur.* A night like this, it warms the blood, no? Well, *someone's* blood. A *vampyr* must restore himself, when business calls." He shivered, but Mauntgraul reckoned the gesture was merely for show, a remembered thrill. "Ah, the wind is so bracing. Keeping one sharp."

The tramp on the steps studied the boy. The boy couldn't have looked more like his opposite, in his suit jacket and slacks, the umbrella he held to keep the rain off his lustrous curls. The tramp, for all his forgetting, had lived long enough to understand a city – even one as changed as this – and the youth at the bottom of the steps, all of nineteen years old, if that, was as powdered and preened as any prospecting catamite. His complexion, paler than a winter sky, bloomed with roses at his cheeks and lips, speaking of rude health. His eyes gleamed with malachite in the depths. *And secrets,* the tramp thought. *Too many secrets.* The puddle that the youth was standing in didn't appear to catch his reflection. If it wasn't for his smell, a rich, antique perfume masking something sweeter and fouler, the tramp would have dismissed him with a growl, told him to go ply his trade elsewhere.

Instead, he said, "I am lost. And yet you found me."

The boy shrugged, but the tramp could tell that he was flattered.

"A simple thing. Webs and whispers. *Sans importance.*"

"Whispers . . ."

"*Oui.* Whispers."

The boy grinned, and here was a curious thing. A kindred spirit, the tramp thought, and so moved, he reluctantly conceded his predicament, Remnant to Remnant.

"I think I have been asleep," he said. "Asleep for a very long time."

"You are still half asleep, I think," the boy said. "The fun half, anyway. Blame that little trinket that jingles in your pocket. Magic is not what it was. Things grow sour. Spells rot. And I'm afraid that the lullaby has driven you mad."

"Trinket?" Now it was the tramp's turn to show his teeth. "It is *mine.*"

"*On se calme.* I don't want it. And we have all been asleep after a fashion. Nonetheless, the Lore is broken. You're not the only one who took the opportunity to dine." The boy dabbed at the corner of his mouth, as though wiping away a spot of wine. "We really should get out of this rain. Do you know how long it takes to do one's hair without the aid of a mirror?"

The tramp had stirred at the mention of food.

"I woke up with a mind to a feast, but . . ." He studied his lacerated palms, his fingers opening and closing. "The times, it seems, have stolen it from me."

"Oh, there are others who will serve," the boy assured him. Taking the tramp's melancholy as an invitation, he climbed the steps and sat down next to him, unmindful of the blood and the shit, his raw, staring eyes. Up close, the tramp should have felt the heat of the boy's body on this cold March night, but he only shivered again, shrinking inside his raincoat. "If you so choose."

"Others?"

"Whispers, *mon ami*. The disciples of saints. How the faithful like to hide themselves, skulking in the cloisters of the world. But spiders pay no mind to holy ground and webs weave everywhere. You might say I have heard the whispers of whispers, their desire and design. Indeed, the Chapter has pulled off quite the *coup d'état*. And the devil take the hindmost, as they say."

"Devil?"

"The trinket in your pocket is but one of three pieces. Long parted and each one a key. Remember. Remember. This dissonance could swell into a symphony. Wouldn't you like to be the one calling the tune?"

He chuckled at his little joke. Confused, the tramp scratched his balls.

"Whispers . . ."

"The Curia Occultus. Ring any bells?"

The tramp winced at the mention of bells. He wanted to get away from this sweet-smelling youth with the pretty white smile, but glimpses of the past were glittering again and a distant heat rumbled in his belly, the temptation of vengeance tilting his head towards the boy.

"And where would one find such whispers?"

"On a mountaintop. Closer to God." The boy had a trace of heat now, the tramp noticed, but his fervour came entirely from his eyes. "And I ask only a small favour in return."

THIRTEEN

There are places under London that not even the rats know.

No one had built London's tunnels, secret or otherwise, to accommodate the wingspan of dragons, so as the dark closed a fist around Ben, an undulation of scales rippled from his snout to the tip of his tail, a beast becoming human. He rolled, feeling every lump of gravel under his backside, into the gloom.

Jia fell from his withering clutches, rudely ejected into the filth. He heard her sit up a few feet away from him, dusting grit off her suit, and he grinned through his bruises, happy to have shaken off pursuit. The choppers wouldn't dare try to navigate the London Underground system, surely. Pedestrians had a hard enough time as it was.

Jia crunched over to him and slapped the grin off his face.

"Never do that again!"

It wasn't a hard slap, as slaps went. Her eyes were harder. He wanted to protest – he'd returned the favour and saved her life, hadn't he? – but part of him could understand why she might not appreciate having a giant red claw close around her, snatching her up off the ground.

All things considered, there was only one safe place in

London he could think of, and he'd decided to keep Jia close at hand. The True Names hadn't baulked at the idea of harming her, he'd noted, the bullets sprayed just as freely in her direction. That bothered him. It said something. Something bad. And he reckoned she had something to tell him. He couldn't make her say it. But he could try.

Jia, a supposed paragon of virtue, was still a Remnant. With few friends left and the envoy's absence, circumstance had thrown them together. Did he trust her? Hell, no. But cards on the table, that didn't mean much. *Who do I trust?* He had to focus on the facts at hand. She was a Chinese unicorn. No. A *sin-you*. According to her, an appointed champion of truth and justice. Sure, she was about as much fun as a wet weekend in Margate, but he reckoned he could trust her to be herself, if nothing else. That would have to do.

With this in mind, he shouted up the tunnel after her, asking her where she thought she was going. She didn't look back. For the inscrutable Miss Jing, it seemed the argument was over.

Ben caught up. Gently, he tugged her elbow. Clearly her vision was up to scratch, judging by the way she managed to navigate the uneven ground. When she shrugged him off, he merely gave a tut. He headed off down a side tunnel, an arched brick corridor on his right, leaving her to it.

Jia hesitated a moment, then she levelled her shoulders and followed him.

Paris wasn't the only city with catacombs. For half an hour, Ben led the way downward through a series of cisterns, channels and sewers, the brickwork changing from Victorian to Roman, the darkness deepening. Jia stumbled along behind him, refusing his offered arm on two occasions, but keeping close to his back. It was obvious that she would prefer to take the lead – anything but rely on him – but this was his territory, his turf. There were places under London, Ben could've told her, that no living soul had ever laid eyes on. From Whitechapel to White City, an unseen metropolis stretched out, a labyrinth of tunnels and vaults, from the vast chambers of the railway lines to abandoned air raid shelters and a host of disused tube stations with subsided and cobwebbed platforms.

Under this layer of modernity lay the skeletons of the past, the wine cellars of kings and queens. The channels of forgotten rivers. The echoing temples of Celtic priests. Lower still and one reached the stratum of bones, the sediment of a thousand wars, some recorded, some not. And under the bones, down winding stairways carved from earth, over bridges that spanned yawning chasms, one would come at last to the barrows.

The lost graves of the Fay.

Ben led Jia through the cavern, marvelling at the stalagmites and stalactites, some of which joined, the towering spindles making a crystal cage of the space, a menagerie for the alien dead. The rock down here was alabaster smooth, touched by something unnatural, warping it into the rarest of stone. Ben hadn't walked in this place for three hundred years, past the slumped and crumbling shapes of the tombs, these monuments to other-worldly lords and ladies, raised back in a time when some said the Fay had been gods.

The First-Born had dwindled and died, victims of some

unrecorded cataclysm. Now, only spectres remained, diminished, weak, but capable of rising still, called from the sleep beyond sleep, as he had learnt to his horror last year. That the vanished race held power untold, magic far surpassing science, Ben could not dispute. Gods? The tales depended on who told them. Every parent is a god to a child. To see a trace of the Old Lands in this depthless place chilled him to the bone.

All the same, he came to a halt, turning to Jia.

"It isn't much. We'll have to wait down here until we figure out our next move."

Or you satisfy my questions.

"This is your lair?"

"Yeah. Like I said, it isn't—"

She was looking at him in that funny way again.

"You are lying, Mr Garston," she told him flatly. Unable to hold her penetrating gaze, he looked away into the shadows, and she let out a sigh, too tired to judge him. "I . . . sense that your lair is nearby, though. Perhaps down that corridor, yes? You know, I could easily find my way back here, if I had to."

"I knew this was a bad idea."

"Then stop wasting time," she said. "It's too late to turn back now."

Shoulders slumped, he shook his head and led her down the corridor in question. Jia must have thought he was leading her into the core of the earth. For all that, he only heard her complain once during the journey, and that was when he came to the end of yet another corridor. Taking in the blank wall ahead, a dead end in the gloom, she let out

201

a groan. Ben rewarded her with a frown and laid his palm flat against the wall, his fingers spread, pressing into weathered grooves. Jia sighed in relief as a section of the wall slid to one side. A warm amber light shone through the gap.

Gold. It was gold. Heaps upon heaps of gold. A collection of coins dating from the Saxon era and on through all the history of the world, the mixed mounds of currencies peppered with goblets, statues and crowns.

Jia traipsed behind Ben through the valleys of treasure, her eyes wide, her feet crunching over jewels, kicking the occasional urn from her path. An enchanted light illuminated the cavern, shimmering from the treasure itself, gathered over centuries into a bed.

Ben coughed and hurried his pace, feeling exposed by this proof of his nature, the greed and possessiveness of dragons. Jia, for her part, made no comment, awe rendering her dumb. For that, he was grateful. No one but him had seen this place in a hundred years. Any criticism and he might change his mind, shove her back into the tunnels under the city. Then coil jealously around his riches in the half-light.

His reason for taking this route was that it had been the only one available. Besides, he couldn't bring himself to leave her behind, abandoning her to her fate – to *their* fate – the world falling to the Ghost Emperor. If the Guild couldn't help them, who did that leave? Somehow he had to find Von Hart and, if necessary, wrest his fragment of the harp from his clutches. Somehow he'd make him pay for his treachery, his rousing of the dragon and destruction . . .

You don't know that. There's more to this than meets the eye.

Whatever was going on here, Jia was the key. Instinct told him as much. In light of this, he was willing to make certain sacrifices, like inviting the *sin-you* into his lair. After all, she had saved his life.

And you don't want to let her out of your sight . . .

Soon enough, Ben reached the edge of the hoard, passing half-finished Michelangelo sculptures, a ten-foot-high Black Sun swastika and a row of open chests filled with bullion. The stacked gold bars were the cause of his argument with Delvin Blain. The dwarf had informed him that there was only so much gold one could fence on the black market; it attracted the wrong kind of attention. Dealing with smugglers was far from wise, particularly for a creature like Ben, whose privacy remained of the utmost importance.

This was excellent advice, Ben had agreed. The Blain Trust had every reason for caution. In the end, the need for discretion had not dampened his wish to donate a portion of his wealth to charities in Somalia and across North Africa. He had decided to take a calculated risk. His hands might be tied when it came to playing the superhero, but he could play the philanthropist, even if he knew that the hoard around him would never be enough . . .

Of course, he said nothing of this to Jia. He led her up the stairs and out of the chamber, up a thousand spiral steps to another brick wall, which again he pressed in a certain fashion, the barrier sliding back.

He stepped through the gap into the cellar of number 9 Barrow Hill Road.

He was home.

★   ★   ★

In the months of his absence, not much had changed. While Jia took a shower, Ben had a look around, relieved to find that the house had sat undisturbed. The bedrooms were pristine and empty. The large framed Blake print, *The Great Red Dragon and the Woman Clothed in Sun*, still hung over the mantelpiece in the living room. Jack, sweet Jack, was waiting in the fridge. Dust covered everything as usual, a shroud for the sham of an ordinary life, and he had to wipe the TV with his sleeve to see the images on the screen.

Putting his feet up, the soles calloused and black, he swigged from a freshly opened bottle and watched the evening news.

The Middle East imploding. The icecaps melting. Refugees fleeing, starving, drowning. Oil spills and earthquakes. Bigots grinning on platforms. The usual circus of human existence, parading with all due pomp and ceremony towards the cliff edge of civilisation.

Ben sighed. Why did he care for them so much, the humans? Was it their fleeting natures that spoke to him, moved him to protect them? He could no longer kid himself that the sentiment was mutual, and his hope – already stretched – was wearing thin. As if a blindfold had been torn from his eyes, he was staring the times directly in the face. Against all his wishes, humans, like Remnants, had become the cause of their own downfall.

Despair was nibbling at the edges of his duty, his *pact*, filling him with doubt. With no official body to guide him (save the one that wanted his head on a plate), where did that leave him? He couldn't turn to the envoy for help and there was no lover to soothe him, make the fight seem worthwhile.

He had lost his way. The Sola Ignis was alone, as ever, but the fire was guttering, about to go out. The Fay had abandoned the Remnants long ago. The humans looked to dangerous science or silent gods. The Remnants were dropping like flies.

And in the end, what's in it for you?

At another time, guilt would have followed on the heels of this thought. He'd have chastised himself for selfishness and gone about drinking himself downstream, away from the problem. But—

An electrical bolt, a detonation of nerves, speared his body, his spine arching against the couch. Veins stood out on his neck, his teeth clenching. Blood bubbled from his trapped tongue, his eyes rolling up in his head as the spasm took hold. The bottle of Jack fell from his hand, thudding on the floorboards and chugging whiskey. Crimson eddied under his skin, scales blooming and retreating, his instincts thrown into confusion, a transformation beyond his control. As he gasped for breath, the room around him fell away, the walls slipping into endless black. The couch under him vanished, the curtain of the *real* ripped back to reveal the nether, a vision into nothingness. Wires, thin and hot, shot through his physique, a drawstring pulling in tight.

Before him, a giant emerged from the darkness, the dome of its head rising from the deep, a pale sun blazing in the dark.

Shuddering, drooling, Ben watched the Ghost Emperor draw closer, taking up the whole of his vision, a viscid, vaporous wall. The behemoth, a colossus of *need*, brimmed with accumulated power, his tendrils and horns a flickering crown. Rigid on the couch, Ben recognised the Lurkers, a host of phantoms swimming through the gulf to join their king, swarming into a deathly whole. Behind the Emperor's visor of bone, the light at his core whirled and flashed, too fierce to look at directly, a radiant maw. Silently he levelled his eyes on Ben, each one burning with blind hunger. His tongue slithered back and forth, the forked appendage wriggling, extending across the non-space to lick at Ben's aura, taste his soul.

Drawn by the souring of magic – Ben had seen the decaying circle for himself – the Ghost Emperor hauled his bulk across the nether to bear against the skein of reality. Frost crackled across Ben's skin, encasing his heat, his eyes drinking in the cosmic horror. His flesh urged to take flight from his bones, drift in flakes towards those weaving tentacles, the squid-like limbs eager to suck up the meat of Creation . . .

He heard an echo, a scream, calling in the dark.

Ben.

"Ben!"

His eyes fluttered open. Jia was leaning over him, shaking him awake. Groaning, he tried to sit up, blood crusting his nostrils and lips. He threw out his arms like a drowning man and Jia retreated, giving him room to catch his breath. Swallowing bile, he wiped mucus and sweat from his face, then spat on the floor between his feet.

"Are you all right?"

"I've been better." He grimaced and scrambled for the Jack, lifting the bottle to his lips and draining the last inch of liquor. He toasted her with the empty. "I've been worse."

Jia didn't look convinced. She had unpicked her braid, he noticed, her hair straggling damply around her shoulders. In her efforts to rouse him, her bathrobe had come loose, revealing the tops of her breasts, pert orbs of skin, porcelain-smooth. *An impression of skin*, he reminded himself, not that it did him any good. Seeing his lingering gaze, Jia blushed and pulled the robe around her, a swathe of green hair shimmering over her chest, her suit re-forming, the show over.

She straightened, tightening her belt.

"You saw him again, didn't you?"

He didn't have to ask her who she meant.

"Looks like your Emperor is paying house calls." Ben bumped his fist against his head. "Maybe I should charge rent on my skull."

Jia snorted. "What would the Ghost Emperor want with you?"

"That thing sniffed me out for a reason." *Twice now.* "I'd like to know why."

"Who can say? I see nothing special about you."

"You flatter me."

"I merely speak the truth. The Ghost Emperor craves the world entire, not some washed-up dragon." He started to protest, but she silenced him with a wave of her hand. "The failing magic draws this evil to the earth like a wolf to unguarded sheep. Why would he turn his eyes in your direction? Is there something you're not telling me?"

Ben climbed unsteadily to his feet.

"Oh no you don't. Don't turn this around," he said. "Let's talk about you for a minute, shall we? What was all that about at Paladin's Court? You followed me from China. You wanted to find the Guild. To warn them, you said. But you were more than happy to talk to the Chapter, even after everything I told you. Or did you just want to get me out in the open?"

"You're paranoid. I—"

"What do you really want, Miss Jing? You know, I didn't come down in the last rain shower."

"I told you. I'm on an urgent mission to—"

"Save it. We both know you used me as bait."

For once, Jia was unable to hold his gaze. She scowled at the TV, at the Blake print on the wall. Anywhere but at him.

"I have to warn them," she said, soft but firm. "You don't know what the Emperor will do."

"And you don't know the Whispering Chapter. What the hell were you expecting? A twenty-one-gun salute?" He crossed his arms, hissing through his teeth. "These are dangerous times. You can't trust anyone. The Chapter wants my balls for breakfast and you were ready to serve them up on a plate."

"My mission is of greater importance than what dangles between your legs."

"Not to *me*, honey. And your mission sounds pretty bogus, to be fair." He was moving forward, watching her retreat in his shadow. "Who are you working for? Von Hart? Everyone and their cat is after the harp. Why should you be any different?"

"You're a suspicious creature," she said. "A cynical drunk in love with his scars. So what if I secure a fragment of the harp? It would help me to find Von Hart. And maybe stop the Chapter from taking your head!"

"So there we have it," he said, raising his arms. "Every Remnant knows the location of Paladin's Court. You turned up on the doorstep just like that." He clicked his fingers under her nose. "Convenient. But the Invisible Church is just that – invisible. You're not the only one who can see through people, Jia. And you were willing to risk my life to get what you want."

"Yes!" she shouted up at him, her fists held rigid at her sides. "Your life. My life. What are they worth? The Ghost Emperor will devour *all*."

"I get it." Her outburst had taken him aback and he held up his hands, framing his complaint. "Still, you should've told me. You should've asked."

Why didn't he just kick her out of his house? What was holding him back? Either way, she knew where he lived now. If she wanted to bring the Chapter down on his head, it was too late to stop her. Better to talk her out of it. To try, at least.

Disgusted with him, Jia swore and turned her back, glaring out of the window.

"If we can save this world, it's a small price to pay," she told him. "Some have already paid it."

And here was the source of her anger, an inkling of emotion under her veneer.

Ben looked at the ceiling, giving his blood time to cool.

After a moment, he said, "At the Court. You said . . . that you lost something."

"It is nothing."

"Doesn't sound like nothing to me."

"I'm alone," she said, covering her face. "The gods have cursed me with a cruel fate. I have no choice. That is all you need to know."

Ben reached out and touched her shoulder, his fingers light. At first, she stiffened, but then she relaxed, turning to face him.

"You're not alone," he told her. What was he even saying? "I brought you here, didn't I?"

"You repaid me in kind."

"Shut up. We all have our scars, Jia."

The pull of her sorrow was strong. It surprised him to find that their lips were inches apart, her chin tipping towards him, her eyes filling his, a mystery waiting to unfold.

"We take our comfort where we can," he breathed.

Jia blinked, startled. Her palm came up, a block of ice on his chest.

"What are you doing?"

"I . . ." Ben coughed, drawing himself upright. "I thought . . ."

Her forehead creased, but she appeared more puzzled than vexed.

"You love another," she said. Another cold statement of fact. No. A judgement. Definitely a judgement.

He didn't have much to say to this. There was no point in lying. He coughed to cover his embarrassment – Christ, he needed a drink – and eddied back across the floor, willing the space between them to crash in like waves, drowning the awkward moment.

But Jia had more to say.

"In my land, we have a story." Her face was a mask, unreadable. "It is one of the *chuanqi*, the strange tales. Sketches, you might call them. Interludes in a broader tale. This tale belongs to Pu Songling, a lowly country teacher, who was no less wise and true."

With that, she went on. "There was a merchant of Qingzhou who often travelled away on business, leaving his wife and his dog at home. His wife, a twisted creature, encouraged the dog to have relations with her, and the dog, in his fashion, grew accustomed to this. One day, the merchant returned home, but when he climbed into bed with his wife, his dog fell upon him and mauled him to death." Ben stared at her. Her gaze was piercing, a thorn through his heart. "'How many things are possible', Songling wrote, 'in the immense universe of heaven and earth. This woman was certainly not the only human to have coupled with a beast.'"

For a minute, silence spun about between them, fraying and cold.

Then Jia said, "You are a coward, Ben Garston. You cannot help me. In the morning, I will leave this place and continue my mission alone."

She pushed past him, her head held high. Her tale was still sinking in, but he grasped its meaning well enough. She had rebuked him for his affair with Rose, perhaps his affairs with humans entirely. He'd wondered how deep her perceptions went. Or what Von Hart had told her. Now he knew. Either way, she had looked into his soul and found him wanting.

211

He'd recovered his voice by the time she reached the living room door.

"It wasn't like that," he said.

She didn't look back.

"You love another," she replied, and left him to his shame.

He had a bad night's sleep. Unformed dreams howled in his head, loss, guilt and consequence. In the morning, with sunlight spearing through the living room windows, he abandoned the couch and the litter of bottles and went upstairs.

Jia lay on her back in the bedroom, her hands crossed over her stomach, as still as a corpse in an open casket. Sensing his presence in the doorway, her eyes blinked open and she sat up, raising an eyebrow at his freshly shaved face and trimmed hair. He'd stood with the scissors in front of the bathroom mirror, letting the curls drift to the floor like autumn leaves. As if he was making a sacrifice, which in a way, he was.

"It's dangerous out there," he told her. "And perhaps you're right. Perhaps that makes me a coward. But I can show you where to find a certain Vicomte. If anyone can, he'll tell us where to find the knights of the Guild. Maybe even the Invisible Church. But first you have to tell me what you want with the harp."

After a moment, Jia nodded. A curt, respectful acceptance.

She opened her mouth to speak and the front of the house exploded.

FOURTEEN

In a flurry of brick dust and splinters, Ben was at the top of the staircase, ignoring the barrage of cuts peppering his hands and face. Half crouching to leap down the steps, he caught himself instead, tottering on the landing. The stairs below were missing, blown to smithereens. Through the noise and the dust, he gawped down on his new open-plan hallway and living room, the Blake print taking flight from the wall, the TV and the sofa aflame. Even the fridge in the kitchen lay on its side, broken bottles of Jack pouring freely from its mangled door.

The sight of the latter drew his face into a scowl.

He heard Jia shout something from the bedroom behind him, perhaps in shock, perhaps a warning, but he wasn't listening. Whatever he had offered her, whatever information, it would have to wait. He had more immediate concerns.

Bellowing, he leapt down into the living room, his sprouting claws buckling the floorboards, throwing up a diadem of wood and glass. Through the gaping hole that had been the front wall, the curtains smouldering, he peered through the smoke and saw the figure standing in the road.

It was the Sister. An assassin of the Whispering Chapter. He'd only made her acquaintance once before, on the

North Sea oil rig a few days ago, but the square set of her shoulders and jaw were imprinted on his mind. Ditto her faded military fatigues, the cross shaven across her skull and the broken grin that hung beneath it.

The bazooka on her shoulder was new.

How did she find me? How did she track me to my lair?

Few Remnants would risk his fury, and even Lambert du Sang wouldn't go as far as to dox him. Would he?

As soon as he thought it, an answer came swimming through the smoke.

It's the lunewrought. *The damn* lunewrought. *Some trace residue of the Fay metal. I'm fucking tainted . . .*

That meant she must've brought the manacle along, looking to make another attempt at his capture. He only hoped she hadn't brought a fragment of the harp with her too, trusting to the fact that the Chapter seemed reluctant to use the artefact – plus he doubted the old woman on the rig would let the thing out of her sight.

Something large, silver and round gleamed on her back, but he had no time to think about that. He watched the Sister discard the rocket launcher from her shoulder, letting the weapon clank to the ground. Her intrusion flooded him with anger, a violation that brought scales rippling over his flesh, his eyes flaring, his mouth widening, distorted by a row of fangs.

"You have got to be kidding m—"

The Sister grinned up at him, answering his transformation by drawing both of her Uzis from the straps at her thighs, snapping them out in front of her and spraying the shattered façade with bullets. The two stone griffins wobbling on the doorstep burst into mossy clouds of shrapnel, joining the ruin of the front door and windows. Plaster rained down, the odd ornament dancing off the mantelpiece, the TV exploding, the floorboards thudding under his feet. Gunfire perfumed the room, acrid in his nostrils, the bullets zipping past his ears. Ben threw up his arms as hot metal whined and sparked off his thickening scales, unable to penetrate his flesh but still hurting like hell. The light fixture, a metal shade, fell from the ceiling and onto his head, stoking his temper.

When his would-be captor ran out of ammo, the muzzles of her guns trailing smoke, the living room was crumpling further with his unfolding mass, his leathery wings pushing at the walls, his tail spilling out into the street, the arrowhead tip thumping down on a parked car. Alarms wailed. Distantly, he heard screaming, his neighbours thrown into panic by the commotion, and he prayed they would stay inside, keep out of harm's way. It was much too late for discretion. As he reared, his horns crashed through the living room ceiling, reducing the bedroom above to rubble. The floor groaned under his claws.

Doesn't anyone knock any more?

He roared. Barrow Hill Road rocked to its foundations. Neck coiling back, horns raking the eaves, his vast shadow fell over the street and the assassin standing there, who quickly removed the round silver object from her back and brought it up before her as he vented a mighty rush of flame.

Fire filled the day, a wall of heat. The deluge slammed into the parked cars, blasting them from their spaces, the parking meters and lamp posts melting into absurd shapes, folding to the pavement on wilted stalks. Tarmac blackened and cracked. A tree went up in a blustering whoosh. The houses on the other side of the street danced in the heat haze, soot painting their façades and windows, their front gardens scorched to ash. The air sizzled and thinned, consumed by an untold heat, as magical as it was fierce, usurping the grip of winter.

When he ran out of breath, Ben glared down at the street, his nostrils smouldering. No human could withstand dragon fire. He expected to see a charred skeleton standing in place of the True Name who had dared to destroy his home.

There wasn't one. Instead, he found himself gazing down at a glowing red disc, the shield large enough to cover the Sister, who was crouching in the road – or almost cover her. He noticed that the toes of her boots smoked a little, a broad black ring around her, but that was far from enough to satisfy him.

What is this shit?

Through his rage, the realisation came to him, another echo of the past. Knights, saints, slayers, and all their wyrm hunting tricks . . . Charmed swords. Diamond-tipped lances. Poison . . . Of course, the Chapter would keep certain relics in its arsenal. After all, the order guarded a fragment of the harp. Why not another of the treasures of Britain? There were several that he knew of, besides the *Cwyth*. Caliburn, for instance, King Arthur's legendary sword. Arawn's Cauldron. The Singing Stones. Because he found himself looking at one of the treasures, Ben was sure, although at first he struggled to place the artefact.

A shield capable of withstanding dragon fire. Wonderful.

The sight tugged at a distant memory, an old tale, something about a wandering saint and a legendary knight, but before it was clear in his mind, he found out the hard way that he'd only grasped the half of it.

The shield pulsed, growing brighter, aglow with some bastard enchantment. The next moment, the same jet of fire that had spewed from his throat roared back at him, blustering around his craggy head. Blinded, he staggered backwards, his shifting bulk tearing at the house, a cascade of rubble rumbling around him.

Joseph of Arimathea. Sir Percival. That was it . . .

The heat couldn't do much to harm him – his scales were naturally resistant, stronger than any charmed shield – but the blast had caught him off guard and, rear legs tangling, he tumbled heavily into the guts of the house, half of the kitchen ceiling shattering over his snout. He shook off the dust in time to see the woman in the road pluck a pin from a grenade with her teeth and lob the explosive in his direction.

The kitchen wall blew out in a rush of heat, hurling a shower of bricks into the back garden. Skull ringing, he looked up to see the Sister, all scars and ugly teeth, climbing the smoking mound at the front of the house, the debris of his sham existence crunching under her boots. Confident of his stunned state, she had discarded the guns and the grenades in favour of a short curved blade, a sickle that was somehow more mean-looking than any of her other weapons. He had felt its sting for himself when he'd chopped off his hand on the oil rig. He didn't much fancy feeling it again.

Peering at him over her shield, the Sister entered the shattered living room and clambered up onto his belly, striding boldly over the paler ridges of scales towards his exposed throat, her sickle swinging.

Ben cursed. He had broken something, something vital, but no amount of profanity would hurry along the healing process. He scrabbled feebly at the ground, trapped by the fallen rubble, penned in by the collapsing walls, his head spinning.

The Sister reached his throat, lodging the sickle into his scales to steady herself as she unclipped an object from her belt. He didn't welcome the sight of that either.

The lunewrought *manacle!*

The radiance of the thing, an unholy silver, glimmered in the True Name's eyes.

He had to get out of here. Had to give himself room to escape.

He shrank back to hominid size, his tail curling in, his wings folding. He maintained a layer of scales for protection, his suit as bulky as armour. His abrupt shift made the Sister lose her footing, sending her sliding to her knees on the littered living room floor.

Grimacing, Ben knocked her blade from his chest, blood pooling around him. Rolling onto his stomach, he dragged himself through the mess, crawling through patches of flame and falling bricks towards the shattered rear wall, to daylight and escape. He'd made it halfway when the Sister emerged from the smoke, stamping down hard on his back.

Ben roared in pain. The butterflies were back again, swarming in front of his eyes, unconsciousness rising to claim him. In a last bid for freedom, he reached behind him and grabbed the Sister's boot, twisting her leg away from his spine. With a cry, she lost her balance, once again crashing to the floor beside him. But she was up on her knees at once, thrusting her bulk towards him. He'd only just managed to flip onto his back when her hand closed around his throat, a vicelike hock knocking the wind from him. Snarling, she brought the manacle down, aiming for his wrist, the circular band ready to snap shut, bring this struggle to an end. The *lunewrought* restraint chilled his flesh, any chance of transformation slipping away from him, drowned in silvery light.

Fuelled by adrenalin alone, Ben shot out his hand. He managed to grab the Sister's forearm, the manacle jarring to a halt an inch from his flesh. The woman growled, pressing down, forcing her weight against him. Then her expression changed. Ben went ahead and squeezed, his fist closing just enough to crunch gristle, snap bone. The assassin tried to mask her agony, beads of sweat dripping from her forehead, her jaw clenching. Vaguely, Ben suppressed a pang of admiration, the sense of it lost as he met her gaze. The fire in her eyes, devout, determined, refused to grow any dimmer.

For a minute, the two of them wrestled in the collapsing house. Outside, distantly, he heard the approaching wail of police cars, the howl of a fire engine. A dog yapping. Neighbours shouting about the End of Days.

Then Jia was there, a flash of green and gold. Retaining human form, the *sin-you* dropped down from the landing, alighting in the room. Before her feet touched the ground (*hooves*, he saw), her butterfly sword was in her hand, a leg darting up over her head, her body a practised spear. She aimed a kick at the Sister's head, knocking the woman to one side, her shield clanging under her. The manacle rolled out of her grip, spinning like a silver dollar in the smoke.

It came to rest between Jia's hooves. Silver and gold. For a moment, the *sin-you* stood there, looking at the thing. Then she looked over at the Sister, sprawled in the smouldering rubble. Finally she looked down at Ben.

Through the butterflies, through the smoke, he tried and failed to read her expression.

But he understood her when she spoke, soft words as she crouched down beside him.

"*Duibuqi.* I'm sorry."

The last thing he knew before everything went black was the manacle closing around his wrist.

Zhàn ~ war

The Bogue, 1841

Where do you see its ending?

That was what her former master, Blaise Von Hart, had said in Xanadu all those years ago. The memory surprised her; Jia didn't tend to think of the envoy much these days. Didn't like the ache in the pit of her stomach and the rush of anger when she pictured his face, so pale, so arcane. So *unknowable*. But she remembered his insistence on the signing of the Pact in the Great Khan's garden, his promise of progress and peace. And his words came winging back to her the moment she saw the ship.

Out there on the Pearl River, the prow of the *Nemesis* broke through the fog, the blade of an axe cutting the morning calm, her great engines rumbling. The "devil ship", that was what the people hereabouts called the iron vessel, the first of its kind in the known world, 180 feet of sheer black metal, funnels, sails, cannons and a trained crew to boot, all armed to the teeth with sabres and flintlock guns. For weeks, the British fleet had lain at anchor in Kowloon Bay, the Daoguang Emperor trembling under his own procrastinating tactics, his sending of messengers back and forth, the semblance of governmental parley that in truth went nowhere, simply played for time. Now the British sailed forth, their patience worn thin, the delicate dance bursting into the flames of war.

Here. Here is the British diplomacy.

On hearing the news of the invasion, Jia had galloped from Canton at full pelt, a blur of green, gold and dust, her single horn spearing through the land. Throwing off her *sin-you* form in a billow of leaves and churned-up earth, she had reached this vantage point on the cape of Anunghoy Island. From here, she could see to all points of the compass and stood scanning the battleground with narrowed eyes, her butterfly swords in hand.

A mile upstream, the green cliffs of Tiger Island guarded the mouth of the river proper, the deep waterway winding fifty-odd miles to the Canton docks. Behind her, down the slope, crouched the village of Humen – an unlikely spot to start a war. The little port lay silent in the dawn, the pink mist curling off the estuary, questing through the empty warehouses, the fishing huts and the taverns, creeping down the alleys between the rickety wooden buildings as though searching for signs of life. All the villagers had fled, leaving only the stench of rotting fish, woodsmoke and wine to speak of their presence. Even the smugglers, those salty dogs who shipped contraband cargo of black spice up and down the river, their clippings slipping like silk between the British and the Emperor, had vanished, gone. Those *fan-quis*! Those foreign devils. Their tongues ever ready with tales for the harbourmasters, their pockets filled with *cumsha*, the gold sand, bribes for the officials to look the other way.

Black spice and gold sand, Jia thought, watching the *Nemesis* crawl upriver. Tea and silk flowed from the country's ports these days as though the Middle Kingdom had sprung a leak. Into the breach, the black spice flowed in return, like sweet fingers stroking the underbelly of the country, Zhongguo a fat fish in the shoals. Quelling the army, sedating the mandarins, soothing the workers, snuffing out the light in their eyes. To a casual observer, the guards in the island forts with their jumble of spears and rusting cannons, the shoemaker snoozing in his jacquard gown on the bench outside his shop, the peasant asleep in the cornfields might appear harmless enough.

Chasing the dragon, some liked to say, but Jia knew better. *Chasing the embers of death.*

Each user symbolised a widening crack in the walls of the Empire, a fatal shift in the foundations of the dynasty, the Qing ready to topple and fall, just like the Yuan and the Ming before them. The Middle Kingdom was half asleep, lulled by the siren song of western progress and free trade. Noble ideals of the British Empire, granted. Noble ideals advanced through mercantile interest, greased by the profiteering ballad of Jardine Matheson & Company that just so happened to have a hundred thousand crates to sell. As *youxia,* Jia couldn't help but admire the strategy. As *sin-you,* she couldn't ignore the bitter truth. And this morning, cannon fire burst and shuddered across the Pearl River to awaken the country with war.

Where do you see its ending? Jia couldn't deny that the omens, the signs, lay all around her, the corruption and perfidy, the bloody cost of human progress. There had been wars before, of course – wars beyond count – but swords and spears were one thing, guns quite another. Over time, the numbers of the dead had grown from mounds into mountains and honour in battle had become no more than nostalgia, a quaint ideal, a thing of the past. The curtain of the future, it seemed, was rising on a stage of fire and smoke.

It is the way of things, Jia thought, trying to reassure herself. *One empire falls, another rises. One dynasty* – but no, the certainty of that escaped her, the sense of unknown tomorrows confounding and troubling her, the age turning towards ruin and war, towards machines like the ship below, machines that, if given free rein, might come to mirror the darkest magic . . . She closed her eyes, waiting for her unease to pass.

I am weary. She was older, it was true, in appearance a thirty-year-old woman, her limbs toned and lithe with the rigours of *wushu*. The ages clung to her and yet her physique lingered at its peak, an illusion of womanhood, a sinewy testament to health. Her long braid remained glossy and black. No wrinkles touched her skin. Yet within . . .

You have no memory of your memories, she thought, with a bitterness that surprised her. *When did you last look into the Eight Hand Mirror? Almost five hundred years ago now, in the mists of time and Mount Song. When you think of your mother and father, Ziyou and Ye, can you remember their faces? Their smell?*

And further back, her mind stretched, mental fingers seeking cracks in a wind-smoothed rock face. She caught a vague recollection from childhood, bidding her parents farewell in the wild-flower meadow outside the palace walls,

Ziyou and Ye slipping underground, the earth covering their equine forms . . . a memory so distant that it ached in her heart, a forgotten scar. Ached alongside the knowledge that she would never again gaze upon their slumbering forms, deep in the cavern under the plains. For centuries, she'd had to content herself that her parents were still there and that, one bright and golden day, when the *Xian* returned and the Nine Hells froze over, the two of them would awaken and come home. They would all be a family again.

The wind. It was the wind that pricked the tear from her eye.

Unable to look away, Jia watched the dark vessel slide into the bay, her shallow draught allowing her access to the delta, a palpable threat to the port city beyond the hills. Canton old and poorly defended.

Chugging steam to mix with the mist, the *Nemesis* growled towards the island forts. White-eared herons struck off the water, taking to the sky. As though the birds were a signal, the troops on the battlements gave a unified roar, their drums echoing across the tide. Man-o'-war junks slipped out from the lee of the shore, their dull red fish-fin sails creaking like the joints of fearful elders pushed into the front line of battle, sticks and clubs in hand. Even from a distance, Jia could see that the Chinese fleet was sorely outmatched, drifting into the shadow of that vast black hull, the *Nemesis* picking up speed, her cannons a primed glut of destruction.

For glory. For England.

Jia sheathed her swords. There was nothing to see here. Nothing she could do. Her mind hardened around her duty, her oath. *To serve the Emperor of Zhongguo, the Middle Kingdom, for all the time to come.* All the same, she would not use her weapons this day. The Daoguang Emperor had dispatched her from Canton for one reason only: survey – spy if necessary – and report back. His Radiant Highness, the Son of Heaven, the Lord of Ten Thousand Years, could rely on hearing the truth from her.

This battle was already over. The war already won.

In true shape, Jia turned and galloped down the hill, heading for the fishing village and the road north. At her back, the sound of centuries-old ramparts breaking apart in rubble and dust, disintegrating in cannon fire. In screams. In change.

Not long afterwards, Jia trotted along the Humen docks. An eerie silence hung in the rigging of the boats and skiffs, the peace broken on occasion by the thunder of guns. The villagers had left in a hurry, heading inland for the safety of the forests, and gulls pecked and squawked at the scraps undeterred. The timber rooftops slumped over the street, cold ashes in every hearth, every chimney clear of smoke. Under the stench of dung and fish, a sweetness lingered, a flowery, tarry scent like rotting sap.

Opium. Death.

When she heard the strain of music coming from somewhere nearby, shocking and oddly familiar in the still, she instantly shimmered and shrank into human shape, her butterfly swords back in her hands, her braid swinging this way and that as she sought the source of the sound.

On assassin's feet, she padded down an alleyway between

two houses, pausing at a gate to a courtyard. The red lacquered archway and the dragons, monkeys and roosters carved around the porch beyond suggested a temple, but Jia knew better. The place was sacred to one faith alone. To the gods of *yen-yen*, the black spice.

The House of the Sleeping Dragon. Suppressing a snort, Jia read the characters beside the arch. *An elegant name for a dive.*

As she padded over the flagstones, past a large copper urn with lily pads floating on the surface, and up to the porch, the music grew louder – a harp, it was the sound of a harp – and the odour of the drug stronger. Crouching to peer over a window ledge, Jia made out the chamber beyond. The familiar sandalwood couches lining the walls. The low tables bearing the usual paraphernalia, the carved pipes of ivory, jade and tortoiseshell. Silver lamps to turn the hard black balls of opium into a sticky gum. Lanterns hung everywhere, unlit at this hour, but clearly betraying the place as a den for smuggler and sailor alike, and the smiling dealers who milked them for silver.

The man who sat on one of the couches, smoke trailing from his pipe, supported this impression, his long golden hair slicked in the fashion of Manchu noblemen, teased and fixed with elephant dung. His red silk robe, spangled with stars, clung to his willowy frame. He swayed back and forth, this failed refugee, cradling a curved spar of silver in the crook of his arm, one porcelain finger plucking at a ghostly suggestion of strings. *Mo shu. Magic.* The melody was soft, yet persuasive, an undeniably pleasant strain in the morning gloom.

The moment that Jia marked the face of the player, her stomach cramped, the mystery unravelling. Emotions warred within her – joy, loss, recrimination, anger. The curtain to the chamber clattered behind her as she stepped through it, announcing her presence.

"You see?" At once, the man's palm fell, the strings vanishing like smoke, the music silenced. He looked up at her, a satisfied expression on his face. "It's true. A fragment of the harp can summon a Remnant. I play but the slightest strain and here you are, awoken from your slumber."

Jia sheathed her swords. All the same, when she moved forward, she did so with a modicum of caution.

"Blaise Von Hart," she said, as if saying his name stamped his presence more firmly on the room. "It's really you."

It had been, what? Four hundred and eighty-five years? Not that she'd been counting. The last time she'd seen him, he had stood on the altar steps of Mount Song, bidding her farewell. Telling her that he'd soon return. Here he sat, with that same old smile on his lips, as though it had only been a few weeks. Part of her wanted to fly into his arms. Most of her wanted to punch him.

"You always were perceptive," he said. "To an extent. You can look into a mirror and see what you want to see. Yet you ignore what's sitting right under your nose."

A frown stole across her brow. Some memories remained painfully clear. Hadn't she seen her heart's desire in the Eight Hand Mirror? Yes. Just as the fairy had said she would. Loath to let him detect her shock at his reappearance, she squared her shoulders and crossed her arms, reluctantly reacquainting herself with the cryptic nature of the *Xian*.

"This . . . instrument you play." Surely that was what he wanted her to notice. "Is that . . .? It's the . . ." Wonder was creeping into her voice; irritated, she forced it out. "Anyway, you're mistaken," she told him. "You sang my name from the walls of Xanadu, did you not? Your lullaby has no power over me. And I have not been sleeping."

"No? Haven't we all been asleep, in our own way?" He waved his pipe, making a moot point of it in the trailing smoke. "Indeed, this is the legendary *Cwyth*, twice forged and twice broken – or at least a fragment of it. Broken or no, the fragment remains a potent tool. One safer in human hands, no doubt. Why would the Guild or the Chapter want to rouse a Remnant? Both have spent centuries trying to rid us from the earth."

Jia snorted. She didn't quite grasp what he meant, but she didn't like the sound of it, all the same.

"If you have something to say, then say it. I have an Emperor to attend."

"Oh, it's nothing. Nothing." Like a cloud passing over the moon, his smile was gone. "We signed the Pact. We do our duty, you and I. And I was the one who came to King John with the harp in the first place, wasn't I? Telling him of the lost magic. Telling him of Arthur and Camlann. Telling him of the Sleep . . . At Thorney Island that distant summer, I revealed the fragments of this, the mnemonic harp."

For a time, a breath between dynasties, Jia had wondered why the envoy had never told her this tale as a little girl. Even later, he hadn't explained why he had brought the shattered relic in his keeping, the three pieces of the fairy harp, to the famous council in London that had sealed the

Remnants' fate. The harp was the axis on which the Lore spun, giving rise to the music that had lulled them all to sleep. It struck her as odd that Von Hart had neglected to illustrate his part in these matters before, crucial as it was. Oh, she had heard the rumours since and pieced together the facts. As an adult, she had come to learn that the envoy extraordinary, the last fairy in their midst, was far more than a wandering sage, blown by the desert winds into her life. Von Hart had come to Xanadu to speak of kings and pacts and lullabies in the west, but he had always been at the heart of things, a pale seed. Back then, she had trusted his intentions and, ever the faithful student, she hadn't thought it her place to question him. Now, standing here in the House of the Sleeping Dragon, she wondered whether his sigh was due to shame, some barely concealed regret. Did he think he had made a mistake?

Before alarm had shuddered all the way through her, Von Hart continued, confirming her fears.

"We were all young once," he said. "I believed the Pact could save us."

Jia, who didn't like his talk of rousing Remnants any more than she liked where she thought the conversation was going, said, "Von Hart, I am *youxia*, Daughter of Empires and Keeper of the Lore." With a disdain she could barely suppress, she narrowed her eyes on the glowing end of his pipe. "I am sure I have no need to remind you."

"Of course not." He flashed her a look that might have been disarming if not for the calculating gleam in his eyes. "I'm merely an old fool, reminiscing about the Bad Old Days."

"Then why do you bring this fragment to me?"

The fragment of the harp, a yard-long conical spar shaped to resemble a horse's head – or a fabulous beast that was much like a horse – glimmered in his lap, all inlaid ivory and wrought silver. With the same thin smile, he pointed the tip of the thing, sharp as a spear, up at her chest.

"Because I wanted you to see it," he said. "*Lunewrought* bears a particular quality. Easily recognisable, to one in the know. Not to mention bearable, to one untouched by its power. To one . . . unbound by the spell."

"Yet bound by the Lore, as we both are." It seemed that she *did* need to remind him, after all. "The Pact we all signed."

"Besides," he went on, as though she hadn't spoken. "I'm not a believer in locking such things away in some dusty and forgotten reliquary. Relics such as these . . . well, they have a habit of being discovered."

"Like the Eight Hand Mirror," she said, her tongue a knife. *Oh, I have not forgiven you, fairy.* "It seems you have a fondness for these trinkets. One might call you a collector."

Silently she cursed herself for letting resentment get the better of her. But he sat there so calmly, so unmoved by his broken promise and the long years that had flowed between them, washing them onto different shores where they could only regard each other as strangers.

"Ah, how astute you are," he said. "I see the years have soured you."

"And my memory of you."

It was impossible to conceal her feelings on the matter, her vision blurring with more than just the arcane shimmer of the harp.

"Touché," he said, in his crisp Germanic accent. It occurred to her then that his alien nature, his other-worldly origin, was why she struggled so much to read him. Humans, Remnants – with either species she could detect the faintest whiff of an untruth, sometimes even when the speaker believed otherwise themselves. Von Hart remained a blank wall to her. Or perhaps a swirl of shadows, behind a curtain of smoke.

"Master – Von Hart – why are you here?"

"Your memory isn't the only thing that has grown sour," he told her, his voice dropping into a murmur. "We are not what we were. The Remnants. How long does the fruit remain ripe when cut from the branch?" He shook his head at the rhetorical question. "Oh, you should have seen us in the Old Lands. How silver, how shining we were! When the Fay branded their circles of protection in the earth to hold the dark at bay. No, none of us are what we once were, humans included. Here we stand on the doorstep of another new age, where men fight over the Middle Kingdom as though for sweets at a *kinderfest*. They are building multiple-barrel flintlock guns. Cannons that can pierce armour at eight hundred yards. There is chaos, Jia. Chaos. There are dark days ahead, child."

"I am no child." Out of all his ominous talk, this was the word that pricked her the most. "I completed my training five hundred years ago. You were there, weren't you?"

"Indeed."

She remembered that day well and sought to remind him of it, a barb hidden in her tone. But he had been muttering about chaos even then, she recalled. Chaos spreading in the land. A worm gnawing at the heart of things. Wasn't that why he'd left? Left and never come back.

Until now.

"My duty then was the same as it is now," she told him. "We do what we must to stand against the darkness."

"Even a hundred years ago, I would've agreed with you," he said. "This world has always been a candle in the dark, a blazing jewel of gods so old we cannot remember their names. Only their ghosts remain, locked in stone, buried under sand, scattered in the storm. Grand Creation! Bounded by a void both outer and inner. The starlit gulfs of space. The abyss of the nether, the Dark Frontier. And in that abyss, phantoms lurk. Beasts of pincer, tentacle and maw, whose eyes scan the infinite dark, hungry for light, searching for a way in."

"I am not afraid of the dark," she said, flinging out her arms. "And I'm a little too old for ghost stories."

"*Gut.* You will need your courage," he replied. "Don't make light of such things. The Lurkers exist and grow in power. Long ago, at the dawn of the Old Lands, when all was silver and bright and new, the Fay stamped their sigils in the earth. Great brandings, wards that stretched from mountain to sea, from ocean floor to the roots of hills, across miles of dunes to the sea again and then beyond, into the wilderness, into ice. In this way, the Fallen Ones sealed the doors of Creation, locking all the paths through the nether. Shutting the darkness out."

"Your circles of protection," she said. Despite herself, Jia looked around the room. Did she expect to see shadows in the walls, a stirring of ghosts? She might not glean the envoy's intentions, but it was obvious that he was trying to frighten her. *Why* remained unclear. Soldiers of all descriptions, British, French, Indian and Portuguese, frequented these back-street dens as much as the smugglers, most of them with an oar in the trade, but there had never been a man here as canny, as artful as the one before her. "Do you mean to trick me?" she asked. "Trap me in a fairy bargain? Extract some terrible price for your tale? We were friends once, Von Hart. You were my master. Like a father to me. But I must warn you. I am not the same doe-eyed girl that you left on the altar steps."

The envoy looked away at this, dropping his gaze. She could tell that her barb had struck home, but any triumph she might have felt evaporated when he next spoke. "And I am not the same fairy. I weaken, as the circles weaken. As the world weakens, now more than ever." His fingers danced lightly through the smoke and now, in the face of all her scorn, she *could* see shadows moving through the walls, the impression of large, hunkering shapes passing over the bamboo screens and the faded paintings, the hint of tendrils, weaving, insectile, sliding over the windows and the furniture. "It's why I left you," he said as, with a face as pale as his, she shrank back, seeking the safety of the middle of the room. "For years, I have wandered, from the Arctic Ocean to the ice shelves of Terra Australis, checking on the old boundaries, the old wards. I didn't find what I hoped to find and I have no news to cheer you. You see, magic is growing sour. Creation rots to the core and the stench of its decay seeps into the void beyond. The ghosts gather, Jia. Gather like flies to a midden heap, seeking the light, the vestiges of the ancient powers like this relic I hold in my hand. The walls grow thin. In time, hungry things will press against them, seeking a way in. Will they catch us sleeping in our beds?"

Jia shuddered. Outside, beyond the courtyard, the boom of cannons echoed down the streets, bringing her back to the here and now. A far-off rumble of collapsing brick. The roar of an engine, coals stoked by diligent hands. All the noise promised destruction and yet, in that moment, she favoured the stark reality of it over the fairy's tale of phantoms and death. And . . . what? What was he getting at? She could barely contemplate the idea.

"This is dangerous thinking," she said.

"I am no more dangerous than the ones out there. The humans. The ruling species. Let us call them what they are."

Oh, how old he looked! How pale. The realisation gnawed at her, as if his words had lifted his curtain of smoke, dispelling some of his glamour. His shoulders, a bony line, betrayed his tension, as if he danced on the edge of something he couldn't name. His sharp eyes snapped around the room, apparently to ward off the shadows, the silhouettes fading now, indistinct shapes thrown by the sunlight through the windows. How could she have thought them otherwise? But Von Hart's weariness, his sadness, was no illusion.

"I know nothing of what you speak." She forced down an unbidden pang of sympathy, her voice a fraught whisper. "Magic circles, shadows, doors . . . these things strike me as your business, not mine. Still, you came here to share more than a tale and to scratch at old scars. That much I can see. So, tell me. What do you want?"

He drew deeply on the pipe, his eyes closing as he inhaled. Even so, she felt like he was watching her, weighing her up. When he exhaled, a soft blue ring wreathed its way towards her, the sides bowing out to resemble an octagon. She batted it away with a tut.

"I mentioned the doors of Creation," he said. "In the old days, there were four of them. Think of . . . think of the Four Guardians of the Celestial Compass, the Turtle of the North, the Tiger of the West, the Phoenix of the South and the Dragon of the East. That kind of thing, *ja*?" Adopting a teacherly tone, he waited for her to roll her eyes before continuing. "From these watchtowers, these gates, the Fay looked out, guarding the world. And roads led out from these gates, Jia, great silver highways stretching off into the unformed gulfs, into the nether and beyond. Our boldest explorers would return from their voyages with wisdom and treasures untold. And sometimes a Lurker, shackled and chained . . ."

Jia's throat felt dry. "Returned from where?"

"Why from Avalon, of course. The Isle of the Apples. The Font of All Worlds. The Fay homeland. These days, the gates are no more, the roads shut. Yet one gate remains, opening onto a road that crosses a gulf so deep, so bottomless, that none dare wander there. Even I, with my most powerful spells, can only navigate this territory by manipulating what's left of the leys and sticking close to earthly bounds. And my crossing must be swift."

"You . . ." She looked at him with renewed wonder. "You would enter such a place?"

"Twice I have done so," he admitted. "On matters of life and death. To tear through the skein of reality is no mean

236

feat. The fabric of the cosmos quickly seals and you risk finding yourself on the wrong side of it. Trapped and forever lost. To keep the earthly plane and the nether joined and stable, one would need a gate."

"And what of your hungry ghosts? Wouldn't these monsters flock to such a gate like wild beasts to a watering hole?"

"Ah, you're a bright one." He nodded, impressed. "Indeed they would. Such creatures tend to avoid touching the roads, the leys themselves, repelled by the wards that protect them. But the wards decay and the ghosts grow bold. And these spells will mean nothing once the gate is opened. Unchecked, the Lurkers would pour through it into the earth, bringing catastrophe with them. One would need to . . . draw their attention away from the gate with an even greater lure. A living source of magic itself . . ."

He had lost her again, his gaze turning inward, his thoughts only for himself.

"I don't like the thought," Jia said. "It sounds wiser to keep this gate of yours shut."

He gave her a knowing look, understanding the depth of her judgement.

"You can see the danger, of course. Without the Fay around to stand guard, what could squeeze and wriggle through it, forcing their way in . . ." he said. "The Fay certainly could. Appalled as they were by human corruption, it's clear that the High House of Avalon had no wish to see the earth devoured. When the Fay left this world, my noble race destroyed the gates, these magical portals, burning them all behind them." Now his expression turned dark, his eyes shadowed, but no less watchful. "All except one."

Jia swallowed. "Go on."

"You remember the old tale, don't you? The one I told you back in Xanadu?" His tone lightened, becoming lyrical again. And again, she had the feeling that he was getting at something, edging towards a conclusion she might not like. "I told you that in the days of the Yellow Emperor, the world of men and the world of mirrors were one. You heard how the humans and the mirror children failed to live in peace and how the mirror children became locked behind glass, forever forced to echo the movements of earthly men and women."

"I do. But what's that got to do with—"

"Well, that was not the end of it," he said. "The Yellow Emperor may have imprisoned the children of the mirror, but no one said the spell would last forever. In time, little by little, some say that our reflections will begin to differ from us. A twitch there. A blink there. One day, humans will hear the clatter of weapons deep, deep in the mirror. The Ghost Emperor will stir, monstrous and pale, his mammoth limbs swimming through the darkness towards the tempting light of earth . . ."

In hundreds of years, Jia had never heard this part of the story before. For a reason that she couldn't quite put her finger on, that troubled her.

"A fascinating tale. But you still haven't answered my questions."

"Oh, but I have. More or less." Von Hart smoothed down his robe, slipping the fragment of the harp into his pocket, a signal that her audience was almost at an end. "Not far from here, on the southernmost tip of the Fan Lau peninsula, there stands an old temple. The place doesn't have a name. It's a ruin built upon a ruin, a finger of stone overlooking the Pearl River estuary. You would struggle to find a place any more remote."

"Von Hart . . ." Her patience was wearing thin.

"Come with me," he said. "Come with me now and I'll show you. There is only so much one can say with words."

"And why should I come with you?"

"To see the truth, Jia. It's time for you to choose on which side of the mirror you stand."

Her eyebrows raised at this, the bare-faced temerity of it. Had she heard him right? There was no way that he, this envoy of a lost and ancient race, a living founder of the Lore, could be asking her to question her oaths.

Could he?

"I know where I stand, Von Hart. I serve the—"

"But you miss them, don't you?" He cut her off, rounding on a point she couldn't quite see – or didn't want to. "Ziyou and Ye?" He tipped his head, regarding her with a look that held no warmth whatsoever. "Please don't tell me you've forgotten them. Of all the evils spoken here today, that would be the—"

"Fairy. Watch your tongue."

"Oh come now. Are you saying that you don't want to look into the Eight Hand Mirror again? Not even one last time?"

A flower of heat burst in her belly, spreading through her chest and neck and into her cheeks. Here he was with his own barb, striking at the heart of her. For a moment, the room seemed as vaporous as the shadows she had glimpsed in the walls, the ground under her feet less solid, less reliable than before. *Oh, to see her parents! To make sure they were all right!* Torn, Jia chewed her lip, bowing her head with the weight of the temptation. Focusing on the boom of cannons outside, she tried to summon up the Emperor's face, a reminder of her mission here, but all she saw was a sequence of masks, each one as human, as fleeting as the last. She only noticed that her fists were clenched when her nails bit into her palms, hard enough to draw blood.

Through gritted teeth, she said, "Flowers in a mirror and the moon in water." *Pleasing but unattainable.* "I know my duty. I heed the Lore. And looking into your mirror will not bring them back."

"But—"

She looked up then, fixing him with flinty eyes. "You abandoned me, Von Hart. You left me to face the ages alone, the rise and fall of dynasties. I should hate you, yet all I feel is sadness, as though at the death of a friend. All the same, I must warn you. The things you've spoken of here today, strange as they are, carry a whiff of rebellion. I am *youxia*, *sin-you*, the Guardian of the East. If you give us cause to cross swords, then I will not spare you. I want you to know that."

Silence sank between them like a stone, carrying their history down to a watery grave.

Then Von Hart laughed, as was his fashion.

"Suit yourself. Another time then."

His grin pricked Jia's patience and she answered between her teeth. "You'll wait forever in your temple, fairy. I will never come."

Von Hart sucked his pipe and exhaled again, the clouds of smoke wafting into the room.

Yes, smoke. It is all smoke. Smoke and mirrors. You can no longer trust the Fay . . .

"Oh yes, Jia," the envoy said. "You will."

When the smoke cleared, Jia was alone.

Alone.

FIFTEEN

Moggio Udinese, Italy

The Alps rose from the valley of the Fella River, a fanged border between Italy and Austria. The shield of the sky shimmered on the mountains, gilding their summits like the cloaks of elderly kings. Drifts covered the foothills. Ice webbed the rocks. All was silent and still.

When Mauntgraul alighted on the precipice, his claws sank up to his hocks, leaving car-sized prints in the snow. Shaking off a blizzard from his wings, he reared on his haunches to survey the scenery, tracing a ridge of pines, a frozen lake and a powdery road far below, sparse traffic snaking along it. The sight of the road made him snort. In his day, most had thought these mountains impassable, a raw and jagged maze.

In his day, he had missed out on his chance of revenge. And today, he would take it.

Oh, it was good to remember himself again. Good to remember the dragon. At his breast, the harp still jingled and chimed, the fragment lodged between his scales, only the tip of the harmonic curve showing. It did not matter. The threat, for the most part, had abated. Its magic weak-

242

ened somehow, grown sour. The fragment was potent yet, but he had found that he could resist its call. Reduce the bells to a background annoyance.

For now.

He had his passenger to thank for that, not that he ever would. Back in London, du Sang had led him through the Soho streets to an abandoned car park where, under a guttering street light, he had spoken to Mauntgraul at length, his tone persuasive and calm, gradually bringing him back to himself. *Wake up. Wake up and remember.* At midnight, the tramp had returned to the idea of a man. The Wandering Moor. And the Moor had thrown off the conceit in serpentine shape, the greatest, most formidable beast of his kind. The white scourge of civilisation. Slave to no one. Rivalled by nothing. King of the wyrms.

Ah, if only that was the truth.

In his aching joints, the throbbing in his skull, Mauntgraul could feel every second of his extraordinary age. The world around him continued to confound him. Sanity, although regained, was but a foothold in a slow landslide. It took a conscious effort to remain focused, to let his thoughts override the tinkling of the bells, the ceaseless murmur of the harp. The truth was – and he would rather kill than admit it – he was afraid. He had found himself hurled into a world that held no place for him, that struggled to credit his existence, let alone submit to his fearsome reputation. If his state of mind had teetered on the brink, enfeebled by centuries of slumber, the snatch of the lullaby had pushed him over the edge. His fear was not solely for the present, either; the future embodied the grist of it. Vengeance was all well and good, long overdue, fitting and deserved, but what then? He was old and he wouldn't live forever. He had seen enough to realise that a world that could not accept his existence would also not suffer it.

Knights in armour were one thing. You may be no one's slave, old wyrm, but you have been bested by the greatest foe of all. Time.

The Vicomte – du Sang honestly believed that he bore such a title – had shown him another way. A better way. In his heart, the flames of vengeance burned hotter than ever and he relished the thought of taking them to the descendants of the Curia Occultus. If nothing else, he would have recompense before the end.

Mauntgraul's tail swished back and forth, the sting on the end of it splashing green splotches on the snow. His blood was up, for he was already winning. By now, Red Ben would have died a slow and horrible death, and Maunt's mother, Rakegoyle, could rest in her watery grave. He'd had no love for the vicious old bitch, anyway. Truth be told, she'd been a wanton and selfish creature, given to violence before thought, which had probably damned them all. The last nail in the coffin of tolerance. Nevertheless, blood was blood. And Red Ben had a habit of getting in his way.

The Red and the White. Blood on snow. Old as dust.

Now the path to vengeance was clear. Du Sang had brought him back to himself. He had given him renewed purpose.

And the beauty of it is, the dragon thought with a sly grin, *I merely owe him what I was hatched to give.*

His unlikely saviour, sitting high up and straddling his withers, finally managed to speak.

"*Voilà!*" Du Sang spat chunks of ice from his mouth and

shook frost from his hair. The upper atmosphere had frozen him stiff, a rigidity that even Mauntgraul's inner heat had not been able to melt, but the curly-haired youth-who-was-far-from-young was well accustomed to the coldest of climes, namely that of unending death. He had no physical need to breathe and his eventual thawing found him ebullient. "This is the place. Didn't I tell you? Who but I could show you the way?"

Du Sang must have thought he was dismounting a horse. With a crack of hardened limbs, he swung his leg over Mauntgraul's neck and promptly fell twenty feet head-first into the snow. The White Dog watched, his long snout peeled back in a sneer, as the youth recovered himself, climbing to his feet and brushing flakes off his suit. Then, after snapping an icicle from the tip of his nose, he trudged up the rocky shelf under the canopy of Mauntgraul's wing and leant against his foreleg as if it were a tree. Mauntgraul resisted the urge to shake the youth off, send him spinning over the precipice and down the mountainside, two hundred feet to the road below. But what was the point? Did the Vicomte even experience pain? Because . . .

"I see a high pass, boy. An ocean of snow. And my eyesight is somewhat keener than yours."

In summer, this place would be a tapestry of meadows rippling with flowers, thick woodlands of ash and pine, all a hale green in the sun. In winter, it was a silent land, dead and buried. One peak looked much like another.

"*Au contraire*, my gargantuan friend." Du Sang was obviously enjoying being useful. "Doesn't your little trinket give you a clue?"

Mauntgraul, firmly set on ignoring the fragment lodged in his breast, cringed as he gave the relic a mental glance. A fierce silver light washed over his mind, as keen as a vulture sighting fresh meat. The harp, he noticed, was restless and warm, clearly agitated by the location. A cacophony flourished in the White Dog's skull, and with a growl he pushed the noise away, back into his forgetting. To focus on the fragment too long, to allow the lullaby to slip through the cracks of his self-control, was to invite the pageant to start up again in all its demented glory.

His irritation was curdling into anger. He still couldn't see anything but snow.

"The pieces of the harp call to each other," du Sang said. "All *lunewrought* is one metal and the artefact longs to be whole. Even the splinters carry the Fay enchantment, able to trap and bind. Don't you see? You could've searched the whole world looking for it, from Tasmania to Svalbard and back again. I have brought you straight to the doorstep. The Cardinal conspires within, awaiting your fiery judgement."

Mauntgraul was glad that the boy pointed. He would've hated to have to ask. He followed du Sang's bone-white finger up from the valley and into the peaks. Up to the highest summit, a shark's tooth rising a mile or two away. At first he could see nothing except a spur of rock, jutting from the steep face of the mountain. Squinting, he picked out signs of habitation even as the Vicomte spoke.

"The Invisible Church," he said. "Not so invisible now, yes? The monastery dates back to Roman times, a watchtower built to overlook this valley. In time, the watchtower became a temple for Benedictine monks, or so the history books would have us believe. We know better, do we not? Up there lies the secret headquarters of the Whispering Chapter."

A draconic appetite brought the monastery sharply into focus. Mauntgraul spied the stretch of a boundary wall, a turret, a bell tower, a domed shrine hanging four thousand feet above the valley floor. From a distance, the place looked abandoned, a medieval ruin, the sheer slopes rendering it unreachable on foot.

That suited Mauntgraul fine. His fangs were showing again, revealing his pleasure.

"I can smell their devotion from here."

His wings shivered, becoming taut, a small avalanche pouring off the ledge and into the gorge below. Claws digging for purchase, he prepared to launch himself into the blue. A furious heat blazed in his belly, spitting emerald sparks. Fresh poison brewed in his glands, rising into the barbed sac on the tip of his tail. His eyes flared, as black as his intentions.

Du Sang waved his arms. "Wait!"

Snow shifted, rock crunching as the White Dog stalled on the precipice. He snorted, the frosty air crackling in the ensuing heat haze. When his head swung around, a pale horror of steer-like horns, du Sang stiffened, frozen again, this time with anticipation.

Mauntgraul's enquiry, soft as it was, came in a hiss of overstretched patience.

"Yesss?"

Du Sang, a porcelain doll under the dragon's gaze, managed to find his voice.

"Forgive me, *monsieur*. Has something perhaps . . . slipped your mind? We had an arrangement. I believe I have upheld my end of it."

Mauntgraul tipped his head, a boulder rolling to one side. The youth with the curly brown hair and the dandy clothes puzzled him somewhat, not least of all with his strange request. He looked hungry again, the dragon noticed, his cheeks sallow and drawn, his eyes dull. The creature under his skin was emerging, throwing off his murderous blush of health, much like du Sang might throw off a coffin lid in whichever pit he chose to sleep. Or perhaps he felt the touch of the sun, shrivelling his hard yet enervated flesh. Du Sang was a dead thing. Long, long dead. His request was beyond a mercy.

"Ah yes. And quite the bargain, too. I came to learn of the Chapter's whereabouts – how do you people say? – *bon marché?*" *And you brought me back to myself.* But that was something he would not say. He peered down at the Vicomte. "You're certain that this is what you want?"

Du Sang coughed behind his hand as if they were dickering over the matter of a bill in a Belleville restaurant.

"*Monsieur*, please."

"Very well. Come here. Closer to the edge."

A touch theatrically, Le Vicomte Lambert du Sang did as instructed, his spine straightening as he pulled down his jacket, his chin lifting to the sky. Thankfully, he refrained from launching into a speech. The boy took a moment, drinking in the frigid meander of the river, the road through the pass and the ridge of pines, as pretty as a Yuletide woodcut. Then he looked up and gave a small nod.

Who knows what goes through his cobwebbed mind? Who cares? A promise is a promise.

Wings spread, Mauntgraul reared back on the ledge, drew in a tremendous breath and spewed livid green flames down at the youth.

Du Sang screamed, but Mauntgraul fancied there was joy in the sound. *Release.* A prickle of envy caught him by surprise as he watched the Vicomte's hair crisp and curl, his clothes blasting from his limbs in tatters, his skin bubbling before shrivelling to black. Echoes replaced his delighted anguish. A jumble of bones, charred and strung together by sinew, slumped off the precipice, spinning down to the pristine valley in a thin spiral of smoke.

De rien . . .

The White Dog gave the youth no further thought. Joy leapt in his own heart, tongues of emerald flame. At his breast, the fragment of the harp throbbed and glittered, chiming in the hope of reunion. Roaring to drown out the sickly-sweet song, a battle cry to shake the mountainside, Mauntgraul plunged off the ledge, his wings straddling the Alpine wind. Gaining altitude between the peaks, the dragon banked, his midnight eyes settling on the monastery.

Time to prey . . .

Five minutes later, at the foot of the mountain, a spindly black shape hauled itself out of the drifts. A scarecrow crawling out of a bonfire, it left a sooty furrow in the snow. Skeletal hands clutched weakly at the ground, fingernails snapping like twigs. Inch by inch, the thing dragged a broken cargo behind it into the blinding daylight, a tangled necklace of spine, ribcage and pelvis. A grinning, carbonised skull creaked wearily in the direction of the pass.

"Shit," it said.

SIXTEEN

When will you learn?

Dawn squeezed through the arrow slit high in the wall, falling on the huddled form of Red Ben Garston. The cell, best described as a stone box, contained a basin, a bunk and a hole in the floor that served as a latrine. Ben, sitting with his head in his hands, took up most of the space. When he stood up to stretch, every hour or so, his shoulders only left a couple of feet to the walls on either side. And despite the swift healing of his cuts and bruises, he couldn't wash the taste of blood from his mouth. Or the ache from his soul. For the last two days, True Names had come and dragged him to a larger cell, where they employed an inventive array of knives, irons, acid, drills and, worst of all, several versions of the same old question, repeated again and again.

Where is Blaise Von Hart?
Where can we find the envoy extraordinary?
Tell us where he hides his fragment of the harp.

Later, exasperated and growing sick of him, the True Names dragged him back to his cell and locked him in. One of them shoved a tray through the bars. A bowl of porridge, some bread and milk. A feast for a sparrow, not a dragon.

The little cell reeked of urine and sweat. The air was thin, telling him that he languished at some altitude. If a natural heat hadn't run through his veins, retained even in human shape, he was sure the nights would've seen him freeze to death.

Why did you even listen to her?

He thought he knew the answer to that. He could tell himself that Jia had given him purpose, reminding him of his Pact. After all, she had spurred him to warn the Guild of the Broken Lance about the unleashed dragon and this Ghost Emperor of hers. But that was only on the surface. Had it been the sadness in her eyes, her veiled sorrow a mirror to his own? Or perhaps it was loneliness, blinding him to her true intentions? Because even now, something didn't quite add up. Much like the harp, all he had was fragments, pieces of a larger puzzle that he was struggling to click into place. No one would ever call him Sherlock. Instead, he had found himself hoodwinked and captured, placed on death row. As he stood in his cell with a *lune-wrought* collar locked around his throat, maybe he even thought he deserved it. Lord knows, the *sin-you*, this paragon of justice and the Lore, had nothing nice to say about him. And sarcasm aside, she had probably spoken the truth.

Who is the real enemy here? Me?

He couldn't even cut his losses; he had nothing left to lose. The Sister might have violated his lair, but he couldn't say he mourned the wrecking of the house. The place had always been a mask, an empty shell, and it was highly unlikely that anyone – either the True Names or the fire brigade – was going to dig through the rubble and break into the

252

caves under the building. If anyone made it past the protective enchantments, they would discover the haul of the century, of course, but for now Barrow Hill Road was the least of his concerns.

What does the Chapter want with the harp? Yeah, I think you know the answer to that one too. Re-forged, the artefact does only one of two things . . .

The Chapter wasn't taking any chances, it seemed. Unconscious, possibly drugged, he had been bundled away from London (he recalled a vague dream of rotors chopping at the air) and up into the mountains somewhere, the Sister removing the manacle and replacing it with the *lunewrought* collar. A canny move, he thought. Unlike his hand on the oil rig, he wasn't about to cut off his own head in order to escape. The silver restraint burned coldly against his flesh, tingling with a subtle magical force. It was a constant source of irritation, as if fingers lightly tickled his neck. The collar might look brittle enough, but the metal was stronger than any on earth, forged as it was from the splinters of the *Cwyth*, the mnemonic harp.

Back in the day, the Curia Occultus had learnt of the *lunewrought*'s legendary power. The Fay metal was anathema to Remnants, a nullifier of transformation and a dampener of ability, much like iron to fairies and garlic to vampires. Over the years, Ben had heard about the odd Remnant captured by the Chapter, rumours of interrogation, even torture, although of course, the Guild of the Broken Lance firmly denied the latter. No one had asked too many questions. In 1215, the Pope had insisted on the Chapter's inclusion on the Curia Occultus and the cult had hidden behind a wall of holy smoke ever since, much the same as any world religion. And, of course, its reputation relied and fed on fear . . .

Still, Ben couldn't deny that some Remnants needed discipline from time to time, sometimes even punishment. And on the rare occasion, he had found himself ordered to deal with them. A part of his oath.

Your love for humans has murdered us all.

Discomforted, he tugged at his collar. The slightest touch and the *lunewrought* throbbed and drew tighter, constricting until he took his hand away. Without the collar, he could've torn his cell apart like orange peel. The Sister had bound him in man form, the red stubble of his shaven head lending him a brutish appearance, one that echoed his mood. His draconic genes glowed in his stomach, an aggrieved and disconsolate heat, his strength and his fire held in check.

Likewise, he was trapped here with his guilt. There was no escape from it. The creeping dread that Mauntgraul was right.

Rakegoyle, Gard, a handful of others . . .

All Remnants fallen by his hand. Fallen to preserve the Pact. *Murdered?* Could anyone call it that? Had his love of humans blinded him so much? His rose-tinted glasses had shattered last year and the frames remained bent out of shape. Had he chosen the wrong side, all those centuries ago? He could've rebelled, rallied the Remnants and taken his fury to the Curia Occultus, fighting for his place in things, his right to exist. Or going down in the flames of freedom . . .

Von Hart. The fucking fairy convinced you otherwise . . .

And still he had given the True Names nothing. As far as information went, he had little to give. The location of Club Zauber remained firmly locked behind his lips.

Ben groaned, rubbing his head. The harpies of doubt circled in his mind, scratching and biting. *Remember. Remember what those Remnants did.* A burning bridge. Devoured people . . .

Traitor . . .

Ben screwed up his face, trying to force Mauntgraul out of his skull. The harpies cackled.

The Pact. Was it really all for nothing?

Noise outside his cell startled him out of his self-reproach. Several footsteps, three or four guards coming down the corridor, the unmistakable clanking of keys.

But for once, the True Names weren't coming for him.

Two of the guards carried Jia between them, supporting her weight, her bare feet dragging on the flagstones. At her back, another True Name ushered them on with a raised gun, an absurd precaution considering the state of the *sin-you*. Strands of hair hung in her face, her long braid half undone. Blood smeared the front of her suit, black on green, and as the agents shoved her into the cell opposite Ben's, slamming and locking the door, he caught the glint of the manacle around her wrist, binding her just like him.

A True Name obscured his vision, a leer spread across his lips.

"We'll be back for you, wyrm. The hour of judgement is at hand."

Ben muttered under his breath, too weary to argue, his concern – his ire – focused on the woman in the cell opposite.

Disappointed, the True Name retreated, leaving the two of them alone.

Ben allowed Jia a minute to get herself together, to realise that her ordeal was over. He knew only too well what they'd put her through and he could see that her assistance with his capture hadn't won her any friends or spared her from interrogation. She smoothed back her hair and pulled herself up on her bunk, her spine straightening, the usual composure. But he could see how she trembled, the pain running through her, barely restrained. He could see her shackled hand clench and unclench, revealing her resentment. Her face was lost in shadow, her breaths heavy and slow. None of these sights prompted his sympathy. Nor did they hold his anger in check.

"So you got me out in the open to draw the Chapter," he said, keeping his voice low, a heated grumble. For all he knew, the True Names were listening, wanted them to talk. "Smart move. Did you think the Cardinal would thank you? Give you a medal? Whatever's going on here, it's bad news for Remnants. And that means you, honey."

She said nothing to this, silence spinning out between them.

"Your plan was clumsy. It stinks of desperation," he told her. "But I'm not as stupid as I look. That whole fight business on the train was a set-up, wasn't it? Ditto healing me. A way to get into my good books, to obligate me. I reckon you knew the Chapter wanted my head in the first place. And if you knew the Chapter wanted my head, then you probably knew why. And let me take another wild guess here. Someone must've told you about it."

Someone.

Again, silence.

Ben banged the bars of his cell.

"Well, you got what you wanted. A free three-night stay at the Invisible Church. And when we check out, we'll check out forever. Is that your idea of justice? Nice one!"

She looked at him then, her eyes sharp. The bruise around one of them shoved his anger back at him, curdling with his guilt. But the sight of her injury didn't catch him off guard half as much as her question, spoken softly yet painfully clear.

"What do you recall of your mother and father, Ben?"

"My mother and fa— What?"

She didn't repeat it, meeting his scorn with the same maddening calm.

"These questions you ask are a mirror," she said, "reflecting your own truth. But for you, the glass remains black. You simply don't want to see. You prefer the comfort of lies."

"I don't see how it's any of your business, lady."

"Walls," she said. "Smoke and mirrors. You know the truth as well as I do. It's just too hard to swallow."

Christ. She's a pain in the arse.

"What the fuck are you getting at? You know, we don't have time for these games."

So she told him. "*The Remnants are dropping like flies.* Isn't that what you said?" Her voice was barely a whisper, her gaze unblinking, steady. Full of sadness, he saw, rather than judgement. "You might as well tell me. This is probably the last time we'll speak. What were their names? Can you even remember their faces?"

"Ah, shut the hell up."

He turned his back on her, another wall. But he was hiding his own surge of sorrow, bubbling under his rage. The truth was, she spoke to the heart of his fear, plucking his despair from him like grey thread from a black pillow. These doubts had been with him all along, right from the start. Small surprise that Jia shared them. If he'd needed any confirmation, du Sang had shown him the present state of the Remnants in Paris, the inflexible nature of the Pact. How stupid they'd been. How naïve! They'd been sold a fairy tale to end all fairy tales. How they'd eaten it up.

One shining day, when Remnants and humans learn to live in peace, and magic blossoms anew in the world, then shall the Fay return and commence a new golden age.

Cut to the present day and most of the Remnants had given up, accepting that the Fay would never return, their reward for signing the Pact a slow march to extinction. Over time, the false promise, the hollow hope had worked like an acid, its corrosive nature gnawing at the heart of things. Wasn't that the way it went? The Lore had shaken in the face of that despair, he thought, shaken and fallen apart. Honour. Duty. Faith. Were these the comforting lies Jia meant? He believed so. And he hated to admit it, but she was right. After years of living under the Lore, he could hardly bear to face the truth.

And, yes, he remembered her. Jynnyflamme, the spawn of Pennydrake. Jynnyflamme. The Sun Tear.

Among his kind, draconic sires tended to remain faceless, a passing wyrm on a few nights' mating, blood and fire crashing through the trees. The female of the species bore the eggs and, once laid, the custom was to then abandon them – in a cave, beside a lake, deep in a Marches forest . . .

It was up to the hatchling to grow and find his or her mother, thus proving the will to survive and thereby earning the ancient teachings of dragonkind. Once upon a time, Ben had made that journey himself. He'd been distracted, heartsick, grieving. And his mother had welcomed him in the Great Forest to commence his training, to kick and to claw the weakness out of him.

He remembered her, all right. He remembered saying goodbye.

"The Chapter welcomes our destruction, Ben," Jia said. "The world has forgotten its true nature. To the humans, we are myths, as good as dead. The circles are breaking, drawing an army of hungry eyes. But the war was over centuries ago. The Ghost Emperor merely comes to sweep up the pieces. Nothing more."

"Is that what you told the True Names? Your mission of warning."

"Yes. But the Cardinal will not listen, as you say. Driven by blind faith, the Chapter opens its arms to a cataclysm. And now it is too late. I have failed."

He spun back to her, letting his anger override the sight of the tears rolling down her face.

"To get to the harp? You still haven't told me why you want the damn thing."

"You think it's safer in the Chapter's hands?"

This checked him for a second. He had seen the ruins of Paladin's Court and the True Names present at the site. He had no way of knowing if the Chapter already had its hands on another fragment, the harmonic curve of the harp. As for Mauntgraul . . . he was reasonably sure that the dragon wouldn't lay a claw on *lunewrought*, even if his wake of destruction happened to turn up the artefact. Its power would frighten him, surely. The last thing he'd want was to find himself bound all over again.

Ben realised that this was a faint hope. Vexed, he said, "That isn't an answer. But you know what, Jia? I'm bored of this. It's pretty obvious why you're after it. The harp is kind of a one-trick pony. If you're planning to do what I think you are, let me tell you now that it's a very bad idea." He swallowed, compassion twisting his voice into an awkward growl. "Why won't you let me help you?"

"I told you. I have no choice."

"And you're afraid I'll try to stop you, isn't that right? You've got your doubts, the same as I do."

"No. I have seen the truth."

He snorted, letting her know that he wasn't a complete fool. "The Ghost Emperor."

Jia met this with silence. She shook her head at some private thought, throwing off something he couldn't read. Some uncomfortable secret, if he knew secrets at all.

"Do you honestly expect me to trust you?" Ben said. "After the stunt you pulled at Paladin's Court?"

She raised her chin a little. "I am Jia Jing, the appointed judge of the court of Kublai Khan, Guardian of the East, Keeper of the—"

"Yeah, yeah. And a former student of Blaise Von Hart," he reminded her.

As soon as he said it, a thought struck him, a flash of

insight so bright that he couldn't believe he hadn't seen it before. In all the events since she'd come bursting into his life, challenging the White Dog on top of the train – appearing so conveniently, he'd noted, in such a way as to gain his trust – he'd missed the most vital clue dangling under his nose.

"Christ, that's it," he said. "You were using me as a stepping stone to get to the Chapter and the harp. But you knew exactly when and where to step, right? Someone had to have told you."

Someone.

"Ben . . ."

It had been there all along, right in front of him. The missing envoy. The Chapter's hunt. That weird message in the fortune cookie back in Paris, conjured up now to confirm his fears, his blood running cold at the thought.

When the time comes, let me fall.

"Jesus. It's a matter of basic maths. One plus one equals two." He laughed, but there was no humour in it. "You probably assumed that the Chapter had nabbed the Guild's fragment of the harp, confiscated the relic during its takeover. And if you came here after the neck and the soundboard, then you must've been reasonably confident of securing the pillar, the third and final piece. Jia, that can only mean one thing."

He grinned, a savage leer of pride. But the *sin-you* didn't look remotely impressed.

"You're a quick learner," she said, in a tone that conveyed that she didn't think that at all.

"You're on no mission of mercy. You're on a raid. And

261

you don't seem to care who gets hurt along the way. I hate to break it to you, but the White Dog won't stop killing. He won't stop smashing shit up. Did you think about that before the envoy went and woke him up?"

Jia looked away, gazing into space.

"Time has taught us other lessons," she said, half to herself. "The value of sacrifice. The price of the truth."

Ben wasn't listening to her.

"Von Hart," he said. "You know where he is, don't you?"

It made sense. She'd lied about her mission, so why wouldn't she lie about her loyalties? As far as Ben knew, Von Hart still had the final fragment of the harp in his possession – but Jia hadn't seemed dead set on finding him, focusing her efforts on the Guild and the Chapter. He'd suspected her complicity back in Barrow Hill Road; her subsequent treachery only cemented the uncomfortable notion. She wasn't working alone. And unlike the envoy, Ben knew that he himself was far from inscrutable. Von Hart must have counted on the fact that he would come to China to challenge Mauntgraul, face down his old rival. That was his duty as the Sola Ignis, after all. The envoy had known that the Chapter wanted his head. Was it such a stretch that the fairy would've sent his student to him, a way to get to the Invisible Church and thus the harp by luring him out into plain sight? Yeah. It sounded like Von Hart, all right.

"And he's still your master, isn't he?"

Before she could reply, a familiar clanking echoed down the passageway, breaking off the chance of further conversation. Frustrated, Ben thumped the bars of his cell again, watching the *sin-you* retreat into shadow, apparently awaiting her fate. Another Remnant giving up.

The face of a True Name eclipsed his vision, the same old leer, the same raised guns. One of the guards fumbled with the keys.

It was too late to get to the truth. The hour of judgement had arrived.

SEVENTEEN

"And the great dragon was cast out, that old serpent who deceiveth the whole world: he was cast down into the earth and his angels were cast down with him."

The words rang out around the walls of the chamber, under the watchful eyes of the saints. Kneeling on the platform in the middle of the temple-cum-courtroom, manacles around his wrists and heavy iron chains binding him to the floor, Ben craned his neck to see them, the looming statues circling the space. His judges and jury. The arched windows, open to the air, had not been kind to the sculptures, the ebb and flow of countless seasons weathering their sombre, hooded faces, eroding crook, halo and sword. Cracks riddled their granite robes.

To his regret, Ben recognised most of them. There was St Margaret of Antioch, who'd been swallowed by a dragon but managed to rip her way out of its belly with her crozier, her staff encrusted with jewels. Then there was St Columba, who was said to have wrestled the Loch Ness monster. St Marcellus, the bane of vampires. St Gildas, who had struck off the head of a giant. St Benedict, who'd bested the devil himself. Swords of God, heroes all, bringing righteous slaughter to the demons in their midst. Ben would've rolled his eyes if his own fabled head wasn't resting on the block. In this case, quite literally.

He considered the block, a square granite lump with a well-worn groove stained a telltale pink, as the Cardinal continued her sermon.

The new Cardinal, Evangelista de Gori – that was how one of the True Names had announced her when she'd entered the chamber – prompted an inward groan from Ben. As she took the high lectern overlooking the court, he realised that he'd already made her acquaintance. Despite her lofty title, she made no concession to ostentation. Her dress, a shin-length one-piece, hung off her frame like the wing of a moth, blending with the sombre surroundings. She was as skinny as a leaf-stripped branch, her hair scraped back into a ponytail, enhancing the cut of her cheekbones, her sharp, no-nonsense nose. The left side of her face slumped somewhat, the palsied nerves disclosing some past seizure or other. Her scars had the odd effect of softening her by a degree, the way in which she bore them conveying a spine of strength. How anyone so elderly and plain could seem so formidable escaped him, but formidable she was. She was also the old woman from the North Sea oil rig.

"This revelation, brothers and sisters," she went on, "was given to St John of Patmos centuries ago, warning us of the end. Warning us to stay vigilant. As we have done from the founding of the Pact to this day, when we seek our absolution."

De Gori stood at the lectern, her spiderlike hands clasping the sides of a gigantic bible, her face turned up to the stained-glass oriels in the roof, the light painting her scars a deep and appropriate red. Flecks of spittle at the corners of her mouth informed Ben that the Italian doyenne was enjoying every moment of her triumph.

"The end comes," she said, "for all imps, grotesques and serpents. They are *abominations*! The children of Lucifer. Demons sent to deceive us. All that comes from the Fay perversion is ruin. These Remnants are a poison in the heart of Creation." She gathered her breath. "Too long have we suffered the compromise, forced to tolerate the evil among us. All we have learnt is that the truly devout cannot make deals with the devil."

This doesn't sound good.

The drab figures lining the tiers of benches around him murmured in assent. How they basked in the Cardinal's fervour! Since that day in 1215 when King John had pressed his seal to the Pact, the Chapter, in all fairness, had found itself facing its own hard part of the bargain, its dream of a holy inquisition outvoted. And even the Pope hadn't deigned to press the matter. England had been tearing itself apart at the seams as it was, teetering on the brink of civil war.

In the following years, the Chapter had faded into history, seemingly content to let the Guild administer and direct the Lore. In hindsight, Ben realised that the older had only been waiting for its chance to seize control, enforce the Lore with an iron rod.

So it came as no surprise to him to see such glee in the Cardinal's eyes, greeting this eventual hour of conquest.

She's on a bloody crusade. She favours the old values, that's what she said. And the old values mean dark days ahead. Oh joy.

"Draco Benjurigan," she said, peering down at him. "Sola Ignis. Remnant and sinner. The Chapter finds you guilty of breaking the Lore."

Ben could barely stand to look at her, this grey spindle of zealous contempt. De Gori was twice the fool if she'd chosen to ignore Jia's warning about the Ghost Emperor, as it appeared she had. Why would she listen to demons? But long-dead saints wouldn't help her when the giant phantom slipped its tentacles through a crack in reality and tore down the fucking walls. Of course, the Cardinal probably wanted that to happen – Jia had told him as much – seeing the coming apocalypse as justification for a life spent on her knees, nibbling on wafers and sipping piss-weak wine.

Ben had met her type before, one too many times. Few things in the world were as blind as faith. As far as slaughter was concerned, it was the best excuse going.

Thinking of Jia, he glanced at the *sin-you* on the bench below him, shackled like himself by *lunewrought*, the manacle around her wrist. A True Name sat on either side of her, guarding her slumped and dishevelled form, her braid loosely tied, her suit bloodstained. Her face was a moon, distant and sad, her eyes downcast, veiled by lashes.

He sent her a silent message.

Any tricks up your sleeve, now would be a good time to play them.

The Cardinal could preach about the end until the cows came home. Either way, Ben reckoned it was the end of the road for him.

On the other side of the chamber, straight-backed, scarred and as visibly pleased with herself as the Cardinal, sat the

Sister. Her cross-shaven rock of a head was tilted to the lectern, but her adoration didn't soften her brutish appearance. She wore the same washed-out military fatigues, but she had dispensed with her sickle and her other array of weaponry. The Arimathean Shield remained strapped to her back, her broad shoulders dwarfed by the relic.

Ben had to content himself with the sight of her arm in a sling and her melted boot soles on the cold stone tier. It was too late for payback now. Broken bones or no, she had vanquished him good and proper – with a little unexpected help, of course. He caught furtive sneers and muttered curses from the other True Names gathered around him. He hadn't won any popularity contests here. And Jia was vastly outnumbered, even if she'd wanted to mount a rescue, which he somehow doubted. Hadn't he served his purpose? If, as he suspected, the envoy was behind her quest for the harp, he obviously hadn't deemed Ben trustworthy or jaded enough to let him in on the game.

Still, that damn message in the fortune cookie. What the hell did it mean?

Looking over at the *sin-you*, he could see her despair, her subterfuge hitting a brick wall, her warning falling on deaf ears. Or rather on *expectant* ears, those of a Cardinal with spread arms, welcoming the End of All Things. What were you supposed to do with that?

"On the count of un-Loreful transformations into Remnant form, whereby humans may have witnessed and recorded said transformations, this court finds the accused guilty."

"Guilty," the assembled conclave murmured as one.

Ben snarled. *About that . . .*

"On the count of acting without due recourse to the Curia Occultus, failure to inform our agents of the Bardolfe conspiracy last year, this court finds the accused guilty."

"Guilty," said the True Names.

I saved your fucking arses.

Cardinal de Gori cleared her throat. Was that a smile on her lips? Hard to tell.

"On the count of un-Lorefully coupling with a human – the most depraved of the crimes listed here today – this court finds the accused—"

"Guilty! Guilty! Guilty!"

The gathering rose to its feet, the hollow intonation ringing between the statues and pillars like an incoming tide. The chorus of voices surrounded Ben on the platform, a whirlpool threatening to suck him down. He clung onto his shock like a raft, straining to stare up at the Cardinal, her revelation shattering his hope like a bullet through porcelain.

Rose. They know about Rose.

It made perfect sense, of course. He'd been a fool to think he could get away with it, his brief, clumsy romance, when the Coven Royal had kidnapped Rose, making her central to their plans. Just how long had the Chapter been watching him, waiting for him to slip up? He wondered what evidence had been presented during his trial *in absentia*. Photographs? Film clips? Recorded telephone calls? He reckoned the lot.

And what did it matter anyway? This was nothing more than a show trial, he knew, masking his murder because he refused to surrender Von Hart. The formalities were for the *sin-you*'s benefit, surely – she certainly loved her protocol, even if she was playing the quisling, withholding the truth of affairs. When his head went rolling across the platform, it would simply serve to force a confession, inform her that she was next . . .

The Cardinal was obviously elated, the stained glass illuminating her scars. The damaged tissue held a pearly sheen as she turned her face skyward to remind all present of his damnation.

"Know that before God and the King and the knights of this realm, no Remnant spared the Sleep and bestowed the freedom of these Lands shall beget issue of like kind, nor influence, adopt or otherwise endow others into their fold. Since we have granted all these things, for the better order of our kingdom and to allay the discord between us, any Remnant found in breach of this clause shall face swift and lawful execution . . ."

The Cardinal knew about Rose. Didn't it stand to reason that the Chapter also knew of her whereabouts? And if de Gori knew of Rose's whereabouts, then that meant his one-time lover was once again in danger. His *child* was in danger.

Stay away. From me. From us.

Ben's roar, choked as it was by his collar, still cut through the chanting of the crowd. Cardinal de Gori, satisfied that her barb had hit home, slapped her hands down on the bible as though to shake condemnation from the pages. He refused to look at her, to let her see his distress.

And more immediate concerns were pressing their case, the *lunewrought* collar growing tighter, the enchanted metal

270

responding to some unseen signal, some controlling charm.

De Gori leant forward and unwrapped something from the lectern before her. At first, Ben couldn't see what it was, but the silvery light washing over her face told him that she'd brought her fragment of the harp to proceedings. Then she lifted the soundboard, her fingers stroking the ghostly strings, a stark tinkling in the air.

The *lunewrought* collar answered, drawing tighter.

"Garston's death will serve as our sacrifice," she said. "We beseech the saints for their aid. We will find the other fragments of the harp, see the devil's instrument made whole. We will bring the fallen fairy before us and compel him to sing us a new song. To change the music of sleep into the music of death."

Ben looked up, watching de Gori's spit pepper the air as she reached the zenith of her plans, revealing an ambition that had carried her over the edge of fervour and into fanaticism. Madness.

"Scripture makes no bones about monsters," she told the court. "Brothers and sisters, we are True Names. Souls native to earth. Together we will be the scourge to cleanse the world. The grandest of all inquisitions!"

Same old story. Ben strained against his bonds to no avail. Cold silver burned his neck, squeezing his Adam's apple. *But if the Chapter doesn't have the harmonic curve, then it must still be in the Guild's keeping. And fairy, much as I'd love to kick your arse, for now you had better stay hidden . . .*

To de Gori, he managed to croak out, "Over my dead body."

She ignored him. The chains around his wrists clanked

taut, a cog under the floor beginning to turn, dragging him forward inch by inch, his head sinking towards the block. Gasping, he understood his fate. Axes were so last year. So *yesteryear*. Lungs fit to burst, he knew that the collar was only going to squeeze tighter and tighter, eventually slicing through flesh and bone, cutting off his head.

Stage goes dark. Audience applauds. No chance of an encore . . .

Grunting, he wedged his knees against the chopping block and grabbed the chains snaking from his manacles, pulling as hard as he could. Veins stood out on his neck, saliva foaming between his teeth, but the under-floor wheel creaked on regardless, his chin touching stone. The *lunewrought* collar had curbed his strength, dousing his inner fire. To all intents and purposes, he was bound here as a man. Incapable of ripping the chains apart.

The butterflies were fluttering again, black flowers spinning before his eyes. Blood drummed in his ears, a forlorn tattoo welcoming him to the land of death. *So many friends waiting to meet you!* He could hear de Gori ranting above him, some screed about sacrifice and fire, rising to the vaulted ceiling and echoing, echoing into a scream . . .

As the scaling cry raced around the chamber, the congregation erupted in panic. The butterflies before Ben's eyes spread their wings in the real world, a cloak thrown over the windows, everything falling into shadow. The chains stopped clanking, growing slack, and by degrees, he felt the *lunewrought* collar loosening, his beheading cut short.

Before he had a chance to draw a hungry breath, a cloud of shattering brick exploded all around him. The floor tipped to one side, the flagstones flying apart like an upended board game, the chopping block a ball and chain swinging from his wrists. Arms wheeling, he slid backwards on his island of rock, the platform pitching in the chaos, a cry flying from his throat.

Shielding his eyes from the billowing dust, he saw a row of pillars caving inwards, the statues in the alcoves toppling. St Margaret wasn't digging her way out of this one. St Benedict was going straight to hell. The looming figures collapsed in sections, swallowed by the sundering floor.

The next moment, the arched windows followed them, the entire valley-facing wall of the temple ripped away by some tremendous force. Like a shipwrecked sailor, Ben clung onto the platform for dear life. A mighty wind rushed into the temple, hurling snow and grit. The True Names scattered, scrabbling away from the crumbling tiers, seeking safer ground.

In the haze, Ben couldn't see any sign of Jia, the *sin-you* lost in the storm. But he could see de Gori high up on her lectern, turning to greet her unexpected guest with a joyous expression and spread arms.

"See? See? An angel comes, answering my call. And he has brought a fragment of the harp!"

It was no angel. Despite the shadow of white wings, his terrible arrival, there was nothing holy about the newcomer. His long, bladed tail snapped out, lashing the chamber like a whip.

Distracted by his imminent death, Ben hadn't sensed the dragon's approach. There was no mistaking his presence now.

273

Mauntgraul, the White Dog, had found his way to the Invisible Church.

The monastery, perched high up on the mountain, shuddered on crumbling foundations. Pinnacles snapped and fell like darts. Gargoyles took to the air, their frozen wings carrying them down. With a mournful clang, the bell tower crumpled. Buttresses budged and cracked, unable to withstand the barrage of the twelve-ton beast.

Wings spread and level, keeping his bulk aloft, Mauntgraul made swift work of the wall, giving himself room to alight. As soon as he did, he reached out a claw for the Cardinal, his splayed talons dwarfing the lectern.

In response, de Gori raised the soundboard before her, once again strumming the strings. Silver light washed out, setting fire to Mauntgraul's eyes. Roaring, he recoiled from the music, the sickening yet pleasurable melody offering sleep and death.

The temple was a shifting archipelago of stone. The chamber rocked and rumbled with the impact, the dragon's retreat sending chunks of architecture crashing over the precipice and down into the valley below. True Names went with them, wailing their final prayers.

To Ben's surprise, Mauntgraul, fangs locked, turned back to the lectern. Approaching through the clouds of dust, the White Dog barged his way into the monastery proper. Or rather the heap of rubble where the boundary wall had once stood, a pulverised, smoking mess. Neck coiling back, his diadem of horns gored the roof, timber and plaster raining down.

It was then that Ben noticed the object tucked between

the scales of the White Dog's breast, the unmistakable gleam of *lunewrought*, the harmonic curve of the harp. The sight confirmed his worst fears. He had hoped beyond hope that Mauntgraul had sought the Guild out solely to take revenge, praying that the order had hidden its fragment well, away from prying eyes.

Can't those knights do anything right?

He should've known better. Mauntgraul, for all his brawn, was no fool. No doubt during his attack on Paladin's Court he had stolen the piece of the *Cwyth* in the Guild's keeping and somehow made his way here. But how?

Ben thought he knew. The harp was all of a piece, bound by one enduring charm. As he'd discovered first hand, the *lunewrought* responded to the proximity of its other scattered parts. Even the collar around his throat was tingling and throbbing, answering the call of its other-worldly source. And above him, it seemed that the two fragments, the one at Mauntgraul's breast and the one in de Gori's grip, looked blurry and distorted in the light, stretching slightly, yearning to join.

Unlike Paladin's Court, the Invisible Church had never advertised its location, particularly not to the Remnant world. Someone must have told Mauntgraul where to find the Chapter. Someone with an ear for whispers, with the command of a million spies . . .

It occurred to him then – seeing as the Chapter had trapped him in human form and in the middle of a collapsing building to boot – that this probably wasn't the best time to draw the dragon's attention. What was he going to do? Fight? It'd be like attacking a shark with an egg whisk.

Before he could stop himself, he was shouting into the chaos, the *wyrm tongue* flying from his throat.

Mauntgraul reared back, his claw closing a foot away from the Cardinal's head. A horrible pendulum, his snout swung around, seeking the source of the interruption. Ben saw the mania shining in his eyes, the same unhinged and troubled glow that he'd witnessed in Beijing. For all the White Dog's strength, he was clearly not himself, but Ben took no satisfaction in the sight, whatever slaughter he hoped to bring.

Noticing Ben, his eyes flared like black suns.

"You!"

"Yeah," Ben said, the earth shuddering under him. "Like a bad penny, right?"

The ridges of Mauntgraul's brow rose in disbelief. Despite his present danger, Ben relished the dragon's surprise. He wasn't sure what he was doing – trying to talk the beast out of his attack was obviously pointless, and any battle, with his neck in a vice, would be over in seconds. Perhaps it was pride, making him reckless. He *wanted* the White Dog to see him, to realise that he'd survived, displaying the fortitude of the Red. To let Mauntgraul know that this wasn't over. Not yet. There were still players in the game.

The White Dog snorted, a plume of heat washing over Ben. Then the dragon gave a grunt. He turned his head, nodding at the crumbling precipice, then back at Ben. No more needed to be said. Ben's survival, while remarkable, wasn't going to last very long.

With a grin, Mauntgraul turned back to the Cardinal.

Ben had never felt smaller than in that moment. But this wasn't about him. It was about the harp.

A furnace swirled in the White Dog's nostrils, his indrawn breath mustering heat, and Ben covered his head as a jet of emerald flame blasted the temple, crisping the dust in the air. Centuries-old stone bubbled and cracked, molten in the heat, the devastating blast of dragon fire. Smoke churned, sprigs of charcoal twisting here and there across the floor, True Names dancing in the haze. *Unlucky.* The smell of cooked meat – never as unpleasant as it should have been – drifted to Ben's nostrils, acrid and sweet.

His threat made, Mauntgraul bellowed at the woman at the lectern.

"*Give it to me!*"

The Cardinal, unlikely to understand *wyrm tongue*, responded in kind.

"Out, Lucifer! I cast thee out! Into the fires of hell!"

Mauntgraul, unmoved, drew in another breath.

Then the Sister was there, pounding up the steps and, one-handed, clumsily, unslinging her shield from her back. In one practised motion, the assassin shouldered de Gori to one side, the Cardinal crying out as she tumbled down the steps, landing in an ungainly heap on the chamber floor, the soundboard tinkling away from her.

The Sister brought up the Arimathean Shield. The broad silver disc reflected Mauntgraul's surprise at this small human obstacle, and the snort of flame that he flurried in her direction seemed like an afterthought, for all its heat and force.

The flames licked around the blessed armour, crackling left, right and centre but leaving the assassin untouched, the Sister steadying herself against the rocking lectern. Ben could've told her that it was a bad idea. The White Dog drew himself up, a laugh rumbling from his throat, tail swishing back and forth, and his amusement burst into a piercing scream.

Ben clapped his hands over his ears, his skull ringing. The Sister wasn't so lucky. Even as the echoes rebounded off her shield, Mauntgraul's shriek, the notorious cry of the *Cornutus Quiritor*, struck the woman with full force. Ben watched, his gorge rising, as the Sister's skin took flight from her bones, the dissonance stripping her of flesh. Her head vanished in a crimson mist, a mess of clothing, bones and viscera slopping to the chamber floor, the Arimathean Shield clanging over her remains like a makeshift headstone.

Give my regards to the saints . . .

Helpless, he watched as Mauntgraul stretched out his neck, a great black eye peering into the chamber. The dragon gave a satisfied grunt at his handiwork, smoke pluming across the scene. When the smoke cleared, he was crooking a claw towards the Cardinal, who was struggling to rise, to crawl towards the fallen fragment of the harp.

She'd only just touched it with her fingertips when a foot came down on her hand with a brittle crunch of bone. Jia stood over her, her bruised face a mask. Dropping into a crouch – and ignoring the Cardinal's furious wail – the *sin-you* retrieved the artefact, rising to her feet in a halo of silver. As Ben looked on, she pressed the manacle around her wrist to the radiant metal, the silver band relinquishing its hold at once, liquefying in rays of light, mercurial beads flowing into the greater fragment. Longing to be whole.

"Jia! Wait!"

If the *sin-you* heard him in the uproar, she didn't pay him any mind. In three quick steps, she crossed the space and picked up the Arimathean Shield.

Mauntgraul lunged for her, but she met the descent of his fangs by hurling the disc, the glowing relic bouncing off his snout with a reverberating clang. As the White Dog recoiled, Jia raced up the steps to the lectern, vaulted over the edge and flew towards the dragon, straight for his breast . . .

Before Mauntgraul had a chance to recover, she had plucked the harmonic curve from between his scales and was dropping to the chamber floor. A woman fell, but a *sin-you* landed, four golden hooves adding to the cracks on the flagstones. The fragments, Ben noticed, had been drawn into her transformation, tightly wound in her mane, a practised effort of will. The dragon turned, a claw lashing out, but Jia was too quick for him. In a blur of green and gold, she galloped towards the shattered wall, navigating the shifting ground stepping-stone style, racing over the torrent of stone. Mane flying, her golden horn spearing the dust, she leapt out into space.

With another terrible shriek, Mauntgraul lumbered after her, his wings unfolding, smashing the dome overhead into smithereens.

When the dust cleared, *sin-you* and dragon were gone.

No.

Bit by bit, the Invisible Church was losing its grip on the rock face, the weight of the collapsing chamber dragging the rest of the edifice behind it, turret, buttress and cloister. Blocks of stone tumbled into the gulf, booming down the slopes and into the valley, an avalanche of ruin.

Ben yelled. The platform went surfing over the earth like a raft towards the edge of a waterfall, the precipice approaching fast. Chains clanking, he spun around on his knees, seeking an escape, and his eyes fell on the statues lining the courtroom, a section of the wall still attached to the ground.

A thin grey figure clung to the feet of a saint, her lips trembling with prayer. Dust covered her from head to foot, but he recognised the old woman even in her fear: Evangelista de Gori, the new Cardinal fallen from grace, watching her little empire crumble.

Cast into hell with the rest of us.

He almost felt sorry for her.

Moments before the dislodged platform sailed out over the gulf, spinning into rubble, he heard de Gori's screech, a desperate parting plea.

"Find her. Recover the harp. Deliver us from evil!"

Then, collared and chained, Ben sailed out over nothing.

PART THREE

Mirror Kingdom

Mirrored in the past, the eye may see
the faces of the centuries-to-be.

Old Chinese saying

Guǐ ~ ghost

Lantau Island, a few days ago

Dust covered the temple steps. Later, Jia feared, there would be blood.

The moment the Zhoukoudian hills started to shake, something long buried stirring inside them, she had galloped to the island as fast as she could. A wailing trail of dust marked her progress from Beijing, a journey of a thousand miles reduced to the passing of a night. Now, a sleek equine shape, a green and gold blur, shot over Tsing Ma Bridge from the mainland, past the traffic and the airport and the theme park and through the wooded peaks where the Tian Tan Buddha looked down on the land, the giant bronze dome of the statue's head gleaming under the flat winter sky. Trees and power lines rattled in her wake. Tourists clutched at maps in the startling gust of wind. The shadow fleeting by belonged to a creature that most would have taken for a horse, had they the eyes to track her, and all of them would have been wrong.

Onward Jia raced, into the wild limits of the island and along the peninsula, passing villages where these days no one lived, a shoreline littered with garbage from nearby

Hong Kong and the rotting barnacled hulls of boats, an old fort abandoned since the Opium Wars and a lighthouse with a shattered lamp. Eventually, with a pop of air, a flurry of leaves and a storm of stirred-up dust, she thundered to a halt on this, the summit of the cape, her emerald mane falling still. When the dust settled, she looked at the steps leading up to the temple, all one hundred of them bearing the imprints of treacherous feet.

The temple loomed above her, a crumbling edifice of untold years. The godless place rested on a cliff edge three hundred feet above the waters, the morning tide swirling between jagged rocks. From here, the southernmost tip of the Fan Lau peninsula, the mouth of the Pearl River opened in a grey-green vista. The one remaining spire of the temple stretched like an elaborate cake up to the heavens, an unsteady tapering finger of stone adorned by tiers of upturned eaves where dragons coiled, their alabaster scales covered in moss. This February morning, the temple stood as ruined, as forgotten as ever – but panic, not peace, blew in on the breeze.

Hooves had drawn to a halt, but feet made the ascent to the doors, bare on the steep stone steps. Caution mingled with Jia's reverence, slowing her approach. Here in this place, so she believed, rested one of the oldest of China's treasures. Hadn't Von Hart invited her here all those years ago to look at the Eight Hand Mirror? The envoy extraordinary kept many secrets and she guessed the temple was one of them.

A woman who appeared to be in her early thirties, her dark hair gathered down her spine in a long braided queue, passed into the shadow of the eaves with head bowed. Her pelt had melted into a tight-fitting suit, a sheen of green silk that covered her muscular curves, allowing her limbs freedom of movement. At her neck, a golden collar had absorbed her mane, locking her true shape in human attire. Sheathed on her back, two butterfly swords, the blades crossed, made a threat of her presence. She required no other armour, even here in the midst of catastrophe. She was a *sin-you*, a Remnant of the Ancient Country, a creature of truth and justice, an appointed judge of Zhongguo. She was also *youxia*, a warrior monk, and her body had long since been honed into a weapon. Her former master had seen to that.

Ahead, the great wooden doors presented a dark and forbidding wall. As Jia drew closer, she made out the carvings that stretched across the panels, the old longevity pattern framing a summer idyll, a master and student sitting reading scrolls under a willow tree, rendered fifteen feet high. For a moment, she was young again, caught by a memory as faded and as lost as all the others.

But this didn't stop her. Jia Jing, the 793-year-old *sin-you*, shot out one leg and kicked open the doors to the temple.

A hollow boom announced her arrival, the echoes racing to the end of the chamber beyond and back again. Somewhere high above, birds fluttered, the admonishing squawk of gulls or terns. Gazing up at the sky, chips of porcelain seen from the bottom of a well, she muttered under her breath, already missing the space and the light outside, a level battleground.

The temple lay dusty and still. Torches guttered out with her entrance, the gloom lit by dull shafts of daylight falling through the narrow windows and gaps in the walls and roof. On either side of the chamber stretched alcoves lined with stubby statues, old gods sulking in the shadows. But Jia knew that she wasn't alone.

"Von Hart! Show yourself!"

Feet whispering over the flagstones, she reached the spirit wall, passing the carved wings of the celestial *long*, the dragon protecting the heart of the temple. Every footstep gave her pain, as though her heart bled out through the soles of her feet. It was hard to come here. Hard to face the envoy as anything other than a friend, however estranged they had become. The walls around her, daubed with wards against fox spirits and *yaksha* demons, meant nothing to her. Let Yama himself come and take her, drag her into the Nine Dark Places, past the Mountain of Knives and the Forest of Swords, down into the fires of hell. Hadn't her road been leading there from the start?

"Fairy, speak to me. What have you done?"

And from the gloom, he greeted her.

"I said you would come, Daughter of Empires." The echoes sounded arch, but she could hear the fear underneath, a bridge trying to reach her. "*Ja*. And come you have, the very next day."

"Von Hart, it was 1841."

He made a tutting sound. Whether he was annoyed with himself or her, she couldn't tell.

"Well, you are here. That's what counts."

"I have come for nothing other than the truth." As she proceeded, seeking the source of his voice, Jia's feet crunched on the litter under her feet, the splintered pews and fallen beams, the grit washed in by the wind. "Have you gone mad? I heard a familiar strain upon the air and tracked the sound to the Zhoukoudian hills. There, I found only echoes. But the hills are shaking to tear themselves apart. Beijing shudders with your treachery."

Von Hart sniffed. When he spoke again, his voice grew louder and then faded, and she realised he was looking around the place, taking in the scene.

"This place is such a dump," he said. "*Ein drecksloch, ja?* This temple, the monks of old said, was a gift from the gods, built from the stones of Mount Kun-Lun where the Five August Ones held court, presiding over the world. Regardless of how the world has forgotten it – forgotten *us*, Jia Jing – the temple still stands as a fortress and a shrine, a stronghold of the real against the Dark Frontier. You are standing at an ancient axis of magic. Still, it's a dump nevertheless."

Whatever he had in mind, whatever he was planning, Jia didn't want to give him any more time.

"That isn't an answer. I've read my history. I know what sleeps under Zhoukoudian. Have you unleashed destruction on us all?"

But she was accusing rather than asking. Why, hadn't he been the one to suggest such a thing, albeit cryptically, in the House of the Sleeping Dragon two hundred years ago? *Why would the Guild or the Chapter want to rouse a Remnant?* he'd asked her. A question, considering recent events (not to mention the name of the tavern), that was as good as a confession. All the same, she wanted to hear it from his lips.

"I'm known for my fondness of gambling games, *mein*

engel. This one, I think, is called roulette, played upon the wheel of fate. We roll the dice. We take our chances."

"You're also fond of riddles." *Why is he so hard to read?* "I am a *sin-you,* the last wakeful one of my kind. I should see the truth before me. Should've seen it all along." She said this to herself as much as to him. "Why is it I can't?"

But he'd already told her, long ago in Xanadu.

I had heard that your kind see much, truth from lie, the real from illusion, and it fascinated me so. How could one stand before such a creature, his heart rendered as naked as a babe? . . . Well, I'll tell you. I am a fairy, one of a race that you call the Xian. *We are known for our glamour and tricks . . .*

"Then tell me," he said. "What do you believe?"

It was a joke, of course. One of his terrible jokes. Her presence here revealed her conviction, loud and clear.

"You have the means. Your fragment of the harp," she said. "Forget this folly. Before the White Dog breaks free."

"A time will come for the dragon to fall," the echoes said. "For now, think of him as a distraction."

"A distraction from what?"

"Why, to keep the eyes of the world averted from us, of course. I can save us, you see. I can save us all. Yet I cannot do so alone. No one must learn of my schemes or guess at my objective."

"Which is what, exactly?"

"There is something that belongs to me. I would have it back."

"I thought you just took what you wanted, Von Hart. Or did you finally find something without a price?"

"Oh, I know who keeps it," he said, and he sounded

genuinely peevish. "Alas, I don't know where they hide. No amount of scrying will do when you don't know where to look. And asking certain Remnants would give too much away. No. It's better this way. Better to remain in the shadows."

Frustrated by his guessing games, her voice dropped into a hiss.

"I'll ask you again. Stop this madness."

"No," he said.

"Then in the name of the Lore, I'm forced to arrest—" she began, but her words dried up in her throat as she reached the middle of the chamber, the light through the roof enough for her to see the dais ahead and the figure standing upon it.

Von Hart was leaning on a lectern on one side of the platform, scratching out a message with a ridiculous quill, the feather belonging to a peacock or an ostrich or some other large bird. He glanced up at her, his piqued expression letting her know that she had caught him at something he would rather have kept hidden. *Scratch scratch* went the quill, and then he tore a narrow strip of paper from the page, holding it up before him between forefinger and thumb. He muttered something, a faint stream of symbols spilling from his lips and bobbing in the air. On the strip of paper, Jia caught an illegible line of characters – a short sentence or two, nothing more – and then Von Hart was blowing on it, the shred drifting aloft. Inexplicably, it curled up in embers and a wisp of smoke, vanishing before her eyes.

"Your spells only seal your crimes," she told him, afraid all the same. She was well aware of the power he held, the other-worldly strength of the creature before her. Could she best him if it came to it? She could try. "I told you. I will not spare you."

"It's a message, that's all. You know, I would've sent a text, but I'm afraid the recipient lost his phone. You could say he was somewhat . . . clumsy."

"A message?"

"A warning," he said. "A request. Before it's too late."

"It is already too late."

"For you, perhaps."

Even in the gloom, he shone a little, whether from the light filtering through the roof or from his alien essence, she couldn't tell. *He's like a candle,* she thought as he stepped away from the lectern, *a tall, thin spindle of wax.* His long robes, a red silk kimono patterned with stars, looked tattered and worn. Perhaps he purchased the same article of clothing over and over and had a wardrobe full of them, for all she knew. This, she suspected, was one of the mysteries he loved to uphold as he went about his inscrutable, and evidently treacherous, business. He had always been a showman. No, a *liar*. His hair no longer flowed to his shoulders; the white-gold strands were short and parted, a severe look against the surrounding rubble. The European style matched his cheekbones, smooth blades framing the sensuous – no, *shameless* – buds of his lips. Hardly a wrinkle marked his face. It was only in his eyes, leaf-shaped, cold and the darkest violet, that she could see the centuries down which he had walked, facing gods knew what horrors, to meet her here in this ruined place on the edge of the realm. The edge of destruction.

I have known him all my life. My master. My friend. The understanding pained her. *And yet I don't know him at all* . . .

He looked ill, Jia decided. Under all his frippery, the stab at sophistication, he looked ill. Glamour or no, he couldn't hide the sweat that glistened on his brow, the tremble of his lips, the suppressed strain. Nor the stink of magic, emanating no doubt from the artefact he cradled in the crook of one elbow, the fragment of the mnemonic harp. She supposed the fragment was even older than he was, though she had no way of knowing that. The ancient piece, one of three in the care of the Hidden Court, was the pillar of the instrument, forged to resemble the head and forelegs of a horse – or a creature very much like a horse – a marvel of ivory and silver, wrought with a craft unknown to the world today. From a short distance, Jia noticed how the fragment glimmered and gleamed just like its bearer, the yard-long conical spar ending in a point as sharp as her fear.

"As a representative of the Curia Occultus," she reminded him, "you were charged to look after your piece of the harp. Not to use it."

"As ever, you see the truth of things," he said. He seemed too weary to argue, whatever invocations she'd disturbed with her arrival taking their toll on him, the insidious grip of magic. "There were three of us, weren't there? In the beginning? The Guild of the Broken Lance. The Whispering Chapter. And me, the envoy extraordinary. This was all my doing, all of it. My grand scheme." He sighed, a sound like the wind swirling in the spire above. "Each of us swore to guard a fragment of the harp for as long as the Lore stood. But like the harp, the Hidden Court has come undone, the old order unmade. And I have been the . . . the . . ." He paused, searching for the word. "*Hausfrau, ja?* Looking after old silver and old glass. Discarded, dormant. Or so everybody thought."

At the words *old glass*, an unbidden shiver ran up her spine, her skin prickling with a guilty memory. She guessed that Von Hart knew that, choosing his words well. Centuries ago, he had come to commence her education in Xanadu, teaching her all about the Empire, the Pact, the lands beyond the sea, the wars between men. In the mist-shrouded mountains, he had trained her in the arts of *wushu*, watching her harden into a warrior, a wandering monk, sworn to uphold the laws of the realm. To uphold the Lore, come what may. Later, their relationship had soured, as all the world had soured, as magic had soured, and she remembered that there had been a price for his wisdom. For his friendship. Always, always a price.

"I have seen much. Sacrifice, compromise, the matter of the Pact. But justice?" He left the answer unspoken, like a flake of ash hanging in the air. "Jia, the founding of the Lore, the slumber of the Remnants . . . I made all my oaths in blindness. I stepped down from the Curia Occultus and turned my back on all that I am. I didn't see that I brought about our undoing, our own slow death. For Remnants and humans alike. You see, to extinguish magic is to extinguish the soul of the world. We sleep as the world dies. In silver, in glass, I have seen the path to our return. And the means of our awakening."

Yes, he had shown her in the first place, hadn't he? His comforting lie. His choice. In that moment, Jia knew with an insight as deep as her Remnant nature that this was all part of the same thread, the same scheme. None of this, his arrival in Xanadu, his lessons on Mount Song, his appearance in Humen and her coming here, was happening by accident. All of it was a game. A gamble. *Roulette*. A game, she now realised, that he had been playing for centuries.

"The harp. You speak of the harp."

"Twice forged and twice broken. Third time's the charm, isn't that what they say?"

Jia could feel her blood pulsing in her head, an increasing throb of alarm.

"This is what you meant by your tale of the mirror children, isn't it?" *Curse him. Does he ever talk in a straightforward manner, free of metaphor and half-truths?* "We Remnants are trapped in the mirror. The Lore is the glass you would have us break."

With a shudder, she conjured up his exact words.

One day, humans will hear the clatter of weapons deep, deep in the mirror. The Ghost Emperor will stir, monstrous and pale, his mammoth limbs swimming through the darkness towards the tempting light of earth . . .

"You would go raising fire," she said. "You would start a war."

Von Hart rolled his eyes. "Such drama, Jia. Must we?"

She took a step forward, shaking her fists up at him.

"You were my master. My friend." But this didn't quite cover it, and her heart threatened to burst, forcing her words into a plea. "Why? Why have you done this?"

293

But he had already told her.

A worm gnaws at the heart of things . . . I believed the Pact could save us . . .

"You lied to me." She pressed her deepest of wounds upon him. "For years, you lied."

"Well, you said you came here for the truth. And the truth you shall have." He broke her gaze to stare into the shadows, perhaps counting the cost of the past. "I made a mistake, long ago. I forged something that I shouldn't have forged. And I chained something that I shouldn't have chained. How was I to know how the ages would turn? How the circles of protection would weaken, magic turning sour? But I am not without my wits, Jia. Am I not Fay, despite my failings?" He coughed behind his hand, a theatrical gesture, and corrected himself. "Few as they are, anyway."

"You have broken the Lore," she told him. "The Pact we all signed."

"*Ja.*"

"And what else? What else, *traitor*?" She spat the word out. "What else did your precious wits have you do?"

Von Hart smiled, moonlight on a winter lake.

"Why, she is standing here before me, Daughter of Empires. Let's call her my get-out clause."

Cold flooded her veins, her inner wounds stinging in the knowledge that he hadn't just betrayed her, breaking the Lore under which they both lived; he had also shaped her. Like molten ore, he had scooped her up in the gardens of Xanadu, a child seething with loss. On Mount Song, he had tempered her into a sword and then left her to rust in the mist, returning years later in the Opium Wars merely to test her mettle. And here he stood, in this nameless temple, poised to challenge her to the hilt . . .

Just like the harp, he had forged her. Made her.

"Blast you, fairy," she told him. "You won't use me like some blunt blade."

"Oh no, *liebling*," he replied. "With you I have fashioned a key."

With this, Von Hart lifted the fragment of the harp above his head, the silvery light illuminating the shadows.

It was then that Jia noticed the bulky object resting further back on the dais. The large angular shape lurked there, *watchful* somehow, and the hairs tingled up on her neck, a sensation that had as much to do with dread as it did with longing.

The Eight Hand Mirror!

As she drew closer to the dais, the mirror became clearer, the gloom in the temple swimming in and out. Breathless, her heart leaping in her breast, she came to a halt at the bottom of the steps, looking up at the dark and achingly familiar surface, Von Hart a pale flame flickering at the edges of her vision, forgotten for now. To all intents and purposes the ancient artefact was simply a large octagonal mirror on a stand, both the frame and the glass covered in dust. Even from several feet away, a coldness was pressing on her cheeks, numbing her flesh. She'd felt this kind of coldness before, this dead weight, this *nothingness* . . . and she had risked the sensation time and again just in order to *see* . . .

She was at the top of the steps before she realised she was climbing them. Von Hart drew back, letting her proceed past him, as though the shadows on the dais were reeling her in, drawing her towards the glass. Two, three steps away from it, she drew to a halt, the chunky octagonal frame stretching over her head, a giant guardian. The glass, as usual, was black, jet black. The darkness in the frame appeared to lack texture of any kind, resembling a . . . *a space. An empty space.* And, as usual, the glass was reflecting nothing – nothing living, anyway – absorbing the vague outline of shapes behind her, the ruined guts of the temple. Not Von Hart. Not her. The mirror had erased her, rejecting or ignoring her physical presence.

Finally, Jia drew in a breath, dust swirling into her lungs. How long had it been since she'd looked in the mirror? Six hundred, seven hundred years . . .?

Like a swimmer testing the water, her fingertips stretched out, hesitant, hungry, to touch the glass . . .

Thud.

Something large and pale smacked against the other side of the glass. Startled, Jia leapt back, her fingers snapping into a fist. Eyes wide, she took in the coiling, vaporous appendage as it withdrew from the glass, sinking back into shadow. But she had seen the vast tentacle, the many slick and questing suckers. It belonged to some gargantuan creature, some half-glimpsed behemoth that she recognised from nightmares, even as her guts clenched in shock. She had caught the hint of a bulbous eye, the colour of old piano keys, and tendrils that might have been follicles or antennae, weaving, insectile in the dark. The intimation of some shining maw, a gruesomely elegant visor of bone, receded into the depths that held it, which, although she had never seen the void before, she knew well enough as the gulf of the nether. Lightless. Endless. It was as though Von Hart had trapped a giant squid in a tank, except she knew that the Eight Hand Mirror, for all its mystery, was just that – a mirror. The frame was barely a foot thick. And she knew that the back of it was flat.

"You see him, don't you?" Von Hart spoke across the ice of her alarm. "The Ghost Emperor shows his teeth."

She tore her gaze from the mirror, turning to face him, her eyes narrow chips of jade.

"Ghosts?"

"They gather here at the door to Creation," he told her. "Converging. Joining. Becoming one." Gently he lowered the fragment in his hand, the shadows settling around them. "A king among phantoms, drawn by the souring of magic and the strumming of the harp."

"Lurkers." Her throat was dry and she could barely muster a rebuke at the horror he'd shown her, the depth of his Lore-breaking. "You rouse a dragon and now you're stirring up this . . . abomination? You'll bring about the death of us all."

"Death comes regardless," he said.

In her mind, Jia could feel the roulette ball, spinning and dancing around his wheel, ready to fall into one of the pockets, each number spelling disaster. And he was playing her too, she knew. Guiding her. Summoning her here . . .

But he was wrong. As ever, she was a servant of justice. A servant of the truth. He had only proved himself a servant of deceit.

Thinking this, she drew herself to her full height.

"I am Jia Jing, the appointed judge of the court of Kublai Khan, Guardian of the East, Keeper of the Lore. And you are no longer my master."

It was hard to go on. Grief threatened to choke her.

Von Hart, however, was not shaken.

"No one is your master, Jia. The Age of Empires is over. Now who will you serve?"

With a whisper of steel, her butterfly swords were in her hands. The sharply edged blades seemed to reflect the eight hundred years of their acquaintance, everything that he had taught her, spiralling off into the past. A bond she stood poised to sever.

"Who if not yourself?"

"I serve the Lore. The Lore protects us."

"Oh Jia," he breathed as she raised the swords, striding towards him. "Who if not your own kind?"

Von Hart drew back as she came near, every bit the maestro revealing a trick at the end of his show. She meant to subdue him, if she could – silence him if necessary. Anything to shut out his voice, the wheeling hints and references that were now consolidating into a whole like the teeth of a key fitting into a lock. A swirl of shadow at the corner of her eye arrested her and she slowed, her head turning, taking in the Eight Hand Mirror.

With her proximity, the glass was clearing. Each receding shadow stole a sliver of her rage, replacing it with longing. She came to a halt, tracing arcs in the dust as she spun towards the mirror, a compass magnetised by need.

How long has it been?

The octagonal frame yawned around her, no longer a

window onto a void, but an underground cave, a darkened shore beside a sunless sea, miles under the northern plains.

Jia's breath frosted the glass as she drew close, her nose all but touching the mirror. Like a woman in a dream, she sheathed her swords, her hands rising to press against the surface before her, the heat of her yearning meeting ice. The sea wind howled through the temple, the triumph of ghosts. Upon sight of the vision in the mirror, a storm was gathering in her breast, hurling leaves of memory around her mind.

Since the end of the Opium Wars, Jia had been wandering, out in the wilds. As Von Hart had said, the Age of Empires was over, the Qing Dynasty crumbling under the weight of the modern world. As the twentieth century dawned, she had stood in a circle of grass on the plains and lamented the bones of Xanadu, the palace long since eroded into lumps in the ground, grassy and unremarkable. There she had paid her respects to her parents, Ziyou and Ye, sleeping somewhere under her feet. She'd wondered if the herd still galloped in dreams, but she didn't linger long. The faded scar of the Silk Road, whence a dusty Italian merchant had come with tales of progress and glory and sleep, had carried her west into the desert. From the ruined cities in the Taklamakan, their crumbling walls shored up by dunes, their watchtowers home to buzzards and the wind, she had walked, galloped and trudged south to Tiger Leaping Gorge, the Jinsha River snaking far below through one of the deepest canyons in the world. Fifty-odd years had passed, vanishing in the dust of her trail. In Yunnan, she scaled mountains and ran through forests, counting the dwindling numbers of elephant, tiger and monkey, sharing meat and fruit with each – and their sense of impending doom. If even the beasts indigenous to earth stood no chance of survival, what hope was there for her? With these thoughts heavy on her mind, she passed over many bridges and prayed in many temples, beseeching gods of justice and mercy as she made her way across the land. Down the long road of history Jia walked, through the Great Leap, the red harvest of dust and death, and through the rise of the Republic. And on and on into the new century, into the modern age.

And when at last she headed north and returned to Beijing, she found a city rising in neon and smog, a miasma obscuring the stars. A new world had risen and it cared nothing for the spirit of the Ancient Country or the children of the *Xian*. For a century and more she had gone in search of old Zhongguo. She had found only ghosts.

Then, yesterday, the Zhoukoudian hills had started to shake, shattering her reverie.

And she had remembered.

Not far from here . . . there stands an old temple . . .

Grim-faced, she had turned her eyes to the south.

Now she stood, the cold glass burning her palms, before the Eight Hand Mirror.

Jia blinked away tears, the cavern in the mirror blurring. In a heartbeat, all her memories came galloping across time as though through the summer dust on the northern plains. The haze parted and she could see them, gazing into the space under that distant and longed-for earth, the cavern carved out for her parents, her herd, by an alien song. The two equine figures lay on the shore beside the underground lake, a soft mound of green hide and golden hooves glimmering in the darkness, locked together in perpetual sleep. Her father, Ziyou, rested his noble horned head against her mother's neck. Ye reclined against his body, her horn bowed to the cavern floor, yielding to dreams, enchanted. Everything was as it had been seven hundred years ago – and yet everything was different.

"No," she said. "It cannot be."

Jia choked, stumbling towards the glass. Her thoughts spun in a whirlpool, sucking her down into all those yesterdays, into the eye of the storm. For a moment, she was a girl again, sitting on the palace steps in the Great Khan's garden, longing for her parents, for the comfort of her slumbering herd. And wasn't this the seed of her sorrow, the restless embryo growing inside her, ripening over the years and birthing doubt? As she looked into the mirror, uncertainty clawed at her heart. That all the things she believed in, her oaths to empire after empire, the Pact and the Lore, should crumble under such a childish need, such a juvenile grievance. It didn't seem right to her. It didn't seem fair. And yet . . .

"Now," Von Hart said, from somewhere behind her. "At last, you open your eyes. You look through the glass and see the bitterest truth."

In the glass, Jia could see Ziyou and Ye, the patchy state of their pelts, silk faded to a stagnant green. With the keen eyes of pain, she could make out the sheen of her parents' hooves, dull, dusty and cracked. The way their tongues lolled from their mouths, dry and sickly-looking. Worst of all, she could see their ribs, stark through their wasted skin, their bellies rising and falling in weak undulations. The two *sin-you* were struggling for breath.

And here was another ghost, whispering to her from a distant childhood. The ghost of her heart's desire.

You can look again, if you wish. Or you can walk away, believing whatever you want to believe. Believing that you have seen an old mirror, a fairy's fancy. Nothing more.

Across the years, he had told her just what she had chosen.

You can look into a mirror and see what you want to see. Yet you ignore what's sitting right under your nose.

There was no mistaking it. Jia could see the truth before her, stripped of illusion and sharpened by despair.

Her parents, Ziyou and Ye, were dying.

Echoes snapped across the dais, cantillating into the temple. The ground shuddered and groaned under her feet, strengthening tremors sending dust and debris rattling from the crumbled spire above. Like ice in the last days of winter, the mirror was cracking under her hands. Fault lines popped and buckled across the surface, zigzagging from her spread palms out to the edges of the frame. In no time at all, a cobweb of fissures covered the mirror, the reflection distorting, the cavern, her parents, gone. Only darkness lay beyond, the black flood of the nether held back by a splintering dam of glass.

Head bowed, Jia stood before the Eight Hand Mirror. Or perhaps it was a door. A door ready to open, punching a hole in the world.

"Jia . . ." Carefully, Von Hart took a step towards her.

Her head swung around, fixing him with eyes as bright as the Nine Hells. And she saw he was burning, yes, a candle in the dark. White flames curled up around his sleeves, rolling up his back, playing in his hair. His flesh, as waxen as ever, glowed as if fed by his personal inferno, by the force of the harp in his hands, his gathering power, his gathering song. Whatever essence comprised his body, the ancient magic couldn't consume him, this last scion of a vanished race.

Her face grew hard, her heart breaking along with the mirror. The blasting cold of the void beyond, opening as the glass shattered inward, tossed her hair into spitting serpents.

"Tell me, master. What must I do?"

EIGHTEEN

Five hundred feet above the mountains, Ben flew without wings. Even in human shape, he could withstand the high altitude, the limited oxygen, the punishing cold. At first, he'd struggled, cursing, his fists beating on white scales. Then, his adrenalin burning out, he had simply fallen into a daze, allowing his cuts and bruises to heal. His near-miss execution and the fall from the monastery pummelled his system with shock; for all his draconic strength, he wasn't immune to it.

But he hadn't fallen far. The air screamed blue murder in his ears, reminiscent of the *Cornutus Quiritor* that gripped him. Mauntgraul, the White Dog, had plucked him from the sky like a raptor catching prey, snatching him from the rubble cascading from the Invisible Church. Wings beating a drum on the wind, the dragon had risen over the Alps and turned his snout to the east.

In intermittent flashes of clarity, Ben came to learn of their pursuit.

For something like a day and a half, without stopping to rest, Jia had galloped south from the Alps and across the Balkans, a living land rocket trailing dust. High above, Mauntgraul followed the trail, his keen eyes scouring the earth. Ben reckoned that the *sin-you* must've been moving at a speed of around two hundred miles per hour, slowing now and then to avoid obstacles, take detours, choose the quickest path. Istanbul passed in a zoetrope of minarets, domes and cobbled streets, Jia racing across the Bosphorus Bridge from Europe into Asia, the suspension cables shuddering. Anyone watching would have seen a dust storm, a freak weather phenomenon, a green-gold missile too swift to register.

No mobile phone snaps for you.

Surfacing again, squinting at the land below, he marvelled at her dexterity. She displayed abilities to rival his own, outpacing the dragon mile after mile. Coupled to this was envy – he was the original green-eyed monster, after all – but mostly there was discomfort, and most of it concerned his wounded pride. It wasn't just his feet dangling in the airstreams or the giant claw closed around him, clutching tightly but giving him enough room to breathe. Stuck in human form, the *lunewrought* collar around his throat, Ben had no choice but to play the captive, a situation that was fast growing old.

Where was Jia heading? Back to China, he guessed. Back to . . . her master? He tried to put the pieces together, stitching suspicion to suspicion, but coming up with little concrete, little he could put his finger on. Had Von Hart really awoken Mauntgraul? Was the *sin-you* really working for him, a secret mission to recover the harp? Did the fairy mean to undo the lullaby, rouse the Sleepers? His rattled brain noted the fact that Jia hadn't denied any of these things. She had used him as a stepping stone to get to the

Chapter, that much was clear, and for some reason, the envoy had sent him a message, a warning, an instruction of some kind. *Let me fall.* With a sensation akin to vertigo, Ben realised that he didn't know the first thing about the *why* of this imagined conspiracy.

All he could do was pick at the threads, tracing them back to the start and disliking the taste of them. Why would Von Hart have wanted the Lambton armour? Why had he given the suit to House Fitzwarren? This implied that the fairy had had his lily-white hand in the Bardolfe conspiracy last year, inspiring, abetting Remnant sedition. This unpleasant thought brought the same old echo from those days last summer, Von Hart in his club.

Perhaps this change in regime is inevitable. Perhaps it is our turn again.

Inevitable. That was the telltale word. If the envoy was complicit in rebellion, it seemed clear that he had his own agenda. He'd rescued Ben, after all, and on two occasions.

He was trying to tell you something, dummkopf. *Whatever it is, he still wants you in the game.*

Was it possible that Von Hart had been working towards the downfall of the Guild all along, feeding the fire that put the Chapter in power? To deliberately place the Lore on shifting ground, throwing up confusion and, of course, the fragments of the harp?

In the spirit of that, wouldn't it make sense if the envoy had awoken Mauntgraul for a similar reason? Had he been so desperate, so determined, that he was willing to risk unleashing a dragon that would certainly want to kill him? Yes, Ben thought so. It would certainly explain his going into hiding. Perhaps the times called for such measures. In the short space of time since the White Dog's awakening, hundreds had died, scooped up from the Wangfujing plaza or caught in the bullet train disaster. The dragon had reduced both Paladin's Court and the Invisible Church to rubble. He wished he could tell himself that concern for humans, those who would fall to the beast, might have stayed the fairy's hand – but no, he had seen too much over the years to trust the compassion of the Fay.

Following this train of thought, he could see how the envoy might've wanted to create a fiery distraction, a twelve-ton venomous smokescreen, while Jia made her play for the harp. It all led back to the same pale source. The same missing player. Von Hart must've known that Ben, as Sola Ignis, would fly to Beijing to face his ancient foe. *The Red and the White*. Of all creatures, he must've known that. And while Ben had been preoccupied with Mauntgraul, Jia had used him to get to the Chapter and the other fragments of the harp.

But something had gone wrong. In such a risky venture, something had been *bound* to go wrong.

The White Dog had paid a visit to Paladin's Court and stolen a fragment of the harp. Then someone – a Remnant with nothing to lose, a million spies and a penchant for jugular veins, Ben reckoned – must have led Mauntgraul to the Invisible Church. The fragments of the harp called to each other, the Fay enchantment all of a piece. Lambert du Sang would have known that, surely. And the harp, it seemed, was drawing the lot of them together, fusing them in chaos and fire in the same way that the relic longed to be whole.

If all this was true – and Ben could only go by his gut, forcing himself to face the worst – then he wondered where that left him.

Smoke and mirrors. You know the truth as well as I do. It's just too hard to swallow.

What had driven Jia Jing, Guardian of the East, Keeper of the Lore, to go against her oaths? What had frightened her so?

I have no choice.

The Ghost Emperor.

With a sinking feeling in the pit of his stomach, he realised that her insistence on the Pact, reminding him of his honour, had all been a ruse.

Truth and justice, my arse. She lied to you, birdbrain. Just because she can see the truth doesn't mean she can't lie.

Jia had stolen the fragments of the harp. Dangling five hundred feet above the mountains, it didn't take a genius to realise why Mauntgraul had stolen *him*: the *lunewrought* collar around his throat.

The harp exerted an arcane pull, magical and magnetic. Responding to the pieces in the *sin-you*'s clutches, Ben's collar was buzzing and tingling against his skin, a cold, wavering compass point. And touched by the harp, the White Dog could sense it, sense its pull and follow, the dragon hungry for the harp, desperate to recover his stolen piece. Jia could've lost Mauntgraul easily enough otherwise. The sureness of his direction, his growing desperation was there in his ragged breaths, the speed at which they flew. As for Ben, he was serving his purpose. The collar waned if they fell too far behind and waxed to an uncomfortable degree when they were following true once more, miles above the *sin-you* on the ground.

A lodestone. He's using you as a living lodestone. Could this day get any better?

He didn't want to think about what would happen when Mauntgraul managed to catch up with Jia – as he knew he must – and he himself outlived his usefulness. The harp was a restless chatter in his head, a tinkling of chimes emanating need. He could only imagine the scale of the music in Mauntgraul's skull, luring him on through the sky, across the mountains and rivers, into the east.

As soon as he thought it, he experienced another tingle, another painful tug at his throat.

Below, the dust trail was fading out, a settling cloud of grit.

"She's stopping," he shouted up at the beast above him. "Set me down, you bloodless bastard."

He couldn't tell whether Mauntgraul heard him or not. Probably not, judging by the wind. Nevertheless, the dragon could see the dust plume fading for himself, probably heard the stolen fragments coming to a standstill. He banked, Ben's stomach lurching, and dived for the snowbound peaks.

A few feet off the ground, he released Ben. He dropped like a stone to the earth, his body slamming into rock, and all he knew was silence.

When he came to, the White Dog spoke.

"Mount Aragats," he said as Ben sat up, spitting out dust. "That's what they call this place. The name means 'Ara's throne', after Ara the Beautiful, a hero of Byzantine legend.

He was so handsome, so strong, that Queen Shamiram waged a war just to have him. In the ensuing battle, Ara was slain and Shamiram, heartbroken and mad, spent the rest of her days trying to raise him from the dead. To no avail."

Ben wasn't in the mood for a story. The view, however, couldn't fail to take his breath away – breath he was surprised to find he had on the summit, retaining a shred of his inherent warmth and stamina. The collar, he knew, restricted transformation and curbed his strength. But it couldn't change his nature.

Mauntgraul, of course, remained unfettered. There was nothing to stop him ripping off Ben's head and tossing it down the slope.

Heart thudding, fists clenched, Ben swallowed his fear.

"You old romantic," he said to the dragon's shoulders. Mauntgraul sat, in human form, on a snowy outcrop that hung thousands of feet over the landscape. The White Dog surveyed that landscape with all the scorn of a descended god. Looking for a dust trail, perhaps. Watching. Waiting. "Let's not forget all the innocent people you've killed."

"Humans!" The White Dog spat the word, echoes bouncing off the surrounding cliffs. "Humans destroy what they love and mourn by the graveside, wishing that their tears could wash away time."

"That doesn't mean they deserve to die."

"Doesn't it?" he said. "Seems to me they threw down the gauntlet when they sealed their murderous Pact."

"That isn't—"

"Fair, Benjurigan?" Mauntgraul stood and turned now,

looking down from his advantage on the bluff. Ben's argument shrivelled up in his throat as he saw the tears rolling down the dragon's cheeks, the slight trembling of his shoulders. His physique was an undeniable model of strength, but the black holes of his eyes only spoke of his anguish. This show of emotion was so unfamiliar, so alien to his character, that Ben let out an astonished breath. "Nothing is fair. This world does not change."

Ben didn't know what to say. There was no enmity in the White Dog's expression, no sign of a legacy of violence, the Red and the White. Mauntgraul, who stood before him in the guise of the Wandering Moor, appeared to have forgotten all about Rakegoyle, his mother. He looked inward, contemplating, watching the progress of some inner war.

It's the harp. The harp has screwed with his head.

The subliminal tinkling, the thrum of Ben's collar, had taken on a palpable presence, emanating from the distant fragments. And the harp was working on him too, he realised, his throat thick with emotion, the hint of memories just out of reach, inviting him to dance . . . At the same time, he wanted to throw up on the snow, sickened by the melody.

The magic of the Fay is growing old. The circles of protection are souring.

He recalled Jia's exact words, silently answering them with his own.

Yeah. Sour enough to poison the mind.

Something was wrong with the magic, that much was clear. Back at the monastery, the Cardinal should've been able to overpower Mauntgraul easily, the strumming of those ghostly strings binding him in human form, peeling back the earth and sending him into the Sleep. Instead, the White Dog had managed to resist, fighting against the song, but the struggle had cost him dearly, Ben saw; the music had driven him mad.

Thinking this, Ben tugged at the collar around his throat, humming against his skin. Somehow, he had to get the damn thing off. He had little to fear from the Sleep himself . . . didn't he? Unlike Mauntgraul, Von Hart had sung his name into the lullaby and secured his place upon the earth. But he couldn't help but wonder how long the magic would take to corrode completely, and what that might mean for the other waking Remnants. Things were falling apart. He'd like the collar to go the same way before he joined the White Dog in bedlam.

The harp was his only hope. In the monastery, he had seen it for himself, the way in which Jia had freed herself. Lunewrought *answers to* lunewrought. If he could just get close enough to the fragments . . .

The collar answered. A cold sting, a solar flare exploding in his mind. Music rose, shrill and bright, threatening to liquefy his brain. He clapped his hands to his ears, his skin crawling, his feet slipping on snow and scree. And into the surge of melody, that voice again, thin, insistent, stabbing his wheeling thoughts.

Ben.

Huh?

Ben. Catch her. Please.

A moment and the voice was gone, an echo that had never been. The radiance receded, the music dwindling to a background hum.

Mauntgraul hardly blinked. Perhaps he was immune to the harp, having grown accustomed to its hunger.

To suppress the urge to vomit, Ben growled.

"You're wrong. Everything has changed."

"Do you imagine so?" Mauntgraul said. He swung out his arms, framing the horizon. "Tell me they don't still squabble over land and money. Crave power over others. Fight with each other over long-dead gods. And what of us, the Remnants? Tell me that they finally accept us. Tell me they no longer fear us. Tell me what has changed from my day to this."

Ben shook his head, but he fell silent. Crazed by the harp or no, Mauntgraul had spoken to the crux of his fear, the creeping despair that had dogged him since Beijing. This creature before him was a monster in every sense of the word, a mass murderer who revelled in gore. But like it or not, the White Dog was speaking the truth.

"This is your progress, Benjurigan. Can you not see? This is why you signed the Pact. Why you sacrificed all. Yet here we are, racing towards extinction. We died out centuries ago, did we not? You. Me. All of us. We are as dead as dreams. Dead as dust."

Ben studied the ground. If his doubts had been subtly skulking in the shadows, his visit to Père Lachaise cemetery had dragged them out into the light, the withering state of the Remnants plain for him to see. So many of them had fallen, both the noble and the debauched. All of them Remnants, regardless. And he'd been warned, hadn't he? *The Pact is no truce at all, merely a cell where you wait for extinction* . . . How could he forget Queen Atiya's words?

Typical of a goddess, they had taken on a prophetic quality. Denial was absurd. The Pact hadn't saved them at all.

Still . . .

"I can't . . . I won't accept that. I swore to protect them."

"From the truth?" the White Dog said.

"From destruction."

Mind wheeling, he recalled the *sin-you*'s words from the mountains outside Beijing, the hint of a larger scheme taking shape in his mind.

The Lurkers are merging in the nether, she'd said. *Something is drawing them to the earth. Something has caught their attention. Something big.*

Or someone.

"Why do you think Jia wants the harp?" he asked the dragon before him. "Can you take a wild guess? I . . . I think Von Hart is planning a rebellion. Summoning an army. Some kind of—"

"Yes. The Pale One. The Lord of Nothing. The King of Emptiness."

Ben's flesh went cold. "The Ghost Emperor."

"*Yesss*," Mauntgraul hissed, his eyes darting around, taking in the rock face as if fearing the phantom's sudden appearance, the giant beast slicing the sky apart to join them on the mountain. "I hear him, you know. I hear him calling to the harp, hungry for its magic. He calls to the *Cwyth* from beyond the world."

"No shit. The harp is what drew him here. Perhaps the envoy—"

"Oh, such music!" Foam bubbled at the corners of Mauntgraul's mouth, his mania taking over. "The hiss of a

314

blade under a fingernail. The last beat of a bursting heart—"
The White Dog choked himself off. "The bells. I hear him
in the bells. But he will not have the harp. Not as long as
I live and breathe. It is mine. Mine!"

"Maunt." Ben took a cautious step forward. "We have to
stop her."

Despite this attempt at partnership, he would never see
the dragon as an ally. History was history. From the old
days to these, Mauntgraul's victims must scale into the thousands, Remnant and human alike. The dragon longed for
the harp. The souring of magic had pushed him to the brink,
a kind of draconic breakdown exacerbated by the modern
age. Ben could see it in his eyes, a glimmer of uncertainty,
even loneliness. And the harp's absence, plainly, was about
to push him over the edge.

Maybe Ben could turn that to his advantage. Somehow.
He had to try.

"Why?" Mauntgraul said. "Oh, fear not. I will have the
harp. You will lead me to it and then I will kill you." He
tipped his head, his tone remaining light, conversational.
"But you make me curious. What do you care if the Sleepers
awaken? You see the worthlessness of the Pact, do you not?
In all this time, have you never wished to see them again,
your kindred? This conflict within you does you no good.
Perhaps you should've chosen the right side."

This time, the White Dog spoke to Ben's hope, his secret
yearning. Perhaps the yearning of all Remnants. An end to
hiding. An end to loneliness. The Remnants awakened, walking
the earth. Perhaps there was still a chance. A chance for—

No. He knew better than that.

"I chose a side. Eight hundred years ago," he said. "This isn't the way. What do you think will happen? You think the Sleepers will wake up all smiles and handshakes after so long underground? You've seen what a giant can do to a city. A flight of dragons. A horde of trolls." He could picture it all too easily. This time, he wouldn't be watching timber houses along an old bridge go up in flames. He'd be watching goblins drag humans into the mines, manticores ripping up power lines, witches getting their warty hands on missiles. "I swore an oath. Break it now and . . . Maunt, there'll be a war."

Mauntgraul grinned. "Rather a war than certain extinction."

Ben tried to argue, but the White Dog was changing, his human physique losing cohesion. His shoulders bubbled and bulged, his neck extending, scales sliding over his flesh. In moments, his wings fanned wide, eclipsing the panorama.

A claw stretched out, closing around Ben. Jia was on the move again. It was time to follow.

Ben cried out. But his anger wasn't just for the dragon. He was thinking about his vision, his flashes of the Ghost Emperor, blazing in some recess of his mind.

And the voice, that voice, calling him from beyond.

This time, he'd recognised it.

It belonged to Von Hart.

NINETEEN

A day or so later, Mauntgraul reached Hong Kong.

Across the bay, the city rose in glittering splendour, her skyscrapers thrusting into the night. Clutched in the White Dog's claw, Ben felt beaten and bruised, at the limits of his endurance, but the view couldn't fail to impress him. The neon climbing frame of the Bank of China building. Jardine House, with its innumerable round windows. The dazzle of the Two IFC Tower soaring over all, rising from behind the bulb-strung piers of the Star Ferry terminal. The dense urban wall flickered in a myriad of colour and light, a fairy palace in the water, illuminating the wooded peak that sheltered the city and the harbour. Few cities shone as bright as Hong Kong. From a hotchpotch of news, Ben recalled that the former British colony currently hovered in an opulent limbo, rendered a special administrative zone, not yet under the full control of the Chinese government. The city was a stolen gem of the Opium Wars, returned to the mainland with sad and reticent fingers.

But the deep black of Victoria Harbour failed to soothe him. The neon hoard waiting below couldn't allay his dread. Around his throat, the *lunewrought* collar was a cold vice, crackling with energy, drawing him and his deathly ride down towards a broad concrete wharf in Kowloon.

Ship containers, mooring winches and forklift trucks spread out under Mauntgraul's claws. The night, cool in the wake of a recent typhoon, held a trace of humidity, the first breath of the coming spring. Diesel, trash and fish competed in Ben's nostrils as he swooped down from the heights. Thankfully, the dockyard was empty at this hour, the tanker moored against the stacked maze of containers and the towering cranes unmoved by the descent of a twelve-ton dragon. It was almost midnight, by Ben's reckoning. And this was a place accustomed to noise. The city rumbled on, sleepless, across the water.

It was also a place accustomed to dragons. Nine of them, to be precise. The hills of the New Territories had been named after eight of the beasts and an emperor, if Ben remembered correctly. Kowloon Peak, Tung Shan, Tate's Cairn, Temple Hill, Unicorn Ridge, Lion Rock, Beacon Hill, Crow's Nest and Emperor Bing sheltered the famed peninsula and harbour. But none of the populace, he knew, would expect to see real dragons. And the emperor who waited ahead was anything but human.

The wharf spread out in a flat concrete rhombus from the western tip of Kowloon, a few miles from where the Pearl River met the South China Sea. It would've made a reasonable landing site, if Mauntgraul had got the chance.

Too late, Ben registered the growing intensity of the collar, chill against his throat. Rousing from a half-daze, he picked out the figure standing below and shock pricked him to alertness.

Braid weaving in the midnight wind, Jia stood on the edge of the wharf, looking out over the water. In human form, she made a lithe silhouette, a thirty-something-year-old woman returned to her homeland. How much, he wondered, had she seen change? Over the years, a city where a village used to stand. A highway dissecting a northern plain. A sky full of machines. He knew he was one of the few who could empathise with her. Whether that meant he could reach her or not, time would tell.

Hearing the snap of wings, Jia turned and looked up at them, and even from a distance Ben could see her weary resolve. The dust of her journey covered her suit. She must have known of her pursuit; the stolen harp would've told her as much, jangling across the miles. Unable to shake off the White Dog, she had decided to stop and face them.

The tense line of her spine brought all Ben's fears flooding to the surface. He shouted a warning, but it came too late. In the crook of her elbow, the *sin-you* cradled the fragments of the harp, their silvery light shining on her face.

Ben didn't care for her expression. There was desperation, yes, but also the same covetousness that haunted Mauntgraul's visage, the sickly glimmer drowning out both resistance and reason. It remained faint, a slow poison, but it was enough to tell him that the harp had Jia in its grip. When her fingers plucked at the soundboard, conjuring spectral strings, her movements were fluid, but somehow automatic. As if the artefact guided her hands.

"Jia! Don't!"

Puissance looped out from the fragment, an argent shudder

troubling the air. Mauntgraul roared – was it laughter? – as the ripples of light washed over him, mirrored in his ivory scales. He greeted the music as one basking in reunion, in exquisite pain, his claw clenching, squeezing Ben's ribs and choking off his cry. The dragon's muscles spoke of resistance, but whether because he'd been stripped of his fragment of the harp or because he was weakened from his journey, his dive for the artefact did him no good.

Collar burning his flesh, Ben felt the scales around him bubbling and seething, serpentine brawn giving way to human guise, caught and bound by the dissonant magic.

Fifty feet up, Mauntgraul shuddered. His wings folded inward, collapsing sails. His snout melted away, his pale flesh blushing, moulding to form a grinning face. A thrashing knot of tail and claws, his body rapidly dwindled in size. With a gasp, Ben found himself released, but he took no joy in his freedom. In Human form, the White Dog and he tumbled from the sky, smacking into the concrete of the wharf.

Minutes passed, stretched out over a rack of pain. The stars wheeled, bleeding fire. Having done its work, the harp fell silent.

Ben groaned. He spat out blood. Nursing his ribs – more than one of them cracked – he clambered onto his hands and knees, one of his legs sprawled out behind him, twisted and broken. *Healing.* A few feet away, Mauntgraul lay, a dark mess of limbs face down on the wharf. But Ben's eyes were only for Jia.

"I don't want to kill you," she told him. "Please. Don't make me."

"We're as good as dead anyway," he said. "Your words. Not mine. If you re-forge the harp . . . Jia, you'll start a war."

"Look around you, Ben. We're already in the middle of one. A war of attrition. And we are losing."

He found that he couldn't argue with this, his blood tasting sour in his mouth. He could tell that she was crying; the harp made her sorrow plain, silver on her cheeks. But he couldn't tell her that she was wrong.

Still . . .

"We swore an oath. All of us. There has to be a better way."

But the Lore is broken. You know that. All bets are off.

"Then show me." She was shouting now, the fragments trembling in her arms. "Show me as the envoy showed me. I can save them. Don't you see? There is still time. I can save them all!"

"Who? The Remnants?" But he guessed that he already knew. In her cell at the Invisible Church, her soft yet pointed question had led him towards a likely conclusion, and she confirmed it now, the wind carrying her bitterness to him.

"You might not remember your parents. I will honour mine."

"Oh yeah? At what cost? The death of thousands? Jia—"

"Better to die for the truth than live under a lie," she said. She struggled to get a grip on herself, control her emotions. This *sin-you*, a creature born to perceive the truth, to uphold justice – how the compromise must've troubled her, an inner conflict wriggling like a worm, gnawing away at her promise . . . Ben could see that. He could also see

321

how some might have taken advantage of it. "If only I had known that at the start."

She shook her head, as if rousing herself from a dream. It was only a moment, a window into her uncertainty, but he could read her doubt all the same. Her *corruption*. He had seen the effects of the harp for himself, the longing and the madness stirred up by the lullaby, a song to melt the hardest of hearts, to derange the soundest of minds. And he saw both in Jia, the unmistakable strain of loss, before her face smoothed into a resolute mask.

"What good am I?" she said then. "What good am I to walk this world as an appointed judge, when I can't shatter the illusion that binds us? We are here, Ben. Remnants among humans. The last survivors of myth and magic. And yet we are forced to hide, to shun the light, exiled, outcast, alone. Left to die. Don't you see? The Lore is the greatest lie of all."

"Is that what he told you? Von Hart?"

"My master has shown me much. Sacrifice. Truth."

I bet.

"And you believe him? You trust the Fay? Jia, whatever he told you, I'm telling you that there is always a price."

She bowed her head at this. As if she couldn't deny it.

"I have no choice."

"There is always a choice," he said.

"Flowers in a mirror and the moon in water," she told him, simply.

He had nothing to say to this, his words lost in a frustrated growl.

"We were locked behind a dark mirror," she said. "And

I have broken the glass. I know on which side I stand."

With a chill up his spine, he remembered du Sang's parting words in the catacombs under Paris, a strange riddle that now seemed to hold the weight of a prophecy.

A shattering of glass. The turn of a key. A black door opening.

"Jia," Ben said. "What have you done?"

Mauntgraul stole her chance of an answer.

"Give me the harp," the White Dog said. "It is mine. And I promise you that your death will be swift."

Despite his threat, Mauntgraul's words came out in a croak. Still, it was enough to make Ben and Jia turn in his direction as he climbed to his feet. Everything about him screamed of enervation, his ribcage showing starkly through his skin, his flesh sagging from his bones. The harp had scoured him, sucking him dry, leaving only waste. He stood in the shadow of the ship containers, his lips trembling between hollow cheekbones, the streaks of hair on either side of his head lit by the fragments in Jia's arms. The harp was all he cared about now. All that he craved.

The harmonic curve, moulded to resemble the mane of a horse – or a creature much like a horse – and the sound-board, shaped into galloping hooves. The dismantled instrument shone with a deep, subliminal radiance, a silvery glow pushing at the air, coupled with the faint suggestion of music, chimes of desire and death.

Neither fragment burned as bright as the lust in the White Dog's eyes, however, black pearls of need fixed upon Jia.

In response, Jia opened her arms to him, a fragment in either hand.

"You want this?" she said. "Maniac. Butcher. Well, you can have it."

Like a snake before flame, Mauntgraul drew back his lips, a hiss slipping between his teeth. Jia spent a second staring at him, her face hardening, the light from the artefact making a mask of her features. No. The mask was gone now, Ben saw, torn away by the radiance, her doubt discarded.

She looked drunk, he realised. Drunk on the power in her grip.

Who was this creature before him? *Sin-you*? *Youxia*? Ben barely recognised her, but he caught her intent. Desperately he thrust out a hand, his fingers splayed.

"Don't—"

Jia paid him no heed. Her arms closed in a swift arc, bringing the fragments of the harp together. The metal glimmered, jangling to shatter stone. There was an odd whispering under the sound, a liquid slithering that set his teeth on edge, *lunewrought* melding to *lunewrought*. He caught a hint of the metal weaving like vines, even as his collar pulsed, responding to the reunion of the harp. As he watched, the equine mane bonded with the hooves of the other fragment, creating the shape of a wishbone, gilded in silver. The *Cwyth* almost made whole.

And the night exploded.

A barrage of light slammed into Ben, the unleashed force of the harp as unforgiving as rock. The deluge of energy swept him up, tossing him like so much flotsam across the wharf. Ropes, barrels and tools joined him, rolling into the silvery flood. With a crack, his back thumped into a stack of crates, the impact sending splinters flying around him, some of them spearing the scales of his suit, making him cry out in pain. All the same, he was lucky. The obstacle prevented him from sliding over the edge of the jetty, a broken toy thrown into the water. As the crates collapsed on top of him, a sparkling dome flowered over the wharf, the skyline bleaching out, erased by an alien power. Ben clapped his hands over his ears, shrinking from the rising melody, trying to shut out its burrowing fingers.

To shut out the music. The music of death. It was bells, sweet bells, a church rattling in an earthquake. It was the breath before every goodbye. In a symphony of a thousand screams, the lullaby spiralled across the wharf, smacking off the waters of the bay and tearing at the sky.

Clutching his skull, Ben squinted through the surrounding wreckage. Jia stood silhouetted in the eye of the storm. In one arm she cradled the bow-shaped V of the harp, the artefact two thirds assembled and throbbing, blazing in the dark. Between the harmonic curve and the soundboard, Ben saw the spectre of strings lacing together and watched, choked by dread, as Jia plucked at them, strumming the appalling notes. Music and light rippled out over the wharf.

And where there was music, there was magic.

The ground. The ground was opening up.

Under him the concrete buckled and cracked, the wharf shifting. Throwing off broken wood, Ben stood and flung out his arms, fighting for balance. He shared an anxious look with Mauntgraul, the White Dog falling to his knees, the ground under him ripped away like a rug. A few feet behind him, the middle of the wharf was bubbling, seething around a widening hole, a whirlpool of rock sinking into the earth. Ben caught the gleam of obsidian, some ensorcelled cavern yawning in the depths, and his cry joined the other dragon's as he felt himself dragged towards it.

Arms wheeling, he tried to run backwards, tottering away from the maw. It was useless. The ground tipped, the churning concrete hurling him onto his back, a makeshift conveyor belt carrying him towards the White Dog. Desperately he flipped onto his stomach, scrabbling for purchase. In his skull, the music took on a strained pitch, a piercing whine, discordant, cruel. The magic, he knew, couldn't touch him – he had been spared the lullaby, after all – but the same wasn't true of Mauntgraul. And as bony fingers closed around his foot, he realised that the dragon meant to drag him into the earth along with him. Into the Sleep.

Howling, Mauntgraul struggled against the music. He had managed to resist the harp before, Ben knew, thwart the spoiling enchantment, and it seemed that he still had some fight left in him. His face was a grimacing knot, his hands clutching at Ben, climbing his legs, using him as an anchor. Ben kicked out, stamping on the White Dog's shoulders, his head, but the dragon was beyond pain, shrieking and flinging his arms around Ben's waist, hauling himself up onto his stomach. Ben gagged, screwing up his face at the stench of blood and sweat, murder and madness filling his nostrils. Limbs locked, the two of them wrestled on the heaving ground, sliding inexorably towards the mouth of the maelstrom.

Still, Mauntgraul was making headway. It occurred to Ben that he meant to exchange his place, put another in his tomb instead. Namely Ben. And Ben, immune to the Sleep, would surely die there, buried and starving, awake and aware, locked under the earth.

Christ.

"I'm sorry," Jia said, as if reading his mind.

He looked up and saw her approach, walking lightly across the wharf. Things weren't happening fast enough for her, it seemed; she came to the edge of the maelstrom, a slender figure in a fluttering cloak of shadow and light, pressing the magic upon them. The music of the harp, strummed by a rebellious hand, went echoing across the waters. Like polished stones, the notes dispersed, skipping and shimmering over the waves, some bouncing with a hollow twang against the hulls of tugboats and neon-lit junks, others fizzling out against the far shore, light bleeding into light. Silver washed out Ben's thoughts, his throat strangled by cold metal, a fanfare exploding in his mind.

Bells. Bells.

Mauntgraul screamed.

The next moment, a great weight was pressing down upon Ben. They were at the lip of the hole now, a dark funnel whirling under them, sucking at their feet. He had seen this cavern before, this bubbling of the earth, many years ago and miles from here in the mountains outside Beijing, the harp blazing in Von Hart's hands. He had seen it more recently too, the cracked shell of Zhoukoudian. In a jolt of horror, he grasped the full extent of the danger, the looming finality, the way the ground would close over their heads, sealing both of them in. Another minute and down they would go, down into the darkness, one of them swallowed by the Sleep, the other by a slow and agonising death.

With a roar of effort, the White Dog was changing, Ben saw, forcing his body against the music, his claws sprouting, retracting, his wings unfolding, then crumpling, a quick tide of dampened transformation. Shrieking to shatter the night, he writhed in the radiance, a surge, a push, his bulk overcoming the penetrating song. Resisting the souring magic, the weakening lullaby. Fangs snapping, his tail came sweeping out, the black barb on the end of it aimed at Jia.

There came a flash of brilliance. A cry and the clang of *lunewrought* on concrete.

Leaping back to avoid his sting, Jia tumbled onto her back, the harp skittering away from her.

At once, the ground slowed, rumbling to a standstill. In full dragon form, Mauntgraul sprang over Ben, his claws splayed, intending to crush the *sin-you*, turn her into mincemeat on the wharf. Instead, she rolled away from his landing, one arm reaching for the harp. Ben was up and on the move at once, leaping towards her, come what may. Her fingers closed around the artefact and she pulled it towards her, meeting resistance as the fused metal relic jerked in her grasp.

She looked up to find Ben crouching over her, his features pained as he clutched the harp.

The *lunewrought* burned his flesh, a frosty heat. He felt its music in his skull like a fire, as though its light would burst from his eyes, his nose, his mouth. But he didn't let go. If it took all he had to stop her, avert her from her dangerous course, then he was ready to die in the attempt.

I'm the Sola Ignis. The lone fire. And honey, this is fucked.

328

Jia shouted something up at him, but he couldn't make out her words, the scaling melody blasting in his ears. And for all his intent, he couldn't hold on for long, a few seconds at best, the *sin-you* wrenching the harp from his grasp.

But not before the collar around his throat rippled and grew soft, the alien metal rendered molten by its closeness to the harp. Roaring, he felt the restraint loosen, then spring free, reduced to mere beads of silver. The drops sailed through the air, a dazzling shower merging with the artefact in Jia's grip, releasing him with a shudder of pain and a gasp of unfettered air.

There wasn't any time to relish his freedom. The White Dog bellowed, pounding across the wharf, a wall of white scales and fangs. The shadow of wings fell over them, veined and vast, bringing certain death.

Ben and Jia exchanged a glance, a frantic meeting of dread.

"You'll kill us all!" Ben spat at her.

"No. I will save us."

Then she was on her feet, scrambling away from him, the harp recovered, clutched to her breast.

Ben turned as Mauntgraul barrelled into him, a claw closing around his chest, dragging him across the wharf. But Ben was changing too, his red-scaled bulk exceeding the limits of the dragon's grip, his wings snapping out, pulling them both into the air over the harbour.

Despite his wounds, his muscles sang with his release, his blood hot in his veins. He roared again, partly in pain, partly in joy, as the two of them soared up into the night, a tangle of wings, tails and thrashing claws.

Mauntgraul, clearly realising that he'd grabbed the wrong prey, fought to release himself, hurl Ben away from him and turn back for Jia and the harp.

Ben wasn't about to let that happen. He held on fast, his talons digging into flesh. Mauntgraul lashed out his tail, his sting darting close, but Ben closed a claw around the base of the vesicle, trapping the barb at foreleg's length, venom splattering the air. The White Dog was a wasted creature, little more than a skeleton now, a collection of scale and bone, eaten alive by the harp. But as the two of them grappled in the sky, their eyes locked and Ben caught a spark of the old fire, the old hatred. Mad or no, Mauntgraul wasn't about to give up. If Ben hoped to stop Jia, first he was going to have to get this monster out of his way. No matter what, he couldn't let the White Dog get hold of the harp. Who knew what evils he'd summon out of the earth? What slaughter he'd leave in the wake of his madness. With his own embers burning in his belly, Ben realised that the dragon was never going to stop.

As Jia shrank to a glimmering dot on the wharf, Ben understood that the time had come to face his destiny.

Blood on snow. Old as dust. The Red and the White.

It was time for an ending. One way or the other.

TWENTY

Across the bay the dragons swept, carried by their flailing wings. As their claws locked, their hind legs scratching for the softer parts of each other, the junks and the ferries below passed by in a radiant blur, tossed on the tides of their passage.

For all Ben's intent, the White Dog had gained the upper hand, his wings spread over Ben, clutching his struggling form. It was clear that Mauntgraul was driving them on, pushing them towards the city. If this was the last engagement, then true to form, he meant to destroy as much as possible. That much was clear. He wrestled above Ben, jaw snapping, teeth connecting with flesh. Roars echoed across the harbour. Blood sprayed the night, hissing into the waters below.

He fought with the last of his strength, Ben knew, a weakened yet no less formidable opponent, fuelled by rage, the insanity left by the absence of the harp. It was all he wanted to do now; perhaps the only thing left that made sense. If the dragon had been in full health, Ben would've stood little chance. As it was, Mauntgraul fought with the fury of the mad, barely pausing in his assault, trying to wrench his sting out of Ben's grasp. Unable to do so, he took advantage of Ben's handicap, landing a series of heavy blows, his claws scoring scales, painting crimson with crimson. And Ben, for his part, had no choice but to defend himself, slashing at the White Dog's snout, his belly, his neck. Anything to stop him, bring him down.

In a jumble of wings and limbs, the two of them crossed the boundary of the southern shore, shooting over the piers of the Star Ferry terminal. Distantly, Ben heard screams rising from the streets beyond, people looking up, shocked by the spectacle flying out of the night. Phone cameras flashed. Traffic screeched to a standstill. The neon blaze of Hong Kong wouldn't spare anyone the sight. There were no shadows deep enough in which to hide. Panic shuddered up from the ground, a city stricken by terror.

Come the dawn, they'll think us a nightmare. A mass hallucination. A fake video.

But the damage, he knew, would remain.

Together Mauntgraul and Ben crashed into the upper floors of the Two IFC Tower, the second tallest building in the city. Glass shattered. Steel screamed. Lights fizzled out. Snarling, the White Dog forced Ben back into the wreckage, the showering debris thumping on his wings, his horns, forcing him downward. Mauntgraul roared, green flames blustering from between his jaws, his heat blackening scale and glass. Ben answered with his own blast, a crimson pennant twisting with emerald, crackling above them as they fell, locked in battle. Claws around each other's necks, the two dragons gouged a furrow through thirty-odd floors, shooting towards the ground. Metal sparked off the ridges of Ben's spine. Office furniture took to the air, spinning out over hundreds of feet. Desks, chairs, computers, reduced to splinters on the road below.

Glancing down the flank of the building, Ben saw people several floors below, their faces pressed to the broad window of an observation deck, the glass cracked and shuddering. Silently he sent them a warning to get back, get away, but it was much too late for that. Another minute and the dragons' combined bulk would crash through the floor like a wrecking ball, taking half the tourists with them. Thrusting his hind legs into the framework, Ben growled and pushed himself clear of the tower, his muscles straining as he forced the White Dog away, out into the open air.

There'll be no more deaths on my watch. Only one, if I can help it . . .

Below, people froze in the road, looking up, their muffled screams stinging his ears. Cars skidded to a halt, passengers spilling from hastily opened doors. He roared, warning the crowds to scatter as he folded his wings, renewing his grip on Mauntgraul. Gravity was his only hope. The wind screaming around them, he let his weight carry the White Dog down, plummeting towards the earth.

And Mauntgraul was laughing, crazed in the thrill of battle, *wyrm tongue* flying from his throat.

"Yes, Benjurigan. Yes. Now you show your teeth!"

With a tremendous boom, draconic brawn met the ground. Cars crumpled under their weight, a ring of rubble and dust fanning out over the road. Mauntgraul's laughter cut short.

Echoes ricocheted between the skyscrapers. Streetlights guttered. Tarmac cracked. In the nearby bars, people looked up at the rattling rows of bottles on the shelves. Faces turned to one another in mute alarm, passing the same message back and forth – *Earthquake! Earthquake!* Shoppers in the Wan Chai district clutched each other in the tremors, frozen amid the shuddering racks of clothes. Souvenirs leapt off the shelves, lucky golden cats waving overtime, fans raining down, plaster models of the city's buildings shattering on the floor like an omen of things to come. Trams clanged to a standstill, their bells ringing, the upheaval punching their tracks out of true. Neon signs sparked and fizzed, bulbs popping in the chaos. Along the peaks from High West to Mount Cameron, the hills overlooking the city, birds took to flight, squawking.

For a moment, all was silence. All was dust.

Sirens wailed in the distance, tyres screeching to a halt some way from the shallow smoking crater in the middle of the road. Not daring to come any closer.

A claw gripped the edge of the crater, bloody and red. Groaning, Ben hauled himself up, a scaled heap of broken limbs. Dragging himself along on his belly, he shook out his wings, debris clattering all around him. For several minutes he lay in the road, breathing heavily, allowing his pinions to straighten, his bones to reset. He didn't have time to fully heal; wounded would have to do. Through his pain, hot knives along his body, he managed to clamber onto all fours, his snout swinging as he cleared his head.

Get up. Get up, you idiot. She'll be getting away with the harp.

He knew it was true. He didn't have a second to spare. The sooner he put an end to the White Dog – he took courage from his wishful thinking – the sooner he could catch up with Jia, wrench the stolen harp from her grasp. What he would do with the relic was anyone's guess. Returning the fragments to the Guild and the Chapter was out of the question. The Lore was over now, he knew it in his bones, and neither organisation had exactly filled him with trust. Maybe he could drop the damn thing in a volcano. Fling it out to sea . . .

In his mind, an echo of Von Hart, calling to him from beyond.

Catch her.

What the hell did it mean? Why would the envoy wrap him up in all this when he was after the harp in the first place, stirring up rebellion? Right from the start, Von Hart had called to him, reaching him through the invasive touch of the Ghost Emperor. Obviously the fairy was trying to tell him something. With some spell or other, the envoy had tried to warn him back in Paris with his weird little message in the fortune cookie.

When the time comes, let me fall.

There was a choice here. And a plea. If the fairy was indeed using Jia as a tool, a way to recover the harp, then it struck Ben that he was using him too. Either way, he'd taken a desperate gamble. It was hardly surprising that he'd try to play the odds. Perhaps Von Hart had thrown in a wild card, keeping one last trick up his sleeve.

Is that why he kept you in the game? Wherever he is, whatever he made Jia do, it seems like he's aiming for damage limitation. She was his student, just like you. And, well, he saved your arse, didn't he? Think, damn it! Whatever the truth behind this Ghost Emperor, he doesn't believe she'll survive her mission . . .

Sprawled in the road, Ben tasted the likelihood of this, sensing he'd hit upon something.

Catch her. Let me fall.

With a knot in the pit of his stomach, he realised that for this plan to work, Von Hart hadn't thought that Ben could stop her, that she'd best the Sola Ignis at every turn. And the worst thing about it was that it was the truth.

Mauntgraul. Jia. Him. All played.

It had been there all along, hadn't it, the deception? Even the message itself, a warning that had been more visual than literal, now he came to think of it. What was a fortune cookie but a western fabrication, an American confection that had nothing whatsoever to do with China? A sweet sham. A clever lie, like Jia Jing's mission of mercy. Ben got that now.

He knew that you couldn't talk her out of it. Tell her that she was wrong.

And all of this to undo the lullaby? To start a war? He couldn't help but feel that there was more to it than that . . .

Never trust the Fay.

Behind him, Mauntgraul spoke.

"I told you that I would show you destruction. See how your world burns."

Ben turned, hauling himself up on his hind legs, claws bunched to defend himself. The White Dog stood on the far side of the crater, his bulk swaying, his wings pale rags. Above them, the Two IFC Tower, a smouldering gouge down its side, flames spluttering from the damaged building. But Ben realised that this devastation wasn't what the dragon meant.

To clarify, Mauntgraul swept out an arm, indicating the road behind him.

There were police cars parked on the corner, their lights flashing in a line across the street. In the illumination, Ben saw the hastily erected barrier, the raised guns of officers crouching behind it. Too far out of range, he reckoned, but how long that would last, how long until soldiers arrived with rocket launchers and grenades . . . he didn't want to think about it. He saw the crowds pressing behind the cars, a sea of faces drawn with shock. The bright audience of mobile phones. The glint of film cameras borne on shoulders, journalists pressing through the throng. He heard the throb of rotors somewhere above, helicopters circling, no doubt with their own cameras poised, recording the monsters in the road.

From New York to Egypt, Beijing to London to Hong Kong, Ben had left evidence of his presence, the clips stacking up, the news stories growing, the age-old doubt evaporating. Seeing the watchful eyes of the crowd, he realised, with shoulders slumped, that the time for hiding was over. The Lore was shattered. The Pact undone. The humans were beginning to learn that fabulous beasts were among them. Myths crashing into the modern world. And as the knowledge spread and the fear grew, he also knew that nothing good could come of it.

"We'll end this," he told the White Dog, his words desperate, fierce. "You and me. And when this is over, I'll go from here. Vanish like smoke. They'll forget. They always do."

Mauntgraul laughed, shaking his head.

"You old fool. They will hunt you down. All of you. You are looking at your death."

"War is not the answer."

"No? Then you hope to bid for peace? These maggots know it not among their own kind. Better to scratch out their eyes."

Despite the bitter truth of this, Ben knew that the White Dog had hit the nail on the head, putting his hope into words. He hadn't even realised the depth of it until he did so, the private resolution that he craved. And Jia, misguided, manipulated, had shown him too. This was no time for despair. The Lore might be over, the Pact no more than a lie, and a catastrophe to end all catastrophes approaching the earth like a runaway train, but there had to be another way, didn't there? Remnants and humans had managed to reach some kind of accord before, however oppressive, however doomed to failure. But times had changed. There was still a chance, surely. He had to believe that.

He was on his own. The lone fire. Standing guard.

It was all he had left.

"I can't . . . I won't let you do that," he said.

Mauntgraul grinned, baring his fangs.

"Come then. Try and stop me."

With that, the White Dog spun and bounded down the road for the line of police cars, his horns lowered, ready to gore. People screamed, scattering, a juggernaut heading right for them. Guns cracked, bullets sparking off the dragon's scales, doing nothing to stop him.

Ben bunched his hind legs and leapt, wings fanning out to carry him over the hole in the road. Tarmac buckled as he landed, stamping down on the White Dog's tail, catching his sting in mid-flail. Thus checked, Mauntgraul howled, his body twisting around, a fist smashing into Ben's snout. Blood flew, a couple of fangs sailing through the air. Flames shot into the night, wild and green, scorching Ben's chest and neck. Bellowing, he scrabbled for purchase, locking his foreleg around the White Dog's head. Together the dragons rolled, crushing the roofs of cars, flattening trash cans and parking meters and crashing into the shops on the left-hand side of the street, bricks and glass raining down.

Ben's fist worked overtime, pounding on Mauntgraul's skull. The dragon's laughter, shrill, maniacal, gradually became a series of grunts, the buildings collapsing around them. Then Ben was lifting the White Dog from the rubble, his wings pumping, catching the wind. Muscles aching, wounds screaming, he dragged the dragon into the air, rising from the ruins in much the same way as two beasts had long ago battled their way from a hill in Wales, released by a legendary wizard to centuries of enmity. The white of vengeance. The red of blood.

"This is what you wanted," he snarled in Mauntgraul's ear, his fangs locked. "Tooth and claw. A reckoning."

"It is . . . the way of things," the dragon growled, wrestling in Ben's grasp.

Up and up the two of them soared, the city receding below them, the Two IFC a smear of neon and flame, the sirens lost to the wind, the crowds reduced to milling ants. Clutching the White Dog's tail, his foreleg locked around his throat, Ben speared directly upward, over the night-bound waters of Victoria Harbour. Mauntgraul struggled, his claws wheeling, scratching at nothing. In Ben's grip, the dragon felt like a bundle of bones, a sack of scales ebbing in strength, reaching the limits of endurance. The harp had done its worst. The Sola Ignis would do the rest.

Mauntgraul roared again, bellowing flame, green heat blustering in a trail behind them as they rose. Ben squeezed harder, choking off his air, restricting any chance of the White Dog's devastating scream. The *Cornutus Quiritor* would do no more harm, not if he could help it.

"Then it's time I repaid your kindness," Ben said. "Like your mother, I will give you . . . a good death."

With this, he snapped in his wings, straightening his tail, moulding himself to the rushing airstream. For a second the wind carried them, the two of them arching through the dark. Then the beasts slowed and fell, their tangled bulk dropping like a stone towards the bay.

Mauntgraul screamed, a curse, a plea, the wind stealing his words away.

With a crash, a mighty hiss of steam, the water closed over Ben's head. The White Dog thrashed under him, an explosion of bubbles and frantic claws, the tide claiming him, snuffing out his heat. Into the dark of the bay they sank, Ben tightening his grip. He heard a muffled roar, submerged rage, as he forced the White Dog down, down into the deep.

Soon enough, the dragon gave up the fight, his mind set on a new battle – to prevent himself from drowning. His limbs opened, thrashing in the waters, trying to saddle the current, pull himself up. Away.

Ben held on fast. Talons out, he tore at Mauntgraul's exposed belly, ripping through scale and flesh, the water darkening around him, a flower of blood and guts.

It didn't have to be this way. You left me no choice.

Ben's lungs were fit to burst as the depths sucked at them, dragging them down, wreathed by spirals of black.

In the dark, he met Mauntgraul's gaze. The dragon's eyes were dimming, growing dull. Hatred replaced by something else, usurped by what Ben could only read as relief. A silencing of the bells, perhaps. An end to days of madness and rage. The last breath of vengeance. Something like that.

At last the White Dog went limp in his grasp, his blood gushing out. His fire quenched.

Ben closed his eyes. Behind them, the butterflies were swarming again, threatening to claim him, seal his fate to the dragon's beneath him.

The dead and the white.

When he opened them again, the White Dog was drifting away from him, released from his claws. He floated, a pale wreck, his long neck and tail weaving, empty of life. His weight was carrying him down, down into the mud and silt, joining Rakegoyle in a watery grave.

And it was a kindness, Ben knew, the darkness crowding in close.

Yes. A kindness.

A kindness for all.

TWENTY-ONE

Gasping, the air filling his lungs, Red Ben Garston burst from the depths of Victoria Harbour. Water fanned off his wings in a sheet, twisting into pearls as he climbed, fighting for altitude. He was weary, his muscles leaden, but what choice did he have but to go on? He was the only one left who could stop the *sin-you*. Stop the re-forging of the harp. Prevent a war between Remnants and humans. Desperation flung him into the sky, dread gnawing at his heart.

The Hong Kong skyline shimmered below, smoke billowing from the damaged flank of the Two IFC Tower, fire engines pumping arcs of water onto the fire. With a pang of guilt, Ben watched the crater in the road and the crushed buildings dwindling under him, further destruction left in his wake. Beijing, London and now here. The chaos seemed like a taste of things to come.

. *And you swore to protect them. That was your oath.*

As he speared through straggling clouds, the neon grid dimming below, he met the stratosphere with a mix of panic and relief – he still lived, still had a chance – his heart thumping as he searched the hills around the city.

She's gone. Gone.

All he saw was darkness, the night threaded by the sodium

riddle of roads and the towns of the New Territories. Above him, planes roared, taking off and landing. Stars winked through the smog, as faint as his hope. A great weight settled on his mind, threatening to force him earthward. Doubt. Despair. Failure. He had seen the *sin-you*'s speed for himself. In Beijing, racing beside the train. In London, shooting down the road from the Heath. And from above, Mauntgraul chasing a trail of dust from the Alps into China, a nigh-on tireless pursuit of days. In the time it had taken him to bring down the White Dog, Jia could've fled anywhere, bearing the re-forged fragments of the harp miles from here, their complete reunion assured.

No. He had lost her. For all his extraordinary eyesight, his own dexterity, there was no way he could find her in such a broad area, the rugged expanse of Hong Kong Island.

As his wounds began to heal, his pain receding, he was left with the sting of self-reproach. He chastised himself for his foolishness. A beautiful stranger from the Far East had crashed into his life with a tale of an ancient and noble purpose, one spurring her into a desperate mission: to alert the descendants of the Curia Occultus to the coming of the Ghost Emperor. On the surface, Ben had had little reason to doubt her, this Jia Jing, a creature that, despite her objections, amounted to the Chinese equivalent of a unicorn. Or vice versa. Purity. Innocence. Truth and justice.

Yeah, right. More like judgement . . .

But doubt her he had. Her true intentions had been there from the start, unravelling in the things she'd said, her barely veiled sorrow, the secret that was driving her on. *I can save them.* Her arrival in his life had been a little too neat, her saving him from the White Dog's venom obviously meant to secure his alliance and thus lead her to the harp. Everyone and their cat was grasping for the artefact. Why not her? All of this, this frantic gamble, had been planned out beforehand. He knew it in his guts. And no prizes for guessing its architect.

Show me. Show me as the envoy showed me . . .

Yeah. She'd confessed as much. After centuries of living in the shadows, even Von Hart didn't know the whereabouts of the Invisible Church, it seemed – but he would have known that the Chapter was looking for Ben all right. Last year he had told him so on the desert sands. *There is going to be a council. Perhaps even a trial . . .* It made a wild kind of sense, typical of the Fay, a race known for its wiles and caprices. Find Ben. Find the Chapter. Recover the harp. It stood to reason that the Chapter would have confiscated the Guild's fragment, didn't it? Usurping the order of knights from power, securing the relic in their keeping . . . Von Hart must've counted on that, some ancient procedure, some clause in the Pact. One way or the other, Jia had meant to steal them both.

If Jia could convince Ben of her mission, draw him out into the open . . . well, with a surge of resentment, he knew that she had managed to do exactly that. Despite his mistrust, his refusal to team up with her, she had played him for a fool.

The plan was a desperate one, yes, a raising of fire to pluck the harp from the blaze, but at the end of the day, the *sin-you* had succeeded.

Jia had followed him to England. Like most Remnants,

she must've known the location of Paladin's Court. Or the envoy would've told her. Ben scowled. Had she banked on him returning to the mansion? With her penetrating insight, had she read the purpose in him even as she reminded him of his duty? A cynical move, at best. At worst, hypocrisy.

And Mauntgraul? One big white distraction. Chaos, confusion to draw the eyes of the Guild and the Chapter, keep them busy. A smokescreen to cover her tracks.

Or did it go deeper than that? Ben wondered. A way to bring him charging into the fray, honour-bound to face his ancient foe, and into the palm of the *sin-you*? If this was the case, then the plan had backfired somewhat. The Chapter hadn't managed to secure the Guild's fragment of the harp. The White Dog had stolen it himself, ultimately forcing Jia to show her hand, her treachery in the Invisible Church. *Lunewrought* had called to *lunewrought*, drawing them all into the heart of the fire, an inferno that threatened to destroy the very foundations of the Remnant world.

And Ben had been touched by the harp, had only recently been released from its binding. Thinking this, he experienced a shred of hope. Could he rely on its magic now? Could he use its taint to his advantage?

High above the city, he closed his eyes.

Yes. A vestige of silver, burning in his mind. A trace of coldness around his throat. Slowing, he spun in the air five hundred feet up, letting the memory, the stain, pull him around, dragging his snout towards the west.

When he opened his eyes, a rough gasp escaped him. Senses prickling, he took in the vision below, a sight that struck him as oddly familiar, despite its new and uncanny nature. An arc of blue light was gleaming under the water, spanning the darkened bay. Vast it was, a broad beam of eldritch radiance stretching under the waves to the distant shore, the hills of an island rising miles ahead, rugged against the stars. Symbols glimmered down there, each one the size of a village, viewed from this height. Some ancient and long-lost power had branded sigils into the earth, each one massive, aglow and indecipherable, bound by the borders of a great wheel, a circle marching off into the horizon.

Even as he watched, the symbols were fading. Corroding. Winking out. Lost in the moonlight.

Not too long ago, Ben had seen a similar vision over the North Sea, the arc stretching off into the European hinterland. He had heard enough since to guess at what it was, recalling Jia's words from the hills outside Béijing.

The magic of the Fay is growing old. The circles of protection are souring . . . And the stench of their corruption draws the Lurkers to its source.

But the circle, it seemed, was also drawing Ben. Tracing the fading curve of the arc, his eyes came to rest on the hills again, the island to the west. Even as his skull jangled, responding to the stolen artefact, he made out the faint line of dust rising between the peaks. The trail moved too fast for him to think it a cloud, a familiar streak of grey smeared across the night, left by a creature galloping at incredible speed from the northernmost tip of the island.

He pictured the partly formed harp wound into a flowing green mane or hooked on a curving horn, borne on impossible winds. Jia Jing was racing for the finish line.

There was a bridge up there, shining in the distance, and

he realised that the *sin-you* couldn't have crossed the waters on hooves alone. First she must've headed inland to reach this place, circumventing the bay. That gave him time. Not much, he reckoned. Hopefully enough.

The circle was fading, vanishing beneath the waves, but by its light, he had found her.

With renewed hope, he spread his wings, shooting west across the waters.

Half an hour later, reaching the far shore and veering south, Ben came to the southernmost tip of the island. A narrow rocky peninsula stretched out into the Pearl River estuary, the waters dark, ships glimmering out there in the distance, the sleepless cargoes of Hong Kong. The moon shone down, gilding the slopes of a cape ahead, the surrounding area wild, deserted. A sea of wind-blown grass and sand.

A good place to hide.

Far below, the ocean pounded against the foot of the cliffs, matching the drumming in his ears, part fear, part a subtle tension in the air.

The temple atop the cape wasn't much to look at. Many steps, crooked and worn, rose up to the ruined building, the great wooden doors thrown wide, the sign of recent entry. Dust still eddied in the air, not quite settled from the *sin-you*'s arrival. The arched entrance was a shadowed mouth, emanating patience. And music, he thought, a faint tinkling from the gloom beyond, betraying the presence of the harp. Above the doors, the tiers of the pagoda, crumbling, adorned with the mossy statues of dragons, rose in unsteady stacks to a single remaining spire, pointing at the heavens like an accusatory finger, or perhaps a plea to forgotten gods who had long since abandoned the shrine.

Ben alighted at the bottom of the steps, his draconic form rippling inward, wings folding and compressing, wreathing into the dark scales of his suit. His tail, arrowhead-tipped, shrank and coiled up into his spine. His snout rolled back, resolving into a human face, his eyes bright, his jaw a grim line. Man-shaped, he could see the evidence of a similar transformation – one that had taken place only minutes before, he guessed – the imprint of hooves on the gritty steps, replaced by the marks of bare feet, leading upward.

He had taken several of the steps, leaping them two at a time, when he realised that something was wrong, an increasing strain in the atmosphere. The night was cold, a chill that he didn't think was entirely due to winter, the way it crept into his bones, his breath frosting the space in front of his nose. Likewise, he heard the rush of the ocean, swirling around the rocks hundreds of feet below, but he felt no wind on his cheeks, on his shaven head, the air around the temple a dead weight pressing down on his shoulders as if to warn him away. He knew this cold, had felt it before. He wasn't likely to forget it. It was the chill of the boundary, a place between the earth and elsewhere, the natural laws relinquishing hold.

Gritting his teeth, he shivered, sensing the touch of the nether.

As he drew closer to the doors, the façade above him confirmed his fears. There were gaps in the bricks, he saw, holes that wouldn't be out of place in any ruin except that some of the blocks weren't completely touching each other, suspended by some supernatural force. Something in the temple was pulling at them, a magnetism that confused their nature, troubling the gravity around him. Skull tingling, Ben let the tide carry him, the air snagging at his chest, his limbs, drawing him on through the doors.

In shafts of moonlight and shadow, he paused on the threshold, fists raised, taking in the scene. Plaster gods, chipped and worn, lined either side of the chamber, glaring at him in the dusty gloom. He ignored the judgement in their painted eyes as he made his way down the nave, heading for the dais at the far end, the darkness waiting there. Above him, directly ahead, there was a place where the moonlight failed, the shadows condensed around what appeared to be a vast octagon, darker than the night outside, the murk in the temple.

He came closer – close enough to feel the currents flowing towards that mouth, that huge lightless maw. In a steady stream, dust trickled past his ears, the hole above him sucking at the shadows, at the night. And it was a hole, wasn't it? Punched in the wall of the world. Tentatively he drew himself to the foot of the dais, frowning up at the bulky object. Close up, its dimensions grew clearer, the octagon resting on a stand, what he could only determine as a breach framed in wood. Leading nowhere.

No, that wasn't quite true. Leading into nothing.

Jia's words came back to haunt him.

I remember when I first heard the Ghost Emperor . . . A new god approaching the earth, pressing his eye against a hole in the world, looking in, hungry. And then reaching out . . .

He recalled du Sang's parting words in Paris.

A shattering of glass. The turn of a key. A black door opening.

He shuddered, sensing that he was looking at the door in question. *The door of Creation.* What else could it be? Only months ago, Ben had found himself on a similar boundary. Lurkers, scenting a build-up of magical force, had been drawn to the oil refinery in Cairo, ready to pull him into the dark – the space between the formed and the unformed – the phantoms reaching out from the endless gulfs that bordered Creation in the hope of feasting on the conjuring source. Looking at the present darkness, Ben felt the same coldness, the same emptiness, with reluctant familiarity. Sure, he was no expert on magic – the fairy was welcome to it – but he had encountered enough *hey presto!* in his time to dislike the taste of it and he could taste its residue here.

The mnemonic harp. Its music was somewhere beyond this place, chiming in the depths ahead. Chiming in his skull. Apart from himself, the temple was empty, a chamber of echoes and dust.

Jia must've stepped through the black door, carrying the fragments into the nether.

Is that where you're hiding, old friend?

Ben had no time to hesitate, to mull over his terror and scars. Squaring his shoulders, he pounded up the steps and leapt into the darkness.

TWENTY-TWO

Into the nether. The Dark Frontier.

For a second or two, his heart in his mouth, Ben sailed into the lightless void. Thankfully, he thumped down on a solid surface, sparks flying from his feet. It took him a moment to realise what he was standing on, recognising the surface from his adventures last year and more recently from his venom-drenched dream. Under him, one of the Silver Leys, forming a narrow shimmering bridge that stretched from the octagonal door at his back into the darkness. He had seen the leys before, sure, how Von Hart possessed the power to direct the residual Fay byways. To steer them *within certain terrestrial limits*, according to the envoy. And as before, he could sense the fairy's hand in things, dragging him into this madness. If he could trust one damn word from the envoy's lips, he guessed that the surface under him, if not exactly physical, held enough strength to support him. At least for now. Still, his relief – the fact that he wasn't falling into the depths forever – wasn't enough to allay his fear.

Stealing a breath, frost fluttering around him, he moved cautiously forward. He determined to look neither left nor right – and especially not down. If he fell, could he fly in dragon form back to the doorway? Would he be able to find it again? If not, then next stop eternity. Falling and falling until he starved. Or until the cold claimed him. Or perhaps a Lurker. *Take your pick.* It was a risk he had no choice but to take, spurring his feet into motion. Heels shedding sparks, he loped along the ley, the bridge into nothingness.

Seconds could have passed, or hours. Each step made him more aware of his size in the immensity, a red-haired mote in the gulf. The ley stretched on, a glimmering tightrope over an endless drop. The earthly laws fell short in this place, unable to assert their physical grip. At times, Ben thought he was moving backwards, the silver road sliding under him, a conveyer belt rotating on nothing. At others, he was sure he was walking sideways or upside down. The width of the ley changed too, sometimes expanding to resemble a highway, then shrinking in a way he couldn't quite trace to the size of a forest path. Sweat rimed his skin. His breath steamed in pale feathers. He looked ahead – always ahead – into the impossible distance. In time or out of it, he eventually noticed the glow up ahead, the orb of a small white sun drawing ever closer.

No. It was no sun, he saw. It was a pale colossus, a beacon of doom hunkering over the ley.

The Ghost Emperor.

Ben recognised the beast from his visions, his spasmodic glimpses of the beyond. The Emperor's gelatinous mass shone against the surrounding darkness like the last star left in the cosmos. Looking up at this king of Lurkers, Ben cringed, taking in the huge horned dome of its head, a crown of spectral light swallowing the whole of his vision. Nausea threatened to overwhelm him, his guts cramping at the sight. The beast's tentacles, six to eight of them, each one riddled with suckers, reached out for the alien road, then recoiled from the sparks that showered at his touch, a motion that struck Ben as both ravenous and tentative, questing for power.

Lurkers, he had learnt, tended to avoid the Silver Leys. Von Hart had told him that the Fay magic had a lethal effect on the half-formed creatures, disintegrating whatever misbegotten stuff comprised their essence. He had seen their aversion for himself last year, when the envoy had chased them away from the threshold of the nether. But magic, he knew, was growing sour. And in turn, the phantoms had grown bold. The Lurkers had gathered, amassing into this shining whole, no doubt endowing the ghost-beast with strength. Strength enough to challenge the boundaries of existence and the charmed highways of the Fay? Ben shivered at the thought.

The void thrummed with power, shuddering through the Ghost Emperor. The energy swept in reefs through his vast endoskeleton, streams of electrical light converging behind his layered grille of bone, his curving, tusk-like visor. The phantom hovered over the ley, a see-through, coruscating giant, his maw a blazing white core, blinding in its intensity.

Jia, Ben noticed, was crouching before the thing like a penitent, the two fused fragments of the *Cwyth* clutched to her breast. Awaiting the third and final piece. Drawing to a breathless halt, he made sure to keep a cautious distance between himself and the *sin-you*, his fists clenched. But he could tell there was no threat left in her, her back turned to him, her bowed head and kneeling body outlined by the flickering light. She didn't turn at his approach, even though he sensed she knew he was there. He took a vague comfort from that; she had let him catch up. The great beast shed pearlescent rays that sparked and recoiled off the ley some distance beyond her.

But too close. Too damn close.

The proximity of the Emperor pressed on him, an amassed weight of energy. Gagging, he fought the urge to double over with his hands on his knees, letting whatever passed for air in these other-worldly depths fill his lungs. He wanted to speak, to reach Jia with his urgency, but before he could do so, a voice filled his skull, booming into the void. A voice that he knew from his visions. From centuries of odd acquaintance. It had never sounded colder.

"So you return, Daughter of Empires. The key has turned. The glass shattered. And you have brought me the harp."

For all its sonorous power, there was a strain in the echoes. Pain.

Shielding his eyes, Ben looked up at the Ghost Emperor. There was something about the beast's maw, something in that thrashing core of light. Something he couldn't immediately place . . . Puissance radiated from the thing, but also intelligence, a conscious intent. He had seen Lurkers up close and personal before and all he'd sensed in them was a blank need, a ravenous hunger, a lust to feast on magic at its source. This was different. There was someone inside the beast, sitting behind its grille of bone, a pale, cross-legged form.

He glared into the blazing sun over the ley, directing his anger at the one who spoke from within it.

"Von Hart," he said. "What the hell are you playing at?"

Ben made out his ancient master, locked in the ghost-beast's maw. Was this the cell from which the envoy had summoned him, reaching out through the walls of reality? Calling to him. A choice. A plea. Even from a distance, he could see that the envoy wasn't himself. His starry robes had burned away and he held his limbs, pure alabaster, in a rigid pose of meditation, surrounded by the flailing brightness. Von Hart clutched an object to his chest, his arms crossed over stark ribs. His white-gold hair was a bristling mop, sizzling with supernatural force.

Angry as he was, Ben experienced a pang of sympathy to see the fairy, usually so poised and impeccable, looking so beleaguered and weak. He wouldn't have counted on the feeling in a thousand years. Grief eddied through him – an emotion that lasted precisely five seconds until he remembered the Lambton armour, the suspected summoning of Mauntgraul, the sense of a wider game playing out, with him as the bloody roulette ball.

He scowled, a need for answers shoving compassion out of the way.

"Ah, Ben." The envoy's voice echoed in his mind. "You heard me. You made it. *Danke, liebling.*"

"Save it. You won't thank me once I get you out of that thing. Trust me."

"Always playing the hero," Von Hart said, his sarcasm plain. "Dare I say I relied on that? But there is only one thing I need from you here. You're too late for anything else."

Catch her. Let me fall.

"You unleashed the White Dog, didn't you? Trying to create a distraction, cover your tracks." Ben swallowed the embers in his throat. "Do you know how many people have died?"

"A sad necessity. A choice of evils."

The envoy said this in a typically dismissive manner, prompting a growl from Ben.

"Don't give me that bullshit. You're gonna answer for this. Somehow, I'll make you—"

"I've already answered, Ben. And so have you. For centuries we've suffered, yoked and shackled under the Lore. There was only one way to break our chains."

By breaking the Lore. By shifting the foundations, causing a breach . . . Again, Ben recalled the Lambton armour, the evidence of Von Hart's hand in things, perhaps fanning the flames of Remnant sedition, the conspiracy last year. He didn't know how deep the envoy's involvement went, but judging by the scene before him, he could take a guess.

You knew all along, didn't you? Ghosts from limbo. The living and the dead trading places.

What had started all this? This breach in the Lore? He wasn't likely to forget it. The breaking of a forgotten tomb. The raising of an old god. How hard would it have been to point Professor Winlock, the noted archaeologist, in the right direction? To place unearthed relics in the hands of the Three, who in turn passed them to human hands? A conspiracy that went even deeper, a web within a web, the envoy extraordinary waiting for his moment, the Pact in tatters, the Lore in disarray. And into the chaos, he had sent his student, his thief, his strange-coloured eyes fixed on the endgame: the undoing of the Sleep.

Just how long had he planned all of this? Years? Centuries? Ben considered the monumental risk, the fairy gambling with the fate of the world. All those who had fallen as a result. Those who had nearly died, including his former lover Rose.

But there was more to it than that. He could feel it in his bones. When he'd been in need, the envoy had been there, plucking him from certain death on two occasions – had it really all been a game? This prompted a colder thought, clutching at his heart. Von Hart might have used him as a wild card, a way to limit the damage caused by his greater plans. But it was also clear that the envoy needed him for something. And he got the feeling that he wouldn't like it when he found out . . .

Ben snarled. All of this had started with the envoy, centuries ago. *Forever* ago. He recalled the painting in du Sang's tomb, Von Hart standing with shoulders slumped, the broken harp at his feet, watching his people depart. Then, one historic day on Thorney Island, he had brought the fragments of the *Cwyth* before the Curia Occultus, re-forging Arthur's shattered harp at the foot of King John's throne. It made a horrible kind of sense that the story would end with him too, the enchantment undone by his lily-white hands.

"The harp, the Sleep . . ." Ben was spluttering, shouting up at the shimmering beast. "It was all your fucking idea in the first place."

Von Hart shrugged. Then he winced, as if the gesture caused him pain.

"I made a mistake," he said, simply. "Times change. So do hearts. I have found another way."

"By becoming this . . . this monster?" Ben spat. "It's you, isn't it? It was you all along. You're the Ghost Emperor."

As soon as Ben said this, he knew he was right. He merely uttered the nub of his fears. It had been there with every strum of the Fay artefact, every note of the lullaby, the raising of dragons and their binding. The telling absence of phantoms.

Jia had told him as much in the hills outside Beijing, he realised that now.

The Lurkers are merging in the nether, she'd said. *Something is drawing them to the earth. Something has caught their attention. Something big.*

"*Ja*," Von Hart said. "One cannot reignite such magic without understanding the cost. I turned the Lurkers' eyes from the earth. I summoned them here, to feed on a living source of magic. As only I could have done."

Looking up at Von Hart, Ben could see the means in his hands, clutched to his scrawny chest: the last fragment, the column of the harp. The Fay had carved the rounded spar, roughly two feet in length, to resemble the chest, neck and head of a horse, all exquisitely moulded in *lunewrought*. Except that it wasn't a horse, was it? He had seen as much in the paintings in du Sang's tomb: Nimue, Queen of the Fay, bringing the fabled instrument to King Arthur in his tent during the Battle of Camlann. Her offering hadn't gone down well, sparking years of abandonment and pain . . .

And here the relic rested in the hands of another, having

spun down the ages through legend and history, shimmering before him in all its other-worldly glory. The top of the column formed a proud bust of blank silver eyes and a windswept mane, a single horn winding conch-like from its pure white brow. The tapering tip was as sharp as a spear.

Dragons and unicorns. The gang's all here.

And ghosts.

"Why?" Ben said, breathless in the dark. "Why have you done this?"

But he thought he already knew.

"The circles are breaking," Von Hart replied. "Magic is souring. The Sleep is failing. The Remnants will die."

Ben shut his eyes at the echoes in his head, squeezing out the light. He wanted to argue, to resist the idea, but du Sang had explained the truth under Paris, the ailing state of the Remnants. Fuck, he'd known it in his bones before then, in the creatures that had fallen by his hand, Rakegoyle, Jordsønn, Mauntgraul . . . and the others brought low, destroyed by the seismic shift in the Lore. Queen Atiya. The Three. He wished he could say that he mourned them, but he couldn't deny their origin, these creations of the Fay. Remnants all.

Coupled to this was the human cost, slayers, knights, True Names – and worst of all, civilians, blind to the mythical beasts in their midst, heedless of the Lore, yet still paying the price.

And he had seen it in Jia's eyes, her haunted look, her choice that was no choice at all.

I can save them.

359

As if rousing from a dream, she stood before him now, facing him with tears on her cheeks.

"It's true, Ben," she said. "I've seen it for myself in the Eight Hand Mirror. I am a creature born to perceive the truth and my master chose me for that very purpose. To turn the key in the door of the world. To shatter the glass of illusion. To pave the road to our freedom."

"To start a war," he told her, bluntly.

A frown troubled her brow. Her knuckles whitened, tightening on the fused fragments of the harp, and he knew that she was expecting him to make a lunge for it. But he was still too far away, and the *sin-you*, he knew, was too fast.

Still she shook the artefact at him, as if warding away her doubts.

"There is no other way! We will wake them and fight for peace."

Ben laughed, a bitter snort. "And do you think for one second that the Sleepers will share your vision? After centuries trapped in slumber?" Reluctantly he pictured it, the dark days to come. "A sky full of dragons. A city facing giants. Witches, Jia. Ogres. Trolls. You think they're going to thank you?"

"The envoy—"

"Will do what? He put them there in the first place. You think they're going to listen?"

"We must all make sacrifices," she said. A mutter, no more.

"You're the one who needs to wake the fuck up. You're talking about a massacre beyond imagining. Magic versus machines. Myths against man. And for what? So you get to see your own kind again? You want to save your parents, isn't that right? A handful of Remnants in exchange for thousands of people. That's what you mean by *sacrifice*?" He grunted, then spat on the ley. "Sounds pretty selfish to me."

Jia glared at him for a moment, but she couldn't hold his gaze.

"How I have ached for them, Ziyou and Ye," she said. "From the walls of Xanadu to the mists of Mount Song and the fires of the Opium War. To gallop beside them, the wind in our manes . . . Here I stand with the harp in my hands. If I wasn't *youxia*, sworn to emperors, then what could have stopped me from running to the northern plains, strumming these fragments and rousing them from the Sleep?" She turned away from him, looking up at the Ghost Emperor. "No, Ben. You are wrong. So wrong. As long as we live under the Lore – under the *lie* – there can be no place for us in this world."

And from the brilliance, her master summoned her.

"Jia. Bring me the harp."

At his echoing voice, Ben watched her spine stiffen, her neck lifting. Then she nodded to herself, blinking away tears. She held the partly forged harp to her breast, the silvery light illuminating her sorrow. Slowly she walked down the ley, leaving Ben to his rage.

But he wasn't done with her.

"If you do this," he shouted, stumbling after her, "there'll be no going back. You'll never wash the blood from your hands."

If he could only catch up with her, reach her somehow . . .

She spat at him over her shoulder.

"My master will re-forge the harp. We'll awaken the Sleepers. We'll save them all."

"No. You'll damn us." He hated the pleading tone of his voice, his hands reaching out for her. "Listen to me. The fairy, Von Hart – he's been playing us all along. He caused the breach in the Lore in the first place, I'm sure of it. You might be right about the magic souring. The Remnants dying. But can you trust him, Jia? Can you trust a word he says? Look at all the people he's deceived. The people who've died. How do you know what the fuck he wants? You said it yourself. He's the Fay."

Jia slowed, coming to a halt. Ben wanted to leap for her, wrestle the harp from her grasp, refuse to accept that this destructive path was the only option left to him. Instead, he halted too, keeping his distance, watching her doubts play out.

"He is my master," she said. "And I am a *sin-you*, born to see the truth from lie."

"Fair enough," Ben replied. "Then ask him."

Jia hesitated.

"*Ask him.*"

She bowed her head, her braid shaking down the curve of her back as she struggled with some inner decision, some inner war. Perhaps she sensed the truth of his words. Perhaps, deep down, she knew it herself. Wasn't that her nature? Oh, how she *wanted* to believe. He could see it in her rigid stance, her trembling shoulders, her tears. A hope that had probably festered through centuries, through years. Making her ripe for the plucking.

Need had blinded her, an illusion, a trick. All he had to do was open her eyes.

Finally she looked up at the Ghost Emperor again.

"Master . . ." but she couldn't put her doubt into words.

"I told you," Von Hart said, his voice booming from the beast's maw. Could Ben hear impatience as well as pain? Fear? He thought so. "A worm gnaws at the heart of things. This is the best way. The only way."

Ben watched Jia's shoulders slump, the harp gleaming in her arms.

After a while, she said, "Smoke and mirrors. You lied to me before."

"I . . . spared you," Von Hart replied. "You weren't ready, my dear. Now bring me the harp. Or do you welcome death?"

"Death comes regardless. Isn't that what you said?"

"Yes. You have looked through the glass and seen it yourself."

"I have," Jia breathed. "You wish to undo the lullaby. To break the enchantment. But that isn't the whole truth. Is it?"

Von Hart straightened at this, his eyes narrowing behind the Emperor's visor, fierce violet slits.

"Remember that I am your master."

"That isn't an answer. What are you hiding, Von Hart? What is your real purpose here?" She spoke through her teeth, a savage hiss. "Will you spare me that too?"

For a moment silence stretched out between them, master and student, as piercing as the light that framed them.

Then Von Hart shook the column in his fist, his fringe falling in his face as he shrieked down at her.

"*Bring me the harp!*"

The ghost-beast shuddered, feeding on the envoy's wrath, his anguish. Light rippled over his bulk, his tentacles quivering, sparking off the ley. Jia took a step back, her face calm, her eyes hard. Once again she was *youxia*, in control of herself. She was a *sin-you*, unmoved by the envoy's dissembling.

"The Sola Ignis is right," she said, nodding. "Another mirror, reflecting truth. Reminding me of my duty. I am Jia Jing, the appointed judge of the court of Kublai Khan, Guardian of the East, Keeper of the Lore. And if death must come, then I choose to meet it with honour."

With this, she turned her back on the Ghost Emperor.

"It won't come by my hand. Not any more."

She looked at Ben. She smiled, a thin knife of acceptance. Of loss. Of hope.

"Ben," she said.

Ben held out his hand.

"Jia . . ."

Von Hart screamed.

The echoes threatened to shatter the nether, the bridge shuddering under their feet. White light washed through the darkness, cast by the Emperor's tentacles, thrashing in the void.

Grimacing, Ben stumbled forward, his hands reaching out, for Jia, for the harp. If he could just get her out of here, away from—

Too late. Sitting in the burning maw above, Von Hart was muttering an invocation, his power flooding into the beast around him, drawing on the strength of phantoms, directing spectral energy. The Emperor lashed out, the tip of a tentacle whipping around Jia's waist, wrenching her back along the bridge.

With a wail, she found herself plucked into the air, into the non-space of the nether. She struggled, kicking at nothing, the beast drawing her towards his radiant maw.

"*No!*"

Shielding his eyes, Ben raced towards her. One of his hands swelled into a claw, ready to rend and tear, release her from the ghost-beast's clutches. But the Emperor had little interest in the *sin-you*, her purpose served. Her complicity denied. With another tentacle, the beast plucked the partly formed harp from her grip, swinging her roughly left and right, then flinging her away, into the darkness.

She landed on the edge of the bridge, an arm and a leg dangling over the edge, scrabbling with one hand at the shimmering surface.

Skidding onto his knees, Ben reached for her, a claw stretching out . . .

A shrill whine filled the depthless gloom. Done with the argument, his resolve unchanged, the envoy offered Ben a ferocious smile, his triumph, his agony, crazed by the shining objects in his hands – chiming in metallic expectation – as he brought the column, the unicorn's horn, up to meet the harmonic curve and the soundboard, re-forging the *Cwyth*, the mnemonic harp.

Silver exploded in the gulf.

The blast forced Ben onto his back, a melodic tide, as heavy as the sea, washing him along the ley. The smell of fusing *lunewrought* coated the back of his throat, pricking ice water from his eyes. Everywhere there was light, glassy beams pushing back the darkness, illuminating the depths of the nether, scorching the void with a boundless and alien magic.

Somewhere above him, a thin thread of chanting, a feverish invocation, wove through the flood of music. Against his better judgement, Ben looked up, peering into the ghost-beast's maw, a white and whirling inferno. He couldn't work out what he was seeing, the mathematics of his betrayal. The words were a garble of echoes, an incomprehensible stream of symbols pouring from the envoy's lips. Von Hart was a spindly silhouette, a charred match in the gusting brilliance, the *Cwyth* made whole in his hands.

Ben found himself in the eye of the storm, the cataclysm blazing above him. The harp was warping, he saw, the triangular instrument rippling and stretching in Von Hart's grasp. Around him, the Emperor pulsed and throbbed, argent veins riddling his vaporous body, his weaving tentacles, radiating from his blinding core. But the creature inside the beast wasn't strumming any strings, Ben noticed, nor summoning the lullaby. He gripped the instrument with both hands, his muscles straining, his bones showing through his skin. He was pulling at the *lunewrought*, his brow creased with a desperate intent.

The realisation struck Ben like a physical blow.

He never meant to play the blasted thing. He means to destroy it. Why?

Aching, he climbed to his feet. He glanced at Jia, watching her drag herself back onto the bridge, pulling herself along flat on her stomach, panting. Wounded, but safe. A situation that he knew wouldn't last.

Up there, locked behind the ghost-beast's maw, Von Hart struggled and screamed, lost in the force that sought to devour the harp, to devour him. His sacrifice. His price. The spark of war. Ben sucked in the cold, the void matching the blood in his veins. From beyond the world, the envoy had called to him. Who knew what energy that had taken, what desperate, dying spell?

There was a choice here.

When the time comes, let me fall.

And a plea.

Catch her.

But Ben would never listen to the fairy again. He'd have his answers or die in the attempt.

The giant phantom loomed over him, a mass of fluctuating light, drinking in the magic of the harp – although the artefact obviously burned him, blackening his ghostly flesh. It only took a second for Ben to see the blisters forming on the Lurker's skin, to guess what was happening.

Squaring his shoulders, he leapt forward, grabbing one of the Lurker's tentacles and swinging himself up. The cold burned his hands and feet, frost puffing out around him, his skin hardening with scales. He moved fast, navigating the limb like a slippery branch, climbing towards the grille of bone, the beast's ornate visor. Arms held out for balance, he could feel the appendage tensing under him, shocked by the warping *lunewrought*. Monkey style, he jumped, landing, scrabbling, on the front of the ghost-beast's maw. Squinting into the light, he peered inside, his lips curling as he met Von Hart's eyes.

"You've got . . . a lot of explaining to do," he managed, grunting as he lodged his feet against the spectral grille and wrenched at a tusk-like bone, as solid and unyielding as quartz.

Von Hart, pale, weak, shook his head, withdrawing against the inside of his cell. Bone – or a substance resembling bone – cracked, loosening. Muscles straining, Ben reached through the gap, his outstretched claw grabbing the envoy with more force than necessary.

And then the world came apart.

The lullaby. The lullaby shrieked in his skull.

Before he could taste his own failure, the chiming resolved into a symphony, deafening and cold. He heard strings, innumerable strings, plucked by a fairy hand and washing over him, a silvery cascade. The strings were the strummed lengths of umbilical cords, stretching from the embryos of gods deep in the womb of the cosmos. The glittering track of a pure white moon, smooth and unscarred, gliding up over the horizon in a ceaseless carousel. The music was the grinding of plates under the sea, the roar of volcanoes breaking the earth, showering lava on the land. Above, he heard the laughter of the speeding stars, spinning, flashing into eternity.

Unseen fingers, diamond sharp, played upon the keys of his soul. The lullaby pressed upon his every nerve, his every thought, hitting every note. In his mind, there swirled hatched eggs and forest caves, village maidens and moonlit kisses, burning bridges and mean-faced kings, white-winged serpents swooping low over blood-soaked plains . . .

The lullaby echoed around him, a maelstrom pulling him into its heart, and he knew it for the song of the universe itself, a rhapsody to summon Creation from the dark. To split atoms, birth cells, fling genes through the primordial muck, bound to an earthly destiny. In the musical storm, Ben saw fish ripple into lizards and lizards rise as apes, eventually flowing into human form, creatures of flesh and flame. He saw the strands shatter, a prism of existence carried on the tide, warping into freakish shapes, strange mutations, the hide and horns of fabulous beasts . . .

And in the brightness, he saw his death. The death of them all.

Clutching his head, he tried to shut out the music, to hang on to himself. The nether went wheeling around him, a shimmering void. The strings snapped, a sharp caesura, the cords broken, the gods falling, falling in the dark. Falling to walk through the dusk of debasement, clinging to the shreds of their art, their lost magic, their magnificent, terrible children. Caught in the eye of the opus, he witnessed the making of his forebears, the seeding of the dragon at an other-worldly hand. A salamander coiled in a glass, which he saw cast into the blackest flame, the liquefied substance imbibed by a naked, screaming man, some long-lost prisoner of history, transformed by the mystic science of the Fay. And then the First-Born surrendered to despair, abandoning the Old Lands and their sorcerous spawn, leaving the Remnants to the fire at the End of All Things.

All this the lullaby showed him, exploding from the harp, shedding the memories of the past and the future. It was the music of death, yes. The souring of magic. His destiny. His ending.

Ben swore, shaking the visions from his head, the sense of them fading, scattering into the gulf. Fear eclipsed their meaning.

The music changed. The knowledge, a blink of enlightenment, gone. Discord whined through the darkness, the gulf washing in to challenge the light.

In Von Hart's hands, the harp jangled and warped, rippling with straining energy. There came a blast, a blinding ring of wildfire like the world caving in. The light punched Ben's skull, his teeth threatening to dance down his throat. The next moment, the *Cwyth* reached its limits of resistance and shattered, the silver and ivory unicorn undone.

Shrapnel showered into the gulf. Chunks of *lunewrought* thudded into the phantom's flanks, the Ghost Emperor howling. Then the great beast himself was flying apart, an explosion like a startled school of fish, deep in the blackest ocean. Lurkers, freed from the magical lure of the harp, shot off in all directions, squirming into the dark.

Below him, the Silver Ley, the bridge, evaporated in sparks and mist. Instantly dispelled. Clutching Von Hart, Ben realised that he was falling, dropping like a stone into the nether, into a bottomless well. A death that would go on forever, dragon and envoy drowning in the immensity, falling and falling until the two of them ran out of breath, starved or froze. Or just went on falling, plunging through the outer limits of Creation, motes in the unformed abyss.

Beneath him, he noticed Jia. The *sin-you* screamed and spun, her hands scrabbling at nothing, her braid flying out, a rope that couldn't save her. Her eyes wide and clear with the shock of her fall.

In the piercing rays, his flesh rippled and surged, the muscles bulging under his suit, blossoming into red-scaled limbs. With a grimace, his face lengthened into a horned snout, his spine shooting out in a bladed tail, the arrowhead tip whipping the dark. Wings, great sails, billowed out, catching the wind, slowing his descent into nothingness.

With Von Hart held limp in one claw, Ben reached out. He reached out for Jia, the tip of his claw inches from her, trying to snag her suit, her braid. Her flesh if necessary.

She looked up at him, her scream silenced as she met his eyes. With impossible grace, she crossed her arms over her chest, her green-gold body becoming rigid, assuming the posture of the *youxia*, the monk, as she tumbled into the gulf.

Her gaze sent a silent message – loud and clear in his panicked mind – squeezing the gristle of his heart.

Farewell.

Ben's roar shattered the void. She smiled up at him, a look that held no triumph, no reproach, only calm acceptance. Then she was spinning out of reach, the tides of the nether sucking her down. Down into the nothing.

Light burst again, drawing back into its fiery source. A second blast, a wave of imploding power, hurled Ben and the envoy away through the boundless darkness. He spun and spun, his sense of direction in this, a place that held none, thrown into lunacy. A mess of wings and tail, a pale figure clutched in his claw, he reeled across the nether, sailing on the echoes of an alien song. A song that was no more.

Eyes closed, trailing tears, Ben fought to master his wings, to saddle the shining tide.

He let it carry him towards that distant eye, a faint octagon ahead, a shadow etched on shadow.

The hole in the world. The black doorway to home.

Xǐng ~ Awaken

Wheeling, tumbling, the wind between reality and elsewhere howling in his ears, Red Ben Garston burst from the large octagonal mirror that stood on the altar in the temple of stones. In a wave of scattering debris, his momentum carried him across the dais and down the shallow steps, a red-scaled wrecking ball. The painted gods in the alcoves watched his ungainly entrance into the chamber, each one exploding in plaster and dust as he crashed along the length of the nave.

As he rolled, the walls shuddering, his body instinctively dwindled in size. His wings folded in, his tail coiled up and his snout shrank, his protean flesh accommodating his return to the world. To all that was solid and real and . . . dying. *Done.* Although the Ghost Emperor, the endless gulf and the one he'd left behind felt only too real to him.

Cradling Von Hart – who, he knew, he must now think of as a *captive*, a situation as fraught with danger and as unlikely to last as the notion itself – the one-time Sola Ignis rolled and rolled, waiting for gravity to catch him, the natural laws to take hold. For the sweet earth to welcome him, whatever cuts, bruises and broken bones it held in store.

With a resounding boom, he finally came to a halt a few feet from the wide double doors leading into the temple. The smoggy glow of dawn across the Pearl River fell on his face like a kiss after the chilly darkness of the nether. For a long minute or so, all was silent apart from the trickle of rubble from above, a slow but ceaseless cascade that told Ben he couldn't lie here forever. With the destruction of the Ghost Emperor and the harp, the spectral pull from beyond the mirror had dissipated, no longer suspending or supporting the bricks above him. Sitting up, he snorted grit and spat out blood, a feather of flame swirling in his nostrils as he grasped what he was seeing. The stones, old and crumbling, were settling. Broken block by broken block. Crack by crack. He could hear the edifice groaning around him, rough echoes in the still, and he knew – in that special way that always told him his troubles were far from over – that soon the remaining spire would fall. Fall and bury him under the stones. He was willing to bet that he'd survive that, a quick switch back to his crimson shell and ridge of horns saving him from an early grave. The envoy, however, would probably be crushed to death.

Ben wished that he felt some deeper concern about that other than a need for answers.

He let out his breath, a slow exhalation of weariness and pain. *No broken bones, thank Christ. That's new.* He'd made the full transformation into human shape and lay spread-eagled on his back in the dirt, his suit covered in dust, his shaven head pale with the stuff. The streaks of blood on his face looked gaudy in the early light. The *wyrm tongue* symbol on his chest rose and fell, rose and fell, as he gathered the dazed thread of his thoughts, his brain spinning, and accepted that he had survived. He was back. Back on solid ground.

But some will never be. The bitter truth of it stabbed him in the middle of his chest. *Jia Jing will never walk in these lands again. You couldn't save her.*

He groaned, shaking his head in his heads. There was no time to rest, surrender to unconsciousness. His ears rang with echoes, the aftershock of the shattered harp rippling out from the mirror on the altar. *The door of Creation.* Blinking, Ben looked up at the thing, regarding nothing more than a blank black octagon, a silent, depthless hole, devoid of magic and monsters. But the sight gave him little relief; he didn't want to guess how long such a silence would last, and the music, the sickly-sweet chiming of bells, did nothing to reassure him. The temple trembled with the sound. And the breeze through the doors behind him, he noted, met and carried the strain, the residual tinkling, silvery and clear, spilling out down the steps.

He shook his head again to clear it. Straining his eyes, green flints in his battered face, he was sure that he could make out a faint light in the space around him that had nothing to do with the dawn. Glimmers of silver borne on the music like tears or drops of blood, the blood of the lullaby. Flowing from the mirror, through the shuddering temple and out into the world.

Not good.

Even in this solid and earthly place, he sensed an ominous prelude in the sound – no doubt to a whole fanfare of shit. *This isn't over. Oh no.* The notes stirred his old serpentine heart despite himself, and he imagined that he was listening to a requiem, the orchestration of a great death, the ending of an age and maybe, just maybe, the beginning of another. A dark one.

A breath before the storm.

Yeah. Ben knew the music wouldn't last. But how far would these echoes go? Would they dissipate over the river, disturbing the dreams of some kraken or other? Or as the story went back in the old days, would the lullaby circle the globe before fading? Before its enchantment was utterly undone? Thinking of all the destruction and terror that the unravelling spell would leave in its wake, he admitted to himself that he simply didn't know. Sweet, sour as it was, the song was brief, like an unexpected pleasure followed by unexpected distaste. A bite of an apple and finding half a maggot. As always, the wheel turned. The balance tipped, back and forth. Well, now the cosmic seesaw had bloody well snapped in half. The Lore was broken, the harp shattered, the lullaby undone. Soon, he reckoned, things long buried would stir and rise. Even gods, and the ghosts of gods, might somehow manage to return, searching for a way back to the light. Ben screwed up his face, bitter memories, most of them recent and raw, pressing against the inside of his skull. Not all of those gods meant well. And as for the Remnants . . .

He knew that the coming storm had a name.

"The awakening. Christ, no . . ."

Next to him, Von Hart coughed and moved weakly in the dust, lying face down in the gloom. His bare limbs were indistinguishable from the rivers of dust streaming from the shifting stones above. The envoy rolled himself onto his back and, in a sudden motion that gave Ben a start, his spine arched in the grit, his fists clenched, his head thrown back on the floor as he vented an echoing howl.

But Ben didn't give a crap about the fairy's grief. All this had been his fault. All of it. He'd taken a gamble and succeeded in re-forging the harp only to break it – for surely that had been his ambition all along, for whatever nefarious purpose – but as Von Hart's cry faded to silence, carried by the wind along with the music into the air, Ben realised that the envoy had also suffered a loss. If this was his victory, then it was a bitter one.

They'd escaped from the nether. One of them hadn't made it. One of them was going to sleep forever.

With a snarl, Ben was up in an instant, up and kneeling over Von Hart, one hand clutching the envoy's throat, the other balling into a fist that was drawn back to his shoulder.

"What the fuck are you playing at? You destroyed the goddamn harp. You summoned the Lurkers to destroy it. That's what you wanted all along, wasn't it? *Wasn't it?*"

In the furnace of his rage, he felt a small shiver of satisfaction as he watched the envoy raise his hands, cringing away from him. His fringe, a mess of white gold, would easily turn crisp and brown in one blast of Ben's fiery breath, and at this thought, Ben forced his anger into a growl, a deep rumble of threat.

"You better start talking. Or I'll drop-kick your bony arse over the cliffs out there."

In response, Von Hart closed his eyes. Playing a sorcerous piece of bait inside the Ghost Emperor and his struggle with the harp had clearly taken its toll on him. He lay here a wasted creature, a fallen creature, a creature of betrayal and deceit. *No. Of rebellion. Of war.* Tears trickled down his cheeks, thin lines through the smears of dust. When he opened his eyes again, he looked up at Ben, regarding him with foggy slits of violet. His gaze said it all. As things stood, he obviously didn't care what happened to him, whether Ben roasted him alive or not.

And the next moment, the envoy extraordinary managed to name the source of his pain.

"Jia . . ."

"She's dead, fairy. Dead or worse." Ben choked on the words, unable to shake off the look on the *sin-you*'s face, her calm acceptance as she'd fallen, tumbling into the nether. Forcing himself to focus on the matter at hand, he shoved his face closer to the envoy's, determined to prise an answer from his lips. "If you're so hell-bent on starting a war, why . . . why did you even bother to contact me? Why send me that message in Paris? Why drag me into this shit?"

When the time comes, let me fall.

Well, fallen they had. Just like the world around them. Everything was falling apart.

In tortured flashes, Ben recalled the strange invitations that had echoed in his skull throughout his journey, a voice he'd been unable to place at first, which had then become horribly clear. Clipped and Germanic. Pained, insistent and familiar, a plea from beyond. And had Von Hart – this murderer, this trickster, this arch-traitor – steered the Ghost Emperor's vaporous bulk to press against the skein of reality, reaching out to Ben in Barrow Hill Road? Drawing him to an appointment on the edge of the nether, the edge of reality itself?

"Talk! You knew that I was too late to stop any of this. What the fuck did you want from me?"

And Von Hart gave him his answer.

"I thought . . . I thought you could save her."

The dragon glared at the fairy for a moment. Von Hart's face had become a blur, washed out by grief. The swell of sorrow in Ben's breast doused his rage. With a heavy sigh, the fight went out of him, his inner heat fading, extinguished by fatigue, a solid block settling on his shoulders. Blinking away tears, he looked again at the empty mirror on the altar, the crumbling temple walls, the floor, counting the cost of his failure.

I couldn't reach her. I couldn't stop her.

Jia had sucked him down into her maelstrom of lies, her private struggle to undo the lullaby, her longing to see her parents again, yet another Remnant losing the plot. He should've seen it from the start. Should've taken du Sang at his word in Paris. The Remnants were dying out, one by one. And why, suspecting that Von Hart was hiding in the nether, hadn't he hit upon the truth sooner?

I'm saying he isn't in the world at all . . . He simply isn't . . . there.

Like a ghost.

A Ghost Emperor.

Under his chagrin, he realised then that his first impressions of the *sin-you* had been right.

Because you did *know, didn't you? You know despair like the back of your hand and you could smell it all over her.*

Jia had doubted herself, he reckoned, desperately wanting to see or hear something that would turn her back from her perilous raid of the fragments, her devastating course of action. *But when the chips were down, you finally managed to change her mind.* After centuries of living under the Lore and upholding the Pact – even after all of that – Ben had struggled to tell Jia that she was wrong, but he sure as hell knew there had to be a better way.

But that hope was gone now. No point wishing for it. He couldn't change the past.

Flowers in a mirror and the moon in water.

In the end, he'd reached her too late. And so she had paid the ultimate price.

This was a cruel game, he thought. A crooked hand laid out by the creature beneath him, this last earthly son of Avalon with all his riddles and machinations. All the same, with the depth of the *sin-you*'s tragedy weighing on his soul, Ben had no energy to hate him. At least not yet. For now, all he felt was loss, a fathomless hollow in his breast as though a cold pale hand had reached inside him and crushed his heart. Like the music, the echoing song around him, Ben was gathering his breath, trying to get his head around the latter-day collapse of the Curia Occultus, the treachery of his so-called friend, the cataclysm of the shattered harp – quite literally, the ending of his world.

"Look," Von Hart gasped as Ben leant forward, reaching for him. "Look around you. The circles of protection have broken."

"Yeah. I got that," Ben snapped, recalling his vision of the shimmering blue arc that had stretched under the sea to Lantau Island, leading him to the *sin-you* and this godforsaken place. "And you can shove your riddles where the sun don't shine."

So saying, he pushed his arms – none too gently – under the envoy's frail body and lifted him from the littered ground. In a trailing cloud of dust, he carried Von Hart through the double doors and started down the many steps. He'd have to leave the mirror here for now, pray that nobody found it. He wanted to find shelter somewhere, perhaps even a ride, a road leading off the peninsula. He wanted to go home. Work this out in his lair.

Chain this bastard up and throw away the key. Just like he threw Jia away.

London was a long way away and Ben would need to rest, heal and gather his strength before returning through the Asian and European skies, the envoy clutched in one claw. That was if Von Hart didn't escape or kill him first. Because the envoy, he knew, would heal quickly enough, and honestly? Ben didn't fancy his chances. He knew he was living on borrowed time.

No. You always have been. She showed you that, at least.

A rumble at his back arrested him, swinging him around on the steps, the envoy groaning in his arms. Looking up, Ben watched the solitary spire above him collapse, a shroud of rubble and dust crashing through the tiers of the ruined pagoda, a cascade of bricks pouring into the chamber below. In no time at all, where a temple had once stood, there was only a smoking mound of bricks, a set of steep stone steps leading up to it.

To nowhere. A dead and forgotten place.

Von Hart put his thoughts into words.

"Good," he muttered, in a pained wheeze. "That'll keep the Eight Hand Mirror buried for a time. Time enough for the echoes to travel through the nether. My work here is done."

Ben bristled at the hint of weary satisfaction in the envoy's voice.

"What are you up to, Von Hart?" he asked, his lip curling, his disgust plain. "Tell me what she died for and maybe I'll let you live."

But when he looked down at the fairy again, he could see that his condition was worsening, his face turning paler, his eyes rolling up in his skull as some kind of seizure took hold. Shivering and clutching his limbs, Von Hart was convulsing in Ben's arms, foam bubbling from his lips. *What the hell?* Appalled, Ben tried to draw back, to set him down, but Von Hart grabbed at him, his long fingers scrabbling at his chest, slipping off the glossy black scales of his suit, the redundant *wyrm tongue* symbol.

"Broken! Broken!" he cried, spittle flying from his lips. "The circles are broken! *Alles ist kaput!*"

Ben gripped him tighter, trying to shake some sense into him.

"No shit, fairy. What in God's name did you think would happ—"

Then the envoy's eyes flew wide, violet orbs of alarm. Or *triumph*.

"The Fay are coming!"

With that, he slumped, his bony limbs falling still. Only the slight rise and fall of his chest informed Ben that he still lived, unconsciousness claiming him.

Terrific.

Under his scorn, Ben shuddered, gripped by a grim epiphany. Reluctantly he recalled the Fay prophecy, uttered years ago by the queen of the vanished race, the false promise that had hoodwinked the Remnants into the Sleep.

One shining day, when Remnants and humans learn to live in peace, and magic blossoms anew in the world, then shall the Fay return and commence a new golden age.

The shattering of the harp. The envoy's talk of echoes through the nether. It struck Ben that perhaps Von Hart had intended to give that prophecy a little push. Had that been his purpose all along? To summon the Fay back to earth?

Muscles aching, eyes raw, Ben continued to make his way down the steps. His questions, it seemed, would have to wait. Whatever Von Hart had meant by his feverish words, it struck Ben that he experienced no joy in them, no pang of longing, only a shiver of fear. He noticed that the music was fading too, the echoes of the lullaby travelling beyond his hearing, spilling out across the river, into China, into the world beyond . . .

Ben gazed into the wilderness dawn, the grassy hills of the island spread out before him. He took a deep breath, considering his next move. *London. And then what?* No one could help him now. And he knew, in a way as deep and as long as his own history, that he would never trust anyone again. The Pact was over. The Lore undone. As for the Sleep . . . well, it didn't look good. For the first time in centuries, he stood in uncharted territory, with no map to guide him. No boundaries. No codes.

Is this what Jia meant by freedom? If she had, he wondered why his sense of doom – and he alone standing in the way of it – felt so much like a cage. Letting out a troubled breath, he accepted that he had indeed been right, although the knowledge brought him no joy.

A war is coming. I can smell it.

And in his mind, the grim understanding. His last real trinket. The only thing he had left.

I'm alive. I survived.

For now.

The sun rose over the Pearl River estuary, shining on a new age.

It wasn't much.

Acknowledgements

I wrote *Raising Fire* through a storm. This book couldn't have happened without the lighthouse keepers and I'd like to thank them here.

Thanks to John Jarrold, my agent, for all his advice and support during the writing of this novel, and for bailing me out when needed.

Thanks to my editors James Long, Lindsey Hall, Joanna Kramer and all of the team at Orbit UK and US for helping me to see the story inside the story and for bringing this book to fruition.

Thanks again to Tracey Winwood for another fabulous cover.

To all at Fox Spirit, fearless genre warriors, you have my depthless gratitude.

Thanks go out to a whole host of reviewers who embraced *Chasing Embers* and hosted the book on my blog tour. To Kevin Hearne, author of the Iron Druid series, for the generous cover quote. To John Gilbert at FEAR Magazine for featuring a relative newbie. To Theresa Darwin at Terror Tree and to the Eloquent Page. To Djibril at the FutureFire. To Danie Ware and everyone at Forbidden Planet for arranging my launch. To everyone at FantasyCon 2016, in particular Lee Harrison, author of *The Bastard Wonderland,*

385

for looking after me at the event and to Georgina Bruce for getting my shoe back. You all made the process of unleashing a dragon into the wild that much more fun.

On a research tip, thanks to the staff at the Beijing Feelinn for letting me stay in their *hutong* home. Thanks to the Wangfujing Bookstore. To my guides at the Great Wall and in Xi'an. Thanks to all the informative staff at the temples in Pingyao (which you should visit if you get the chance!). Thanks to Lee who got me to the Yellow Mountains. And to the Hong Kong Heritage Museum.

Special thanks to Joyce Chng, author of *Wolf at the Door* and *Dragon Dancer* (https://awolfstale.wordpress.com/) for checking my Chinese characters and for her insightful advice on Asian representation.

On a personal note, I can't thank Liz and Khalid enough for helping me out when things went adrift. Likewise, thanks to Ben and Karl for giving me the necessary shelter to finish this novel. Thanks to my family for their love and support. It meant a lot.

And to all the readers and writers that I've met on this journey.

Thank you.

Look out for

BURNING ASHES

by

James Bennett

The Lore is over. For Ben Garston, the fight is just beginning.

The uneasy truce between the human and the mythical
world has shattered. Betrayed by his oldest friend,
with a tragic death on his hands, there isn't enough
whiskey in England to wash away the taste of Ben's
guilt. But for a one-time guardian dragon, there's no
time to sit and sulk in the ruins.

Because the Long Sleep has come undone. Slowly but
surely, Remnants are stirring under the earth,
unleashing chaos and terror on an unsuspecting
modern world. Worse still, the Fay are returning,
travelling across the gulfs of the nether to bring a final
reckoning to Remnants and humans alike.

A war is coming. A war to end all wars. And only Ben
Garston stands in the way . . .

www.orbitbooks.net

extras

www.orbitbooks.net

about the author

James Bennett is a British writer raised in Sussex and South Africa. His travels have furnished him with an abiding love of different cultures, history and mythology. His short fiction has appeared internationally and the acclaimed *Chasing Embers* was his debut fantasy novel. James lives in London and sees dragon bones in the Thames whenever he crosses a bridge.

Find out more about James Bennett and other Orbit authors by registering for the free monthly newsletter at www.orbitbooks.net.

if you enjoyed
RAISING FIRE

look out for

WAKE OF VULTURES

by

Lila Bowen

Nettie Lonesome lives in a land of hard people and hard ground dusted with sand. She's a half-breed who dresses like a boy, raised by folks who don't call her a slave but use her like one. She knows of nothing else. That is, until the day a stranger attacks her. When nothing, not even a sickle to the eye can stop him, Nettie stabs him through the heart with a chunk of wood and he turns to black sand.

And just like that, Nettie can see.

But her newfound sight is a blessing and a curse. Even if she doesn't understand what's under her own skin, she can sense what everyone else is hiding – at least physically. The world is full of evil, and now she knows the source of all the sand in the desert. Haunted by the spirits, Nettie has no choice but to set out on a quest that might lead her to find her true kin . . . if the monsters along the way don't kill her first.

Chapter 1

Nettie Lonesome had two things in the world that were worth a sweet goddamn: her old boots and her one-eyed mule, Blue. Neither item actually belonged to her. But then again, nothing did. Not even the whisper-thin blanket she lay under, pretending to be asleep and wishing the black mare would get out of the water trough before things went south.

The last fourteen years of Nettie's life had passed in a shrivelled corner of Durango territory under the leaking roof of this wind-chapped lean-to with Pap and Mam, not quite a slave and nowhere close to something like a daughter. Their faces, white and wobbling as new butter under a smear of prairie dirt, held no kindness. The boots and the mule had belonged to Pap, right up until the day he'd exhausted their use, a sentiment he threatened to apply to her every time she was just a little too slow with the porridge.

"Nettie! Girl, you take care of that wild filly, or I'll put one in her goddamn skull!"

Pap got in a lather when he'd been drinking, which was pretty much always. At least this time his anger was aimed at a critter instead of Nettie. When the witch-hearted black filly had first shown up on the farm, Pap had laid claim and pronounced her a fine chunk of flesh and a sign of the Creator's good graces. If Nettie broke her and sold her for a decent price, she'd be closer to paying back Pap for taking her in as a baby when nobody else had wanted her but the hungry, circling vultures. The value Pap placed on feeding and housing a half-Injun, half-Black orphan girl always seemed to go up instead of down, no matter that Nettie did most of the work around the homestead these days. Maybe that was why she'd not been taught her sums: Then she'd know her own damn worth, to the penny.

But the dainty black mare outside wouldn't be roped, much less saddled and gentled, and Nettie had failed to sell her to the cowpokes at the Double TK Ranch next door. Her idol, Monty, was a top hand and always had a kind word. But even he had put a boot on Pap's poorly kept fence, laughed through his mustache, and hollered that a horse that couldn't be caught couldn't be sold. No matter how many times Pap drove the filly away with poorly thrown bottles, stones, and bullets, the critter crept back under cover of night to ruin the water by dancing a jig in the trough, which meant another blistering trip to the creek with a leaky bucket for Nettie.

Splash, splash. Whinny.

Could a horse laugh? Nettie figured this one could.

Pap, however, was a humorless bastard who didn't get a joke that didn't involve bruises.

"Unless you wanna go live in the flats, eatin' bugs, you'd best get on, girl."

Nettie rolled off her worn-out straw tick, hoping there weren't any scorpions or centipedes on the dusty dirt floor. By the moon's scant light she shook out Pap's old boots and shoved her bare feet into the cracked leather.

Splash, splash.

The shotgun cocked loud enough to be heard across the border, and Nettie dove into Mam's old wool cloak and ran toward the stockyard with her long, thick braids slapping against her back. Mam said nothing, just rocked in her chair by the window, a bottle cradled in her arm like a baby's corpse. Grabbing the rawhide whip from its nail by the warped door, Nettie hurried past Pap on the porch and stumbled across the yard, around two mostly roofless barns, and toward the wet black shape taunting her in the moonlight against a backdrop of stars.

"Get on, mare. Go!"

A monster in a flapping jacket with a waving whip would send any horse with sense wheeling in the opposite direction, but this horse had apparently been dancing in the creek on the day sense was handed out. The mare stood in the water trough and stared at Nettie like she was a damn strange bird, her dark eyes blinking with moonlight and her lips pulled back over long, white teeth.

Nettie slowed. She wasn't one to quirt a horse, but if the mare kept causing a ruckus, Pap would shoot her without a second or even a first thought—and he wasn't so deep in his bottle that he was sure to miss. Getting smacked with rawhide had to be better than getting shot in the head, so Nettie doubled up her shouting and prepared herself for the heartache that would accompany the smack of a whip on unmarred hide. She didn't even own the horse, much less the right to beat it. Nettie had grown up trying to be the opposite of Pap, and hurting something that didn't come with claws and a stinger went against her grain.

"Shoo, fool, or I'll have to whip you," she said, creeping closer. The horse didn't budge, and for the millionth time,

Nettie swung the whip around the horse's neck like a rope, all gentle-like.

But, as ever, the mare tossed her head at exactly the right moment, and the braided leather snickered against the wooden water trough instead.

"Godamighty, why won't you move on? Ain't nobody wants you, if you won't be rode or bred. Dumb mare."

At that, the horse reared up with a wild scream, spraying water as she pawed the air. Before Nettie could leap back to avoid the splatter, the mare had wheeled and galloped into the night. The starlight showed her streaking across the prairie with a speed Nettie herself would've enjoyed, especially if it meant she could turn her back on Pap's dirt-poor farm and no-good cattle company forever. Doubling over to stare at her scuffed boots while she caught her breath, Nettie felt her hope disappear with hoofbeats in the night.

A low and painfully unfamiliar laugh trembled out of the barn's shadow, and Nettie cocked the whip back so that it was ready to strike.

"Who's that? Jed?"

But it wasn't Jed, the mule-kicked, sometimes stable boy, and she already knew it.

"Looks like that black mare's giving you a spot of trouble, darlin'. If you were smart, you'd set fire to her tail."

A figure peeled away from the barn, jerky-thin and slithery in a too-short coat with buttons that glinted like extra stars. The man's hat was pulled low, his brown hair overshaggy and his lily-white hand on his gun in a manner both unfriendly and relaxed that Nettie found insulting.

"You best run off, mister. Pap don't like strangers on

his land, especially when he's only a bottle in. If it's horses you want, we ain't got none worth selling. If you want work and you're dumb and blind, best come back in the morning when he's slept off the mezcal."

"I wouldn't work for that good-for-nothing piss-pot even if I needed work."

The stranger switched sides with his toothpick and looked Nettie up and down like a horse he was thinking about stealing. Her fist tightened on the whip handle, her fingers going cold. She wouldn't defend Pap or his land or his sorry excuses for cattle, but she'd defend the only thing other than Blue that mostly belonged to her. Men had been pawing at her for two years now, and nobody'd yet come close to reaching her soft parts, not even Pap.

"Then you'd best move on, mister."

The feller spit his toothpick out on the ground and took a step forward, all quiet-like because he wore no spurs. And that was Nettie's first clue that he wasn't what he seemed.

"Naw, I'll stay. Pretty little thing like you to keep me company."

That was Nettie's second clue. Nobody called her pretty unless they wanted something. She looked around the yard, but all she saw were sand, chaparral, bone-dry cow patties, and the remains of a fence that Pap hadn't seen fit to fix. Mam was surely asleep, and Pap had gone inside, or maybe around back to piss. It was just the stranger and her. And the whip.

"Bullshit," she spit.

"Put down that whip before you hurt yourself, girl."

"Don't reckon I will."

The stranger stroked his pistol and started to circle her. Nettie shook the whip out behind her as she spun in place to face him and hunched over in a crouch. He stopped circling when the barn yawned behind her, barely a shell of a thing but darker than sin in the corners. And then he took a step forward, his silver pistol out and flashing starlight. Against her will, she took a step back. Inch by inch he drove her into the barn with slow, easy steps. Her feet rattled in the big boots, her fingers numb around the whip she had forgotten how to use.

"What is it you think you're gonna do to me, mister?" It came out breathless, god damn her tongue.

His mouth turned up like a cat in the sun. "Something nice. Something somebody probably done to you already. Your master or pappy, maybe."

She pushed air out through her nose like a bull. "Ain't got a pappy. Or a master."

"Then I guess nobody'll mind, will they?"

That was pretty much it for Nettie Lonesome. She spun on her heel and ran into the barn, right where he'd been pushing her to go. But she didn't flop down on the hay or toss down the mangy blanket that had dried into folds in the broke-down, three-wheeled rig. No, she snatched the sickle from the wall and spun to face him under the hole in the roof. Starlight fell down on her ink-black braids and glinted off the parts of the curved blade that weren't rusted up.

"I reckon I'd mind," she said.

Nettie wasn't a little thing, at least not height-wise, and she'd figured that seeing a pissed-off woman with a weapon in each hand would be enough to drive off the curious feller and send him back to the whores at the Leaping

Lizard, where he apparently belonged. But the stranger just laughed and cracked his knuckles like he was glad for a fight and would take his pleasure with his fists instead of his twig.

"You wanna play first? Go on, girl. Have your fun. You think you're facin' down a coydog, but you found a timber wolf."

As he stepped into the barn, the stranger went into shadow for just a second, and that was when Nettie struck. Her whip whistled for his feet and managed to catch one ankle, yanking hard enough to pluck him off his feet and onto the back of his fancy jacket. A puff of dust went up as he thumped on the ground, but he just crossed his ankles and stared at her and laughed. Which pissed her off more. Dropping the whip handle, Nettie took the sickle in both hands and went for the stranger's legs, hoping that a good slash would keep him from chasing her but not get her sent to the hangman's noose. But her blade whistled over a patch of nothing. The man was gone, her whip with him.

Nettie stepped into the doorway to watch him run away, her heart thumping underneath the tight muslin binding she always wore over her chest. She squinted into the long, flat night, one hand on the hinge of what used to be a barn door, back before the church was willing to pay cash money for Pap's old lumber. But the stranger wasn't hightailing it across the prairie. Which meant . . .

"Looking for someone, darlin'?"

She spun, sickle in hand, and sliced into something that felt like a ham with the round part of the blade. Hot blood spattered over her, burning like lye.

"Goddammit, girl! What'd you do that for?"

She ripped the sickle out with a sick splash, but the

man wasn't standing in the barn, much less falling to the floor. He was hanging upside-down from a cross-beam, cradling his arm. It made no goddamn sense, and Nettie couldn't stand a thing that made no sense, so she struck again while he was poking around his wound.

This time, she caught him in the neck. This time, he fell.

The stranger landed in the dirt and popped right back up into a crouch. The slice in his neck looked like the first carving in an undercooked roast, but the blood was slurry and smelled like rotten meat. And the stranger was sneering at her.

"Girl, you just made the biggest mistake of your short, useless life."

Then he sprang at her.

There was no way he should've been able to jump at her like that with those wounds, and she brought her hands straight up without thinking. Luckily, her fist still held the sickle, and the stranger took it right in the face, the point of the blade jerking into his eyeball with a moist squish. Nettie turned away and lost most of last night's meager dinner in a noisy splatter against the wall of the barn. When she spun back around, she was surprised to find that the fool hadn't fallen or died or done anything helpful to her cause. Without a word, he calmly pulled the blade out of his eye and wiped a dribble of black glop off his cheek.

His smile was a cold, dark thing that sent Nettie's feet toward Pap and the crooked house and anything but the stranger who wouldn't die, wouldn't scream, and wouldn't leave her alone. She'd never felt safe a day in her life, but now she recognized the chill hand of death, reaching for her. Her feet trembled in the too-big boots as she stumbled backward across the bumpy yard, tripping on stones and bits of trash. Turning her back on the demon man seemed intolerably stupid. She just had to get past the round pen, and then she'd be halfway to the house. Pap wouldn't be worth much by now, but he had a gun by his side. Maybe the stranger would give up if he saw a man instead of just a half-breed girl nobody cared about.

Nettie turned to run and tripped on a fallen chunk of fence, going down hard on hands and skinned knees. When she looked up, she saw butternut-brown pants stippled with blood and no-spur boots tapping.

"Pap!" she shouted. "Pap, help!"

She was gulping in a big breath to holler again when the stranger's boot caught her right under the ribs and knocked it all back out. The force of the kick flipped her over onto her back, and she scrabbled away from the stranger and toward the ramshackle round pen of old, gray branches and junk roped together, just barely enough fence to trick a colt into staying put. They'd slaughtered a pig in here, once, and now Nettie knew how he felt.

As soon as her back fetched up against the pen, the stranger crouched in front of her, one eye closed and weeping black and the other brim-full with evil over the bloody slice in his neck. He looked like a dead man, a corpse groom, and Nettie was pretty sure she was in the hell Mam kept threatening her with.

"Ain't nobody coming. Ain't nobody cares about a girl like you. Ain't nobody gonna need to, not after what you done to me."

The stranger leaned down and made like he was going

to kiss her with his mouth wide open, and Nettie did the only thing that came to mind. She grabbed up a stout twig from the wall of the pen and stabbed him in the chest as hard as she damn could.

She expected the stick to break against his shirt like the time she'd seen a buggy bash apart against the general store during a twister. But the twig sunk right in like a hot knife in butter. The stranger shuddered and fell on her, his mouth working as gloppy red-black liquid bubbled out. She didn't trust blood anymore, not after the first splat had burned her, and she wasn't much for being found under a corpse, so Nettie shoved him off hard and shot to her feet, blowing air as hard as a galloping horse.

The stranger was rolling around on the ground, plucking at his chest. Thick clouds blotted out the meager starlight, and she had nothing like the view she'd have tomorrow under the white-hot, unrelenting sun. But even a girl who'd never killed a man before knew when something was wrong. She kicked him over with the toe of her boot, tit for tat, and he was light as a tumbleweed when he landed on his back.

The twig jutted up out of a black splotch in his shirt, and the slice in his neck had curled over like gone meat. His bad eye was a swamp of black, but then, everything was black at midnight. His mouth was open, the lips drawing back over too-white teeth, several of which looked like they'd come out of a panther. He wasn't breathing, and Pap wasn't coming, and Nettie's finger reached out as if it had a mind of its own and flicked one big, shiny, curved tooth.

The goddamn thing fell back into the dead man's gaping

throat. Nettie jumped away, skitty as the black filly, and her boot toe brushed the dead man's shoulder, and his entire body collapsed in on itself like a puffball, thousands of sparkly motes piling up in the place he'd occupied and spilling out through his empty clothes. Utterly bewildered, she knelt and brushed the pile with trembling fingers. It was sand. Nothing but sand. A soft wind came up just then and blew some of the stranger away, revealing one of those big, curved teeth where his head had been. It didn't make a goddamn lick of sense, but it could've gone far worse.

Still wary, she stood and shook out his clothes, noting that everything was in better than fine condition, except for his white shirt, which had a twig-sized hole in the breast, surrounded by a smear of black. She knew enough of laundering and sewing to make it nice enough, and the black blood on his pants looked, to her eye, manly and tough. Even the stranger's boots were of better quality than any that had ever set foot on Pap's land, snakeskin with fancy chasing. With her own, too-big boots, she smeared the sand back into the hard, dry ground as if the stranger had never existed. All that was left was the four big panther teeth, and she put those in her pocket and tried to forget about them.

After checking the yard for anything livelier than a scorpion, she rolled up the clothes around the boots and hid them in the old rig in the barn. Knowing Pap would pester her if she left signs of a scuffle, she wiped the black glop off the sickle and hung it up, along with the whip, out of Pap's drunken reach. She didn't need any more whip scars on her back than she already had.

Out by the round pen, the sand that had once been a

devil of a stranger had all blown away. There was no sign of what had almost happened, just a few more deadwood twigs pulled from the lopsided fence. On good days, Nettie spent a fair bit of time doing the dangerous work of breaking colts or doctoring cattle in here for Pap, then picking up the twigs that got knocked off and roping them back in with whatever twine she could scavenge from the town. Wood wasn't cheap, and there wasn't much of it. But Nettie's hands were twitchy still, and so she picked up the black-splattered stick and wove it back into the fence, wishing she lived in a world where her life was worth more than a mule, more than boots, more than a stranger's cold smile in the barn. She'd had her first victory, but no one would ever believe her, and if they did, she wouldn't be cheered. She'd be hanged.

That stranger—he had been all kinds of wrong. And the way that he'd wanted to touch her—that felt wrong, too. Nettie couldn't recall being touched in kindness, not in all her years with Pap and Mam. Maybe that was why she understood horses. Mustangs were wild things captured by thoughtless men, roped and branded and beaten until their heads hung low, until it took spurs and whips to move them in rage and fear. But Nettie could feel the wildness inside their hearts, beating under skin that quivered under the flat of her palm. She didn't break a horse, she gentled it. And until someone touched her with that same kindness, she would continue to shy away, to bare her teeth and lower her head.

Someone, surely, had been kind to her once, long ago. She could feel it in her bones. But Pap said she'd been tossed out like trash, left on the prairie to die. Which she almost had, tonight. Again.

Pap and Mam were asleep on the porch, snoring loud as thunder. When Nettie crept past them and into the house, she had four shiny teeth in one fist, a wad of cash from the stranger's pocket, and more questions than there were stars.

Enter the monthly
Orbit sweepstakes at
www.orbitloot.com

With a different prize every month,
from advance copies of books by
your favourite authors to exclusive
merchandise packs,
**we think you'll find something
you love.**

facebook.com/OrbitBooksUK

@OrbitBooks

www.orbitbooks.net